And
ANOTHER
THING...

Also by EOIN COLFER

Artemis Fowl

The Arctic Incident

The Eternity Code

The Opal Deception

The Lost Colony

The Time Paradox

EOIN COLFER

DOUGLAS ADAMS'S
HITCHHIKER'S GUIDE TO THE GALAXY
PART SIX OF THREE

And
ANOTHER
THING...

HYPERION

NEW YORK

Lyric from "History" by Tenacious D, reprinted by permission of Time For My Breakfast and by permission of Buttflap Music.

"My Way"
by Claude Francois, Jacques Abel Revand, Gilles Thibaut and Paul Anka
Copyright © by Architectural Music (BMI) and Jingoro Music (BMI). International Copyright Secured. All Rights Reserved. Reprinted by Permission.

"My Way"
English Words by Paul Anka, Original French Words by Gilles Thibault
Music by Jacques Revaux and Claude Francois
Copyright © 1967 Societe Des Nouvelles and Editions Eddie Barclay.
Copyright © 1969 Chrysalis Standards, Inc.
Copyright Renewed
All Rights for the USA Administered by Chrysalis Standards, Inc., Editions Jeune Musique, Warner Chappell Music France, Jingoro Co. and Architectural Music Co. All Rights Reserved. Used by Permission.

Library of Congress Cataloging-in-Publication Data

Colfer, Eoin.
    And another thing— / Eoin Colfer. — 1st ed.
        p. cm.
    ISBN 978-1-4013-2358-5
    1. Prefect, Ford (Fictitious character)—Fiction. 2. Dent, Arthur (Fictitious character)—Fiction. 3. Interplanetary voyages—Fiction. I. Title.
    PR6103.O4427A84 2009
    823'.92—dc22
            2009028285

Hyperion books are available for special promotions and premiums. For details contact the HarperCollins Special Markets Department in the New York office at 212-207-7528, fax 212-207-7222, or email spsales@harpercollins.com.

Book design by Shubhani Sarkar

FIRST EDITION

10 9 8 7 6 5 4 3 2 1

For Jackie, Finn, and Seán, who miss me when I am away, but not as much as I miss them. If you want to remind yourselves what I look like, there should be a picture of me at the back of this book.

AND ANOTHER THING . . .
EOIN COLFER

If you own a copy of the Hitchhiker's Guide to the Galaxy, then one of the last things you would be likely to type into its v-board would be the very same title of that particular Sub-Etha volume. As presumably, since you have a copy, you already know all about the most remarkable book ever to come out of the great publishing corporations of Ursa Minor. However, presumption has been the runner-up in every major *Causes of Intergalactic Conflict* poll for the past few millennia. First place invariably going to "land-grabbing bastards with big weapons," and third usually being a toss-up between "coveting another sentient being's significant other" and "misinterpretation of simple hand gestures." One man's *Wow! This pasta is fantastico* is another's *Your momma plays it fast and loose with sailors.*

Let us say, for example, that you are on an eight-hour layover in Port Brasta without enough credit on your implant for a Gargle Blaster, and if upon realizing that you know almost nothing about this supposedly wonderful book you hold in your hands, you decide out of sheer brain-fogging boredom to type the words *the hitchhiker's guide to the galaxy* into the search bar on the Hitchhiker's Guide to the Galaxy, what results will this flippant tappery yield?

Firstly an animated icon appears in a flash of pixels and informs you that there are three results. Which is confusing as there are obviously five listed below him, numbered in the usual order.

. . . .

Guide Note: That is if your understanding of the usual numerical order is from small to large and not from derivative to inspired, as with Folfangan slugs, who judge a number's worth based on the artistic integrity of its shape. Folfangan supermarket receipts are beauteous ribbons, but their economy collapses at least once a week.

. . . .

Each of these five results is a lengthy article, accompanied by many hours of video and audio files and some dramatic reconstructions featuring quite well-known actors.

This is not the story of those articles.

But if you scroll down past article five, ignoring the offers to remortgage your kidneys and lengthen your pormwrangler, you will come to a line in tiny font that reads, *If you liked this, then you might also like to read* . . . Have your icon rub itself along this link and you will be led to a text only appendix with absolutely no audio and not so much as a frame of video shot by a student director who made the whole thing in his bedroom and paid his drama soc. mates with sandwiches.

This is the story of that appendix.

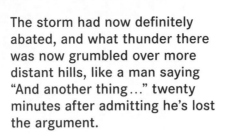

The storm had now definitely abated, and what thunder there was now grumbled over more distant hills, like a man saying "And another thing..." twenty minutes after admitting he's lost the argument.

DOUGLAS ADAMS

We have travelled through space and time, my friends, to rock this house again.

TENACIOUS D

So far as we know . . . The Imperial Galactic Government decided, over a bucket of jeweled crabs one day, that a hyperspace expressway was needed in the unfashionable end of the western spiral arm of the Galaxy. This decision was rushed through channels ostensibly to preempt traffic congestion in the distant future, but actually to provide employment for a few ministers' cousins who were forever mooching around Government Plaza. Unfortunately the Earth was in the path of this planned expressway, so the remorseless Vogons were dispatched in a constructor fleet to remove the offending planet with gentle use of thermonuclear weapons.

Two survivors managed to hitch a ride on a Vogon ship: Arthur Dent, a young English employee of a regional radio station whose plans for the morning did not include having his home planet blasted to dust beneath his slippers. Had the human race held a referendum, it's quite likely that Arthur Dent would have been voted least suitable to *carry the hopes of mankind into space.* Arthur's university yearbook actually referred to him as "most likely to end up living in a hole in the Scottish highlands with only the chip on his shoulder for company." Luckily Arthur's Betelgeusean friend, Ford Prefect, a roving reporter for that illustrious interstellar travel almanac *The Hitchhiker's Guide to the Galaxy,* was more of an optimist. Ford saw silver linings where Arthur saw only clouds, and so between them they made one prudent space traveler, unless their travels led them to the planet Junipella, where the clouds actually did have silver linings. Arthur would have doubtless steered the ship straight into the nearest cloud of gloom, and Ford would have almost certainly attempted to steal the silver, which would have resulted in the catastrophic combustion of the natural gas inside the lining. The explosion would have been pretty, but as a heroic ending, it would have lacked a certain something—i.e., a hero in one piece.

The only other Earthling left alive was Tricia McMillan, or Trillian to use her cool spacey name, a fiercely ambitious astrophysicist cum fledgling reporter who had always believed that there was more to life than life on Earth. In spite of this conviction, Trillian had nevertheless been amazed when she was whisked off to the stars by Zaphod Beeblebrox, the maverick two-headed Galactic President.

What can one say of President Beeblebrox that he has not already had printed on T-shirts and circulated throughout the Galaxy free with every uBid purchase?

Zaphod Says Yes to Zaphod was probably the most famous T-shirt slogan, though not even his team of psychiatrists understood what it actually meant. Second favorite was probably *Beeblebrox. Just be glad he's out there.*

It is a universal maxim that if someone goes to the trouble of printing something on a T-shirt, then it is almost definitely not a hundred percent untrue, which is to say that it is more than likely fairly definitely not altogether false. Consequentially, when Zaphod Beeblebrox arrived on a planet, people invariably said yes to whatever questions he asked and when he left they were glad he was out there.

These less than traditional heroes were improbably drawn to each other and embarked on a series of adventures, which mostly involved gadding around through space and time, sitting on quantum sofas, chatting with gaseous computers, and generally failing to find meaning or fulfillment in any corner of the Universe.

Arthur Dent eventually returned to the hole in space where the Earth used to be and discovered that the hole had been filled by an Earth-sized planet that looked and behaved remarkably like Earth. In fact this planet was *an* Earth, just not Arthur's. Not *this* Arthur's at any rate. Because his home planet was at the center of a plural zone, the Arthur we are concerned with had found himself shuffled along the dimensional axis to an Earth that had never been destroyed by Vogons. This rather made *our* Arthur's day, and his usually pessimistic mood was further improved when he encountered Fenchurch, his soul mate. Luckily this idyllic period was not cut short by Arthur and Fenchurch bumping into any *alternate universe* Arthurs who may have been wandering around, possibly in Los Angeles working for the BBC.

Arthur and his true love traveled the stars together until Fenchurch vanished in mid-conversation during a hyperspace jump. Arthur searched the Universe for her, paying his way by exchanging bodily fluids for first-class tickets. Eventually he was stranded on the planet Lamuella and made a life for himself there as sandwich maker for a primitive tribe who believed that sandwiches were pretty hot stuff.

His tranquillity was disturbed by the arrival of a couriered box from Ford Prefect, which contained the Hitchhiker's Guide to the Galaxy Mark II in the form of a smarmy pan-dimensional black bird. Trillian, who was now a successful newswoman, had a delivery of her own for Arthur in the shape of Random Dent, the daughter conceived with the donated price of seat 2D on the Alpha Centauri red-eye.

Arthur reluctantly took on the role of parent, but was completely out of his depth with the truculent teenager. Random stole the Guide Mark II and set a course for Earth, where she believed she could finally feel at home. Arthur and Ford followed, to find Trillian already on the planet.

Only then was the Mark II's objective revealed. The Vogons, irritated by the Earth's refusal to stay ka-boomed, had engineered the bird to lure the escapees back to the planet before they destroyed it in every dimension, thus fulfilling their original order.

Arthur and Ford rushed at semi-breakneck speed to London's Club Beta, pausing only to purchase foie gras and blue suede shoes. Thanks to the old dimensional axis/plural zone thing, they found Trillian *and* Tricia McMillan coexisting in the same space-time, both being screamed at by an emotional Random.

Confused? Arthur was, but not for long. Once he noticed the green death rays pulsating through the lower atmosphere, all of the day's other niggling problems seemed to lose their nigglyness. After all, confusion was not likely to slice him into a million seared pieces.

The Vogon prostetnic had done his job well. Not only had he lured Arthur, Ford, and Trillian back to the planet Earth, but he'd also managed to trick a Grebulon captain into destroying the Earth for him, thus saving the crew several hundred Vog hours' paperwork with the munitions office.

Arthur and his friends sit powerless in London's Club Beta and can only watch as the ultimate war on Earth is waged, unable to participate, unless involuntary spasming and liquefaction of bone matter counts as participation. On this occasion the weapons of destruction are death rays rather than Vogon torpedoes, but then, one planet killing device is pretty much the same as another when you're on the receiving end . . .

CHAPTER I

According to a janitor's assistant at the Maximegalon University, who often loiters outside lecture halls, the universe is sixteen billion years old. This supposed truth is scoffed at by a clutch of Betelgeusean beat poets who claim to have moleskin pads older than that (rat a tat-tat). Seventeen billion, they say, at the very least, according to their copy of the Wham Bam Big Bang scrolls. A human teenage prodigy once called it at fourteen billion based on a complicated computation involving the density of moon rock and the distance between two pubescent females on an event horizon. One of the minor Asgardian gods did mumble that he'd read something somewhere about some sort of a major-ish cosmic event eighteen billion years ago, but no one pays much attention to pronouncements from on high anymore, not since the *birth of the gods* debacle, or Thorgate as it has come to be known.

However many billions it actually is, it *is* billions, and the old man on the beach looked as though he'd counted off at least one of those million millions on his fingers. His skin was ivory parchment, and viewed in profile he closely resembled a quavering uppercase S.

The man remembered having a cat once, if memories could be trusted as anything more than neuron configurations across trillions of synapses. Memories could not be touched with one's fingers. Could not be felt like the surf flowing over his gnarled toes could be felt. But then what were physical feelings but more electrical messages from the brain? Why believe in them either? Was there anything trustworthy in the Universe that one could hug and hold onto like a Hawaliusian wind staunch in the midst of a butterfly storm, apart from a Hawaliusian wind staunch.

Bloody butterflies, thought the man. Once they'd figured out the wing fluttering a continent away thing, millions of mischievous lepidoptera had banded together and turned malicious.

Surely that cannot be real, he thought. *Butterfly storms?*

But then more neurons poured across even more synapses and whispered of improbability theories. If a thing was bound never to happen, then that thing would resolutely refuse not to happen as soon as possible.

Butterfly storms. It was only a matter of time.

The old man wrenched his focus from this phenomenon before some other catastrophe occurred to him and began its rough slouch to be born.

Was there anything to trust? Anything to take comfort from?

The setting suns lit crescents on the wavelets, burnished the clouds, striped the palm leaves silver, and set the china pot on his veranda table twinkling.

Ah, yes, thought the old man. *Tea. At the center of an uncertain and possibly illusory universe there would always be tea.*

The old man traced two natural numbers in the sand with a walking stick fashioned from a discarded robot leg and watched as the waves washed them away.

One moment, there was forty-two and the next there wasn't.

Maybe the numbers were never there and perhaps they didn't even matter.

For some reason this made the old man cackle as he leaned into the incline and plodded to his veranda. He settled with much creaking of bone and wood into a wicker chair that was totally sympathetic to the surroundings, and called to his android to bring some biscuits.

The android brought Rich Tea.

Good choice.

Seconds later the sudden appearance of a hovering metal bird caused a momentary lapse in dunking concentration and the old man lost a large crescent of his biscuit to the tea.

"Oh, for heaven's sake," grumbled the man. "Do you know how long

I have been working on that technique? Dunking and sandwiches. What else is left to a person?"

The bird was unperturbed.

"An unperturbed bird," said the old man softly, enjoying the sound of it. He closed the bad eye that hadn't worked properly since he'd fallen out of a tree as a giddy boy, and examined the creature.

The bird hovered, its metallic feathers shimmering crimson in the sun's rays, its wings beating up tiny maelstroms.

"Battery," it said in a voice that reminded the old man of an actor he had once seen playing Othello at London's Globe Theatre. Amazing what you can get from the tone of a single word.

"You did say battery?" said the man, just to confirm. It could possibly have been flattery, or even hattery. His hearing was not what it used to be, especially on initial consonants.

"Battery," said the bird again, and suddenly reality cracked and fell to pieces like a shattered mirror. The beach disappeared, the waves froze, crackled, and evaporated. The last thing to go was the Rich Tea.

"Bugger," muttered the old man as the final crumbs dissipated on his fingertips, then he sat back on a cushion in the room of sky that suddenly surrounded him. Someone would be coming soon, he was sure of it. From the dim caverns of his old memories, the names Ford and Prefect emerged like gray bats to associate themselves with the impending disaster.

Whenever the Universe fell apart, Ford Prefect was never far behind. Him and that accursed book of his. What was it called? Oh, yes. *The Pitchforker's Pride Is a Fallacy.*

That, or something very close to it.

The old man knew exactly what Ford Prefect would say.

Look on the bright side, old mate. At least you're not lying down in front of a bulldozer, eh? At least we're not being flushed out of a Vogon air lock. A room of sky is not too shabby, as it happens. It could be worse, a lot worse.

"It will be a lot worse," said the old man with gloomy certainty. In his experience, things generally got worse, and on the rare occasion when things actually seemed to get better, it was only as a dramatic prelude to a cataclysmic worsening.

Oh, this room of sky *seemed* harmless enough, but what terrors lurked beyond its rippling walls? None that were not terrible, of that the old man was certain.

He poked a finger into one of the wall's yielding surfaces and was reminded of tapioca pudding, which almost made the old man smile, until he remembered that he had hated tapioca ever since a bullying head boy had filled his slippers with the stuff back in Eaton House Prep.

"Blisters Smyth, you sneaky shit," he whispered.

His fingertip left a momentary hole in the clouds, and through it the old man caught a glimpse of a double-height sash window beyond, and outside the window, could that be a death ray?

The old man rather feared that it was.

All this time, he thought. *All this time and nothing has happened.*

Ford Prefect was living the dream. Providing *the dream* included residence in one of Han Wavel's ultraluxury, five-supergiant-rated, naturally eroded hedonistic resorts, filling one's waking hours with *permanent damage* amounts of exotic cocktails, and liaisons with exotic females of various species.

And the best bit: The expense of this whole self-indulgent and possibly life-shortening package would be taken care of by his Dine-O-Charge card, which had no credit limit thanks to a little creative computer tinkering on his last visit to the Hitchhiker's Guide offices.

If a younger Ford Prefect had been handed a blank page and asked to, in his own time, write a short paragraph detailing his dearest wishes for his own future, the only word he might have amended in the above was the adverb *possibly*. Probably.

The resorts of Han Wavel were so obscenely luxurious that it was said a Brequindan male would sell his mother for a night in the Sandcastle Hotel's infamous vibro-suite. This is not as shocking as it sounds, as parents are accepted currency on Brequinda and a nicely moisturized septuagenarian with a good set of teeth can be traded for a mid-range family moto-carriage.

Ford would perhaps not have sold either parent to finance his sojourn at the Sandcastle, but there was a bicranial cousin who was often more trouble than he was worth.

Every night, Ford rode the fleshevator to his penthouse, croaked at the door to grant him entry, then made time to look himself in the bloodshot eyes before passing out facedown in the basin.

This is the last night, he swore nightly. *Surely my body will revolt and collapse in on itself.*

What would his obituary say in the *Hitchhiker's Guide*? Ford wondered. It would be brief, that was for sure. A couple of words. Perhaps the same two words he had used to describe Earth all those years ago.

Mostly harmless.

Earth. Hadn't something rather sad happened on Earth that he should be thinking about? Why were there some things he could remember and others that were about as clear as a hazy morning on the permanently fogbound Misty Plains of Nephologia?

It was generally at about this maudlin stage that the third Gargle Blaster squeezed the last drop of consciousness from Ford's overjuiced brain and he would giggle twice, squawk like a rodeo chicken, and execute a near perfect forward tumble into the nearest bathroom receptacle.

And yet every morning when he lifted his head from the en suite basin (if he was lucky), Ford found himself miraculously revitalized. No hangover, no dragon breath, not even a burst blood vessel in either sclera to bear witness to the previous night's excesses.

"You are a froody dude, Ford Prefect," he invariably told himself. "Yes, you are."

There is something fishy going on here, his rarely-heard-from subconscious insisted.

Fishy?

So long and thanks for all the . . .

Wasn't there something about dolphins? Not fish, true, but they inhabited the same . . . habitat.

Think, you idiot! Think! You should be dead a hundred times over. You have consumed enough cocktails to pickle not only yourself but several alternate versions of yourself. How are you still alive?

"Alive and froody," Ford would say, often winking at himself in the mirror, marveling at how lustrous his red hair had become. How pronounced his cheekbones. And he seemed to be growing a chin. An actual chiseled chin.

"This place is doing me good," he told his reflection. "All the photo-leech wraps and the irradiated colono-lemming treatments are really boosting my system. I think I owe it to Ford Prefect to stay another while."

And so he did.

On the last day, Ford charged an underwater massage to his credit card. The masseur was a Damogranian pom-pom squid with eleven tentacles and a thousand suckers that pummeled Ford's back and cleaned out his pores with a series of whiplash tapotement moves. Pom-pom squids were generally hugely overqualified for their work in the spa industry, but were tempted away from their umpteenth doctorates by the lure of high salaries, plankton-rich pools, and the chance of massaging a talent scout for the music industry and maybe getting themselves a record deal.

"Have you done any talent scouting, friend?" asked the squid, though he didn't sound hopeful.

"Nope," replied Ford, bubbles streaming from his Plexiglas helmet, face shining orange in the pleasant glow of rock phosphorescence. "Though I once owned a pair of blue suede shoes, which should count for something. I still own one; the other is closer to mauve, due to it being a copy."

The squid nipped at passing plankton as he spoke, which made conversation a little disjointed.

"I don't know if . . ."

"If what?"

"I hadn't finished."

"It's just that you stopped speaking."

"There was a glint. I thought it was lunch."

"You eat glints?"

"No. Not actual glints."

"Good, because glints are baby gloonts, and they're poisonous."

"I know. I was merely saying that . . ."

"More glints?"

"Precisely. You're sure you're not a talent scout then, or an agent?"

"Nope."

"Oh, for Zark's sake," swore the squid, a little unprofessionally. "Two years I've worked here. Talent scouts and agents coming out of your suckers . . . they promised. Not one. Not bloody one. I was studying advanced kazoo, you know."

Ford couldn't resist a lead-in like that. "Advanced kazoo? How advanced can kazoo studies be?"

The squid was wounded. "Pretty advanced when you can play a thousand of them at the same time. I was in a quartet. Can you imagine?"

Ford gave it a go. He closed his eyes, enjoyed the *whup-pop* of the suckers on his back, and imagined four thousand kazoos playing in perfect subaquatic harmony.

Sometime later the squid enveloped Ford in half a dozen tentacles and gently flipped him over. Ford opened one eye to read the squid's badge.

I am Barzoo, read the tag. *Use me as you will.*

And underneath in smaller print:

I am allergic to rubber.

"So, Barzoo. What kind of stuff did you play?"

The masseur got his tentacles a-pumping before he answered, whipping up a flurry of currents.

"Old songs mostly. Covers. You ever hear of Hotblack Desiato?"

I have heard that name, Ford realized, but he couldn't quite pin the memory down. Every day things got a little fuzzier.

"Hotblack Desiato. Wasn't he dead for a while?"

Barzoo cocked his head, thinking about this. The squid's beak hung open, ignoring the tiny streaks of plankton flashing by.

"Hey, if you can't remember, don't worry about it. I'm having a few memory problems myself in this place. Little things like how long I've been here, what my purpose in life is, which feet to put my shoes on. Stuff like that."

The squid did not respond and its tentacles rested heavily on Ford's torso, like old rope.

Ford hoped that Barzoo had not suddenly died, and if the squid *had* passed on to the energy stage, would the suckers lose their suck or go into some kind of death-suck mode? Ford had no desire to spend the rest of his holiday having tentacles surgically removed from his torso.

Then Barzoo blinked.

"Hey, buddy," sighed Ford, bubbles spiraling from his helmet. "Welcome back. For a second there, I thought . . ."

"Battery," said the squid, beak clicking on the T's. "Battery."

I never noticed before, thought Ford. *But that squid looks a lot like a bird.*

Then the underwater massage cave dissolved and Ford Prefect found himself deposited in a room composed of blue sky.

A familiar figure sat in the opposite corner.

"Ah," said Ford, remembering.

. . . .

Guide Note: Remembering is generally a two-stage process involving dialogue between the conscious and subconscious parts of the brain. The subconscious opens proceedings by throwing up the relevant memory, an act which releases a spurt of self-congratulatory endorphins.

Well done, matey, says the conscious. *That memory is really useful right now, and I couldn't remember where I'd put it.*

You and me, pal, says the subconscious, delighted to have its contribution acknowledged for once, *we're in this together.*

Then the conscious reviews the memory in its in-tray and sends a message down to the sphincter telling it to prepare for the worst.

Why did you remind me of this? the conscious rails against the subconscious. *This is awful. Terrible. I didn't want to remember this. Why the Zark do you think I shoved it to the back of my brain?*

That's the last time I help you out, the subconscious mutters and retreats to the darker sections of itself where nasty thoughts are housed. *I don't need you,* it tells itself. *I can make myself another personality out of these things you've discarded.* And so the seeds of schizophrenia are sown with kernels of childhood bullying, neglect, low self-esteem, and prejudice.

Luckily, Betelgeuseans don't have much of a subconscious, so that's all right then.

. . . .

"Ah," said Ford again, followed quickly by "Crap."

He stepped gingerly across the floor of sky, noticing with a jolt of surprise that one of his legs flickered slightly for a moment.

I'm not real, he realized, which was enough to stick a pin in his permanently buoyant mood, but he recovered quickly, something that the room's other occupant didn't seem to have managed just yet.

"Look on the bright side, old mate," he called to the Earthman. "At least you're not lying down in front of a bulldozer, eh? At least we're not being flushed out of a Vogon air lock, remember that? A room of sky is not too shabby, as it happens. It could be worse, a lot worse."

And it shortly will be if I'm right about what's going on here, thought Ford, but he didn't voice this opinion. Arthur looked as though he'd had quite enough bad news for one day.

Interplanetary news reporter Trillian Astra spent a few anxious moments in the press bathroom before heading into the auditorium for possibly the biggest interview of her life. In the course of a celebrated career, Trillian had spent a year undercover in prosthetics working as a Vogon clerk in the Megabrantis Cluster. She had lost her left foot to frostbite when mine raiders on Orion Beta had ram-raided a madranite shaft, and more recently she had been attacked by a holistic orthodontist when she had the temerity to question the effectiveness of tooth-straightening chants.

The Galaxy knew Trillian's name. At the height of her career she was feared by shady politicians, movie moguls, and pregnant single celebrities from Alpha Centauri to Viltvodle VI, but on this day she felt the specter of fear at her own shoulder.

Galactic President Random Dent. Her daughter. Simulcast from the University of Maximegalon live to an audience of five hundred billion.

She was nervous. No, more than that. She was terrified. Trillian had not seen her daughter since . . .

My God, she realized. *I cannot remember precisely the last time I saw Random.*

Trillian tried to calm herself with ritual.

"You're looking good for an old bird," she said to the mirror.

"Do you really tink this, dahling?" said the mirror, obviously highly offended by what paraded before its sensors. "If this is good, then you are having the low standards."

Trillian bristled. "How dare you. If you had seen what I have seen. If you had been through what I've been through, then I think you might agree that I look pretty damn good."

The mirror's sighs rippled the eight gel speakers mounted in its frame.

"Enough with the history lesson, dahling. I don't factor in the past, I just comment on the present. And right now, let me tell you, you look like Eccentrica Gallumbits, in her third cycle. And believe me, honey, by that old whore's third cycle things were mostly liquid and gas. If I were you, I'd buy myself a good towel and a bathrobe and just . . ."

Trillian reached across and pounded her fist against the mirror's mute button.

When did they start to give mirrors character traits? She could remember when only very special doors and top-end androids had the Sirius Cybernetics Corporation's Genuine People Personality feature.

Maybe Trillian didn't want to hear what the mirror had to say, but she could admit to herself that it was right.

She did look old. Ancient in fact.

That's because I am Zarking ancient. A hundred and five Earth years old. What's left of me.

Over the years Tricia McMillan had been chipped away by her job as Sub Etha reporter, and soon only Trillian would remain. This was not simply a metaphorical statement; Trillian Astra had always been prepared to sacrifice everything for the network. Her friends, family, various body parts.

She lost the foot on Orion Beta during the mining hostilities; seventy percent of her epidermis seared off by a plasma splash on the front line at the Carfrax Gamma Caves, left hand and forearm mangled by a desert crawler tread during the Dordellis Wars, and her right eye poked out by a flag on a little pointy stick during a WangoPango teenybop ice capade on Gagrakacka.

So what was left of Tricia McMillan was an original brain (with added nu-fluid), one rebuffed eye, a couple of cheeks (one buttock, one facial), an assortment of minor bones, and two and a half liters of human blood. The other three liters were not technically blood at all but tears harvested from a hive of silver-tongued devils, small mammals indigenous to the Hastromil system. They are relentlessly exploited because of the usefulness of absolutely every part of their beings, from their hinged silver tongues, to their very thought waves, which can be harnessed to an aerial and used to boost video signal reception if you live down a hole. The same philosophers who cite the Babel fish as proof that God doesn't exist also cite the unfortunately initialed STD as proof that Satan does. An argument which even a potato with a charge running through it could see undermines their initial point. But what do they care? Head doctors love controversy.

Ironically, Trillian was in Hastromil to cover a rally to protect the STD when she was run over by a silver-tongue float, constructed even more ironically from silver-tongue hides, which irony she then trumped by receiving a silver-tongue transfusion while wearing a *Protect the Silver-Tongue* T-shirt. It was later reported, by Trillian herself, that all this localized irony overload had caused the death of eleven empaths attending the rally. Twelve, if the empath known to be already depressed was added to the statistic.

Trillian smooshed the plaskin on her cheek. It was smooth but a little overstretched. The guy at the checkout had promised that her face would loosen out with wear. But it never had. On bad days, Trillian thought her face looked like a skull pushed into a balloon.

A network executive had once described her as "a slim, darkish humanoid, with long waves of black hair, an odd little knob of a nose, and ridiculously brown eyes."

Not anymore.

Today was one of those bad days.

Random. After all these years.

Every time she looked into her daughter's eyes, it was like staring into pools of her own guilt.

Trillian slapped her palm against the mirror.

"Ow! Hey!" said the mirror, overriding the mute.

Trillian ignored it.

She needed to pull herself together. She had at one time been the Galaxy's most respected reporter and that was an achievement. She would force her regret into its box down in the pit of her stomach and go do her job.

Trillian plucked at a strand in her helmet of coiffed sim-hair, squared her shoulders, and walked into the auditorium to interview the daughter who had been conceived in a lo-grav fertility satellite clinic near Barnard's Star.

Trillian shuddered. As if morning sickness had not been bad enough without lo-grav thrown into the mix.

Random had every right to feel displaced: Her father was a test tube; her home planet, insofar as she had one, had been destroyed in several dimensions; and her mother had taken one look at her and decided to vigorously pursue a career that would take her far from home for long periods.

No wonder Random was a little frosty.

President Random Dent sat cross-legged in a hovering egg chair onstage, chanting quietly.

"Bicuspid lie behind canine behind lateral incisor behind central incisor. Toooooth find your place."

The curtain had not yet been drawn, but she could hear the hubbub of the crowd through the heavy material. The curtain was velvet, not holographic. An expense grudgingly borne by the university at Random's insistence. While in no way anti-progress, the President believed that there was still room for tradition in the Galaxy.

She smiled softly as her mother was led onto the platform. From a distance a person could be forgiven for thinking that their roles were reversed and that Trillian was the President's daughter, but up close the truth was plain. Surgery shine was written all over Trillian's face.

The reporter's step faltered as she caught sight of her daughter, but she recovered herself well.

"You look well, Madam President," she said in that typical reporter's accent, which was somewhere between Sector ZZ9 and Asgard.

"As do you, Mother," responded Random.

Trillian settled into a second egg chair and consulted her notes.

"President Random Frequent Flyer Dent. Still using too many names?"

Random smiled in the calm manner of one who has been tantrum-free for decades. "And you, Trillian Astra. Still using the wrong one?"

Trillian smiled tightly. This was not going to be an easy interview.

"Why now, Random? We haven't seen each other more than a dozen times in the past twenty years. Why now, when my career is on the wane? I go from beauty pageants on New Betel to the biggest interview of my life."

Random smiled again. A gentle creasing of her outdoorsy face. Her gray-streaked hair stiff with sunshine and salt water.

"I know it's been a while, Mother. Too long." She stroked a tiny ball of fur around her neck and it mewled softly. Trillian saw tiny teeth and a tail and her heart sank.

"I've heard about that thing. Your constant companion. It's some kind of little gerbil, isn't it? Cute."

"More than a cute gerbil, Mother. Fertle is my companion. A flaybooz. Fully grown. A font of knowledge, all transmitted telepathically." And then she dropped the bomb. The career killer. "We were married yesterday."

Trillian's skin felt tighter than it had a minute ago. "You were married?"

"It's a mental bond, obviously. Though Fertle does like me to tickle his tummy."

Keep it together, Trillian told herself. *You are a professional.*

"Let me get this straight. You communicate *telepathically* with . . . Fertle?"

"Of course. Communication is what keeps families together. Haven't you heard?"

At this point, Trillian stopped being a reporter and started being a mother.

"Less of the payback jibes, young lady. This is your life we're talking about. You are Random Dent, the President of the Galaxy. You united the tribes of Earth. You oversaw the official first contact ceremony." Trillian was on her feet now. "You spearheaded the economic drive into space. You negotiated for equal rights for aliens."

"And now I want something for myself."

Trillian strangled an imaginary Fertle, six inches in front of the real one. "Not a gerbil, though. Not a Zarking gerbil. How is a gerbil going to give me grandchildren?"

"We don't want kids," said Random blithely. "We want to travel."

"What are you talking about? It's a rodent."

"He," said Random pointedly, "is a flaybooz, as you well know. And I thought you, of all people, would understand our relationship. The formidable Trillian Astra. Champion of all people, except her daughter."

Trillian thought she detected a chink of light in the gloom. "Wait. What? This is about me? You are going to destroy your life to get back at me? That's one hell of a twisted revenge cocktail, Random."

Random tickled her husband till he snickered. "Don't be ridiculous, Mother. I wanted you here to introduce your son-in-law to the Galaxy. It will be your crowning moment as a journalist, and it will bring us together as a family."

Trillian saw it all then, the genius of Random's coup de grâce. If she announced this union in full 3D spectro-vision, then she would be a laughing stock. If she did not, then her daughter was lost to her forever and would probably milk the situation for enough sympathy to win another term in office. At the very least, the flaybooz would vote for her, and there were zillions of those.

Trillian's frame jerked spasmodically. *Married!*

"Forget it, Random, you're not using me to put a spin on your relationship. As soon as I get out of here, I'm going to track down your father and he can deal with you."

Random shook with laughter, frightening her husband. "Arthur! Do you have any idea how far he would go to avoid confrontation?" She paused, cocking her head to one side. "Fertle says, and I agree, that *you* have to announce this, Mother. The Galaxy is expecting big news."

"Absolutely not. I refuse to be manipulated."

"You'd rather be controlled by the networks, like the robot you are. I can hear you buzzing from here. I can smell your circuits. Is there any part of you that's real? Can you put me in touch with my human mother? Or perhaps you know where her backbone is buried."

Trillian was almost relieved that the façade of civility had been scorched away.

"Screw you, Random."

The President nodded. "Yes, Fertle. This is how she is. Are you surprised now that I am difficult to read? At all the defenses I have erected around my brain?"

Trillian was almost shrieking. "You are talking to a bloody yo-yo!" Fertle seemed to react to this.

. . . .

Guide Note: Though flaybooz have no ears, they are extremely sensitive to vibration and can actually explode in extreme circumstances. Thor, the Asgardian and sometime rock god, held the record for spontaneous flaybooz detonation when he debuted his new tune "You Wanna Get Hammered?" from a chariot in orbit around Squornshellous Delta. The record had previously been held by intergalactic rock stars Disaster Area, who dropped a speaker bomb into a volcano crater where the flaybooz were enjoying a static electricity festival.

. . . .

Fertle's fur bristled and he opened a tiny mouth that now seemed to have a beak.

"Battery," said Fertle in a voice of wire and claws.

"What?" said Trillian. "Did I just hear a flaybooz speak? Now, that would be news."

"Battery," said Fertle again, this time with some urgency.

The velvet curtain rose slowly, but there was no audience behind it, just an auditorium of sky and two humanoid figures.

Random and Trillian stood and gaped, family resemblance clear for once in spite of the various surgeries and implants.

"What's happening?" said the President, her voice higher suddenly. "Mother. What's happening? Where are my journalists?"

"Don't panic," said Trillian, trying to keep the quaver from her voice. "Something is happening here."

"Something is happening?" shrilled Random. "That's it? All of your years in the field and all you can come up with is *something is happening*? This is a kidnap attempt, that's what it is. We've been transported somewhere."

Trillian squinted at the humanoid figures, who seemed to be growing increasingly familiar, as though scales of forgetfulness were falling from her eyes.

"Kidnapped. I don't think so. Not by these two. They're harmless . . . mostly."

Random adopted her favorite presidential power position: feet planted, arms crossed.

"You two men. What have you done? I demand to know where we are."

The shorter man noticed the new arrivals; it was pretty likely that he would, as one of them was shouting at him.

"I think the question should be *when* we are and possibly who put us here, followed by is there a drinks trolley?"

Random scowled. "Is there a drinks trolley indeed. Be flippant all you like, young man. I know that underneath you're as scared as we are."

The young man smiled. "I'm Betelgeusean, Random. We don't do underneath."

Random lost the urge to riposte when the sudden recognition of the second man hit her like a Surprise-O-Plasm pie in the face.

"Father? Daddy? Dad?"

"Pick one," suggested the Betelgeusean. "It will make conversations easier."

Trillian took off across the room of sky, moving faster than she had in years.

"Now, let's see what your father has to say about this marriage."

Random suddenly seemed a lot younger. "Daddy!" she howled. "Daddy! My stupid mother hates my husband."

The father figure dropped his head and wished for tea.

CHAPTER 2

Ford Prefect explored the room of sky, breathing on the walls to see if the surface fogged, pulling horrible faces to check for a recoil factor, and eventually touching it gingerly through his sleeve. When the material of his shirt did not have its electrons excited to a higher temperature, Ford deemed it safe to poke the wall with his finger. He did so and the wall rippled, sending images flitting across the room, of flaybooz wedding ceremonies, beach huts, and wild parties. When the ripples died, so did the residual memories, and the wall was azure sky once more.

"Do you mind?" said a voice that seemed to come from everywhere. "My needles are on red as it is, to coin an archaic phrase. If you could just sit still, I can hold this construct together awhile longer."

"So you're saying that this whole room is a construct?" said Ford, poking the wall again.

"Would you . . . Didn't I just say . . . Yes, yes it's a construct. This waiting lounge is all in your head. In all of your heads. It is a virtual room. Is there another way you would like me to impart this information?"

Ford scratched his chin and was disappointed to find that it was not as chiseled as it had been at Han Wavel.

"How about a video?"

The sky walls disappeared altogether, replaced by several representations of a robotic bird, tapping a claw impatiently.

"Ah," said Ford. "The Hitchhiker's Guide to the Galaxy Mark II. I thought as much. I haven't seen you since . . ." Ford flipped through his solidifying memories. "Since you tried to get the Earth blasted to pieces."

"Not since then," said the bird. "Not since way back then. Imagine."

"You've upgraded your feathers to gold, I see."

"It's a construct, Betelgeusean. I appear as I wish to appear. So did you, back at the resort. Remember the chin?"

Ford sighed wistfully. "I do. That was so froody. The shadows I could cast with that godlike chin."

"I've seen a few gods," remarked the bird. "Some of them are not so great in the chin department. Why do you think Loki cultivates that beard?"

Ford paced a little. "Back to my question. How about a video?"

H2G2-2 scowled, which is not easy with a beak. "Didn't you hear me? The needles are on red. I can't hold the waiting lounge together for much longer."

"Nothing fancy. Just some 2D animation, old school stuff. I know you can do it if you really want to."

The bird rolled its eyes dramatically then disappeared from one of the walls. In its place a black screen opened and on the screen were four neon stick figures. One had rather outlandish boob circles and another hadn't much in the way of chins.

"Ha ha," called Ford to the sky. "Very humorous."

A cartoon bird appeared on the screen and hovered above the four humanoids.

"Welcome," said the bird, "to this video demonstration which I like to call: *Constructs for Idiots.*"

Ford raised a finger. "Does that mean that the people in the constructs are idiots, or that you're explaining it to idiots?"

The bird ignored him. "As a pan-dimensional, mega-advanced, omniscient travel guide, equipped with the very best Organ-O-Brain, capable of running over ten trillion simultaneous calculations . . ."

Ford rapped on the screen. "Could you keep it down and hurry it up. I feel pretty sure that there is bad news coming, and it might be better if I get to grips with it first. Some people in this room don't handle bad news so well. I'd like to have a chance to massage the truth a little before I present it."

"Well, if you'd stop wittering on . . ."

"I am stopped. Go ahead please . . ."

The bird cleared its throat in a wholly unnecessary manner. "As I was saying. As such an advanced biohybrid organism, it was a simple matter for me to poke a neuron beam into the dream center at the back of each brain—yours was pretty hard to find, by the way, Betelgeusean—and then link the neural networks through a central server—that is to say, myself."

Ford frowned. "Show me some moving pictures," he said.

On-screen blue beams fanned from the bird's wingtips, entering the humanoids' heads through one ear, then exiting through the other ear and converging on the H2G2-2's forehead.

"So you sent us to sleep and gave us a dream."

"I gave you life, for a long time."

"But it was virtual life, we didn't go anywhere?"

"Correct. Anywhere or anywhen."

"Which is not a word. Organ-O-Brain? Really?"

"I was trying to be succinct."

Ford poked the wall again, this time with two fingers, watching the memory ripples run around the walls and intermingle. "It's all a dream then. And not just this room?"

"No," said the voice coldly. "Not just this room."

More poking. "How far back?"

"Club Beta."

"Club Beta. That bongs a gong for some reason. Club dingly dangly Beta." Ford stopped pacing. "Holy shankwursters!"

"I will thank you," said the Hitchhiker's Guide Mk II, "to mind your language. I am fully programmed to take offense."

"Aren't we all."

• •

Guide Note: This is literally true of the Cyphroles of Sesefras Magna, a gas giant in the Pleiades system. The Cyphroles are tiny invertebrate free-swimming gastrozoa who absorb the hostile energy emitted by their predators and use it to power their own systems. This makes the predator angry and so the Cyphroles swim faster through the gas ocean. Sesefras Magna gas dragons have learned to approach the Cyphroles casually, whistling a little tune or pretending to search for a few coins they have mislaid. The Cyphroles always fall for these tricks, as nature gave them large energy filters and tiny bullshit detectors.

. . . .

"Club Beta? In London? But that was . . . I don't even remember how long ago that was."

"It was then and it is now. My perception is unfiltered, so I see all points of my existence simultaneously."

"How about us impoverished beings with filtered perceptions?" Ford didn't like this bird much, and believed that he wouldn't like it even with a few Gargle Blasters eating at his stomach lining.

"You are still in the club. No time has passed."

Ford grabbed clumps of his ginger hair. "Why? For Zark's sake, why?"

Mk II rolled its pixelated eyes. "You try to do someone a favor. Honestly."

"Favor?" spluttered Ford, not giving a damn who heard. "If you wanted to do us a favor, you could have transported us away from the exploding planet."

"That would have been in direct contradiction with my program. I have prolonged your life by several decades."

"Who asked you to? Not me."

"Random Dent made the request. She is my secondary master. When the human minor realized that the entire planet was about to be destroyed, she expressed regret that she had not been allowed to live her life as she would have wished. Granting that wish did not conflict with my primary directive."

"What about the rest of us?"

"Mistress Dent included her parents and their chinless, dim-witted friend in her thoughts."

Ford was wounded. "Chinless? She thought that?"

"Oh yes," said the bird with obvious relish. "Several times."

Something occurred to Ford. "Secondary master? Who is the primary?"

"You are not entitled to interrogate me," snapped Mk II.

Ford borrowed a tactic from the Sesefras Magna gas dragons. "I know that. Of course a wondrous being like yourself doesn't have to answer to a lowly Betelgeusean like myself. But it would be a lovely treat for me to understand the complexities of your plan."

The bird cocked its head. "I know what you're doing."

"Obviously."

"I experience every moment simultaneously."

"No point in arguing then, is there? You already know what you're going to do."

"Good point. Very well, the Vogons created me so that I could cajole you back to Earth before the Grebulons destroyed it."

"Which is happening *now*."

"Now, as you know it. Yes."

"Will we be rescued?"

"Probably not."

"So you gave us the lives we wanted."

"No. I gave you free will and a construct. You followed your own paths under my supervision."

Ford winked at the bird. "I get it. I see now. You wanted to experience real time."

Mk II dropped its beak slowly, crossing its wings across its breast. "I lived your lives with you, never knowing what was coming next. It was exhilaratingly . . . random."

"And now?"

"Now? Now I know *exactly* what happens. A hundred years of maintaining four universes have depleted my power source. I only lasted this long because I periodically combined two constructs for the past virtual twenty years. Perhaps I should have thought of that sooner, but linear time is so immediate. In five virtual minutes this room will disappear, and you will be left on Earth facing the planet-killer beams of the Grebulons."

Ford's throat was suddenly too dry and his thoughts too cohesive. How he missed cocktail hour.

"Five minutes?"

"And counting," said Mk II, fading from view. In the places where the bird had been there appeared several digital readouts that said 4:57, then 4:56. You get the picture.

"Humans think digital watches are pretty neat," Ford murmured absently, then turned to face the three humans, who were busy doing their utmost to avoid being the least bit civil to each other.

The old man wasn't as ancient as he had been barely a moment before. He could tell this by the tautness of the skin on his hands and the renewed sharpness of his hearing.

I can hear every word these two women shriek at me. Oh joy.

"Arthur!" yelled the elder of the two, actually yelled. He hadn't been yelled at in . . . decades. "Are you even listening to me?"

Trying not to, thought Arthur, keeping his head down.

"I hate her," screamed the teenager. "She abandoned me and now she wants to control me. How does that make sense?"

"Arthur?"

"Daddy?"

"I am speaking to you, Arthur Dent."

Arthur Dent. It fit him. It was him.

"Arthur Dent," mumbled Arthur Dent, and he wasn't happy to hear it.

"Is that all you have to say? After all these years."

"I'm an old man," said Arthur hopefully. "Leave me alone."

"Old?" said the woman. "What are you talking about, old? You look exactly the same as you did the last time I saw you. *Exactly.* How did you do that?"

It was as Arthur feared. All those years alone on his beach and now he was back in the universe with people shouting at him and no idea what was going on.

"How did I do what?"

"Stay so young. I'm *younger* than you and I look like a silicon implant after a night in the toaster. Oh, why did I bother with all these refits? I should have retired. Or brought Random along with me. Other parents do it."

Arthur resigned himself to the fact that there was no wishing himself back to the beach, and made eye contact. He saw a slim, darkish, young woman, with shoulder-length curling black hair and chocolate eyes, wearing a dark, shimmering trouser suit.

Memories poked through to his consciousness.

"Trillian. You look beautiful."

The brown eyes blinked. "Screw you, Arthur. I didn't come here to be patronized."

"Sorry. You look beautiful, miss."

"Arthur. I chose Zaphod at the party, so live with it and drop that torch you're carrying. You need to see me as I am. My foot buzzes, for heaven's sake."

"Does it really? I didn't notice, and I *would* notice, because my hearing has become pretty sharp just recently."

Trillian placed two fingers on her left tibia, searching for the vibration that generally thrummed along her shinbone, keeping her awake at night.

"No buzzing."

"Mother," said Random behind her. "Mum."

Trillian noticed her fingernails were all her own. No acrylic falsies.

I am young. Young-ish. How can this be? Time is running backward.

"Mum!"

"Just a minute, Random. Tickle your bloody yo-yo or something."

"Fertle is gone, Mum. I'm no one again."

Trillian realized the enormity of what had happened and rushed to comfort her daughter.

"It's okay, darling. We have our lives to live over."

Random clenched her fingers into tiny fists. "I don't want this life. I want to be president of the galaxy. Is that too much to ask?"

The President was gone, and in her place a tearful teenage Goth.

• •

Guide Note: The "Goth" phenomenon is not confined to the planet Earth. Many species choose to define their adolescent periods with sustained truculent silences and the heartfelt belief that their parents took the wrong baby home from the hospital because their natural parents could not possibly be so mind-warpingly dense and boooring. While the adolescents of Earth advertise their feelings of isolation by wearing black clothing and listening to rock bands with names like Bloodshock and Sputum, the Hooloovoo (a super intelligent shade of blue) demonstrate their dissatisfaction with the Universe by holding their breath until they turn deep purple, while the Tubular Zingatularians (deep sea crustaceans) drive their parents demented by literally talking out of their arses.

Trillian realized that her daughter was a child once more and she hugged the girl with something close to ferocity.

"We have each other again. Daddy's here too." Trillian's rush of enthusiasm was enough to make her dizzy. "All the things we can do together. Camping and getting earrings and stuff. So many protests to march in. You'll love those. Down with international conglomerates and all that. The future is yours. You *will* be galactic president again. I promise."

Ford Prefect stepped into the conversation, waving his towel like a peace flag.

"I hate to be the one leaving a bag of Sooflinian pooh on your dream doorstep, but there may not be time to mount an election campaign for this particular planet. There might not even be time to secure the party nomination."

Trillian asked Ford a question she had historically posed at least once per conversation. "What the hell are you talking about, Ford?"

Ford raised his hands high, like a preacher. "All of this, it's a construct."

Guide Note: Throughout recorded history people have used constructs to avoid reality. The cheapest way to escape despair is to take refuge in one's imagination. During the day, a person might be forced to work in a quimp slattery, but in the evening that same person can be transformed by sheer force of will and imagination into a rumper of feltsparks.

Of course billions of people have no imaginations, and for these people there are Pan Galactic Gargle Blasters. After two of those babies, the dullest, most by-the-book Vogon will be up on the bar in stilettos, yodeling mountain shanties and swearing he's the king of the Gray Binding Fiefdoms of Saxaquine.

Unfortunately this method of escape from reality only lasts for a couple of weekends, by which time the escapee will be quite dead. Cause of death usually being a rebellious liver packing its bag and exiting the host torso via the nearest viable exit.

Because liver desertion is not a nice way to go, most species have invented some form of construct to escape their daily lives. The most primitive constructs are cave paintings, unless you are a gilled creature, then it is difficult to get the paint to stick; and if you try it on dry land, then the paint will be sticky but so will your gills. Cave paintings lead to more sophisticated works, lead to books, first with pictures, then without. Back to pictures with television. Onward to 3D experiences, finally interactive, multisensory, holographic constructs. Better than the real thing. In the case of the Flargathon Gas Swamps, much better than the real thing.

The Gaseans of Flargathon were so peeved by their name and by the constant stink of spirogyra invading their nostrils that they hired the hyperintelligent Magratheans to build an idyllic construct that would be permanently occupied by every Flargathonian, except for a rotating staff awakened to service the virtual reality and keep the gas mines pumping. The construct was designed by the Magrathean A-Team of Drs. Brewtlewine, Zestyfang, and La-Sane, who had won a Golden Lobe for their work on New Asgard. After fifteen years the construct was ready to be plugged in and was named DB-DZ-DLS in the team's honor.

For years things were rosy, all happy snores and money in the bank, until the computer happened to randomly wake up five people who did not have the population's best interests at heart. These people, let's call them assholes, realized that while the cats were indulging themselves in their favorite virtual fantasies, the mice could strip the planet bare and live like les grandes fromages in the real Universe.

It took them ten years, but the assholes managed to gut the old planet while the Magratheans were simultaneously building them a brand-new one. A nice Neptune-sized, terrestrial world (hold the swamps), slingshot into orbit in the Alpha Centauri system. They named the planet Incognitus and immediately enforced a worldwide no extradition rule. Five years later the Gaseans awoke to find their suspended animation diaper bags overflowing and their planet smelling worse than ever.

And the moral of the story is? There are a few actually: Some people are bastards and should never be left in charge. And a Magrathean will always take the money, no questions asked. Finally, always fit composting diaper bags just in case. Because you really never know. No one really ever knows.

• •

"Four minutes, Ford," said Arthur Dent seconds later, feeling confusion and powerlessness appear at his shoulders like two mates from secondary school who were great fun at the time but now refused to move on like everyone else and still thought fart cushions were *hilarious.*

"That is so bloody typical of this galaxy. I finally get my daughter back and now you tell me we're all about to be blown to pieces in four minutes."

Ford punched his shoulder jovially. "No, no, we go back to reality in four minutes. It will take the Grebulons at least thirty minutes to carve up the whole planet with death beams. It would be a lot quicker and more cost-effective with nukes. Ask the Vogons; you wouldn't catch them using death beams."

"You are wrong, Ford," said Trillian, pale with worry and anger. "I remember Club Beta. We survived that. Our Babel fish transported us to Milliways. I remember it clearly."

"Clearly? Do you really?"

"Maybe not clearly," admitted Trillian. "It was a long time ago."

"No," blurted Random. "It wasn't Babel fish, it was unicorns."

"Unicorns," breathed Arthur, and he knew then that Ford was right, the Guide Mk II had let them supply their own method of escape. His own had involved uniting of all the Earth's superpowers. Clearly impossible.

"Yes, *Arthur.* A squadron of space unicorn rangers came to save us. I remember Sparkle Gem True Hoof, we were pen pals."

Arthur hurriedly changed the subject before anyone could get started on the unicorn theory.

"In four minutes this room will disappear, Ford. We'll be left facing Grebulon death beams, and *you* thought it would be a *great* idea to waste half of that time with your election campaign imagery?"

"I didn't think it was a *great* idea," said Ford, who didn't get sarcasm unless he really concentrated, which he only did about once a year, usually when he had one last chance to press the correct button or the ship exploded.

"I thought it was an *okay* idea. On a scale of one to ten, maybe four point five."

"Ford!"

"Yes, Arthur old mate."

"You're doing it again. Wasting time. Shouldn't we be coming up with a plan?"

Random wiped her tears on a sleeve. She would swallow down the world of hurt and bear up, just as she had always done as President. Hadn't she persevered when the celebrity chefs of Earth had downed spatulas because of the influx of cheap and flashy Dentrassis labor?

• •

Guide Note: Dentrassis chefs are extremely foul-mouthed and launch into long tirades even when things are going right, and so make excellent TV chefs. Also, because of their time-hop pods, they do not have to "prepare one earlier" until the end of the show.

• •

Had she not forged ahead when the Blagulon Kappans had parachuted twelve million cows into mainland Europe in an attempt to increase the methane content of the atmosphere?

Luckily there were not many vegetarians on that continent and the cows did not last long, especially since they were Ameglian Major cows who literally begged to be eaten. Most of them didn't have to ask twice. Many of them never got to ask once. And quite a few were being flambéed before their parachutes hit the ground.

I will take control, thought Random with a determination that actually was beyond her years.

She shrugged her mother off.

"Listen to me, everyone. I've been in tighter spots than this. What we need to do is hook your Hitchhiker's Guide up to the Grebulon communications system and I will negotiate with them, as future President of the Galaxy."

Ford patted Random on the head. "Hush now, dearie. Grown-ups talking."

"You pormwrangler!" swore Random most unpresidentially.

"Thank you very much," said a touched Ford, who had always been proud of his skill at the pormwrangling pits of Bhaboom Lane. "But let's do compliments later."

"Later?" said Arthur. "What later? We don't have a later, thanks to your Mk II."

"It's not mine," objected the Betelgeusean.

"You stole it, Ford. You posted it to yourself, care of me. I think that makes it yours."

"Ah, you see. I *stole* it. Therefore it's not mine. You're winning my argument for me."

2:37 said the digital readout.

2:36

then

0:10 . . . 0:09

"Hmm," said Ford, scratching the plane in space where his chin was obstinately refusing to be. "That's a little strange."

"I know," agreed Arthur. "Surely the numerical system hasn't changed. We've only been away a couple of seconds."

"Well, if the numerical system's been changed, they might not even be seconds."

The bird reappeared, its image striated with lines of interference. "Sorry. All this arguing is draining my battery. Negative energy."

And Mk II disappeared, taking with it the tranquil room of sky. Arthur, Trillian, Random, and Ford found themselves deposited on the men's room stairs in Stavro Mueller's swanky (until very recently) Club Beta, their memories of virtual lives dissipating like mist in the sunlight.

This is real life, Arthur realized. *How could I ever have been duped by that beach? How could it be real when no one was trying to kill me?*

The air was alive with screaming, the cacophonous wrenching sounds of civilization collapsing, the thrum and buzz of Grebulon death rays and the chittering of a million rats fleeing the city, which the four arrivees could understand thanks to the Babel fish universal translators in their ear holes.

"I saw it in those dog intestines," squeaked one lady rat named Audrey. "I foretold the end for the two-footers by a big green space light. No one would bloody listen. Nobody."

"Come on, Mum," scoffed her eighteenth son, Cornelius. "You said a dark stranger would cross our path."

"Them're dark strangers, firing them death beams. What would you call 'em?"

Cornelius twitched a whisker, the rat equivalent of rolled eyeballs. "That's one interpretation. You need to be more specific, Mum. People are laughing."

"Cheeky beggar," said Audrey and scampered off down a drain.

The rest of the rats said things like:

"Oh, no!"

"Oh, Muroideam!" (Father of the rat gods.)

"Aaaargh! Dark stranger, my arse!"

Arthur Dent sat on the stairs in the midst of the whole imbroglio feeling strangely peaceful. There was nothing to do but be happy for having loved someone once and having been loved in return. It was big, dying. BIG. But not as big as it had once seemed.

At the foot of the stairs, a sobbing Random was being comforted by both Trillian and Tricia McMillan.

Stupid bloody plural zone, thought Arthur. *You leave one Earth and come back to another. The Earth I left was destroyed and the one I returned to has a Tricia McMillan who never traveled through space with Zaphod Beeblebrox.*

Ah, the infinite multitudinous possibilities of my home planet. The things I might have seen on another Earth, just down the probability axis. I might have made myself a nice cup of tea.

"Regrets," he sang absently. "I've had a few. Like all those days, spent in detention."

Frankie Martin Jr. What a crooner.

The green rays scythed closer now. Arthur could feel their heat burning one side of his face.

That's going to peel, he thought.

"Hey, look," said Ford brightly. "My blue suede shoes. Froody."

CHAPTER 3

The Tricia McMillan who was native to this Earth, and who had never been artificially sustained in the H2G2-2's construct, had an idea.

"I will talk to them, dear," she said to the girl who was possibly her unborn daughter from what was periodically another dimension. "The Grebulons listen to me. I'm something of a pinup for them."

And she was gone down the hallway, seconds before the hallway itself was gone, frittered by the beams, like confetti in the wind.

Arthur was too numb to be horrified. Instead he experienced a strange prickling jealousy.

At least Tricia died with some sense of purpose. She found an answer to her question that was not bloody forty-two. All I can do is sit here and be helpless.

Arthur felt a sense of disbelief that he had come to know well in his Galaxy traveler phase. He had often secretly suspected that he was insane. There was no *Heart of Gold*, no Zaphod Beeblebrox, and certainly not a Deep Thought. As for the planet-building Magratheans. Patently ridiculous. More ridiculous even than the talking mice who were supposed to rule the planet.

"S'cuse me, guv'nor," said a rat skirting Arthur's foot.

"Sorry, mate," muttered Arthur, automatically raising his shoe.

It was all insanity. And he was being observed somewhere by a cluster of undergraduates who were doubtless hungover from the previous night's rugger celebrations and couldn't give a toss about Patient Dent's delusions.

If they don't give a toss, why should I?

Behind him the gents' door splintered and flew over his head. Moments later very suspect water began seeping through the seat of his trousers.

Ford chuckled. "It's true what they say. It *does* always flow downhill."

"Do you think we should make a run for it?"

"Run where? The whole planet's going up, my friend. Our running days are over. And those guys are out of hitchhiking range." Ford rummaged in the satchel around his neck and pulled out what looked like a roll-up cigarette. "Ahhhh," he sighed happily. "I've been saving this."

Arthur was delighted to have something to be interested in. "What is that?"

Ford squinted at him. "That's more *sarcasm*, is it?"

"No. It's a genuine question born of ignorance."

"Well, in that case, happy to enlighten you, buddy. It's a cigarette."

"Oh." Arthur felt his interest waning.

"But not just any cigarette," continued Ford, holding the roll-up as though it were a grail of the rather holy kind.

"Got a wide-bore death ray inside it?"

"Course not."

"How about a matter transporter?"

"You know, that would be useful. But no."

"So, it's just strands of tobacco wrapped in paper, then?"

"Tobacco? Paper? Honestly, Arthur, you humans only use ten percent of your brains, and you fill that fraction with tea-related information. This is a Fallian albino marsh worm. Deceased obviously. Spends its life absorbing hallucinogenic gas from the vents. Then dies and turns stiff-ish."

Arthur glanced upward. A death ray had just sliced off the top floor, without even slowing down. A rather large airplane pinwheeled through the patch of sky above, and Arthur fancied he could hear someone singing "Kumbaya."

"Is this a long story? Only I imagine our minutes are numbered. And the number is a single number. Between one and three maybe."

"No, nearly at the good bit. Hitchhikers call these joysticks. One puff and you feel blissfully happy. Love everybody, forgive your enemies, all that stuff. Two puffs make you curious about just about everything, including the horrible death that is probably coming your way for you to have lit this baby in the first place. *This is going to be great,* you tell yourself. *I am about to experience an energy shift to a new plane of existence. What will it be like? Will I make new friends? Do they have beer?"*

"Third puff?" asked Arthur, fulfilling his role in the storytelling partnership.

Ford rummaged in his satchel for a light. "After the third puff, your brain explodes and you feel a little peckish."

"Ah," said Arthur, wondering how many hitchhikers had expired before they figured out the third puff thing.

"Here we go," said Ford, pulling out a plastic lighter with the legend *The Domain of the King* in blinking lights on the shaft. "One puff or two?"

Arthur had never been much of a smoker. Whenever he tried a cigarette, he felt so guilty about what he was doing to the lungs his parents gave him that it made him feel quite ill. Once, at a teenage party, Arthur did attempt to lounge about on the patio toying with a Silk Cut Blue, but ended up throwing up on the hostess in an effort to not throw up on her Chihuahua. He still shuddered at the memory, and looked around to see if anyone from that party was pointing at him.

"Not for me, thanks. Dicky tummy."

"Okay, pal," said Ford, sparking the lighter. "Blissful happiness, here I come."

"I'll say so long now then, Ford. I wouldn't have missed a minute."

"Really?"

"No. Not really. There were a few minutes I could have done without."

The minute when Fenchurch disappeared, for example.

Ford had taken a single puff from the joystick when a giant jelly cactus popped into existence in the center of the lobby. It wobbled for a moment, then turned into a huge bloodshot eye. The eye cast itself wildly about the room, then rolled back and became a quartet of pompom squids, playing thousands of kazoos in perfect harmony.

"Beautiful," said Ford, wiping a tear from his eye. "That makes me so . . . There aren't the words."

The squids hit a high note then disappeared in a flurry of rainbow-gilded bubbles, which popped musically to become a white spaceship. A glittering teardrop with a few celery-stalk fins.

"The *Heart of Gold*," breathed Arthur. "You have got to be joking."

. . . .

Guide Note: This spaceship was so essentially cool that one look at its brochure could skip a teenage male a couple of decades into the future, straight into the middle of his own midlife crisis. The *Heart of Gold* was powered both by conventional engines and the revolutionary Infinite Improbability Drive, which allowed the ship to be everywhere at once until it decided where it wanted to be. Coincidences, déjà vu, and increased amounts of junk mail were all side effects of the *Heart of Gold*'s unconventional drive field.

. . . .

Ford ground the tip of the joystick on the sole of his shoe, then popped the cigarette into his satchel. He jumped to his feet. "Let's go, Arthur. Don't look so surprised. The Earth gets destroyed and we get rescued by Zaphod. That's the way it always goes, give or take a few details and half a dozen light-years. What a trip. A cosmic trip."

"So why the joystick?"

"One puff only, my man. Blissfully happy. I find it helps before a re-union with Zaphod."

Arthur stumbled down the steps. "But what about Tricia? Isn't she supposed to come with us?"

"Hey, Trillian is the same person. Fate can only take one of everyone. Be happy for Tricia, she's on another plane. Pure energy. Can't you see the colors?"

Arthur scowled. "The green death-ray colors? Yes, I can see those. I would prefer to see them from a great distance, so can we please get out of here?"

"Absolutely, Arthur. If we don't go soon, my froody shoes will be ruined. Although the blue one might turn a nice shade of purple, which would make me enormously happy."

Arthur gently shepherded Random toward the glowing white ship. "Come on. We need to leave now."

"Fertle," mumbled the girl. "I want my Fertle."

"I want my Fertle!" chuckled Ford, playfully tickling Trillian. "Catchy, isn't it?"

The white spaceship shuddered and a door opened smoothly, telescoping to the ground. Zaphod Beeblebrox, Galactic President, interplanetary fugitive, and committed self-serving entrepreneur, appeared in the doorway, planet-sized ego shining through his bright eyes, golden hair bouncing in shoulder-length curls. Very outer-ring, but he carried it off well.

"Okay, let me get this straight," Zaphod said, tapping his temples. "Hello, Earthlings. I have once again come to save you." Then he seemed to notice the ongoing planet destruction unfolding before him. "Hold on just a minute. This isn't Ireland!"

Ford ran up the gangplank to embrace his semi-cousin.

"Zaphod! I am so happy to see you."

Zaphod blinked. "Happy to see me? You must be smoking something."

They piled into the *Heart of Gold* and zipped up to a couple of hundred feet, employing the ship's Dodge-O-Matic program to evade the death beams until the Infinite Improbability Drive was powered up, to blast them wherever it was they expected never to be.

Ford Prefect was the only one of the ship's occupants who thought to look down, and he saw a forlorn-looking H2G2-2 hovering beside Club Beta's single remaining chandelier. It casually dodged a buzzing death beam and then with a *why bother* shrug collapsed in on itself like an origami bird being folded by invisible hands, until all that was left was a diamond of blackness that zipped around the roofless hall, decapitated a rat out of sheer badness, then winked out of all existences in all times.

Good riddance, thought Ford, and went in search of a drink.

Had Ford not gone in search of a drink, he might have seen a tall, thirty-ish man, wearing a bathrobe and slippers, stumble into the Beta Club clutching his towel. The man barely had time to glance skyward in confused wonderment before an emerald death ray blasted him and his ginger companion to atoms.

Guide Note: This was one of the many deaths of Arthur Dent. Now that one Arthur had managed to break the cosmic pattern and skip dimensions to be rescued, the pattern unraveled for the rest, and they were picked off one by one, by improbable accidents hurriedly cobbled together by a ticked-off Fate.

One Arthur was electrocuted by malfunctioning headphones as he produced a local radio show discussing recent UFO sightings in the area.

A second Arthur woke up one morning convinced that he could fly, and no amount of persuasion could prevent him from scaling a radio tower and hurling himself off.

A third was crushed by a buffadozer during a protest to save his house. The buffadozer did not suffer any physical damage but was traumatized by the event and went on to sue the council, specifically naming a certain Mr. Prosser in the suit. Prosser was subsequently given the axe.

Yet another Arthur was drowned in a freak rainstorm shortly after giving the two fingers to a truck driver who had cut him off on the motorway.

The list is almost endless. Suffice it to say, without cataloguing every single one of the various deaths misadventure or adventure, accidental (or on purpose), Occidental, dental, mental, rental, retail, fetal, fecal, decal (smothered by Saran Wrap), to name but a few, that only one Arthur Dent survived in any dimension after the final, once and for all, no-tricky-loophole destruction of Earth. The same is true of both Ford Prefect and Trillian, but not Random or Zaphod, who were sticking to their pan-dimensional roles well enough to earn gold stars.

Related Reading:

Someone's Out to Get Me by Arthur Dent (2803)

He Believed He Could Fly by Mrs. A. Dent (1103)

The last remaining Arthur Dent sat in his usual place on the floor of the *Heart of Gold*'s flight deck, bumping his head repeatedly on a familiar shelf, and yet he did not feel comforted. It may have been the green death rays flashing past the view-screens, or it may have been that somewhere, deep in his primal essence, in the stardust that made up his atoms, Arthur realized that *he* was the last Arthur Dent in the universe. Truly alone in the magnitude of stuff.

All Arthur could have verbalized was that he missed his towel and would have paid a large sum of money to have somebody with soft bosoms hug him and tell him that things were going to be all right.

Trillian and Random were pretty depressed by the whole destruction of their home planet thing too and huddled together underneath the refrigerator. Ford Prefect, however, was positively ebullient, thanks to the single puff on his petrified worm.

"This is *great!*" he enthused, clapping Zaphod on the shoulder. "Look at those death beams. Did you ever think you would live to see a Grebulon death lattice from the *inside*?"

"*Grebulons*, wow. Those guys are vicious," responded his cousin with equal enthusiasm. (Zaphod was basically a one-puff man all the time.) "What a light show. Do you remember those thermonuclear warheads at Magrathea?"

"I do," said Ford fondly. "They were something. Foxy beggars, with their little jinks and turns, but we shook 'em."

"We sure did, cousin. And we're going to shake these Grebu-guys too."

Trillian winced as a ray scorched the spaceship's port fin. "Can we just get out of here?"

Zaphod spun like a disco dancer and shot Trillian with two finger guns. "Pow pow, cutie. Miss me? Bet you did . . . so would I."

"Later, Zaphod. Can the ship take us to safety?"

"Not so simple. We can't shoot through the lattice without being sliced up like Halitoxican party grevlova. We have to let the Improbability Drive run a few numbers and get its head around the problem."

"The computer has a head now?"

Zaphod danced a little Betelgeusean foreplay jig. "Finally someone makes a *head* comment. I was starting to think you guys were all on the joysticks."

"Sorry, Zaphod," Arthur snapped. "We're a little distracted by impending violent death."

"Sure, the computer's got a *head*," continued Zaphod, ignoring Arthur's thread of the conversation. "Come on, people. Don't you notice anything different about me?"

They got it at the same time.

"Goosnargh," said Ford.

"What the . . . ," said Trillian.

"Blooming 'eck," said Arthur, sounding a little like a cockney rat.

Zaphod Beeblebrox had, perched rakishly on his shoulders, a single head.

• •

Guide Note: Zaphod Beeblebrox's two heads and three arms have become as much a part of Galaxy lore as the Ravenous Bugblatter Beast's cranial spigot, or Eccentrica Gallumbits's third breast. And though Zaphod claims to have had his third arm fitted to improve his chances at ski-boxing, many media pundits believe that the arm was actually fitted so that the President could simultaneously fondle all of Eccentrica's mammaries. This attention to erotic detail resulted in Miss Gallumbits referring to Zaphod in *Street Walkie-Talkie Weekly* as the "best bang since the Big One." A quote which was worth at least half a billion votes in the presidential election and twice as many daily hits on the private members section of the Zaphod Confidential Sub-Etha site.

The origin of Zaphod's second head is shrouded in mystery and seems to be the one thing the President is reluctant to discuss with the media, other than claim that two heads are better than none. A comment which was taken as a direct jibe by Councillor Spinalé Trunco of the Headless Horsemen tribe of Jaglan Beta. Zaphod's response to this accusation was "Of course it's a jibe, baby. Dude's got zero heads. Come on!" Early images do represent Zaphod with two heads, but in many shots they do not appear to be identical. In fact, in one vidcap, which has famously come to be known as the "I'm With Stupid" shot, Zaphod's left head appears to be that of a sallow female, attempting to bite the right head's ear. A Betelgeusean woman later surfaced claiming to be the original owner of the "sallow female" head. Loolu Softhands told Beebelblog that "Zaphod wanted us to be together, like all the time, so we conjoined. After a couple of months he found out that he liked the two-headed thing more than he liked me. So we went out for a few Blasters one night and I woke up back on my own body. Bastard."

Zaphod has never refuted Miss Softhands's story, leading to speculation that his second head is a narcissistic affectation, an allegation President Beeblebrox claims not to understand.

Related Articles:

"Head to Head with Mr. President" by Loolu Softhands

"It's Just One Boob After Another" by Eccentrica Gallumbits

• •

Ford embraced his cousin.

"You finally took it off," he said while simultaneously chewing his lip, which is not easy. "Removing a head sounds like the action of an imbecile, but for some reason I am totally in favor of it."

Arthur knew the reason. His friend was still riding the worm.

"Are you sure that was a great idea, Zaphod? Didn't that head *do* stuff?"

Zaphod raised a single finger, the way a person might if they were about to make a significant announcement. "Shut your mouth, monkey. I am talking to my cousin."

"I thought we were past that, Zaphod. Haven't we been through enough?"

Zaphod reared backward. "Oh. Hey, Arthur. Is that you, buddy? My other head had better eyesight. Plus I didn't recognize you without the pool garment."

"Dressing gown."

"Whatever. Important information only at this point, I think. Death rays and so forth."

"Is it *important* that we know where your other head is?" shouted Arthur, keeping his syntax as stripped back as possible.

Zaphod clapped his hands. "Oh yeah. Yessir. You are all going to love this."

He crab-danced to the low crescent bank of computer controls. "Ladies and gentlemen, here he is, give him a big hand because *your* lives are in *his* hands."

"Death rays!" howled Arthur, as the Dodge-O-Matic sent the ship into a tight pirouette. "Can we get on with it?"

Ford cradled Arthur's cheeks in his palms. "Life is about moments, Arthur," he said seriously. "That's the secret. Moments are longer than you think. If you add up all the good moments, then, you know. It's like ages."

It really infuriated Arthur that there might be something in that reasoning.

"Very well, Ford. Do you think it might be possible for the ladies to see Zaphod's other head?"

"Don't patronize us," said Random.

"Of course not, sweetie."

"Screw you."

Zaphod stamped a silver boot heel. "Can we get back to my moment? The head, remember?" He tapped a short, sequential code into the computer.

"Not much of a code, is it?" commented Arthur. "One two three?"

Zaphod scowled at him. "Eyesight and numbers. I am sooo bad at life's minor things. I'm more of a forward-thrusting, back-lit, great-discovery-making champion of the boudoir. Head number two takes care of the little man stuff. Or as I call him . . . Left Brain, because he was on the left, and he's the brainy one."

"Show us the head!" shouted Arthur.

Zaphod thumbed a red button and a crystal sphere emerged from a bucket of gel in the console, rising smoothly to float at a median eye level.

"The gel is full of things, you know," Zaphod explained with standard vagueness. "Stuff that's good for the things that need to be done."

"Please shut up, brother," said Zaphod's second head, which rested on a cushion of wires and fuses inside the sphere. "You're embarrassing yourself. And me."

Left Brain resembled Zaphod almost exactly, apart from some styling differences. Where the Galactic President was flamboyantly highlighted and may or may not have been wearing eyeliner, Left Brain's hair was close-cropped with a severe parting and his eyes shone with laser-sharp intelligence and strength of purpose.

"The gel is an electrolytic compound which feeds my organic cells and powers the anti-grav field around the sphere."

"And the speakers, LB," said Zaphod. "A man's gotta have sounds."

"Yes, ZB," sighed Left Brain. "The speakers. Now don't you have someone to wink at in the mirror?"

Zaphod leaned heavily on the console. "Some days I think maybe separating was a mistake. But since Left Brain took over the ship from Eddie, we haven't exploded once. Not one time. And the causing wars thing is way down. That's good, right?"

"Now that the ship is not being run by my imbecilic predecessor, our life expectancy has risen by eight hundred percent."

Random, a politician, nodded appreciatively at the statistic.

Arthur rapped on the sphere. "Hello . . . Zaphod . . . Left Brain. Are you driving the ship? Can you get us out of here?"

"Please don't touch the glass, Earthman. You have no idea how many times I have to spin around in the gel to get smears off."

"Sorry."

"To answer your questions. I am currently interfacing with the Dodge-O-Matic program so that we can avoid the Grebulon death rays. Their lattice is closing as we speak, so the sooner we engage the Improbability Drive, the better."

"How soon is that likely to be?"

"In ninety seconds. Several minutes before the death rays can possibly destroy the ship."

"You're sure about that?"

Left Brain did not appreciate the question. "You're new here and we've just met, so I'm going to explain this. I am the ship, the ship is me. There is no misinformation."

"New? I've been here before, mate. And we *have* met, only the last time . . ."

"I was still attached to Zaphod, the idiot."

"Wohoo!" yelled Zaphod. "He nailed you there, Arty. Don't go toe-to-toe with this guy."

"Subjugated by his raucous personality," continued Left Brain. "Dominated by his irrepressible hedonism."

"I warned you, Earthman. Don't say I didn't warn you. Left Brain will skin you alive and make fritters with the shavings."

Left Brain swiveled, focusing his gaze on Zaphod. "This shiftless monkey kept me locked inside my own head until I planted the separation idea during a drunken binge. Zaphod is such a gobemouche that he actually believes the notion was his own."

Zaphod's eyes clouded. "Gobemouche? Say, what now?"

Although Arthur was worried about the ramifications of the heads' sibling rivalry, or split personality, or whatever the correct medical term might be, he decided to choke down his misgivings for Random's sake. They were saved after all. Random was safe and that was all that mattered. Arthur knew from experience that losing his home planet would crush his spirit in the near future, possibly around teatime when there was no tea, or perhaps following a particularly beautiful holo-sunset, but for now he was determined to put on a brave face for his daughter.

"Okay, everyone," he said, his voice as bright and hollow as a lightbulb. "Emergency over for the moment. Why don't we all strap ourselves in for an Improbability jaunt?" He chuckled. "We all know how wacky they are."

Random patted the spot on her chest where Fertle used to be. "Wacky, Arthur? Wacky? You're not fooling anyone. And that was the most forced chuckle I have ever heard, *Arthur*. You'll never be half the man my husband was."

And once again, everything is my fault, thought Arthur. *Maybe I should fake being cheerful more often, then perhaps people would fall for it.*

"I don't suppose this computer has learned to make tea?"

A red light flashed on Left Brain's dome. "Stop talking now, Earthman. The word *tea* has been flagged. The last time you asked for *tea*, you backed up the entire system during an alert."

Another forced chuckle from Arthur, followed by a little shuffle and a quick exit to the viewing gallery.

"I'm just going to check the death-ray lattice thing. See how we're getting on. Can I get anyone anything?"

No one bothered to reply.

. . . .

Guide Note: "Can I get anyone anything?" is a standard get-out-of-room-quick card and can be played whenever uncomfortable circumstances, ranging from mild embarrassment to major impending doom, are fast approaching. Most cultures have a variation on the "can I get anyone anything," and they are so obviously rhetorical that they barely merit a question mark. Betelgeuseans ask: "Did anyone hear a plopping sound? Like a tennis ball into a bowl of custard? Anyone? I better go check it out." The Jatravartid version is: "Did someone hear the door crystal? I bet it's Poople. Late as usual. I better go and let him in before he fills his handkerchief."

• •

To Arthur's relief, no one broke interstellar protocol by actually asking for something, and he was able to sneak off to the viewing gallery and pretend he was back on his beach.

Ford rapped his knuckles on the console, listening to the *bong*. "I had forgotten that bong, Zaph. You know, noises and things. You forget all about them, then experience them again and remember how important they are to you. Then you wonder where all the memories were all that time you weren't thinking about them."

Zaphod had no trouble tuning into this wavelength. "I always thought my memories were across the hallway in head number two. And if I needed them, head number two just beamed them over."

"Wow. That is like it. Like the essence of what I'm trying to communicate. Did you guys, like, look in each other's eyes, you know, when he was shooting the memories across?"

"Absolutely not," said Left Brain, bobbing a little in spite of his gyroscopic field. "His theory is ridiculous. We both have a cortex."

Ford danced around the sphere, cradling it like a crystal ball. "Yeah, but you have the big brain. You're the smart one hooked up to the Infinite Improbability Drive."

Left Brain could not contain a little satisfied smirk. "That is true. I control the drive. It is part of me now. I feel its every uncertainty."

Ford's eyes were glazed but still intelligent. "So explain to me how I was expecting you."

Left Brain's glass turned a little green. "What?"

"Yep. That's right, smarty-pants-less. I knew you guys would show up."

"That's ridiculous. How could you know? The odds that the only person in the Universe who could rescue you would turn up exactly when you needed him were 150 billion to 1 against. Acceptable odds for the drive."

Ford begged to differ. "Depends how you cal-cu-late, mate."

"There is only one way to calculate," said Left Brain stiffly.

"Oh, no," said Ford in the tone of one who has spent far too many hours in cheap hotels with no credits for the Boob-O-Whooper and is forced to read his own guidebook. "There are many ways to calculate. The Vl'hurgs' entire mathematical system was based on entrails."

- -

Guide Note: This is not entirely true. Dried velohound penis was also involved.

- -

"And I myself," continued Ford in a voice so superior it would have caused single-cell life forms to accelerate their evolution so that they could use their fab new opposable thumbs to pick up a rock and beat him to death. "I myself base most of my calculations on emotions."

"Emotions!" spluttered Left Brain all over the inside of his own bowl. "Emotions? How can you afford to have only one head and still be so stupid?"

"I like being stupid. You see things clearly. Being stupid is like squinting through the sunlight."

Each statement rocked Left Brain's sphere like a slap from a wet towel. "Sunlight? What are you saying? Stupidity is ignorance and darkness."

"So you *planned* to come here. These are the coordinates you selected?"

"No," admitted Left Brain. "The exact spot had already been destroyed, so the drive moved us to safety."

"So out of all the spots in the Universe, the ship brings us here."

"Coincidence. Backwash from the Improbability Drive."

"This is more than coincidence. Zaphod comes to the rescue of his favorite cousin. How unlikely is that? It's happened before near enough to this very same planet. One more time and it's a pattern. And the last time I checked, patterns are not very improbable."

- -

Another Guide Note: This last was a lie, as Ford Prefect had never once checked the probability of patterns. Ford rarely checked anything apart from how full his glass was and general froodiness levels. He once paid a month's salary for a froody detector which only worked if the operator's own froodiness was sufficient to power it. Ford tried it once in the bathroom, then forced it into the trash compacter along with the receipt.

• •

Left Brain rocked back on his X-axis. "Yes, it is true that patterns are not good models for improbability."

"Generally true?"

"Generally."

"*Generally* doesn't sound very improbable. Doesn't sound very zenzizenzizenzic to one against. Sounds more like even money to me."

"Y-Yes," stammered Left Brain. "You make a good point."

"Are you sweating, man? Can robot heads sweat now?"

Left Brain was indeed perspiring profusely. Little spider-bots emerged from the sphere's collar, feasting on the moisture drops.

"I am *not* a robot," protested Left Brain.

"Hey, you're floating in a glass bubble, hooked up to a computer. Spiders coming out of your neck. The last time I checked, those things all scream robot."

• •

Guide Note: Again no checking. Total buffa-biscuit.

• •

"Although," mused Ford, stroking close to his chin. "The total cock-up of the Improbability Drive is very *organic being* territory."

"Total cock-up," said Left Brain nervously. "You really think so?"

"Absolutely. But let's dwell on that later, and at great length, to much embarrassment for one of us. Now, how about you fire up that drive and send us somewhere that actually *is* improbable."

Left Brain's dome light pulsed a sickly green and streams of numbers flashed across the glass. "Improbable? But how to calculate? How to . . . Everything I believe in. Numbers are fallible? Can that be true? Can it?"

Ford was beginning to sober up. "Hey, buddy. Forget it. I'm just twisting your pormwrangler. Tell him, Zaphod."

Zaphod draped an arm around his cousin's shoulders. "It's true, buddy. You've been wrangled by the best. Ford here once made a Voondonian grand high friar attack him with incense sticks."

"For a *bet*," said Ford, who wouldn't like people to believe that he went around incensing incensed friars for *no* reason.

Left Brain was in some distress. "The computer sings to me of numbers, but you. You two *buffa-biscuit* heads with your *buffa-puckey*!"

"Hey, less of the buffa," said Ford, injured. "I'm just trying to bond. You know, impress you with my offbeat intellectualism."

"It's just all . . . It's just too . . . Numbers. Emotions. Zark!"

And then Left Brain went into a loop. A very short loop. One word, over and over.

"Zark . . . Zark . . . Zark . . ."

Zaphod's third arm popped out from underneath his ruffled silk shirt, slapping Ford on the crown of his head.

"Idiot. You froze him."

"You kept the arm then."

Zaphod tucked his spare hand across his chest into the left pocket of his spray-on trousers.

• •

Guide Note: Not a euphemism. Zaphod bought a pants sprayer on Port Sesefron which promised to "reach those hard to reach places." After the first application, Zaphod turned the power down a bit. There was a special nozzle for pockets.

• •

"I mostly use the third arm for ceremonial stuff. Stick a purple sleeve on, and hey presto it's a sash."

Ford flapped his lips, unimpressed by Left Brain. "It didn't take much to freeze him. You should have waited for version 2.0."

Trillian strapped herself into a luxurious Tilt-O-Chair beside Random, who was sulking hard enough to feed a family of Cyphroles for five hundred years.

"Why aren't we somewhere else, Zaphod? I can still see death rays."

Zaphod betrayed his cousin with a thumb jerk. "Ask Ford im-perfect. He froze the ship."

Arthur chose this moment to stroll back onto the bridge. "Froze the ship? Did you say froze the ship?"

Arthur's old memories were reasserting themselves by the second, and to his chagrin, he found them not entirely dissimilar to the new ones.

I miss being surprised, he realized. *These days I go straight from calm to terrified.*

"What is your problem, Ford? Are you wired somehow to screw things up?"

"*He's* wired, not me," said Ford, pointing to Left Brain, who was now bobbling against the ceiling like an escaped balloon.

Arthur sensed that something was missing on the bridge.

"I don't know what it is," he said, testing the air with his fingers. "But something was here a second ago and now it's gone."

Zaphod was delighted to have some relevant information. "Let me fill you in on that, Earthman. When the Dodge-O-Matic is activated, the computer paints the walls with an off-white light. Phototherapeutic brain calming stuff."

"And the light is off."

"Badabingo!"

• •

Guide Note: Badabingo is a board game played by lifers on the prison moon in orbit around Blagulon Kappa. A game for up to a hundred players, the object of it is to get all your little horsies around the board and back to their stables. At which point a six is needed before you can twist off the horsies' heads. Once the last horsey is beheaded, the leader jumps to his feet and shouts "Badabingo." After that it is up to him to stay alive until the riot squad arrives.

• •

"Which means the Dodge-O-Matic is also off."

"Green stick in the green hole, boy."

Guide Note 2: The "green stick in the green hole" cry is a reference to a simple matching game used in the very special adult ed classes on Betelgeuse V where President Beeblebrox grew up. A Striteraxian equivalent would be: You display inordinate pride for someone who has completed a task which could have been performed by a lesser primate in a shorter time. The Silastic Armorfiends were never very good at references, but they were quite excellent at getting to the point. Usually the point would be made of toughened steel and coated with venom.

"Which means we can be diced into cubes by that death-ray lattice thing, just like the entire planet."

Zaphod snorted like this was the craziest thing he had ever heard. "The Earth ain't going to be diced, Arty. Those death rays will superheat the surface and totally vaporize the entire planet. Any second now."

"That's comforting. What about us?"

"Oh, yeah. The lattice has already figured out how to box us in. We're gonna be diced. No doubt about that. Green stick and all that. I was just beginning to take ownership of this haircut too."

Arthur pressed his face to the porthole. Outside, in space, the green rays sliced soundlessly through the blackness. Vast emerald pendulums, boiling the planet below where they touched. As the rays swung closer, Arthur saw that they were comprised of pulsating bars, crackling with internal lightning.

A really fat, evil one was swinging inexorably their way.

My daughter is going to die, he realized. *And that really upsets me. I bet it's Thursday.*

He pulled his face away from the glass with a soft pop.

"There must be something we can do. We're not beaten yet, are we?"

Ford was waggling his joystick under Zaphod's nose. "Do you think that if I have another puff now, that would constitute a second puff, or another first puff?"

"Couldn't we somehow jump-start Left Brain?"

Zaphod frowned. "Tricky one, cousin-o-mine. Maybe if *I* have a puff, the answer will come to me."

Arthur found that his surprise gland was alive and functioning after all.

"Don't you care that we are all about to die? How can you not care?"

Ford winked at him. "In a spot like this, Arthur, what does it benefit a man to care?"

"I don't know, Ford. I truly do not. But I have a daughter there, in that seat. That's what I know."

There was a knock at the door.

"Get that, would you, Earthman?" said Zaphod.

Arthur was kind enough to provide both a delayed reaction and a double take for the entertainment of the Betelgeuseans.

"You get it. It's your . . . arkkkkk!"

"You're funny, buddy!" howled Zaphod, punching his shoulder.

"Didn't I tell you, cousin? I've been telling you for years. Arthur is a riot."

"Riot? Badabingo."

"Did you hear that? Can there be someone at the door, in space?"

The knock sounded again. A booming bong that made Arthur feel as though he were inside a belfry.

"Don't worry about the bong thing," said Zaphod. "It's just a recording. I can set it to ding-dong if you like. Or a pootle-tink bird, my favorite."

Green light glowed through the porthole. The window began to bubble.

"Open the door!" yelled Arthur, waving his arms for emphasis. "Open it quickly."

"I can't," said Zaphod, not seeming too upset. "Little Ix broke the ship. Remember?"

Trillian stroked Random's hair once, then crossed the bridge to the emergency hatch.

"Improbability? You want improbability? You two idiots staying alive this long, now *that's* improbable."

She reached into what seemed to be a solid panel and pulled out a crank.

"Emergency manual handle. Remember?"

"Hey, sugar. It's not my ship. I just stole it."

Arthur grabbed the handle and cranked until the sweat dripped down his jawline. This did not take as long as one might imagine, as the Grebulon rays' proximity was turning the drifting *Heart of Gold* into a very effective cauldron.

"Come on, Arthur," urged Trillian. "Come on."

Arthur opened his mouth to argue that he was coming on as fast as he could and could she please give him a break as he had spent the last century or so on a beach taking no strenuous exercise whatsoever and where the hell did she get off dropping his surprise teenage daughter on Lamuella then zipping off to cover a war that never happened? Arthur was about to say all of this, then thought that maybe he would crank harder instead.

Surprisingly, just thinking these things made him feel a little better.

Arthur's cranking powered a small plasma cell that sent a charge through the hatch and excited the molecules sufficiently to precipitate a phase transition, turning the portal to a gas.

"Now, you see, that's not what I thought was going to happen at all," puffed Arthur.

A tall, green humanoid alien stood in the air lock, wringing his hands. He was an impressive specimen, if your criteria for being impressed included developed musculature, wide intelligent brow, dark, tortured eyes, and a suit so sharp that just thinking about it could give a person a migraine.

"Babel fish?" said the alien in cultured, but slightly testy, tones. "Please tell me Babel fish."

Zaphod threw his hands in the air. "Babel fish all round."

"Oh, thank Zarquon," said the alien, stepping inside. "Honestly, if I had to go through one more room full of grunts and blank stares. What is it with people? Just buy a dozen fish and let them breed."

"People are so cheap," agreed Zaphod.

The alien stopped in his tracks. "What? No. It couldn't be?"

Zaphod flicked back a sheaf of hair. "Yes it is, baby."

"Zaphod Beeblebrox. Galactic President Beeblebrox?"

"Alive and procreating, sir."

"I do not believe it. Well, this is a turn-up for the files. You pull over in the uncharted backwaters of the unfashionable end of the western spiral arm of the Galaxy and who do you find bobbing around in the atmosphere but . . ."

"Zaphod Beeblebrox," completed Arthur, eager to move things along. "Listen, I hate to be a worrywart, but those death rays are getting awfully close. That big one in particular."

The green alien ignored him. "Mr. President. I've wanted to say something to you for a very long time. I've *prepared* something. Can you spare a second? You would really be doing me a favor."

Zaphod took a step back, just in case the alien could not see every inch of him.

• •

Guide Note: Technically, there were no aliens on the ship, just space travelers. As soon as the "alien's" identity is revealed, we can abandon that classification.

• •

"Of course you may say a few words. My colleagues would be honored. I am naturally too important to feel honored, but I would be mildly amused."

The *alien* bowed slightly, reached into his suit jacket for a wafer computer, located a text file, and cleared his throat.

"You, Mr. President . . . ," he began.

"Yes, proceed."

"You, Mr. President . . ."

"Old news, move on."

"You, Mr. President, are the most philosophunculistic, moronic, steatopygic excuse for a politician that it has ever been my good fortune to not vote for, and if I thought for one second that this crappy Universe deserved any better, then I would pay, out of my own pocket you understand, to have you assassinated."

Zaphod half-caught the last insulting term. "Steato . . . what?"

"Steatopygic. Fat-arsed."

"Fat-arsed!" gasped Zaphod, pawing at his own lips. "Fat-arsed?"

Arthur's memories were still coming back, so it took him a second even with such well-phrased stimuli.

"I know you. You're the guy with the insults."

The alien took a photo of Arthur with his computer, then searched for a match in his files.

"Ah, yes. Arthur Philip Dent. Jerk and complete arsehole. I've done you already, my records tell me."

Zaphod rested his hands on his knees. "Fat-arsed. I feel faint."

* *

Guide Note: This "alien," it can now be revealed, was Wowbagger the Infinitely Prolonged, who became immortal due to an accident involving a particle accelerator and an unwillingness to sacrifice two of his elastic bands. It must be pointed out that elastic bands held a special significance to Wowbagger, as in his culture, elastic bands are religious symbols representing the circuitous and elastic nature of the god, Pollyphill-Ah. After his accident, the arch promonate of the Church of C&E proclaimed that Wowbagger's newfound immortality was a definite sign to the faithful. Wowbagger proclaimed that it was a definite pain in the arse and it had put him right off elastic bands. After several millennia wallowing in sulky boredom, Wowbagger set himself the challenge of visiting every occupied world in the Universe to sample their indigenous beers. This was the beginning of what historians call his amber period, during which Wowbagger put on a lot of weight and discovered a talent for insulting people. One morning Wowbagger realized, after his morning retch, that he actually enjoyed insulting people more than drinking beer and so decided to switch challenges in midstream. His new task, he determined, would be to insult every single sentient being in the Universe in alphabetical order. Because Wowbagger was such a good-looking guy, and his spaceship had such distinctive lines, the media soon got wind of his quest, and Wowbagger would land on a planet to discover the entire population lined up, in alphabetical order, screaming to be insulted, which kind of took the good out of it for him.

* *

"You came through the death ray lattice?" asked Arthur urgently. "In your ship."

Wowbagger shrugged. "Of course. My ship is made of dark matter and powered by dark energy. These Grebulons operate with mere baryonic materials. They can't understand my ship, never mind stop it."

"Can you shut them down? The beams?"

Wowbagger pocketed his wafer computer. "No. They are loose in real space. The Earth is doomed, which is a pity, as there are many people left to insult on your planet. But at least I got Beeblebrox, eh. Out of order, true, but you make exceptions for his caliber of idiot. So not a total disaster of a day." Wowbagger rubbed his hands briskly. "Anyway. A pleasure to meet you all, probably won't be the next time."

Trillian switched on her reporter's smile. "Mr. Wowbagger. Trillian Astra. We met on New Betel. You were kind enough to give me five minutes."

"Ah yes. New Betel. I'd just done the king, hadn't I? Called him a festering pustule. That was a bit of a low period for me. Everything was festering or septic."

"Maybe you read my article in *WooHoo*?"

"I never read press. You start believing it, you see. Look at Beeblebrox there. He actually believes that he's some froody superstar, instead of the philosophunculistic bumpkin that he actually is."

Zaphod was just pulling himself together from *fat-arsed* when the bumpkin comment socked him in the gut.

"Bumpkin? Ooooh. What . . . You *monster*."

Trillian persisted. "I wonder, could you give us a lift? Just as far as the next planet."

"Impossible," snapped Wowbagger. "I travel through dark space. Mortals are not supposed to see dark space, it affects them."

"We're prepared to take that risk. We wouldn't be any trouble."

Wowbagger raised an eyebrow. "Beeblebrox wouldn't be any trouble? I doubt that. He's a fugitive from someone or other, isn't he?"

Trillian hoisted Zaphod erect. "The President will behave himself. Won't you, Zaphod?"

Zaphod mumbled something.

"See? He said, *Will do*."

"I thought he said, *Kill you*."

Arthur bobbed in front of Zaphod, trying to catch his rolling eyes.

"You didn't say that, mate. Did you? No. Because that would be insane, right? Threatening to kill the one person who could save our lives."

Zaphod drew himself erect, breath growling deep in his throat. "He called me a fat-arsed bumpkin. I cannot allow him to live."

"Oh crap," said Ford.

Wowbagger's mood shifted from polite boredom to impolite boredom. "Don't you think people have tried to kill me before? In my line of work, I attract enemies like a flaybooz attracts lint."

Random sobbed into her fists.

"I keep track of my pursuers for my own amusement. Currently I am being chased by over a hundred bounty hunters, sixteen government vessels, a few unmanned Smart-O-Missiles, and half a dozen wannabe immortals who want to eat my heart and steal my powers. If only it were that easy. I long for death, I crave it the way this idiot craves publicity. I have been alive long enough to realize that there is no such thing as perfect love. That's too long."

"I could kill you," said Zaphod. "I've got some juice in this Universe. I know people who know stuff. Did you ever go a few rounds with the Ravenous Bugblatter Beast?"

Wowbagger snorted. "That old bag of bolts? I hope you can do better than that."

Arthur cupped his hands around his face and peered though the porthole. The beam was almost upon them now. Arthur thought he could hear a whine of energy, though he knew that was impossible.

I probably can't hear the screams of the dying, either, he thought.

"Trillian," he called over his shoulder. "I really think it would be rather a good thing if Zaphod stopped talking. Do we have any stun guns?"

Zaphod was only getting started. "I can do better. You ever take a shot from a spiderwitch?"

"I have, actually. I mix them into my cocktails. No adverse effects."

"What about a plasma axe? Those things will split your atoms for you."

"Not my atoms. I was hit with four of those so-called unshatterable axes by a band of Silastic mercenaries after I called one of their mothers a hurst-toting mawg face. Guess what? They shattered."

"I know a guy who can get me six ounces of Consolium. You hold that in your armpit for five minutes and the job is done, baby."

Wowbagger was losing what modicum of interest he had in the conversation. "Consolium is a myth, Beeblebrox. Spare me your fatuous tale-spinning."

"I know gods!" said Zaphod, desperately. "Other immortals. I bet they could cut you down to size."

The death ray loomed huge now, causing the ship to vibrate, seeming to slice through space as it passed.

"Trillian!" called Arthur.

"Please, Mr. Wowbagger."

"You know gods?" asked the green immortal, reluctantly intrigued. "You are actually acquainted with real gods? Class A?"

"I have Thor's address right here on my communicator. One word from me and you're hammered."

"Gods have tried to kill me before."

"How did that go?"

"Oh shut up, Beeblebrox."

"Never a major god, I'll bet," said Zaphod. "Never a class A."

Wowbagger nodded thoughtfully. "No, never a class A. I've never had much time for those major supreme beings. Tosspots every one of them. But surely a blow from Thor's legendary hammer, Mjöllnir, would be enough to put my lights out. You can arrange this, Beeblebrox?"

"I'm the only one who can."

"It's true," said Ford. "Old Red Beard owes Zaphod a favor."

Arthur could see nothing but green.

And so I lose my daughter again. How much heartbreak can one man bear?

Wowbagger pressed a button on his wafer computer. "You had better not be spiraling my sinkhole."

Zaphod hooked a thumb into his sash/fake arm. "This is no spoof. You called me a fat-arsed bumpkin. *This* is a matter of honor."

Wowbagger spoke tersely into his computer. "Extend the shield," he said.

A white glow crackled across the porthole and the death ray passed harmlessly over them.

CHAPTER 4

Planetary catastrophes are no big deal. They happen all the time. Expanding stars sterilize the surfaces they once nurtured. Asteroids plow into hydrocarbon oceans. Planets wobble a little out of orbit a few light-years too close to a black hole and tip over the event horizon. Ravenous quantum beings devour every last drop of energy on their home worlds before turning on each other.

Guide Note: This last was the subject of a reality show broadcast in the Sirius Tau system called *Last Behemoth Standing*. Twenty-five thousand cameras were dropped into the atmosphere of Levy Wash, a world ravaged by four colossal free-flying creatures, and billions of viewers watched them fight it out for world domination. Unfortunately, Pinky, the voters' favorite Behemoth, jumped free of Levy Wash's atmosphere and leapfrogged the camera network's wireless trail back to the star system's populated cluster. Pinky stripped three worlds down to the mantle before the federation army froze her with liquid hydrogen. Ratings broke all records for the first two planets, but by number three the audience grew jaded and switched to *The Cheeky-Chuu Chronicles,* a show featuring a small rainbow bird endowed with superpowers by a mysterious birdbath.

Related Articles:

"The Worst Idea Ever" by Gawn F'zing (ex–network president and current federal penitentiary inmate)

"Life Beyond the Beak" by Big J Jarood (ex–child star)

Arthur Dent watched his world die for the last time. The porthole frame made the whole event look like it was happening on TV. An early episode of *Doctor Who,* perhaps, when the special effects were charming but not so sophisticated.

I can almost see the wires, thought Arthur.

The death rays were the fat tubular kind favored by late-twentieth-century television animators, and the Earth itself looked like a football covered in papier-mâché.

But it is real. Horribly so.

The rays converged on the planet, peeling it like a blue green apple. Arthur was sure that he saw New Zealand curl away from the Antipodes, a thousand-mile-long tail of steam and debris flowing behind it.

I miss my beach, thought Arthur. *I miss not knowing anything for certain.*

Soon the planet was engulfed in a roiling cloud of steam and ashes. The death rays converged into a point like the tip of a pencil and, with one mighty push, skewered the unfortunate Earth utterly, rending her from pole to pole.

Not real, thought Arthur, hiding behind his fingers. *Not real.*

I brought that planet *to the stars,* thought Random Dent, her eyes blurred with tears. *I built the bridges that cured cancer, made poverty history, gave Goldflake their first Galactic number one single. Now it's all gone. All those people. All that future. My little Fertle.*

Trillian closed her eyes. She had seen enough devastation throughout her career to last at least one lifetime. Even Wowbagger's. A lot of the destruction hadn't been real, but that didn't mean she could forget having seen it.

And what did I achieve? With all that Galaxy-trotting reportage? Who was saved or helped?

Nobody.

And who was hurt and lost?

I was. And my daughter.

But even as she thought this, Trillian Astra felt a little itch in her hand where a microphone used to be.

Someone should be covering this, said a tiny persistent voice inside her. *The people need to know.*

VOGON BUREAUCRUISER CLASS HYPERSPACE SHIP
BUSINESS END

The Vogons were not *bad* people as such. It was true to say that nobody liked them, and that their interpersonal skills didn't extend much beyond trying not to spit on the person they were talking to, but they weren't bad. That is, they would not blast your planet into atoms without the proper paperwork. *With* the proper paperwork, however, they would travel to the end of the Universe, and to as many parallel ones as necessary, to see the job done. And, to be fair, most of them couldn't care less if they *did* spit all over the person they were talking to.

• •

Guide Note: There is actually a documented case of a tiny Jatravartid being drowned during a conversation with a Vogon clerk. The Jatravartid had the temerity to present a petition and claim it was a legal document. During the ensuing coughing fit, the Jatravartid was first stunned by a semi-solid phlegmbule and then quickly submerged.

Related Articles:

"Twenty Thousand Games to Play in a Vogon Queue" by Magyar Ohnfhunn. (written in a Vogon queue)

"TTGTPIAVQ II" by Magyar Ohnfhunn (written toward the head of the queue)

And

"All Vogons Are Bastards and Must Die" by Magyar Ohnfunn (written just after the hatch came down on his fingers)

• •

The Vogons are unusual as a race because they exhibit the generic characteristics of doggedness, lack of compassion, and a very good ear for exceedingly bad poetry. All Vogons are like this and there are no exceptions.

• •

Guide Note: There are rumors of the existence of an underground group of Vogons on an outer Brantisvogon world who call themselves Tru-Heart Vogs.

They like to sit in a circle and just say things without first submitting paperwork.

● ●

Physically Vogons are not attractive creatures. If beauty is in the eye
of the beholder, then the beholder won't be a Vogon, because even Vogons
know how ugly they are. A Vogon head resembles nothing more than a
giant prune with extra deep wrinkles for the eyes and mouth. The body is
a vast green buttery mound of flesh with too few bones per square foot
and too many folds and flaps. The limbs are weak and ineffectual, and
seem almost random in their placement. If a disturbed child were given a
hard-boiled egg, a raisin, and some spaghetti strands to play with, whatever the child came up with would look like one Vogon or other.

So if all Vogons are repulsive, bureaucratic sadists, how does one get
ahead in their society? It is a matter of being more Vogon-ish than the
rest. The Vogons have a word for it. When one of their number distin-
guishes himself in the ruthless prosecution of his orders; when the
man-hours and body count are ridiculously disproportionate to the im-
portance of the task, when a Vogon forges ahead where others would
have been discouraged by plural zones, hordes of Silastic Armorfiends,
or the tears of widows—that Vogon is spoken of in the halls of power as
having *kroompst.*

As in: *That Prostetnic Vogon Bierdz, you see what he did to that or-
phanage? Barely a stick remains. That boy has real kroompst.*

Yeah. He's a kroompster. He's got kroompst coming out his krimpter.

Whenever a senior Vogon uses the term *kroompst,* all others present
must respond by throwing up both arms and echoing the word with
much enthusiasm and spittle.

The term *kroompst* could have been invented for Prostetnic Vogon
Jeltz. In his distinguished career as fleet commander, he had never once
failed to complete his assigned duties. When the inhabitants of Rigan-
non V objected to their world being nudged into a wider orbit, with their
groundless claims of *planet death* because of the instantaneous ice age
that would surely follow, who had set off a colorful fireworks display in
their aurora borealis to distract the Rigannonons from the buffer ships
coming in from the south? Jeltz, of course. And when the tiny Blue Belle

Tweeters had neglected to tick either the yes or no box on the final page in the third volume of their Objection to Planning Permission submission, who was it who had razed their forest habitat in spite of the protestors tied to the trees? Once again, it was Jeltz. And now, in his finest hour, he had with only a single ship at his disposal arranged for *all* Earths in *all* parallel universes to be destroyed by Grebulon death rays, because the last thing interstellar travelers wanted was surprise planets popping out of plural zones every third trip.

If the planning office had a tough job that needed doing, then Prostetnic Jeltz had the kroompst to get it done. In fact, Jeltz's photograph hung on the Wall of Kroompst, alongside all the bureaucratic greats in Vogon history: Vrunt the Naysayer, Sheergawz the Rubberstamper, and Jeltz's nemesis, Hoopz the Runaround. And now Jeltz himself. All the photographs were taken from behind, as was the tradition in the Hall of Kroompst, wherein stood the Wall of Kroompst.

Jeltz sat in his command chair on the bridge of his ship, the *Business End*, wondering what epithet would be bestowed on him back in Megabrantis.

Jeltz the Destroyer. That had a ring to it, but it did seem a little random. He rarely destroyed a world without paperwork.

Jeltz the Unswerving. Nice one, but it did make him sound like a race pod pilot.

Whenever Jeltz played the epithet game, he always came back to his father's pet name for him.

Jeltz the Utter Bastard. That said it all, really. Jeltz remembered one of his own early poems.

"Utter bastard," he said in a voice of distant rumbling thunder.

> "*Play thee,*
> *No more,*
> *By the crabby hole.*
> *Lay down thine mallet*
> *And flap flippy floppy arms,*
> *At a world of sun and tight skin.*
> *Learn hate well,*
> *My little, Utter Bastard.*"

Jeltz felt something collect at the corner of his eye. A speck of dust he supposed, flicking it away.

Constant Mown, a subordinate, appeared at his shoulder, sporting one of those chin-cup drool-catchers so fashionable among the youngsters.

"Prostetnic Jeltz?"

"Obviously, Constant. I wear a name tag to help people to find me. It saves time when you are dealing with idiots."

The subordinate bobbed. "Yes, Prostetnic. Of course, sir."

"Did you want something, Constant Mown?"

"You said to inform you when we were ready for hyperspace."

A contented sigh dribbled from between Jeltz's lips. *Hyperspace.* It was said that Vogons only experienced the emotion known as happiness when they were lost in hyperspace. The skin was pulled back, bones pushed together. A person felt almost evolved in hyperspace. And there was a lack of control that had a dark deliciousness to it, and there was a small chance that one could end up anywhere, without the proper visa.

"Very well, Constant. Plot our course through Earth space. Might as well be the first to use the route, now that there is no Earth in the way and no Earthlings left to complain."

Constant Mown bobbed twice, then froze, head cocked like a confused Squornshellous Zeta mattress.

"Problem, Mown?"

Mown was reluctant to deliver news of *any* kind. In his experience news delivered to superiors invariably ended up being bad news, even if it had seemed good when one opened one's mouth to deliver it.

"No, sir. No problem. As you said, there is no Earth . . ."

Jeltz burbled with his pendulous bottom lip. "And no Earthlings. The order clearly states that no Earthlings are to be left alive. The Imperial Government does not want some displaced humanoids demanding their day in court."

"Indeed, Prostetnic. Well said, nice sentence structure."

Jeltz rubbed his side where the kidney-drain chafed his skin. "*Are* there Earthlings left alive, Constant?"

"There are rumors of a new colony in the Soulianis nebula," admitted Mown, the words leaking out of his face.

Jeltz gurgled for a long moment. "Soulianis? Isn't the mythical Magrathea supposed to be in Soulianis?"

"Correct, Prostetnic. Well remembered."

A vein fluttered in one of Jeltz's eyelids, a manifestation of his annoyance. Another common manifestation was flushing whoever had delivered the annoying news out an air lock.

"You said rumors, Constant Mown. What kind of . . . rumors?"

"They . . . the Earthlings . . . put an advertisement in the *WooHoo* magazine personals."

"An advertisement!" spluttered Jeltz, offended for some reason. "Show me."

"Of course, Prostetnic."

Mown scuttled across to a computer terminal, flexed his fingers, then punched the operator in the tender spot between the shoulder blades until he brought up the appropriate page on-screen.

"There it is, Prostetnic. The link is dead now; they are not taking any more résumés."

Jeltz read the advertisement carefully, gargling all the while. "Nice of them to provide coordinates," he noted. "What would you do, Constant? In my place. Would you allow these Earthlings to live? After all, their planet was the main target. Would you follow your orders to the letter and make the long journey to Soulianis to obliterate this colony?"

Mown did not hesitate. "We are Vogon, Prostetnic. I cannot even file the paperwork until the Earthlings are dead."

"That was the correct response, Mown," said Jeltz. "Eleven jumps to Soulianis, I think."

The constant bobbed an affirmative bob. "I will program the drive immediately, Prostetnic. We can charge the Unnecessarily Painful Slow Death torpedoes on the trip. Hyperspace static will give them a little extra sting."

Jeltz nodded approvingly. "You, Mown, are an utter bastard."

Mown tried to salute, flinging a tiny arm across an expansive gullet in the direction of his head.

"Thanks, Dad," he said.

Arthur Dent woke to the sound of surf on the beach.

Whoosh on the way in, rattle on the way out.

The familiar noises came from below and to the left of his bed. Exactly as they should. The pootle-tink birds were beginning their morning show-off antics, clapping broad wings and singing their slightly risqué songs, hoping to attract the attention of a rainbow-plumed female.

I am home in my beach house. All that other stuff, with the Earth exploding and the green aliens, was all a nightmare. It was nice to see everybody, but why does there always have to be genocide?

Arthur felt a sense of relief and he breathed it in, inflating his lungs, relishing his daily decisions.

Rich Tea or Digestives. Maybe Earl Grey today. Why not?

Arthur lay still, letting his bones warm up. No sudden moves at his age, whatever his age was.

Come to think of it, maybe the dream hadn't been all bad. He'd fairly raced up the ramp to Zaphod's ship. Not a single ball joint had popped out of its socket. And the nose hair, he hadn't missed that.

Maybe I should get a trimmer. Nothing fancy.

No! It starts with nose hair trimmers and the next thing you know there's a Zylatburger bar on your doorstep. No commerce. No contact.

Arthur opened his eyes and was momentarily relieved to see the interior of his wooden hut, but then he noticed something on the corner of the ceiling. A digital countdown, with words before it. He closed his bad eye and read the words, which amazingly enough were in English.

Seconds to reality read the words. Then a countdown. Five seconds to reality apparently.

Five . . . four . . .

More reality, thought Arthur. *Bugger.*

At zero the beach was switched off and Fenchurch appeared on Arthur's ceiling, smiling that off-kilter smile of hers, those arched eyebrows like slashes of oil pastels. Blue eyes twinkling.

I can see you, darling. This is real.

But, of course, it was not.

"Hello," said Fenchurch. "Welcome to consciousness. If you enjoyed your tailor-made easy-wake experience, please leave the program a feedback star. Would you like to leave a star at this time?"

"What?" said Arthur.

"Would you like to leave a feedback star at this time?" said the computer, upping the volume a notch.

"Um . . . Yes. Have a star. Have two. Why not?"

Fenchurch smiled, and it was painful to watch. So beautiful.

"Thank you, Arthur Dent. It has been my pleasure to monitor your dreams."

And just like that she was gone.

Again.

No less painful than the first time.

Reality was a small room on Wowbagger's longship with gray interactive walls and a cubicle in the corner. Arthur realized that a hot shower would be extremely nice, but not too long, or he might relax and start thinking about Fenchurch.

Not thinking about Fenchurch was going to be difficult, Arthur realized as her face appeared on the shower door.

"I am your chamber's Body Optimizer," said the computer's interpretation of his dreams. "Tell me what you want. Please start your sentence with: I want . . ."

Simple enough. "I want a nice shower," said Arthur. "And a shave. I want to feel good."

"Shower, shave, and feel good. Are these the things you want?"

"Affirmative," said Arthur, getting into the spirit of it.

"Please enter the cubicle, Arthur Dent."

Arthur unbuttoned his shirt, then had a thought. "Fenchurch . . . Ahmm, computer . . . could I have a little privacy?"

"I am the computer. There is no privacy."

It was ridiculous, Arthur knew. This was not Fenchurch, this was a still shot plucked from his memory.

"Nevertheless, could you shut your eyes?"

"I don't have eyes."

"Turn off your cameras then and take the face away."

"While you are in the Optimizer only. After that I will resume monitoring."

"Knock yourself out," said Arthur, dropping his clothes into a hamper, which made a sneezing noise.

"Holy shit!" said the computer.

"What kind of language is that for a computer?"

"I got this phrase from *your* memory. Apparently you used it all the time at the BBC."

"I had good reason," muttered Arthur. "Bloody producers."

"These clothes have a stink-o-factor of twelve and are carrying several viruses, not to mention the twelve million dust mites, which I just mentioned. Your speech patterns are very strange. At any rate, these garments really have to go."

"Wait!"

"No waiting, Arthur Dent. Those mites could get into my circuits and then where would we be? Floating dead in space, that's where. Kiss your shorts good-bye."

The hamper growled and shook slightly as Arthur's clothes were incinerated.

"Now, into the cubicle with you. Five minutes and then my cameras are back on."

Fenchurch's face disappeared and Arthur stepped tentatively into the stall.

"No peeking."

"Four fifty-nine, Arthur Dent. Four fifty-eight . . ."

"Okay. I'm in, I'm in." Arthur glanced around. "Won't I need a towel?"

"Whatever for?" asked the computer.

Arthur barely had time to wonder what kind of shower he was in for when dozens of glowing lasers shot from crystal nodes set into the walls, bathing him in crimson light.

Arthur's first thought was that he had been lured into a death cubicle, but when he opened his mouth to scream, a laser shot inside and scraped his tongue. He lifted an arm to cover his mouth and another laser trimmed and buffed his fingernails. The laser scrubbing was thorough and not altogether unpleasant once Arthur relaxed and accepted what was happening. Dirt and skin cells were sloughed off and collected by a recycling vacuum in the tray. He selected a hairstyle from a v-catalogue and his scalp tickled as the lasers coiffed his locks.

"Smile please, Arthur Dent," ordered the computer.

Arthur complied and his teeth were whitened by a jittering beam.

I feel good, Arthur realized. *Better than I have in years.*

The cloud of skin, hair, and grime settled, and Arthur stepped from the cubicle to find a suit lying on the bed. As soon as he saw the suit, Arthur cringed. It took him a minute to figure out why.

"Bugger me," he breathed. "Eaton House."

It was his school uniform from preparatory school, complete with striped tie and green cap.

Fenchurch appeared on the wall. "Do you feel good, Arthur Dent?"

Arthur covered himself with a handy pillow. "Eh . . . Yes. Yes I do. Can't I have something else to wear?"

"You dreamed of this, Arthur Dent. So I made it in your size. There are no more clothing credits for this cycle. Is there something wrong with these garments?"

Arthur ran his finger along the green jacket's crimson lapel.

"No. Nothing *wrong*, I suppose. It's just that this is a school uniform."

"It is clean."

"Yes, I know."

"Free of viruses and dust mites."

"Good point, but hardly age-appropriate."

"And it has nostalgic value. I have helped you to recapture your youth, Arthur Dent. Don't I get a thank-you?"

"I suppose so."

"You suppose? Holy shit!"

"Okay. All right. Thank you."

Fenchurch was miffed. "After all I have done for you. The twenty-twenty vision and the kidney stones."

"What?" said Arthur, alarmed.

"Didn't you notice your improved vision? I fixed your retina. Also my scanners detected a cluster of kidney stones, so I pulverized them."

Arthur closed his good eye and realized that his other eye was also a good one.

"That's amazing. Shouldn't you have asked?"

"Should I? Wowbagger allows me independent choice in basic health matters. If you step back into the cubicle, I can return your eye to its original state."

Arthur blinked and realized almost instantly that he enjoyed being able to see properly very much indeed.

"No. No, Fenchurch. I like this twenty-twenty thing. Thank you very much."

The computer smiled. "You are welcome, Arthur."

"And the kidney stones. An entire cluster. That would have been painful, I imagine. So, thanks for that too."

"And the clothes?"

"Perfect," said Arthur graciously. "If you would just make yourself scarce, I can put them on."

"Feedback star?"

"Go on then."

"Thank you, Arthur."

Fenchurch fizzled out and Arthur put on his school uniform. *Could be worse,* he thought. *Could be short trousers.*

"Thank you, Fenchurch," he whispered.

Arthur bumped into Trillian in the corridor.

"Blimey," he said taken aback. "You look fantastic, Tricia . . . Sorry, Trillian."

"Really, Arthur?"

Arthur Dent had that particular English personality defect where he dissected any compliment he gave shortly after giving it, effectively hobbling himself.

"I mean . . . you always look fantastic. It's not that you didn't look fantastic before. You look extra-fantastic now. Mega-fantastic, I suppose I should say, seeing as we're in space and all that."

Trillian wore a smart electric blue trouser suit and wedge boots to her thighs.

"The computer picked this outfit out of my head. I wore it to interview the president of the Sirius Cybernetics Corporation. Or rather, I dreamed I wore it, in the construct."

"Well, whatever. It suits you."

"The computer treated me to a face peel," Trillian confided, leaning in close. "And balanced out my vitamin and mineral levels. I feel like I could run a marathon."

"Me too."

Trillian tugged the sleeve of Arthur's jacket. "No need to ask where you went to school then."

"Lucky I wasn't dreaming of the nightclub in Cottington, or I could be wearing shoulder pads right now."

"Nice cap though."

Arthur hurriedly snatched the hat off his head, stuffing it in a pocket. "Didn't realize I had that on. Habit, I suppose. Have you seen Ford?"

"I have, actually. He trotted past me on his way to the bridge."

"Anything different about him?"

Trillian frowned. "His hair did seem unusually shiny. Oh, and it was blue."

Arthur was not surprised. "It was only a matter of time. The computer in your room, what did it look like?"

"My cat, Copernicus. Imagine that. Very clever trick that. How about you?"

Arthur stared through a porthole into the deep and endless blackness of space.

"Just a computer. No face. It didn't look like anyone."

WOWBAGGER'S LONGSHIP, THE *TANNGRISNIR*

Wowbagger's sleek golden interstellar longship sped silently toward Alpha Centauri, dark matter engines revolving behind it, solar sail fluttering above, and the *Heart of Gold* slung underneath like a baby flaybooz in its parent's pouch.

• •

Guide Note: Contrary to an almost universal norm, it is the male flaybooz who nurtures the young. A full-grown flaybooz can fit up to fifty young in his pouch, but generally there is only room for a couple, as males like to carry around a small tool kit in case of emergencies, maybe a few beers, and a copy of *Furballs Quarterly*.

• •

Ford Prefect poked around the bridge and was hugely impressed. "This is something, Wowbagger. Dark matter. Seventy percent of the

Universe is made of this stuff and we can't even see it. How do you make a ship from dark matter?"

Wowbagger shrugged. "The *Tanngrisnir*? I bought it from a guy a few centuries ago."

"That's it? You bought it from a guy?"

"He swears he stole it from Thor. The Thunder God? It's his longship, hence the retro design."

"I know who *Thor* is. I am a reporter."

"Tanngrisnir was one of his goats, apparently. I was going to replace the horned ram figurehead, but I've heard that Thor is a bit dim and I was worried that he wouldn't recognize the ship with a new symbol on the prow. I had hoped that maybe he would come after me, dash my brains out with the big hammer."

"Wishful thinking," guessed Ford.

"Looks like it. No sign of him so far." Wowbagger leaped from his chair. "Look, can you not touch that?"

Random was twiddling a glowing button on a console.

"Excuse me," she said, but meant something entirely different.

"It's just that I've been on my own for a long time now. I have things just the way I like them. One push on the wrong knob and we could all end up on the outside looking in. Which would be a slight annoyance for me, but a lot more serious for you people."

"So what is that button you are so sensitive about?"

"That is my coffeemaker."

"What?"

"It took me decades to get the foam just right."

"Oh, for Zark's sake."

"Everything is Zark with you. You might show a little more gratitude. I just saved your lives."

"I didn't ask you to," said Random, eyes blazing beneath her long fringe.

Wowbagger was beginning to regret inviting these people aboard, but the hyperspace jump would have killed them on their own ship. No shields, no buffers, no gyro. They would have been shaken like beads in a rattle. A rattle traveling at incomprehensible speeds, with no fitted safety belts.

"I am delighted to say, young lady, that I will not be the object of your detestation for much longer."

"But I like detesting you," said Random sweetly.

. . . .

Guide Note: Given Random Dent's instant and irrational hatred of Wowbagger the Infinitely Prolonged, it was inevitable that he would eventually become her stepfather. The well-known actor Angus deBeouf, who played a psychiatrist on the hit show *Psych-O-Rama* for seven seasons, postulated that single mothers feel an attraction to males that is proportional to the revulsion their teenagers feel toward that same person. Though not actually a qualified psychiatrist, Mr. deBeouf does have four brains and silky hair, so his opinion carries considerable weight, especially among that section of the Galactic population that wears slippers in the afternoon.

Related Articles:

"The Happy Teen. A fairy tale" by Jimmy Habrey K.

"Trust Me, I Play a Doctor" by Angus deBeouf

. . . .

Wowbagger plucked a face mask from its niche in the wall and strapped it over his nose.

"I had forgotten what people were like," he said, breathing deeply. "Use this experience. Take from it the strength to go on."

"Do you mind sucking your magic gas *after* dropping us off?"

Wowbagger replaced the mask. "It is not magic gas, oddly dressed child. I bottle the atmosphere from my home world. Full of carbon dioxide and toxic chemicals, but it calms me." He smiled broadly to demonstrate his calm. "Now please do not touch anything else on my bridge or I will vaporize you on the spot, you odious adolescent. When I was young, teenagers didn't talk back to their elders or they got a dunking in a bucket of toadstool mandarins."

"When was this? Just after the Big Bang?"

"One more. Just say one more thing. I have some toadstool mandarins around here somewhere."

"That bottled atmosphere isn't working, is it?"

"No," admitted Wowbagger. "Actually it's giving me a bit of a head-ache. Or maybe you're the cause of my headache."

Random fell back on the old reliable.

"I hate you!" she screamed and stormed off to her room, presumably to replicate more black clothing.

"Don't feel too badly," said Trillian, hurrying after her daughter. "She hates everyone."

. . . .

Another Guide Note (a little too close to the previous one, but educational): Toadstool mandarins are a form of toxic jellyfish whose tentacles are loaded with entheogenic venom. The effects of a mandarin sting are threefold. The first is a sharp stinging sensation; the second a nasty red welt, which may fester if not treated with a salve of toadstool mandarin doo-doo. And the third is a bolt of self-awareness, thanks to the entheogens in the venom. Having been stung, a victim's typical reaction will be something like:

Owww. Zark, that hurts.

Then:

Oh no. Look at this nasty red welt. I'm in the swimsuit competition later.

And finally:

What? I'm a latent misogynist with father issues!

If a person is allergic to mandarin venom, one sting will prompt total self-awareness, leading to either immediate catatonia or a career as a talk show pundit.

. . . .

Wowbagger managed to lure the males to the conference table with the promise of a Dragon Slammer, an alcoholic drink so fantastic that it made the Galactic Blaster taste like bilgewater. This argument didn't impress Zaphod much, as he had developed a bit of a bilgewater habit during a particularly boring state cruise on the Tranquil Sea of No Surprises Please on the planet Innocuadamis during his inaugural year as President.

They sat around an obsidian table which glooped and grew as more people pulled up chairs.

"So what about this Dragon Slammer then?" asked Ford, finger-combing his thick azure locks. "Better than a Pan Galactic Gargle Blaster? I'll believe it when I wake in a week on the other side of the Galaxy, with no kidneys, three wives and a tattoo."

Wowbagger smiled confidently. "Oh, I think you're going to like this one, Mr. Prefect. It's quite special."

"Not replicated, I hope. Only the real thing."

"But of course."

A hover tray flitted from the galley and smoothly deposited a crystal tumbler before everyone seated at the table.

Zaphod sniffed the contents of the tumbler. "Smells like water to me, partner."

"It *is* water," confirmed Wowbagger. "Pure mega-mountain springwater from Magramel."

"Big deal."

"Wait for it, Fat Arse."

"There's no need for that. I've already promised to have you killed."

Wowbagger touched the table, which rippled and produced a bowl of small speckled eggs.

"These are sea dragon eggs. The sea dragons are tiny *Syngnathidae* found in the shallow tropical waters of equatorial Kakrafoon."

"Should I be writing this down?" asked Ford jauntily.

Wowbagger forged ahead. "The males hatch every ten years and live for four seconds. When they die, their essence, soul if you will, is released into the water."

"I am reluctantly interested," said Zaphod. "Soul drinking. Sounds wonderfully depraved."

"Do as I do," instructed Wowbagger.

The green immortal popped an egg into his drink, then waited as an infrared lamp caressed the tumbler from below. Seconds later the egg became translucent and a small sea dragon could clearly be seen wiggling around inside it.

"It's like a dragon, only from the sea," said Zaphod with childlike awe.

The dragon chewed its way from the egg, paddled around awkwardly for a moment or two, then clasped a claw to its heart and began to vibrate. A tiny golden cloud of lightning spread from its heart to permeate the water.

"Down the hatch," said Wowbagger and swallowed the lot.

Ford and Zaphod followed suit and were immediately blown from their seats. They lay spasming on the ground and singing the Meli-Meli scene from Pantheoh's *Hrung Disaster* opera in perfect harmony. From a floating diagnostic gel cube in a bank of sensors and wires, Left Brain took the third part.

"Hmm," said Wowbagger. "All I ever get is heartburn."

Arthur decided to give the Dragon Slammer a pass.

Twenty minutes later, Ford and Zaphod were back on their seats, giggling at each other.

"Very well," said Wowbagger, clapping his hands. "Fat Arse and his baboon have been entertained. Now can we please get down to business?"

· ·

Guide Note: The phrase "down to business" is thought to have originated on Chalesm, where industrial espionage was so sophisticated that businessmen were forced to strike major deals down in mine shafts, underneath tarpaulins, wearing disguises, and talking in code through voice boxes. All of which precautions ensured that none of the businessmen had a clue as to what deal they had actually struck. One union representative made a planet-wide announcement that he had secured pensions for all members when he had actually promised to secure his member to a pensioner. The strikes continue.

· ·

This sounded a little complicated to Arthur. "Business. What business? Aren't you simply going to drop us off at the nearest spaceport?"

"Not until you kill me."

"Aren't you immortal?"

"Were you not listening? Fat Arse *promised* to kill me."

"Come on," objected Zaphod. "Now you're just being mean."

"I am Wowbagger the Infinitely Prolonged. Being *mean* is my vocation. Haven't you figured that out yet?"

Zaphod stood as regally as he possibly could with the left side of his body still jittering. "I promised to kill you and so I shall. Does anyone else hear singing?"

"Not me," said Ford, tipping the dragon eggs into his satchel. "Can't hear a thing. Especially not opera that is not there."

"A Beeblebrox's word is worth something in this galaxy. So there's no need to *keep* calling me Fat Arse."

Wowbagger winked at him in a manner so infuriating it could have animated rocks. "I'm just keeping you motivated, Beeblebrox. I imagine you distract easily."

"He does," said Ford, chuckling.

"Hey!"

"Well, you do. Remember that time with the groon-pole and the bucket of flitter pies? You really should have kept your mind on the job that time."

"Point taken. Let me hear it again."

Wowbagger was happy to oblige. "Fat Arse."

"Okay," said Zaphod. "I'm ready. Just let me plug Left Brain out of whatever he's plugged into and I'm ready to go."

Wowbagger raised a finger. "You mean *we're* ready to go?"

"Oh no," said Zaphod, climbing onto the console to reach Left Brain. "The gods don't like visitors. Thor will speak to me because he owes me a favor and I'm more stupider than he is. I go to Asgard alone."

He reached into the cube of shimmering gel and hauled Left Brain free with a slooshy pop.

"How are you doing, buddy?" he asked, peeling sensors from Left Brain's gourd.

"A little sleepy," said Left Brain, blinking rapidly. "Do I have to wake up?"

"I'm afraid so. We need to fly."

Wowbagger handed him a wafer computer. "Keep in touch with this. It's on a dark energy network. Good anywhere in the Universe. We can rendezvous once you have Thor, and please tell him that I stole his ship, it might give him a little incentive. Don't make me track you down."

Zaphod pocketed the computer. "Right. I'm all set. All I need is two million credit chips and I'm out of here."

"Two million credit chips?"

"Just thought I'd ask."

"Focus, President Steatopygic. Focus."

Zaphod actually snarled. "You are so dead."

"Now you're talking," said the green immortal.

CHAPTER 5

Anything can be real. Every imaginable thing *is* happening somewhere along the dimensional axis. These things happen a billion times over with exactly the same outcome and no one learns anything. Whatever a person can think, imagine, wish for, or believe has already come to pass. Dreams come true all the time, just not for the dreamers.

Think of something crazy, or if that's too taxing just throw random adjectives and nouns together.

Indignant seaweed? No problem. The resentful hijiki of Damogran. The hijiki strands, acerbated by shoals of triple stripe yellowheads casually nudging them aside to nibble on the tender coral polyps, banded together and wove themselves into an impenetrable barrier separating the reef from the fish. The knock-on effect of this was that the reef became sterile and died. The hijiki had tied themselves too tightly to disband and perished along with the hated yellowheads.

How about murderous clowns? Too easy. Add in a vegetable obsession. Type that into your Hitchhiker's Guide v-board and you will get over a million hits. The top one being the story of Bling & Blong of Circus Minimus, two tiny clowns who both fell in love with Gerda the Amazing Cucumber Lady. After months of feuding, Bling loaded a custard pie with acid and melted his little brother during the matinee. Gerda belonged to him, but so distracted was he by guilt that one evening he accidentally ate his fiancée and choked to death himself on the engagement ring.

How about this one? How about an ex-two-headed President of the

Galaxy who bought a tiny tropical planet from the Magratheans at a knockdown price then sold it to rich Earthlings so they could live on in comfort after their planet had been destroyed?

How crazy would that be?

THE *TANNGRISNIR*

Arthur lay on his bunk looking up at the sky, to where Fenchurch hovered on a cloud wearing the same dark jeans, high boots, and sodden T-shirt that she'd worn when he first saw her, passed out in the back of her arsehole brother's car.

"Does the T-shirt have to be wet?" asked the computer.

"What? Oh, God, no. Sorry, of course not. I am such an idiot."

"Just trying to be accurate, I expect. I can portray this Fenchurch person naked, if you'd like."

"No, no," said Arthur in what he would have liked to think of as an immediate fashion. "A dry T-shirt is fine. It was raining that night so I was wet too, if that gets me off the hook at all."

"No need to explain," said Fenchurch's rendered head. "Guests often take advantage of my realistic representations. I have a celebrity catalogue if you would like to browse through it."

"Perhaps some other time," said Arthur. "Can you show me these Grebulons?"

"Of course. Do you seek closure, Arthur Dent? If you step into the cubicle, I could laser the memories."

"No. I need to see them because of how I feel now."

"And how is that, would you say?"

Arthur's smile was guilty as an orchard thief's. "I don't feel too bad, to be honest. Pretty happy, in fact, all things considered. I miss my beach, but you know, I thought losing Earth would hit me harder, but it hasn't. Maybe if I can actually look into the faces of those responsible, I might feel a little worse."

"I've got high-definition, honeycomb speaker systems, 3D, and super-deep perception wrapped up in a little remote camera no bigger than a human head," said the computer confidently. "Not to mention Point 'n' Pitch and a Wow-O-Wang warbler. Let's see if I can't make you feel like shit."

"What?"

"Your words, not mine."

Fenchurch disappeared and the blackness of space appeared on the ceiling. Arthur recognized the solar system and the ten planets in elliptical orbit around Sol. The deep blue of Saturn, Jupiter like a giant malachite pebble. Continent-sized boulders spun and shuddered in the asteroid belt beyond Mars, huge thunderclaps shaking Arthur's bunk as the rocks collided.

"Was that the ship or the show?" asked Arthur nervously.

"I put the sound in," admitted Fenchurch. "Give me a little poetic license. All these speakers, and space is a vacuum."

Farther out they flew, whizzing through the blue black vastness of empty space, wisps of charged interstellar gas crackling across their vista. Past the dwarf planet Pluto they journeyed, to a slightly larger planet, a completely ice-bound body, shining smooth but for the pockmarks of palimpsests and the gray industrial pods of an alien spaceship anchored on its surface.

"The Grebulons," whispered Fenchurch. "Looking for something else to monitor."

The detail was incredible. Arthur could see every plate of armor, every twist of cable.

He reached out to touch the hull and the entire scene lurched and zoomed.

"That's the Point 'n' Pitch," said Fenchurch. "Careful with that. People have been known to throw up."

Arthur peered through a porthole, feeling like a Peeping Tom. He saw soft sofas and magazine racks. Amiable-looking humanoids ambled along the carpeted hallway, stopping to chat politely or exchange what appeared to be astronomy trading cards.

This was not the kind of behavior a person expected from destroyers of worlds. Arthur looked, but not one of the Grebulons was laughing maniacally, nor did they appear to have misshapen minions.

"They look so nice," said Arthur, a little disconcerted by how easy it would be to like these people.

Fenchurch's snort was so spot-on that Arthur wanted to weep. "It's always the nice ones. You look up the Sub-Etha the day after a planet gets blown to smithereens, and it's zigabytes of the neighboring worlds saying how the rampaging mass murderers were always so polite on trade missions. How they always sent kittens at Cattybagmas, how they kept to themselves mostly."

Arthur used the P 'n' P to zoom in on a Grebulon woman with a clutch of admirers gathered around.

"Would you like me to put a wet T-shirt on her?" asked Fenchurch wickedly.

"Look in their eyes, Fenchurch."

The computer sent a dark energy beam through the porthole. "Not the brightest, are they? I can't scan back further than five orbit cycles with these people."

"Why would they do it, then?"

"Maaaaaybe, someone put them up to it."

Arthur's stomach lurched as his perspective was shifted at hyper-speed. They withdrew from the surface and past the inferior planet of Pluto, just in time to catch the rear end of a huge ship, blue rings of light spinning up to enter hyperspace. The ship was yellow and ungainly and would never feature on a froody Sub-Etha spaceship show where middle-aged ex–racing drivers threw it around a test track while making jolly xenophobic remarks and claiming not to understand all the knobs and dials. This ship was clumsy in the way that comets are not.

"Vogons," said Arthur, surprised not a jot. "Jerks every one of them. Complete arseholes."

"Ah. Your people."

Arthur managed a spurt of indignance. "Not my people. That bunch *killed* all of my people."

"Well, not all of them."

"Nearly all. Three of us, that's all that are left."

"Soon will be."

"Soon? What do you mean *soon*?"

"Well, I had a little rummage in their computer. Apparently the Vogons are off to the Dark Nebula of Soulianis and Rahm to hunt down a colony of Earthlings."

"What? Earthlings? What the hell is a dark nebula? Shouldn't you play ominous music when you say things like that? Can their computer give you any details?"

On the ceiling/screen the whirring blue circles suddenly froze, turned white, and disappeared, along with the Vogon ship.

"Too late," said Fenchurch. "Even my instruments cannot hack through hyperspace."

Arthur tumbled from his bed, absently jamming the school cap onto his head.

"We must warn them, surely. Should we warn them? Should we go to this dark nebula place? Bom bom bohhhhm."

"Don't you miss your beach, Arthur?"

And from Arthur's mind the computer plucked a memory of his beach hut and plastered it on the ceiling.

"I miss it terribly. Every day was the same. No exploding planets or people screaming at me or aliens invading my personal space. Why do people always feel it necessary to stand nose-to-nose for a simple conversation? Plus, on my island, I could stray as far as I wanted off the subject and nobody tried to drag me back on course."

"So why would you follow the Vogons? They never fail. Why give yourself the heartache?"

"I need to go because a large part of me doesn't want to go. What kind of Earthling would I be if I didn't want to save my species?"

"An alive one. Not blown to atoms by Vogon thermonuclear warheads. A little archaic, but they do the job."

"We have to turn around, or power up a drive. Push the go-faster button. Something."

"Calm yourself, Arthur Dent. Wowbagger goes where his schedule takes him."

"He was going to Earth wasn't he? To insult Earthlings?"

"True."

"Well then. The last Earthling colony appears to somehow be in this dark nebula. Couldn't Wowbagger insult the Earthlings there?"

"It's feasible. You state your case well, Arthur Dent."

. . . .

Guide Note: Throughout recorded history the ability to "state one's case well" has generally had about as much success as "talking things out reasonably" or "putting aside our differences." The people who use these tactics generally mean well and would make excellent motivational speakers or kindergarten teachers, but on no account should they be put in charge of situations where lives are at stake. Malapropos comments such as "I know we haven't always seen eye to eye . . ." tend to send negotiations spiraling toward disaster, especially if the other species' representative suffers from globular organ envy or thinks you are being a patronizing git. Successful negotiations are invariably conducted from a position of power, or at least the perception of power. Strolling into a meeting wearing a comfortable robe and smelling of incense, with a sincere desire to iron out difficulties, is, perversely, a surefire way to get everyone killed. General Anyar Tsista, the acknowledged prince of negotiators, once claimed that while on the job he never used a sentence that did not include at least one Zark, two shits, and half a dozen asscracks. His final pronouncement contained only a single shit, and was uttered in the form of an authoritative command to his bowels which had locked up as a result of too many hours seated around the negotiation tables. Unfortunately, because of their thin bowel walls, Golgafrinchans are prone to catastrophic bowel ruptures, so General Anyar Tsista's final utterance was also what killed him.

• •

"You're absolutely right," said Arthur. "I do state my case well. I ought to state it to Wowbagger immediately."

"Perhaps not so articulately," suggested Fenchurch's image. "May I propose a Zark and perhaps a couple of pormwranglers?"

Wowbagger sat in his favorite vibro-chair on the bridge, trying not to talk about himself. Outside the corona of the ship's force field the destruction of the Earth had pulverized the moon, resulting in an elliptical dust ring that was heading for Venus.

"Look, Trillian Astra. Another planet is about to die. Ask me about that, or something else. I have seen many wonders."

Trillian was not in the mood to be distracted. An in-depth profile of Wowbagger would have Sub-Etha editors drooling into their nonfat local lacto-laxo sim-coffees.

"The people want to know about you. Who is this green alien who travels the universe insulting everyone in alphabetical order?"

"Ah, you see, that's not the way I do it anymore. The whole alphabetical order thing was amusing for a while but then I became a slave to it. People were expecting my insults and began returning the favor."

Random looked up from a page on which she was drawing a series of savage-looking flaybooz.

"Saying stuff like *You're a pathetic loser?*"

"To paraphrase, yes."

"Or: *I didn't know lizards wore suits.*"

"Once or twice. I'm trying to talk to your mother . . ."

"Or: *Is that smell considered pleasant where you come from?*"

Trillian wrapped her daughter in an embrace that looked suspiciously like a headlock.

"I'm not leaving you, darling. Never again. So there's no need for all this hostility."

"I wish you *would* leave," said Random, scowling. "Without you around I turned out pretty well."

Trillian disguised gritted teeth as a loving smile and turned back to her interview. "So, you have abandoned your alphabetical trademark?"

"Yes," said Wowbagger. "I do planets now. It's much simpler and I don't need to listen to every insult-slinger in town trying to take me on. I simply pull into orbit and drop a data bomb into the atmosphere. Everyone gets an e-mail and a sound file. Believe me, if you press that play button, then you are left in no doubt as to how I feel about sentient beings."

"And how do you feel about them?"

"They're mortal. I despise them."

"So underneath all this aloofness is a simple maledicent."

"What? You think I enjoy using foul language?"

"Don't you?"

"Well, yes. Immensely. But it's not just that . . ."

And then Wowbagger told Trillian something that he had never told anyone. Perhaps it was the almost hypnotic tone of her slightly husky voice, perhaps it was time to tell someone.

"I want them to kill me. I want them to try."

Oh God, thought Trillian. *Recorder chip, don't fail me now.*

She glanced down at her wristwatch and was relieved to see the audio readout flickering.

"That's quite a statement."

"I s-suppose it is," said the green space traveler.

* *

Guide Note: This was Wowbagger's first stutter since visiting the Castor system where the swearword *g-g-grunntivartads* increases in potency with each added g.

* *

"I am amazed to hear myself saying that."

"As am I, Mr. Wowbagger."

"I think it's time you called me Bowerick."

"Bowerick?"

"My first name. My father had a sense of humor. Bow Wowbagger?"

"Oh, yes," said Trillian, suddenly caring a little less about her recorder.

The universe cannot suffer tender moments like this to last for very long, and there were contenders for the honor of trampling roughshod over this one. First was Random Dent, who was taking a moment to compose a disgusted disparagement before she stalked from the bridge for the second time. But the winner was her father, Arthur Dent, whose comedic arrival nicely counterbalanced the saccharine nature of the moment, thus restoring order to the Universe.

"Right, you zarkers!" said Arthur, rushing onto the bridge. "We need to turn this turd bucket around and get our pormwrangling tails to the Dark Nebula of Soulianis and Rahm."

"*Bom bom booohm!*" trumpeted the computer, just trying to help.

And then for one final cosmic laugh:

"Was that a bit harsh? Sorry, everyone. What is a pormwrangler, anyway?"

CHAPTER 6

THE PLANET NANO

Far out in the fringes of the Dark Nebula of Soulianis and Rahm, there is a small planetoid that hangs on one of the nebula's curling tendrils like a Christmas tree decoration. This dwarf planet, catalogue number MPB-1001001, ignores the universal law of gravitation to maintain a spinning position 150 million kilometers from the surface of Rahm. At these particular coordinates, the nebula's clouds of interstellar dust, hydrogen, and plasma have been parted by gas streams and magnetic fields to reveal an oasis of clear space devoid of debris and bathed in a nourishing solar wind.

The tiny planet, Nano, succeeds in defying the pull of its star chiefly because of its huge mass, composed mainly of super-dense matter excreted from white holes, but also because of its revolving dynamic core powering over five thousand servo mechanical thrusters. This discrete positioning ensures consistently temperate weather conditions and encourages life to flourish in the planets' fertile vastitas, azure oceans, and abundant number of fjords . . . an abundance which is unusual in a planet that has never known an ice age.

Nano's geography is a cartographer's dream. A single pangaeaic continent spread along the equator, surrounded by azure seas which are brimming with fish literally waiting to be caught.

· ·

Guide Note: In this case the word literally is not simply a misrepresentation of the word figuratively. The Ameglian major steelback fish are reared with stories of paradise at the other end of the line and hang around fjords just waiting to be saved. The inaccuracies of these stories would be obvious to most the moment they were dragged from their natural habitat by a hook and tossed whole onto a sizzling pan, but such is the faith of the steelbacks that they simply flap their way through the Twelve Psalms of Deliverance and wait for their promised golden ball of plankton to appear.

The registered name of this continent is Innisfree, after the lake isle in Sligo, Ireland, on the recently vaporized planet Earth, where the movie *The Quiet Man* was set. The larger of two towns on the continent is called Cong, after the village where *The Quiet Man* was actually shot. These names have been selected by Nano's registration officer, a certain Mr. Hillman Hunter.

Hillman Hunter was not a particularly religious man, but he did have faith in the traditional order of things, when the traditional order was stacked in favor of the entrepreneur. Hillman Hunter believed in money, and it was very difficult to make money in times of anarchy. How was a fellow to put a few bob together when the little men did not respect their betters and there was no Big Man to tell everyone how to behave? Men needed some god or other to show them their place in the world, and ideally that place would be far below Hillman Hunter's.

Guide Note: The notion that religions can be useful tools for keeping the rich rich and the poor abject has been around since shortly after the dawn of time, when a recently evolved bipedal frogget managed to convince all the other froggets in the marsh that their fates were governed by the almighty Lily Pad who would only agree to watch over their pond and keep it safe from gurner pike if an offering of flies and small reptiles was heaped upon it every second Friday. This worked for almost two years, until one of the reptile offerings proved to be slightly less than dead and proceeded to eat the gluttonized bipedal frogget followed by the almighty Lily Pad. The frogget community celebrated their freedom from the yoke of religion with an all-night rave party and hallucinogenic dock leaves. Unfortunately they celebrated a little loudly and were massacred by a gurner pike who for some reason hadn't noticed this little pond before.

● ●

Hillman Hunter had come to believe that this new world should have a god to issue commandments, smite sinners, and declare which forms of conjugality were pleasing in his eyes and which forms were just wrong and gross. Because Nano had been undeniably made by the planet-building Magratheans and not God, it did not have a deity to rule over it, which was causing some debate in the community. The natural order was falling apart and all sorts of people were beginning to consider themselves equal to those who obviously were equal, which is not what religion was about at all. Hillman decided that a presiding god was needed to restore the pecking order, so on this particular Thursday, in a small conference room beside the town's municipal building, he was holding interviews for the position.

THE TOWN OF CONG, INNISFREE, NANO

A huge anthropoid was seated uncomfortably in the interview room's office chair, its grotesque, scaled torso squirming in the confines of the small seat. Tentacles dripped from its chin like fleeing slugs, and hard black eyes glittered from the depths of a pulpy face.

Hillman Hunter shuffled the pages of the creature's résumé.

"So, Mr. Cthulhu, is it?"

"Hmmm," said the creature.

"Good," said Hillman. "A bit of the ineffable, I like that in a deity." He winked conspiratorially. "Still, it wouldn't be much of an in-depth interview if we couldn't get a few facts out of you, eh, Mr. Cthulhu?"

Cthulhu shrugged and dreamed of days of wanton genocide.

"Anyway, let's get the show on the road," continued Hillman brightly. "Or as my Nano used to say, let's get the steamers on the shovel, which was a reference to cleaning cow doings off the driveway after the herd had been driven through. That's how I started, Mr. Cthulhu, selling dried cow biscuits for people to burn on their fires. And look at me now, bejaysus, I'm running a planet."

Hillman laughed suddenly with a noise like a rusty machine being fired.

"Sorry, Mr. Cthulhu. I smoked like a train back in the old country and I haven't had a minute to check in for the new lungs. Being in charge of this crowd of bloody eejits is running me ragged." He danced his fingers down the pages of Cthulhu's résumé. "Let me see. What do we have here? What caliber of a deity am I dealing with? Ah . . . I see here you were in people's minds a lot a few centuries ago thanks to Lovecraft. Not much since then?"

Cthulhu spoke in a voice of meat and metal. "Well, you know. Science and all that. Put a bit of a kibosh on the god business." Clear gel dripped from his tentacles as he spoke. "I kicked around Asia Minor for a while, trying to drum up a little fear. But people have penicillin now, even poor people have reading material. What do they want gods for?"

Hillman nodded along with Cthulhu all the way. "You are so right, sir. So right. People think they are too good for gods. Too smart. But not here on Nano. We are the last outpost of Earth, and we will not be destroyed because we have driven away our protector." By the time he had finished his little speech, Hillman's chubby cheeks glowed a proud red. "Next question. Our last god was a *less is more* kinda guy. Sent his son down, but didn't show up too often himself. I think, and no disrespect to the man himself, that was probably a mistake. I honestly believe that he would put his hand up to that himself now if we could ask him. What I'm asking you, Mr. Cthulhu, is: Are you going to be a hands-on god or an absentee landlord?"

Cthulhu was ready for that one; he had been practicing his answer for that very question with Hastur the Unspeakable only the previous night.

"Oh, hands-on, absolutely," he said, leaning forward to make clear eye contact as Hastur had advised. "The days of blind faith are over. People need to know who is blighting their crops or demanding virgin sacrifice. And now I am going to look away, but only because prolonged eye contact will drive you insane."

Hillman shook the sudden torpor from his head. "Good. Good. Quite a stare you have there, Mr. Cthulhu. Handy weapon to have in the arsenal."

Cthulhu accepted the compliment with a flap of one prodigious tentacle.

"Let's move on, shall we? Where do you stand on the whole Babel fish argument? Proof denies faith and so forth."

"My subjects will have proof and faith," rasped Cthulhu agitatedly. "I will bind them to slavery and trample the weak underfoot."

"I seem to have hit a nerve there," chuckled Hillman. "Again, I think you're on the right track; maybe you might want to pull back a little on the slavery and the trampling. We have quite a lot of weak people here, but they are big supporters of the church, whatever church we eventually pledge to. Money builds temples or as my Nano used to say: *Many mickles make a muckle.*"

"Mickles?" said Cthulhu, confused, and it is not easy to confuse a Great Old One.

Hillman scratched his chin. "I never knew what a muckle was, or a mickle for that matter. But it takes many of one to make the other, if you see what I mean."

"Hmm," said Cthulhu.

"So. An old standard next. Presuming your application is successful, where do you see yourself in five years' time?"

Cthulhu brightened. *Thank you, Hastur,* he beamed into space.

"In five years I will have razed this planet, eaten its young, and stacked your skulls high in my honor." He sat back satisfied. Succinct and informative, a textbook answer.

A spluttering cough blurted from Hillman's lips. "Skull stacking! Come on, Mr. Cthulhu. Really? Do you think that's what gods do today? These are interstellar times we've got here. Space travel, time travel. What we need on Nano is what I like to call an Old Testament god. Strict, sure. Vengeful, fantastic. But indiscriminate eating of young? Those days are gone."

"Shows what you know," muttered Cthulhu, crossing his legs.

Hillman tapped the résumé. "I have something highlighted here. Under current status it reads, 'dead but dreaming.' Could you elaborate on that? Are you dead, sir?"

"It could be said that I'm dead," admitted the oozing anthropoid.

"You don't seem dead."

"Ah, yes, but this tiny form is not me." Cthulhu poked his body as if he were not familiar with its workings. "This is my dream of me made substantial by dark and terrible forces. I wear this form until my true self is called back to service. My true self is quite a bit bigger."

"Sorry to harp on this, but you are dead?"

"For the moment. Yes. I would have to say yes."

"But gods cannot die. That's the whole point."

Cthulhu wished Hastur could be with him. Hastur was always quick with the comebacks.

"Well . . . that's true. But I suppose, technically—and I stress that *technically*—I am not actually a god. I am a Great Old One. A demigod, you might say."

Hillman closed the file. "Oh," he said. "I see."

"It's more or less the same thing," persisted Cthulhu. "I do all the same things. Apparitions. Impregnating. You name it. I have cards for the lounges in Asgard and Olympus. Gold cards."

"These things are all well and good, but . . ."

"Don't bother," said Cthulhu disgustedly, gel splattering the desk. "You people are all the same. Never give the little guy a chance."

"It's not that, sir. I have nothing against your kind, but the advertisement did specifically say 'Grade A God.' I'm sure you can do lots of things, but we're looking for someone with a bit of substance. Someone who's in it for the long haul. Certainly not someone who can die."

Cthulhu rose from his chair in a furious rage. "I will crack open your skull," he thundered. "I will visit pestilence on your land." But he was not needed and was already fading. "I will tear your head from your torso and drink your . . ."

And then he was gone, leaving nothing behind but the smell of a harbor at low tide.

Drink my what? wondered Hillman Hunter, scribbling the words *NO CALLBACK* in highlighter on the cover of Cthulhu's résumé.

Blood probably. Unless it was my cerebrospinal fluid.

He leaned back in his chair and turned on the back massager. Hillman was a positive kind of guy, always willing to look on the bright side, but this hunt for a god was getting depressing. Not one of the interviewees had met his standards. Excello, the robot god. Vladirski, the vampire lord. Hecate had a few useful skills, but a she was female. Goddess of Nano? Not bloody likely.

And as if the god-hunt wasn't trouble enough, he had to deal with all the strife from the other colony. Killing people over cheese, did you ever hear anything more ludicrous? A bit of cheddar was lovely on some crusty bread, but hardly worth dying for. And there was the problem of the staff, who were deserting the town in droves. Some days Hillman Hunter felt like just staying in bed.

"All you need is a nice cup of tea and a few biscuits!" Hillman said in a squeaky impersonation of his grandmother, a voice he often used to motivate himself. "Then you'll be grand."

Even the thought of tea made him feel better. What was an Irishman without tea?

"Get up off your backside, Hillers," he said in Nano's tones. "Those people need you."

It was true. The colonists did need him, especially after the kidnapping of Jean Claude. What Nano needed was a real live god to thunderbolt a bit of discipline into its residents. But how did you attract a grade A god to the unfashionable fringe of the western spiral arm of the Dark Nebula of Soulianis and Rahm? It would take one hell of a benefits package, that was for certain.

Hillman took a note of Cthulhu's Sub-Etha address, just in case.

. . . .

Guide Note: The gods came into existence a few millionths of a second after the Big Bang, which basically means that they did not create the Universe; rather, the Universe created them. This is a sore subject in the halls of the holy and is totally off-limits around the dinner table. If a journalist has the temerity to broach the topic, he could find himself punished in a strange and imaginative way. Most of the gods have been alive for so long that they have assembled entire libraries devoted to the topic of strange and unusual punishments. As recently as ten thousand years ago there were seminars on Olympus devoted to the subject. These seminars were discontinued as an increasing number of the minor deities were treating the gathering as an excuse to drink and fornicate, which resulted in a glut of new hybrid godlings who had no mythology to go home to. While the seminar ran, it handed

out a yearly award in the shape of a spiked puffer fish in honor of Loki's famous stroke of turning a sex addict into a puffer fish who would poison
anything he tried to embrace. Among the more memorable Puffies awarded
was the one given to Heimdall who, in a fit of pique, turned a gang of builders who were overcharging him into the wall that they had refused to complete. Another one went to Dionysus for his punishment of Sir Smoog
Nowtall, the Blagulon Kappan actor who performed the one-man show *Playing to the Gods,* which was slightly critical of its subject matter. Dionysus,
whose area was theater, was a liberal fellow and would have let the play
run, had it not been for a scene where he himself was depicted as a flatu-
lent, bingeing fool. So enraged was Dionysus by the scene and the positive
notes it garnered that he condemned Nowtall to an eternity of being the
rear end in a pantomime donkey suit where the bum cheeks before him
were the heads of his two fiercest critics, forever reciting their most scath-
ing reviews. Classic.

Gods had a great time of it for millions of years; swanning across the sky in
their chariots, showing up in different places at the same time, being all-wise
and stuff, but then science developed to the point where it could duplicate
many of their tricks. Blighting a crop was no longer as big a deal as it used to
be. There were virgin births all the time; in fact many societies preferred virgin
births, as they cut out the need for in-laws, and parents didn't have to imagine
their children doing anything nasty with strangers. The last straw for godkind
came when Fenrir, the giant son of Loki, tried to impress his dwindling flock by
driving his space cycle into a white hole. The only part of Fenrir intact after the
jump was one of his molars, which is now a glowing asteroid orbiting Sagar 7,
and can do nothing but influence the tides and communicate vague messages
to clairvoyants. The gods were horrified (all except Odin, as it was foretold that
Fenrir would devour him at the time of Ragnarok, so he had a little giggle into
his fist), and they retreated to their home worlds, vowing nevermore to consort
with mortals. (The actual sentence was: *Mortals, screw 'em.* Which does not
read as godly as a sentence containing the words *vowing, nevermore,* and *consort.*) So serious were the Aesir about this vow that they surrounded their world,
Asgard, with a shell of ice, leaving only one point of access, Bifrost the rainbow
bridge, which was guarded by the all-seeing god Heimdall.

Visitors were not encouraged.

In fact visitors were actively discouraged from attempting to dock by ravenous flesh-eating dragons, soul-sucking siren succubae, and Flyting, a scurrilous Norse technique of insulting a person which focused on genitalia and parentage.

The gods wanted nothing to do with mortals. Especially investigative journalists, more especially holy people looking for some kind of heavenly reward. But the most unwelcome person in Asgard was Galactic President Zaphod Beeblebrox, and each of the dragons had been given one of his old shirts to sniff.

● ●

THE HEART OF GOLD

The *Heart of Gold* flew through the multicolored and varitextured space of everywhere. With the Infinite Improbability Drive engaged, the ship became part of the Universe itself until the coordinates slotted into their tumblers and popped the craft out at the correct destination with the interstellar travel equivalent of a *ta-dah*, scaring the hell out of the person parked in the next bay. But until that moment anything could happen, especially anything that was highly improbable, which of course then made it probable, which rendered it improbable again, repeating ad infinitum.

Most people preferred to shut their eyes during improbability flights, to shield their psyches from the impossibilities occurring around them, but Zaphod taped his eyes open so that he wouldn't miss a thing.

During the trip to Asgard, Diona Carlinton-Housney, one of Zaphod's favorite singer/prostitutes, broke through from the afterlife to sing possibly prophetic lyrics in hysterical falsetto.

"Oh, Zaphod, baaaby, the fist is gonna fall."

Hey, thought Zaphod. *My name in a song. Froody.*

"Zaphod, my baaaby," sang Diona. "You gotta climb that wall."

Zaphod tried to clap along, but his hands were miles away, arms stretching into space.

"You look good, Diona. Great, in fact. No decomposition or anything. I always hoped the afterlife would be like that."

Diona placed three hands on her hips, using a fourth to hold the microphone stalk.

"You're not listening to me, Mr. President."

"I don't want to listen. I want to ask stuff. Do you get many sub-etha channels where you are? I love *CelebStalk*. Do you get that?"

Diona waved away this talk of entertainment, continuing with her song. "Zaphod, baby. You gotta walk across that bridge."

"How about alcohol?"

"You tell him what his secret name is, Zaph, baby, and he's gonna let you in."

"Yeah, okay. Bridges, whatever. But seriously, have you had something done, because I think you look better now."

Diona's eyes flashed. "Your grandfather told me not to come. That boy is an idiot, he said. He won't listen, he never does."

"It was cryptic," protested Zaphod. "Cryptic is hard."

"Cryptic! It was a goddamn nursery rhyme. Any fool could figure it out."

Zaphod frowned. "Something about a wall and a bridge."

"And the secret name. Come on, Mr. President. This is important."

"Wasn't there a fist in there somewhere? I like things with fists, especially when the thumb is sticking up. I saw a cartoon once where the stupid guy sticks his thumb into his own eye and . . ."

"Oh, for Zark's sake," Diona said, and turned into an ice sculpture of herself, which then proceeded to melt, dripping upward into the ceiling. As each drop touched the panels, it exploded with a tinkling *oh*.

"That girl always could sing," Zaphod murmured, then settled back and waited for probability to assert itself.

He could see two incredible new colors that his brain could only describe as *dangerous* and *shifty,* and jagged indents were being hammered into the spaceship walls as though the *Heart of Gold* was being rammed by a colossal spiked creature.

"Whoa," yelped Zaphod as a spike shot up between his legs. "How soon for normality, Left Brain?"

Left Brain popped up from an electrolytic gel flask on the main console.

"Who knows in an environment like this," he said, gel dropping in blobs from his frictionless orb. "In actual time, five seconds, but not necessarily in the order or regularity that we are accustomed to."

Normality returned with a whinny of tiny ponies and a procession of animated, chanting skeletons across the bridge.

"I can see right through you," they chanted. "Can you see right through me?"

Then ponies and skeletons were gone and the bridge was as normal as it was ever likely to get, considering the ship's navigator was the captain's disembodied head.

Zaphod pulled on the tape strips on his eyelids. "Are we normal, LB?"

Left Brain zoomed around the main cabin, touching base with the various infrared sensors set into the instruments.

"Affirmative, Zaphod. The Improbability Drive has spiraled down and we are in real space."

"Excellent," said Zaphod, unstrapping himself from his flight seat. "I have trouble telling the difference sometimes, between what and what-not."

He leaped to his feet, gangling across to the wraparound view screen, his silver boot heels tinging on the ceramic floor.

"Okay. So what do we got here? A planet covered with ice. That's exactly what I did not expect to see. Or rather I expected to see it from the inside. Why are we outside the barrier, LB? Oh why, oh why?"

Left Brain screwed one eye shut, the face he made when analyzing streamed data.

"The Aesir have installed a new shield since our last visit."

Zaphod pounded the air like a frustrated philosopher trying to force an existentialist concept into a pragmatist mind.

"Those crafty immortals with their little beards and horny helmets. I thought shields didn't work on improbability drives."

Left Brain hung momentarily wordless, running millions of calculations a second, refining his syntax, paring away any superfluous language until he arrived at:

"You thought? Don't make me laugh."

Zaphod executed a misconceived Du-Bart'ah spinning kick, which missed the hovering orb by several feet and made his groin tendon sing like a violin.

. . . .

Guide Note: President Beeblebrox's kick was misconceived because the ancient art of Du-Bart'ah had been developed by the Shaltanacs of Broop Kidron Thirteen, who were a happy and peaceful race. The spinning kick was employed to knock Joopleberries from their shrubs with minimal disturbance to the plant itself. Any attempt to use Du-Bart'ah for aggressive reasons would activate the subliminal conditioning in the training chants and turn the attacker's body on itself. Zaphod did not know this, as he'd learned the technique from a hologram on the back of a ZugaClusters box.

• •

"Really, Zaphod," said Left Brain, hovering to a safe altitude. "We have a task to complete, there is not time for your usual petty antics."

"There is always time for antics," moaned Zaphod from his fetal position around a chair stem. "Antics get me out of bed in the morning."

Left Brain knew this to be true, but he had never understood why. "Is that why we are here, Zaphod? So that you have something to do?"

Zaphod twanged his tendon gently. "I am Zaphod Beeblebrox, LB, and with the life I've had, it's only a matter of time before I run into a humongous anticlimax. I aim to put that off as long as possible."

Left Brain screwed one eye shut. "I don't think that's going to be a problem. Not with the amount of firepower pointed at us."

"Excellent," proclaimed Zaphod, strained tendon forgotten. "It seems like ages since we've been up against impossible odds with no reasonable chance of survival."

"Not long enough," Left Brain said and transferred the incoming call onto the main screen.

"No," said Heimdall, God of Light, emphatically.

"But I haven't . . ."

"No!" repeated Heimdall, his huge bald head filling the screen, his eyes boiling red like gas giants.

Zaphod tried again. "You don't even know what . . ."

"No. No. No. I don't care what it is, Beeblebrox. No is the answer. Now *improbable* yourself off somewhere else before I set the dragons on you."

"Just hear me out," pleaded Zaphod.

"Nope."

"Five seconds, what could it hurt?"

"No. Any question you could ask me, the answer would be no."

Zaphod spat it out quickly. "Is Thor home?"

"No, he bloody isn't!" roared Heimdall, the tips of his waxed mustache quivering.

"Really?"

The Asgardian god bared his teeth. "Actually, yes. Yes, he is home. You're in bloody Asgard, aren't you?"

"He is! Could I . . ."

"No. It's back to negatives again, my friend. And when I say *my friend*, I actually mean *my hated enemy whom I would like to see disemboweled and then sprinkled with salt*."

"Come on, Heimdall. Forget all those misunderstandings and negotiate a little. This is important."

Heimdall's cheeks were so red that it seemed quite possible that his head would explode.

"Misunderstandings? Misunder . . . Zark me. You have a lot of nerve, Crap-prod. You have enough sheer bloody gall for an entire bucket of gallstones."

. . . .

Guide Note: Gall stones: light gray pebbles found on Damogran. Very cheeky.

. . . .

"What say we put the past behind us, where it belongs, and just start again? We can do that, can't we? We're both rational adults."

"*We're* both rational adults, but you should see Thor now. He's just a bag of nerves with a helmet on top after what you did to him."

"That's why I want to talk to the boy. To explain."

Heimdall took a moment for some breathing exercises, blowing into the gloved fingers of one hand which he wiggled before his face.

"Explain?" he said finally. "You want to explain?"

"Yes, that's all I want from you wonderful gods," said Zaphod in tones that would have had the Sucky Crawlers of Sycophantasia reaching for their sick bags. "A chance to explain, and possibly make amends for, my previous mistakes."

"Amends, eh?" Heimdall said. "I suppose you do need to make amends."

"Yes. Yes, of course I do. I repent and I deserve penance."

"I know what you're doing there," said Heimdall, scowling. "Pushing my *god* buttons. Who do you think you're fooling?"

"I'm serious. Look at this face."

Heimdall leaned in until his eyes filled the screen. These were eyes that could slice through the fat of a normal person's lies and find the bone of truth within.

"Very well, Zaphod Beeblebastard. Come outside and let's talk about amends."

"Come outside? Into space? Won't that be cold?"

"Fear not, mortal. I will extend a bubble of atmosphere to you."

"Just step outside then?"

"Out you come, Zaphod. Alone. You have one minute to decide."

Left Brain hovered at Zaphod's shoulder.

"I think you should probably go," he said. "Don't worry about me. I'll be fine here inside the ship. I'm sure the atmosphere bubble will hold its integrity."

"Can you check it?"

Left Brain squinted for a moment, then spasmed as lightning flashed inside his dome.

"The Asgardian computer doesn't share information, apparently." Little spider-bots clicked along the glass, nipping at the scorch marks. "There isn't a line out from the entire planet. If you go out there, you are on your own."

Zaphod sighed and straightened his coat. "People like me, LB, the truly great ones. We are always alone."

LB nodded. "That was good, but I wasn't ready with the lighting. Give me a second, then try it again."

"Okay. Something warm. And not directly overhead. Makes my hair look thin."

Left Brain interfaced with the ship's illuminations, putting a yellow spotlight on Zaphod's face.

"Ready?"

"What would you say my motivation was?"

"Greatness. Pure undiluted greatness."

Zaphod nodded gravely, accepting the truth of this. He steepled his fingers and spoke slowly.

"People like me . . ." he began, then Left Brain opened a tube and shot him into space.

. . . .

Guide Note: As divine dynasties go, the Aesir, the gods of Asgard, are not exactly the biggest pseudopods on the amoeboid. Adored on less than a thousand worlds, they can fairly be classed as middle-tier gods. Zeus, the father of the rival Olympians, has often publicly claimed that he has "pulled fluff balls from his navel that were bigger than Asgard," but this is more than likely simply an attempt to exacerbate Odin's legendary planet envy. Odin and Zeus have had a "bit of a thing" going for several thousand years, ever since Zeus accidentally turned Odin into a wild boar during one of his "take human form and plant some wild oats" visits to the planet Earth. But even though the gods of Asgard have not achieved the same level of penetration as the Olympians or even some of the novelty gods, such as Pasta Fasta, who began his career as a restaurant chain icon, they are significant for what they have contributed to popular culture, most notably the horn, which they use to decorate their ceremonial helmet, create music, and, most importantly, fill with beer. Scientists have postulated that without the phrase *Do you fancy a horn of beer?* in their lexicon, several worlds would never have emerged from their cataclysmic planetary war phase.

. . . .

Heimdall, God of Light, left Zaphod thrashing in the inky void for twenty-nine seconds before lobbing out an atmosphere yo-yo to reel him to safety. In those twenty-nine seconds Zaphod Beeblebrox was forced to think on the inside of his head rather than transmitting his thoughts directly to the universe as he preferred. His tangent-ridden reflection resulted in the oft-quoted "Beeblebrox's Inner Monologue," of which there are two published versions: The official one, which Zaphod produced after a weekend on the writer Oolon Colluphid's estate, and the unofficial version, which was picked up telepathically by Left Brain and included in his memoirs, *Life in a Fishbowl.* Both accounts will be presented and you can make up your own mind which is more accurate:

The official version:

And so, the moment has arrived. I grieve bitterly, not for myself, but for those who have been denied the ecstasy of knowing Zaphod Beeblebrox. People will recognize the name, I suppose. Beeblebrox has done a few small things in his short existence. How will I be remembered? As a supernova perhaps, a celestial body that blazes in the night sky, a light in the darkness, granting those that felt its heat on their faces a moment of wonder and perhaps hope. This would be enough. There are those who heap praise upon my shoulders, lauding me as a prophet, a revolution-ary, or a great satisfier of women. I accept the praise with gra-cious modesty, but if I could choose my own epitaph, I would simply say that Zaphod Beeblebrox surprised everyone. In a good way.

And the unofficial version:

Oh, Zark. Big . . . Big . . . BIIIIIIIG. Space everywhere, but no air! My hair will collapse. And I always bloat in zero g. Heimdall, you total bastard. Look a ball of ice. Smoothie, shiny, wish I could lick it. What underpants am I wearing? For the autopsy, you need to think about these things. New ones with drainage, I hope. Ford, dude. You were froody, we were froody together. But I was slightly more froody. I bet this gets big coverage. It's not every day a Galactic President gets dumped out of an air lock by his own head.

There was a third version, which flickered just below the surface of Zaphod's consciousness. Left Brain didn't hear it and Zaphod didn't re-member it.

So, Zaphod's buried personality monologued internally. *As I did not hold my breath, there will be no lung damage, but that does mean that I have more than half a minute before oxygen-deprived blood reaches my brain. I could have done so much more with my time . . .*

The Light God watched Zaphod spasm, with no little satisfaction in his all-seeing eyes. He stood on the lip of Bifrost, the portal between Asgard and the rest of the Universe, counting down the seconds until he would have to choose between rescuing Thor's old manager or letting him die.

It hardly seemed like a choice at all, since Heimdall hated mortals in general (except the noble Sigurd of legend) and Beeblebrox in particular, but letting men die in the vicinity of Asgard was definitely frowned on by Odin, as martyrs had a tendency to live forever. Which was ironic, as they were dead. Or maybe it was paradoxical, not ironic. One of those tricky terms that Loki bandied around to fluster him. Heimdall was a soldier and didn't crowd his brain with extraneous vocabulary. *Hunt, kill, burn, flay.* Those were the kind of words he liked. Especially *flay,* but it was difficult to work into everyday conversation.

Heimdall pouted for a moment, then sent a gloopy plasma string undulating from the tip of the Gjallarhorn, the legendary harbinger of Ragnarok. The Gjallarhorn might seem to the casual observer like your typical twenty-foot, old Norse yelling horn, but in the hands of a god it became a tool of great power, and a handy vessel for beer drinking games.

At the tip of the plasma string there was a bubble of atmosphere which Heimdall fly-fished in space until he managed to snare Zaphod. The plasma shell would give the Betelgeusean quite a shock when he jittered through to the breathable air inside, but Heimdall was not in the least worried about that. The god's only concern about Zaphod Beeblebrox's pain was to ensure that there was plenty of it in his immediate future—his immediate past too, if he could get a time pass from Odin.

He reeled Zaphod in and landed him on the Rainbow Bridge.

. . . .

Guide Note: The term Rainbow Bridge is an example of how gods in general are given to rhetoric and aggrandizement. Osiris did not just have a flu which knocked him sideways for a few weeks, he died and rose again. Aphrodite did not just have a wardrobe full of low-cut blouses and an inexhaustible supply of dirty limericks, she was irresistible to all males everywhere. And the Rainbow Bridge was not just a spectacularly engineered suspension bridge of ice and steel, it was, according to the Aesir, an actual bridge of rainbows.

Zaphod jittered for a minute while the plasma evaporated, then moaned as he realized that his silver boot heels had melted passing through the charged shell.

"Oh, come on," he moaned. "Do you realize how many silver-tongued devils' tongues went into those heels? This is the worst day of my life."

Heimdall loomed over him, his grin several yards wide.

"I am delighted to hear it."

"That *rainbow* bridge is made of ice and steel," said Zaphod in petulant revenge for the boot heels.

"Silence!" roared Heimdall. "Or you shall be flayed!"

"I'm already afraid."

"No, not afraid."

"Not afraid. Afraid. Make up your mind."

"I said *flayed*. Flayed! The skin peeled from your body!"

Zaphod gulped comically. "Now I am afraid. Is that allowed?"

Heimdall pinched his nose and quietly recited the first verse of the Völsunga saga, which generally calmed him down, but this time even Sigurd's exploits could not soothe his pounding heart.

While Heimdall was reciting, Zaphod processed the loss of his heels and decided he had bigger porms to wrangle. He jumped to his feet, immediately fell over, tried to cover the embarrassing fall with a backward tumble, stood upright once more, tottered around for a second until he found a gait that worked with no-heeled high heels, then treated himself to a three-sixty spin.

"Wow," he concluded. "I have to say, Heimdall. This is one hoopy world you guys have here. I mean wow. Is that a waterfall? How big is that?"

Heimdall tried one last verse before replying. "It's the fountain of youth, if you must know. Frigga fancied a water feature."

"That's great. Landscape gardening, it's the future."

"No, it isn't," said Heimdall gloomily. "Ragnarok is the future. The gods will perish and the universe will drown in blood."

Zaphod nodded. "Now that would be a fountain worth seeing. But for now, let's stay positive, eh, big fella? We're not drowning in blood yet."

Heimdall was indeed a big fellow, especially seen from directly below. Gazing up at a god's crotch can do wonders for a person's lack of low self-esteem. Especially when the crotch contours are tightly bound by the leggings of a red-striped neon blue ski jumpsuit. Heimdall spent his days and nights on the ice and so apparently had decided to dress the part. He had eschewed the traditional mammaloid leggings in favor of snowboarding boots, and there was a pair of orange tinted ski goggles perched on his forehead and a stripe of sunblock on his nose.

"So. Hate to hurry things along, but you know, my old buddy, Thor. Any chance you could see your way clear to letting me in to see him . . . ?"

Heimdall's vision of the apocalypse faded and he peered down at Zaphod.

"Amends, you said. You wanted to make amends."

Zaphod pasted on his most disarming smile. "Well I would say that, wouldn't I? In my defense, I didn't mean a word of it. I was under duress."

"You know the drill, Zaphod."

"Not tasks! Come on, Heimdall. That's so oldy-worldy. I thought you guys were getting with the times."

"Asgard does not change."

"What about that water feature? That wasn't there on my last visit."

"Significantly. Asgard does not change *significantly*. Three tasks, Beeblebrox, if you really want to talk."

"Three! I don't have time for three. Your tasks take forever. I'll do one."

"Three," insisted Heimdall, eyes bulging in their sockets.

"One!" repeated Zaphod.

"I'm just going to kill you, screw it."

Zaphod rocked back on his biological heels, then rocked forward a step. "You're bluffing, big boy. I know the rules here. No one gets struck off the coil on Asgard without the Big O's say-so."

"Don't push me, because I'll call him."

"Yeah? What's stopping you? Maybe Odin doesn't give out his number to gatekeepers."

Heimdall shook his massive head. "Don't do it, Beeblebollocks. Don't make me call the guy. He's no fan of yours."

"Call him, go ahead. You won't though, because he's number one and you're . . . you don't even have a number. Odin could be enjoying a nice horn of honey meade and your call might make him drop it, then holy Zark it's Ragnarok."

Heimdall pointed a finger the size of a torpedo. "Right. That's it. I am calling."

"Are you? Looks like you're talking to me. Lot of flapping lips, not much number punching."

"Be this on your own head, Zaphod," muttered the god. "All I wanted was three tasks. Four, tops." He waggled his horn in a certain way and it collapsed into itself until it fit neatly into the god's palm. "This is it. No turning back."

"Of course there is, if you're full of buffa-biscuit."

"Buffa!" croaked Heimdall in the choked tones of a Folfangan phlegm ferret having its throat tickled for the precious pharmacopeia in its mucus. "Buffa, you say!" He punched in a number on the horn's keypad and hummed his way through a few seconds of ringing.

"Yep, hello. Odie, it's me," he said into the horn.

Heimdall closed one eye and endured a few seconds of abuse from the father of the gods.

"Okay. Sorry, I do realize that you have a lot of golden plankton balls to churn out, and I know mead stains. Freeze your shirt, then the mark comes right out. Listen, I've got someone here, a mortal. I just want the go-ahead to kill him."

More abuse. Zaphod could easily catch the tone from ten feet below phone level.

"I know we don't . . . I am aware of policy . . . Of course I read the document . . . The bullet points anyway . . ."

Zaphod drifted away from the conversation, already impatient with a situation that did not feature him. As a child, Zaphod had been diagnosed with ADHDDAAADHD (ntm) ABT which stood for Always

Dreaming His Dopey Days Away, Also Attention Deficit Hyperflatulence Disorder (not to mention) A Bit Thick. Even as an adult Zaphod could not manage the condition, because he could never remember what he suffered from.

A couple of D's, he had told his pill guy on Eroticon VI, *maybe an H,* and was prescribed ointment for DDH which was Double Dose Hemorrhoids. Zaphod stopped using the ointment after a couple of days because he couldn't keep it down.

So even though Heimdall and Odin were discussing his immediate future and the amount of discomfort contained therein, Zaphod found himself distracted by the twinkly lights of Asgard. It was an amazing sight, even for one accustomed to the shiny shiny of wide wonderful space.

Size-wise, Asgard was no Megabrantis Delta, but what was there made a big impression. For a start, there was the whole *encased in ice* thing, which cast a flickering silver blue light show over the entire surface. The surface itself was littered with the kind of dramatic topographic features that would drive a Magrathean to industrial espionage. Mighty, gushing rivers; high, snow-peaked mountains; and fjords as intricate as a twitterflitter's electrocardiogram readout. Glistening ice fields coexisted impossibly alongside tracts of golden corn, all bathed by sunrays which could not be traced back to any star. Towering castles breached the clouds, dragons coiled around their turrets. It was a dreamworld, if the dreamers were testosterone-fueled males who were never forced to behave like adults.

Heimdall was saying something.

"Hmm?" said Zaphod.

"I got the green light," said the god, smiling happily.

"What green light? What do you want a green light for?"

"It's a saying. The green light means go."

"Go where?"

"Nowhere. I'm not going anywhere."

"Then why do you need a green light?"

Heimdall pinched his nose. "Forth Sigurd fides till he comes to the dwelling of a mighty chief called Heimir; he had to wife a sister of Brynhild, who was known as Bekkhild, as she had bided at home, and learned woman's work, whereas Brynhild followed unto the wars, so was she called Brynhild."

"I see," said Zaphod, wondering if he might use the craziness as cover to nip across the bridge.

As if reading his mind, which he probably could, Heimdall blocked his path with a massive fur-trimmed boot.

"I told Odin it was you."

Zaphod was suddenly a little more nervous than he had been. "And what did he say?"

"He said that you were a well-known public figure, so to make your death confusing"

"Confusing?"

Heimdall bent double, shaking the Gjallarhorn to its original length.

"You're shaking your horn to its original length," noted Zaphod.

"I'm going to summon the dragons."

"So that they can kill me in a confusing way," Zaphod surmised.

Heimdall's grin seemed wide as a crescent moon. "That's right, Beetlepox. I'm going to instruct them to kill you by accident but make it look like murder."

"Oh," said Zaphod. "What about the tasks? There must be a golden axe somewhere you guys need me to find."

"You wanted one task," said Heimdall. "That's exactly what you're getting."

Zaphod blew into his hands. "Good. Great. Can we get on with it then? I am freezing. My spare neck hole really feels the cold, which incidentally is the title of my next album."

"It's a simple task," said Heimdall innocently. "All you need to do is cross the bridge."

Cross the bridge, Zaphod thought. *That sounds familiar. Then again, bridge is a common enough word. And often used in a metaphorical sense.*

"Which bridge?"

"This bridge!" roared Heimdall, his beard quivering. "This bloody bridge that you're standing on."

"Okay. Just trying to get the details straight. Cross this bridge I'm standing on. Anything else?"

"There's a tube of false atmosphere so you won't drift off. If you make the first wall, you need to climb it."

I gotta climb that wall. Familiar. But the word wall *is even more common than* bridge.

"So, cross and climb. Got it. And no hidden tricks?"

"Apart from the dragons trying to tumble you into the abyss? No."

Zaphod frowned. "So the dragons are not friendly dragons, singing songs and stuff, like in the kiddie stories."

"They do sing death dirges."

"Really? What rhymes with flay?"

A rare flash of perceptive wit from Zaphod at the worst possible moment.

"Oh, very good. You just cut ten seconds off your head start."

Heimdall adopted a heroic stance, which is not easy when one is clad in a garish ski suit, but in fairness the god carried it off. He raised his horn and blew a long, undulating series of notes that sounded suspiciously like the old Betelgeusean nursery rhyme "Arkle Schmarkle Sat on a Schmed," but with a semitone more implied violence.

Zaphod felt a sudden chill in the scar tissue where his second neck used to be. He turned on the spot where one of his silver heels had until recently twinkled, and then he ran like blazes through the tube of false atmosphere across the so-called Rainbow Bridge.

VOGON BUREAUCRUISER CLASS HYPERSPACE SHIP
BUSINESS END

Constant Mown sat in the hyperspace cradle in his home office, shivering, as the *Business End* lurched out of hyperspace in much the same way as a drunken Betelgeusean reporter might lurch out of a convenient bush with an empty bladder. The reporter being the one with the empty bladder not the bush, unless the bush happened to be a howhi shrub, which expels its seed in a slightly acidic solution when its foliage detects moisture. In essence, you pee on it and it pees on you.

Eight more jumps to go, thought Mown. *And then we get to wipe out another species.*

And in truth, the idea did not give him as much satisfaction as it should. Surely there was no greater pleasure for a Vogon than to close the file on an enforcement order, but Constant Mown was perhaps not as much of an utter bastard as his father liked to think. In fact in recent months when Mown searched inside himself for that tough Vogon core necessary to carry out some of his more distasteful duties, instead of steel and kroompst he found sensitivity and even empathy. It was horrible, awful. How was a constant ever to become a prostetnic with wishy-washy emotions like those swilling around in his thinking gourd?

I don't want to be a prostetnic. I don't even want to be an enforcement bureaucrat.

Oh sure, Mown gave good Vogon on the bridge. Threw his little spaghetti arms around saluting daddy, waxed euphoric about the Unnecessarily Painful Slow Death torpedoes, but his blood pump wasn't in it.

I don't want to kill anyone, even with the right paperwork.

Mown had to take a few deep breaths before composing the next thought.

There are things more important than paperwork.

He said it aloud.

"There are things more important than paperwork!"

Suddenly there was bile in Mown's throat, but the little Vogon was so worked up that he couldn't enjoy it. Mown tumbled from the hyperspace cradle and scrabbled along his bedside draining board until he found a drool cup to spit into.

That was better.

Had he really said that aloud? What was happening to him?

Mown lowered himself gently onto his cot, an act that would have surprised the hell out of his shipmates. Vogons did not generally have the wherewithal to lower themselves gently onto anything. Plonking awkwardly and collapsing ignominiously were the main options open to the Vogon race. Getting up again was even worse than sitting down. Rising from anything lower than a bar stool generally involved a bruised coccyx, a complicated system of weights and pulleys, and several pints of splutter. But Mown possessed something heretofore unheard of among the Vogon. Mown possessed a modicum of grace.

Mown wiggled a couple of fingers beneath the mattress lining and pulled out a small pink piece of plastic contraband. He slipped the item underneath a soft thigh and quorbled nervously for a few moments, building up the kroompst to bring it out into the open.

"This is the last time," he promised himself. "One look, then I'll get rid of it. Never again. The absolute last time."

Look at me, said the pink thing, warm through the fabric of his trews. *Look at me and see yourself.*

Mown's fingers tip-tapped on the frame and then with a sudden surge of courage he grabbed the plastic handle and yanked it out.

The item was a plastic Barbie mirror, purchased in a cheapo knick-knack market on Port Brasta. Authentic Earth memorabilia. Mirrors were forbidden on board ship, because Vogons got depressed enough without looking at their own mugs in polished glass.

· ·

Guide Note: Vogons survived until they died through determined extrospection. Apart from disdainful dabblings in the poetic arts, most Vogons try to focus their attentions very much on other species in order to avoid dwelling on their own various physical and psychological shortcomings. Vogons rarely spend time in flotation tanks, they never meditate in steam lodges, and they most certainly do not gaze at their misshapen warty faces in mirrors. The only race to ever have successfully perverted a Vogon planetary demolition order were the Tubavix of Sinnustra, who sent a reformatting screen virus to the Vogon fleet which turned all their monitors into mirrors. Five minutes after the virus had uploaded, the Vogon turned their torpedoes on each other.

· ·

Mown looked at himself in the mirror and felt no revulsion whatsoever. In fact he liked what he saw.

Oh my god, he thought. *What's happening to me?*

Something had happened to Mown. A few months previously, his block of breakfast gruel had been cross-contaminated with the tip of a toadstool mandarin tentacle, which released just enough entheogens into Mown's system to prompt him to acknowledge something he had already suspected.

I do not hate myself.

This was a revolutionary, if not heretical, thought for a Vogon to construct, and would surely have had Mown expelled from the Bureaucratic Corps had he admitted to it on his psych test. If the bureaucratic corps had a psych test.

Constant Mown had been doing more than just having the thought lately.

"I do not hate myself," he whispered to the mirror. "In many ways I am not altogether too bad."

And if Mown did not hate himself, what did he have to project onto the universe? If not love, then certainly an affable diluted version.

I like myself so maybe, perhaps, others could like me too.

"Not if I kill them first," said Mown morosely to his own reflection.

It had pained him to see the Earthlings eradicated once; if it happened again, he might just come to hate himself.

Mown closed his fingers around the tiny mirror.

There must be a way, he thought. *A way to save the Earthlings and not get myself flushed out of a torpedo tube.*

CHAPTER 7

THE *TANNGRISNIR*

Wowbagger's ship red-shifted from the real universe into the mysterious omni-layer of dark space. The view through the portholes was so utterly exotic that an average being could only handle a few seconds of it before either lapsing into catalepsy or replacing the actual view with some pleasant imagining that revealed a lot about the person doing the imagining.

Ford Prefect actually blushed.

"Goosnargh!" he squeaked, covering one porthole with his satchel. "I've seen a few things in my day and in my night too, but that right there . . . that is . . ." And he fled the bridge, deciding that there were times in a man's life that it was better to be alone rather than discuss the view, which he had a sneaking suspicion originated in the recesses of his own mind, particularly the recess that had been conceived one winter afternoon during the meat festival of Carni-val when he'd been dressed as a pollo-bear and had become entangled in a tower of stacked chairs, only to be rescued by a gaggle of three-legged student liposuckers who demanded a very curious reward.

"What's his problem?" wondered Random. "All I see is nothing and more nothing. An eternity of nothing to see."

"You are lucky," said Bowerick Wowbagger. "There are worse things to see than nothing. Nothingness, for example."

"Wow, that's cheery. You should write greeting card messages."

"Listen, odd child. You may learn something."

"From you? No thanks. I think I'd rather stay stupid."

"Your wish has already been granted."

Random bristled a tad more than she was already bristling, which was a shade more than the average berry-snouted spikehog that had just smelled a hunting dog. "How dare you, don't you know who I am?"

"A member of the Cult of Ridiculousness from the Stammering Mud Flats of Santraginus V?" offered Bowerick.

"That's ridiculous."

"Oh, my mistake. The Cult of *Ridiculous* from the Stammering Mud Flats of Santraginus V."

• •

Guide Note: This conversation had similar elements to the exchange which precipitated the collapse of the actual Cult of Ridiculousness from Santraginus V. The COR at their zenith had several dozen names on their mailing list, but the entire organization self-destructed following a particularly contentious Friday Q&A session when committee treasurer T'tal Ychune challenged chairman Oloon Yjeet as to the validity of the society's name. The minutes read as follows:

Yjeet: The chair recognizes Treasurer Ychune.

Ychune: Of course you recognize me. I'm your cousin. We shanked vorkle dumplings together, or would you prefer to forget about that?

Yjeet: Please, T'tal . . .

Ychune: That's Treasurer Ychune.

Yjeet: (sigh) Please, Treasurer Ychune, can we try to keep this civil?

Ychune: You'd know all about civil, wouldn't you? Very civil it was of you to drop around with some spare contraceptives to my betrothed last week. Most civil.

Yjeet: I explained that.

Ychune: (bark of bitter laughter) Oh yes, the water balloon story. How could I forget?

Yjeet: Was there something official you wished to present?

Ychune: There certainly was. I move that the society's name be changed from the Cult of Ridiculousness to the Cult of Ridiculousity.

Yjeet: Are you serious?

Ychune: Totally. Ridiculousness is a little dated, a little slapstick. I think Ridiculousity gives us a little gravity.

Yjeet: Gravity? We're a society that celebrates the history of absurdist comedy as portrayed on cereal box cards. Gravity. That's ridiculous.

Ychune: Aha! You're making my point for me.

Yjeet: (stands abruptly) Yjenean loves me, not you. Get over it. And you can keep this stupid society.

Ychune: (also standing and pulling a large machete that he had somehow concealed in his regulation striped comedy shorts) It's not stupid, it's ridiculous. There's a difference.

The rest of the transcript is rendered illegible as blood streaks have dissolved the ink. Only three phrases can be deciphered in the final lines, and these are: "electronically tested," "call those comedy shorts," and "of course elephants dream." Draw your own conclusions.

• •

Random crossed her arms and shifted her weight as if leaning into a strong wind. "I know what you're thinking, *Bowerick*. You're thinking that any second now I'll run out of things to say and resort to *I hate you* and a stomping exit."

"I *was* rather hoping our exchange would end in the traditional way."

"You don't get off that easily a second time. I've got the gripes of a pensioner and the energy of a teenager, so I can argue all day if that's what you want."

Bowerick Wowbagger pinched the bridge of his nose. "That is so removed from what I want, you have no idea."

Trillian actually wrung her fingers as the exchange escalated. She was so far in the red as regards good parenting credits that she had no idea where the high moral ground was. Even if she could occasionally glimpse it as a myopic hiker glimpses a mist-sodden hill at night, she had no idea who currently occupied it or how to scale its slopes, should she accidentally bump into them.

"Random," she snapped, then reeled it back in. "I meant to say *Random*. Softly, like that. Raaandom."

"What are you babbling about, Mother?"

Trillian felt the old virtual animosity building up, but she choked it back down. "I want to be gentle with you, understanding. But *babbling*?

Babbling, Random honey? I'm more than a mother, I'm your friend. But I don't babble, darling."

Random turned her Goth lasers on Trillian. "Really? Seems to me like you're babbling now. Babbling and hovering. Shouldn't you be off covering a dog fair or something? Leaving me alone again with some perfect stranger perhaps?"

Before Trillian could choose a reply then temper it with compassion born of guilt, Bowerick Wowbagger decided that he'd had enough for the moment.

"Ship," he said. "Tube the younger female."

The mouth of a transparent tube popped down from a tube in the suddenly liquid ceiling and wavered over Random's head. It mimicked her movements, then *whoomped* down as soon as its predictive software reckoned it knew where the target was going next.

Random was enclosed in a soundproof tube and sent asleep with a shot of twinkling green gas. Her face twitched and then assumed a strange expression that it took Trillian a moment to identify as a smile.

"Now I'm going to cry," she said, gazing fondly at her drugged and imprisoned daughter. "I haven't seen a smile like that for years. Not since Random was appointed junior judge in preschool. She loved handing out those demerits."

"The child is dreaming. I can show you the recording if you like," offered the green ship's captain.

There was a ball of anger clogging Trillian's throat, and now she had a legitimate reason to cough it up.

"How dare you!" she cried, eyes wide, chin thrust forward. "You sedated my daughter."

Wowbagger picked up a small pink sliver from the floor. "And I cut off her index finger."

Trillian gagged on her ball of anger. "You what? You bloody what?"

"Technically the ship did it. That tube has sharp edges—she must have stuck her finger out at the last second. Possibly to deliver some obscene gesture."

"My girl, my little girl. You sliced . . ."

Wowbagger tossed the digit toward the ceiling, which absorbed it into the plasma. "Now, now. Not *sliced*. Sliced implies deliberate intent. It was an unfortunate accident at worst."

Trillian hammered on the tube with her palms. "Arthur! This lunatic is cutting up our daughter."

"Hardly cutting up," said Wowbagger, consulting his wafer computer. "The computer has already grown a new finger for her."

Trillian checked. It was true, a brand-new pink index finger was steaming gently on the end of Random's metacarpal. There was no blood, and the teenager did not seem in the least uncomfortable.

"Your daughter is relaxed and dreaming," continued Bowerick Wow-bagger.

He winced at whatever was on-screen. "Though perhaps it's better if I don't show you the dreams. They're a little matricidal."

"Wake her up!" demanded Trillian.

"Absolutely out of the question."

"Wake her up immediately."

"Not likely. She is insufferable."

"And you're not, I suppose."

Wowbagger considered this, rubbing a thumb with his forefinger to focus his thoughts, as was traditional among his people.

• •

Guide Note: Wowbagger's people had believed this action to be an old number one concubines' tale until scientists discovered pockets of natural adenosine blocker secreted below the thumb pads. A brisk thumb scratch unleashes as much energy as five medium cups of a caffeine beverage. Many people become addicted to the little highs and spend all day on the couch twiddling their thumbs.

• •

"I think some people find me insufferable," he concluded. "But I would bet that no one likes that child, unless they are blinded by familial bonds."

"So now I'm blinded?"

"I can't think of another reason why you would tolerate this person. She is vile, grant me that much."

"I will not grant you a thing!"

"Have you heard how she talks to me? How she talks to you?"

Trillian's cheeks were on fire. "We've had our problems. They are *our* problems. Now release my daughter."

Wowbagger winced at the thought. "How about I put her in storage for a while? I can have the computer melt some of that nicotine from the walls of her lungs."

"Don't you dare put her in storage!" shouted Trillian, resisting a strong urge to stamp her foot. Then: "Nicotine. Has she been smoking?"

"For a few years, according to my readings."

"Smoking! Where did Random find time to smoke? I don't think I've ever seen her breathe in with all the complaining she does."

"Storage? Go on."

Trillian was tempted. "No. No, but maybe a lung scrape."

Bowerick waved his fingers over a few sensors, and Random's tube was suffused with flickering laser waves.

"Random will have to sweat that tar out over the next few days. She may experience some nausea."

"Good. That should teach her a lesson. Smoking."

Bowerick reached his hand into an amorphous gel table and pulled out a mug of tea.

"I think we should leave her in there until we reach the nebula. Nobody suffers, everyone's a winner."

Wowbagger had a charming way about him, and Trillian found herself forgetting the severed digit. After all, Random was perfectly fine. In fact, she was better than fine. She was mint.

"No . . . I couldn't. Could I?"

Wowbagger shrugged. "From what I've gathered, you're hardly mother of the century, so what's a few more days apart?"

And right there the charmingness ended.

"How bloody dare you! You uncouth green alien."

"We are in open space, so technically there are no aliens here."

"You have no idea what I've been through. You are in no position to judge me!"

This was the stage of the conversation where Arthur would have sidled from the room in search of some vital but unnamed object in an unspecified and hard-to-reach location. Even Ford would have taken one look at Trillian's face and known to shut his cocktail hole, but Wowbagger, having nurtured a death wish for several millennia, instinctively pointed his green prow toward dangerous situations.

It's unlikely, his subconscious said. *But perhaps this Earthwoman, this undeniably attractive Earthwoman, could do me some grievous bodily harm.*

Wishful thinking.

"Actually I do have an idea what you've been through. The computer mined your memories. I have it all on file."

"You perused my memories?"

"Of course. I was taking you on board my ship. You might have been a mass murderer. With any luck."

"You had no right."

"Oh, here we go with the journalist speak. What happened to *We'll be no trouble, Mr. Wowbagger*?"

"I asked you to take a few hitchhikers on board, not to dig our memories out of our heads."

"Again, you're using the wrong verb. There were no digging implements involved."

Trillian clenched her fists so fiercely that her phalanges creaked.

"You pedantic, smarmy, ass!"

"Ah yes. I had forgotten how fond you people are . . . were . . . of lower life form–based insults. What's next? Cheeky monkey?"

"Oh, I can do better than that."

"Really? I'll get my notebook. I'm always on the lookout, you know."

Trillian thrashed like a combatant being restrained by invisible arms. "That's right, Wowbagger. Make a list of insults, so you can while away your meaningless life making people miserable."

"As opposed to spending your life away from your child—reporting on other people's misery?"

"At least I'm not making them miserable."

"Really? Why don't you ask the girl in the tube?"

They were well matched and Bowerick was warming to the contest. He tossed his mug into the ceiling and gave the human female his full attention.

"Go on then, Trillian Astra. Give me something new I haven't heard a million times before."

"Zark you, Bowerick."

"What do you think? New?"

"Do you think I'd waste my time trying to impress someone who mutilated my daughter?"

"I think so. You media personalities are always trying to impress the Universe. Think of me as a viewer."

Trillian might have smiled; there were teeth involved. "A viewer? I never tried to cater to viewers in your demographic."

"And which demographic would that be?"

"The lunatic fringe. The sad loner brigade."

"A loner *brigade*?" said Bowerick, smirking.

"You're hiding, Wowbagger. In this ship, behind words. You are a sad, lonely, stupid man. Wasting the incredible gift you've been given. Imagine the things you could have done."

Wowbagger could not hold her eyes. "I've seen things you people wouldn't believe. Attack ships on fire off the shoulder of Orion. I watched C-beams glitter in the dark near the Tannhäuser Gate. All those moments will be lost in time, like tears in rain."

"You are pathetic."

"That was one of my favorites movies. I've watched a lot of movies."

"And insulted a lot of people."

"That too."

"All over a couple of elastic bands."

"Zarking bands. We know now that the whole elastic band doctrine was buffa-biscuit."

"You had eternity and you wasted it."

Bowerick leaned hard against the wall, disappearing up to the shoulder. "I did. I did and I want to die."

"So do I."

Bowerick was surprised at this, and by how much it upset him. "*You* want to die?"

Trillian placed a hand on his smooth green cheek. "No, stupid. I want *you* to die."

"Finally, we agree on something."

Trillian stared into Wowbagger's emerald eyes.

"How soon do you have to die?" she asked.

Bowerick had been around long enough to spot an opening when he heard one.

"Not immediately," he said and leaned down to kiss Trillian Astra.

She was shaking a bit, but not as much as the girl in the tube, who had just regained consciousness.

ASGARD

It tickled the sir's divine fancy to set impossible tasks for mortals then pull up a bar stool to the view pool and watch the unfortunate prince or suitor burst a gut trying to do his god's bidding. Slaying the fiercest dragon was a favorite, as was climbing the tallest tower or crossing the widest desert. Anything with a superlative in it. The best impossible tasks were the ones that were so close to possible that the poor eejit being run around in circles could almost touch victory, when failure crept up behind and administered a fatal dose of gruesome death.

Tasks were generally handed down in groups of three, so the one being tested could taste success on the first two and even develop a bit of a cocky swagger, which made for much higher high fives when the testee god delivered his killer blow on task three. Odin insisted on wild-card rules, so that in theory the mortal always had a chance at success, but in the history of task-setting, only one man had successfully completed three tasks, without dying somewhere in the process. Truth be told, that man had actually been Odin himself in one of the human disguises that he was so proud of.

Oooh, all the other gods were forced to coo. *What an amazing mortal who looks nothing like Odin.* And pretend that it was totally nonridiculous that a mortal could move faster than the speed of cameras and change size whenever it suited him.

You would think he'd have made an effort with the fake name, Loki had mentalbrained to Heimdall. *I mean, Wodin. Come on.*

Zaphod Beeblebrox had managed to negotiate from three tasks down to one, which in effect meant that he would fail and perish two tasks early, a fact which would have a devastating trauma-inducing effect on absolutely no one inside the ice shell except Zaphod Beeblebrox.

The Galactic President found himself listing to one side as he pelted along the Rainbow Bridge.

My balance is all off without Left Brain, he realized. *And my breathing too.*

He was sucking down big breaths, but only a fraction of the air was making it to his lungs.

There's a leak somewhere.

In actuality there was no tracheal leak, it was simply that Zaphod's lungs were accustomed to a pair of windpipes feeding them, but now there was only one and it was struggling to do the job. It did not help that the carbon dioxide–oxygen mix was a little too CO_2 heavy for most mortals, so the closer Zaphod got to the planet's surface, the woozier he became.

"Compliments to the under-brazier!" he yelled, because it seemed appropriate.

And though this may seem like a nonsense sentence hodgepodged together by a doped and dopey brain, this particular phrase happened to be that day's password for the Helheim pressure cannons located below the Asgardian iron mines. Which would have mattered not at all, had not Zaphod's delirious utterances been picked up by the fading beams of Heimdall's call to Odin and transmitted to the wireless earpiece of Hel, the mistress of Helheim. Even then, no action would have been taken without the fail-safe Bong-O-Code, a complicated series of taps known only to the big knob gods, which had to be physically hammered into the vein of iron that ran through the stone of Hlidskjalf, Odin's gigantic watchtower and throne, all the way down to Helheim. However, as the iron of Asgard has a little divine magic in its molecules, there is a certain amount of communication between the vein and any metal that has been removed from the vein, the bridge for instance. And as Zaphod tore across Bifrost, the corrugated nubs of his melted heels sent a flurry of pings and bongs vibrating into the bridge with every footfall. Pings and bongs which perfectly matched the fail-safe Bong-O-Code for the Helheim pressure cannons.

Highly unlikely. Forty-seven million to one against. Piddling odds for anyone or anything inside the footprint of an Infinite Improbability Drive's spool-down corona of coincidence and serendipity.

Zaphod's sense of balance was further discombobulated by the mini-cyclones burrowing through the tube of false atmosphere and thrumming about his head and shoulders.

Dragon wash, he realized. *The beasties are close.*

If Zaphod's sense of balance was a little discomfited, then his other senses were positively assaulted by the approach of the dragons to his rear. They soared through the true atmosphere, improbably graceful, long necks undulating with each wing beat, fire snuffles playing around their nostrils. Several scaly heads poked into Zaphod's peripherals, but the creatures didn't seem to be in any hurry to nudge him off the bridge.

They're toying with me. Bloody flying rodents.

"Evening, gents," he called breathlessly. "You can't be bought off, I suppose? I have a really good replicator on the ship. Whatever you guys want. Name it."

The dragon with most horns swooped in close to act as spokesman for the group.

"Whatever we want," it said in a voice like meat being sucked through a bottleneck. "Wow. Okay. Let me think. We could spare him, couldn't we, boys?"

"Sure."

"Could do."

"Why not?"

It was an encouraging start, Zaphod thought.

"So what do you want? Tell me what I can do for you."

The horned dragon chewed on a flap of skin hanging from its nose.

"Could you fit us all on your ship?"

"Of course I could," Zaphod said and huffed, without for a second considering whether this were true.

"And you could transport us to a new world? A young world brimming with life?"

"That is not a problem. Off the top of my head I can think of a dozen, and this is my stupid head."

The dragon inched closer, so the blue flames at its salamandroid nostrils singed Zaphod's hair.

"And could we kill every last being on the planet?" it said in a growled whisper.

"And the trees," called one of his mates. "We want to burn down the trees, for a laugh."

"And the trees," said the spokesdragon. "Even dragons need to relax."

Zaphod was amazed that he could run and talk at the same time. "What was the bit before trees?"

"Kill everyone—oh, and lay eggs in their corpses. That's very important to us. Can you arrange this, little mortal?"

"Whereabouts in their corpses?" asked Zaphod just to make conversation.

"Oh, you know. Hollows, crevices. Eye sockets are good."

And though he didn't think he had it in him, Zaphod ignored the fire in his lungs and picked up the pace.

Why do you always do these things, stupid? he silently berated himself. *Do you even know why you are here?*

He didn't. The reason would come back to him when he had a second to think. If he had a second.

Deep in the bowels of Asgard there moldered a magma-powered deep-sink sewage treatment megacube. Below this and to the left a bit, in what might reasonably be called the rectum of Asgard, sat the region known as Niflheim. At the lowest extreme of Niflheim, on what might be fairly referred to as the interior sphincter of Asgard, sat Helheim.

Hel, the mistress of said sphincter, lounged on the pile of inflated serpent intestine cushions that littered her throne, stroking the baby dragon stole around her neck.

"What do you think of my new stole?" she asked Modgud, her corpse-eating familiar, who was currently wearing the form of a giant eagle.

Modgud squinted. "I think it's still alive, sweetness."

Hel wrung the little dragon's neck with a perfunctoriness that suggested much experience.

"What do you think now?"

"I don't know," mewed Modgud, who had always been a bit petty for a corpse eater. "It seems so . . . lifeless."

Suddenly Hel sat bolt upright in a flurry of squeaking cushions.

"I just got the . . . It's the th-th-thing," she stammered, twisting a communicator earpiece deeper into her ear hole.

Modgud rose up on his claws. "What, sweetness? You just got what?"

"The password phrase, from Odin."

"Which one? The *change the sewage filter* one?"

"No. No, you stupid bird. *Compliments to the under-brazier.* That's the password for the pressure cannons. We're under fire."

Modgud was wounded by the personal attack, but decided for the good of the planet that he would let it fester for now.

"Now, now, sweetness. Hold up there. No call for hysterics. Don't you need some kind of confirmation?"

Hel dabbed her brow with a hairy forearm. "Yes. Yes, of course I do, dear friend. The fail-safe Bong-O-Code. Sorry about the *stupid bird* comment."

"Oh, forget it," said Modgud, good-naturedly. "You're in a high-pressure job." While inside he swore to up the daily doses of poison. Maybe he couldn't kill this witch, but he could have her writhing on the toilet for half the day.

Hel's relieved smile froze as the fail-safe Bong-O-Code vibrated up through her torso from the iron throne she sat upon.

"What is it?"

"Shut up, idiot. I'm counting bongs."

Modgud preened for a few moments while his mistress counted.

"War!" she said at last, springing to her feet. "Asgard is at war. Finally my chance to get out of this dump and back to the surface. If my defenses save the day, then it's so long loser craphole."

"Loser?"

Hel rolled her eyes. "You are so sensitive for a corpse eater. Warm up the cannons."

"Which ones? Not all of them?"

"Yes, all of them."

"What am I shooting at?"

"Not the bridge, Heimdall's on the bridge. But anything else that moves!" snapped the she-devil. "We might lose a few dragons, but there are aliens inside the shell."

Loser craphole, thought Modgud sulkily, opening a window on his wrist computer. *At least we acknowledge the existence of technology down here. At least we're not relying on archaic phone calls and bong codes.*

"I can mentalbrain what you're thinking!" screeched Hel. "Something about tents and cake!"

Modgud activated the cannons with a few taps on his screen.

God help us, he thought. *But not the gods we have here. Some other ones that are a bit less . . .*

The corpse eater did not finish the thought, just in case Hel got her mind reading spot-on for once.

Zaphod was running out of breath, and what little he did have left sprinkled his lungs with pins and needles. The dragons swirled around the bridge now, at least a dozen of them, shunting each other with playful shoulders, nipping at tails. They loosed fireballs close to their target, stripping chunks of ice from the bridge.

Still, thought Zaphod. *Killed fighting dragons in Asgard. Not a bad way to go. Better than slipping on a wet spot and tumbling into a boring hole. A pity I couldn't reach that wall.*

Wall. Hadn't Diona Carlinton-Housney said something about a wall?

I shall make reaching that wall my new short-term goal, decided Zaphod with the same full tank of foundation-free reasoning that characterized most of his life-changing decisions. *If it's the last thing I do, I will reach that wall.*

Two lurches later his legs gave out and he was reduced to dragging himself along the bridge in a three-handed scrabble.

"Wall, dammit," he croaked. "Wall."

The dragons thought this was hilarious, and one of them even pulled a cell phone from under a scale to call his weekend buddies.

"Honestly, you have to see this idiot, Burnie. You remember that guy with the wooden legs? Remember we lit him up like a torch? This guy is even funnier. Get up here now."

More dragons. Froody.

The beasts' wings dipped inside the atmosphere tube, as they tugged at Zaphod's clothing with their sharp little claws.

"Come on. This is an official presidential jacket. Don't you lizards know who I am?"

Bifrost jumped with the impact of giant footsteps as Heimdall jogged leisurely along the bridge, grin wider than the crooked mayor of Optimisia with dental implants who has just won the planetary lotto on his birthday and discovered that his chief love rival from high school was recently cuckolded and that the prosecution's case against him has collapsed.

"You didn't make it," said the god, eyes magnified by the orange lenses of his ski goggles.

"Are those prescription?" wondered Zaphod.

"You didn't complete your task, Babblepox."

"It's Beeblebrox," shouted the frustrated Galactic President. "You may not realize this, but every time you mispronounce my name I feel bad. I'm a positive kind of person, but for some reason that really hurts. It's not funny."

"I think it's funny, Feeblejocks," said Heimdall, using his godly voice projection powers to broadcast his comments to the dragons, who chuckled fireballs and smacked wings. "What do you think, my beautiful pets?"

"I think it's a buffa-bucket of hilariousness," answered a red-striped alpha male hovering above the bridge, his rear legs dangling, which is harder than it looks. "If you ask me, Boss, mispronouncing this mortal's name is as close to . . ."

More sounds came out of his mouth, but they weren't words as such, just shrieks and a few initial consonants, which were probably on their way to being swearwords before the pain blotted out any commands from the dragon's parietal lobe.

"What the . . . ," said Heimdall before his jaw dropped. The red-striped alpha had simply burst into plasma flame, taken from behind by some sort of missile.

"Wow," said Zaphod. "I've often wondered what would happen if a dragon held its breath."

Another dragon was hit, in the shoulder, sending it spinning toward the surface of the planet, leaking inkblots of blue black smoke.

"Aren't you going to react?" asked Zaphod. "Don't you have the whole superspeed reaction thing? Or is that just the major gods?"

Heimdall was goaded into action.

"Fly, my beauties," he called. "Hide on the surface."

The dragons dropped out of their hovering pattern and scattered for cover as far away as they could get from whatever was attacking their comrades. Fast as the dragons were, many could not outrun the slew of spiraling missiles that were hugging the bend of the planet, breaking from the pack when they locked onto a target.

Heimdall collapsed his horn and put an emergency call into Hel-heim.

"Hel? We are under attack here."

"I know," said the she-devil. "Don't worry, I've sent a few dozen shells your way. Can you see the enemy?"

Heimdall was known for being so alert that he needed no sleep. They used to say in the taverns of Scandinavia that he could see grass grow and hear a leaf fall on the other side of an ocean. But that was a long time ago, and these days Heimdall often snuck off for a snooze after his latte and had been known to miss the sound of autumn altogether.

"I don't see them. Just missiles coming up from the southern hemisphere."

Hel hmmed. "The southern hemisphere you say. Not through the Bifrost Arch?"

"Nope. I'm looking at the arch. Up from the south definitely."

"And you can't see any aliens? Maybe green chaps, with lasers or some such?"

Heimdall squeezed Gjallarhorn's shaft until it squeaked. "No. No zarking aliens, okay? Just groups of blue torpedoes with pinkish trails. A bit like ours if I remember."

"No no," said Hel in the tone of a guilty teenager blocking her mother at the door to a bedroom that is full of boys and drugs, stolen jewelry, and possibly music playing backward. "They couldn't be like ours. Ours have red trails. A light red, some would call it puce."

Heimdall growled as another of his dragons took a hit. "I don't care what some would call it. Shoot them down, Hel. Can you do that?"

"Erm, yes. I should think so. The computer has . . . eh . . . isolated their frequency, so we should be able to send a self-destruct signal, which I am doing . . . now."

The remaining missiles exploded in flashes of pink and electric white, gears and pistons thunking into the ice shell.

"Well done," said Heimdall, tears of relief on his tanned cheeks. "Odin shall hear of your labors this day."

"Will he? Would you? That's marvelous. Of course I could have destroyed those missiles much sooner had they actually been *our* missiles, because I already have those frequencies. So obviously they weren't *our* missiles and why would they be, but in case anyone asks, they weren't. Anyone like Odin for example. Not ours. Got it?"

Heimdall was about to answer, when he noticed that Zaphod Beeblebrox had discovered new reserves of energy and was racing just as fast as he could toward the wall.

If he gets over that wall, I am bound to parlay.

In spite of this truth and the recent losses to his dragon brigade, Heimdall's face was smeared with a grin. Beeblebrox had nearly reached the wall, but *nearly* was about as much use as a flaybooz in any activity involving thumbs—bottle opening, for example, or playing the lute, or perhaps hitching a ride. The Betelgeusean might as well have been standing still for all the good it would do him. Nothing could outrun a god in real space. Even with one footfall to go, Beeblebrox might as well have been a light-year away from the wall, wearing a lead jacket and neutronium boots.

Catch Beeblebrox, Heimdall thought, and before the electrical impulses containing this notion had time to fade, he had Zaphod by the throat and pinned to the wall.

"I don't know what you did to my lovely dragons. Whatever it was, it won't help you now."

Zaphod felt as though a mammaloid were squatting on his chest. Not a nice vegetarian mammaloid either, who had probably sat down by accident and would lumber off as soon as it heard Zaphod's voice. No, a vicious mutant carnivore mammaloid who had gone against the advice of its parents and the herd in general in making the decision to tenderize its prey with buttock bounces before consuming it.

"Stupid mutant mammaloid," huffed Zaphod, woozy with all the running and CO_2 inhalation.

Heimdall's grip tightened a knuckle. "Is that it? Are those the last words of the famous President Needlefrocks?"

Zaphod remembered something. "I'm not the only one with a nick-name, am I?"

The god twitched nervously. "What are you talking about?"

"Don't bother denying it. You guys all have like a secret pet name. A name of power. Thor told me all about it one night on tour, after an open-air gig in a quarry on Zentalquabula. We were so hammered you have no idea. I kissed a Silagestrian."

"Liar," hissed Heimdall.

Zaphod was hurt. "I'm not proud of it, but I kissed that Silagestrian all right and its handler."

"No mortal can know our monikers. It is forbidden. You lie."

Heimdall's huge, smooth face was inches away from Zaphod. His anger shimmered in the air around them, and Gjallarhorn glowed red with godly power. Zaphod took all of this in and said: "Lie? Me? That's a bit strong, isn't it? I'm just repeating what Thor told me. Don't kill the messenger and so forth."

"Don't say it. I am warning you, mortal."

Even Zaphod saw the absurdity of that warning. "Or what? You'll do something nasty like send dragons after me or squeeze my head off?"

It occurred to Heimdall that he should get on with the head squeez-ing before Zaphod could get the name out, but a sudden nervousness gagged him for a vital moment. And instinctive exploitation of vital mo-ments was one of Zaphod's few areas of expertise. The others being his much reported Big Bang technique, his three-handed preparation of Gargle Blasters, and a system of inverted blow-drying that gave his quiff that extra bounce.

"Come on, Bent Stick," he said. "Let me up."

And Heimdall did. He had no choice once his divine moniker had been invoked. The god took a dozen steps backward then turned his back in a sulk.

"Someone . . . Anyone . . . calls me Bent Stick on Asgard and I am bound to civility. Bloody Bent Stick? What sort of a divine name is that?" he grumbled, kicking loose lumps of ice through the wall of the atmosphere tube, creating localized rainfall on the planet's surface be-low. "Loki suggests it and of course Odin thinks it's hilarious. Loki says, he says, *Look at Heimdall out there on his ski slope with that old bent stick of his.* And the bossman nearly swallows his beard laughing. So from that day on it's Bent Stick this and Bent Stick that. I used to have a great name. I was Asgard's Eye. But apparently that's too tricky to pronounce after a few tankards, so now I'm Bent bloody Stick."

The giant god's shoulders hitched repeatedly, and he looked from the back very much like someone who might be having a little self-pitying sob.

"Hey, come on," said Zaphod, picking himself up. "Why the long face? You've got stuff going for you."

"What do I have going for me? I'm stuck out here on this stupid bridge with a bunch of reptiles for friends." He stamped a foot, sending tremors rippling across Bifrost. "Do you know what they're doing in there now? Do you know?"

"Well, no I . . ."

"Orgies!" shouted Heimdall. "Old school orgies. And look at me, out here chasing mortals. I could be in there, covered in jartle resin, up to my neck in . . ."

"Okay, big fellow, there are a few pictures that even I don't need floating around in either of my heads."

"Loki has got two palaces. Two! After all the stunts he's pulled. And he sits at Odin's table. And why? *Why?* Because he can remember jokes." Heimdall turned, his beard wet, his eyes despairing. "Bloody jokes! I am guarding the planet here. Hello."

Zaphod tucked his third hand into a pocket. "You know what I see?"

"What?" said Heimdall, his jutting bottom lip casting a shadow.

"I see a hero."

"Don't you patronize me, Feeb— Beeblebrox."

Zaphod punched the god's thigh. "I'm not patronizing you, silly. What you are is a genuine hero. And there are only a dozen of those in the Universe. Me, you, and four others."

Heimdall's nod was barely perceptible, even for a chin as big as his. "Maybe. Odin doesn't see it like that."

Zaphod stood on tiptoes. "Can Odin hear me now?"

"Probably not, inside the tube. Unless he's specifically listening."

"Well then, forgive me for saying it, but Odin doesn't deserve you. In fact, I'll go further. Maybe *Odin* needs to take a look at himself and ask: *Who should be sitting beside me now? A gutless trickster? Or my loyal guardian?* I think a lot of people would like to hear that question answered."

"Gutless? You think so? A lot?"

"We may be mortal, but we're not stupid. People *like* you, Heimdall. They adore you."

"Maybe once they did."

"Now. Still. Did you know that they have a Heimdall cult on Algol? Those sun simians can't get enough of you."

"Really? Algol, you say?"

"And on Earth, you were, well, a god. Statues all over the place."

Heimdall chuckled. "Yes, Earth. They loved the whole horn thing." His eyes misted, and for a moment the Light God was doing encores in Scandinavia, until he realized that Zaphod was playing on his weaknesses.

"No," snapped the Light God, wiping his nose. "It's over. We're over. No parlay with mortals."

"You have to. I know your secret name."

"Oh sure, spring that one on me. That's low, even for you."

Zaphod placed two of his hands on his hips. "I invoke your secret name and demand my right to entry, Heimdall God of Light, also known as Asgard's Eye."

Heimdall snorted not unhappily and hefted Gjallarhorn. He tapped a section of the wall and the entire edifice crumbled to dust. Dust which flittered into the atmosphere squeaking, "Free. Free at last. Heimdall, you bastard."

"I have to let you in," said the God of Light. "Thor is probably in the Well of Urd drowning his sorrows, he more or less lives there these days. You can have one beer with him, if he will permit it."

"One beer," said Zaphod. "I'll just sip."

If Left Brain could have intercepted this thought, he would have laughed bitterly and proclaimed that there was about as much chance of Zaphod Beeblebrox *just sipping* as there was of a mouse giving a straight answer to a simple question.

CHAPTER 8

THE *TANNGRISNIR*

Ford Prefect was also heading toward a beer moment. The Betelgeusean reporter was determined to enjoy the peace and quiet of dark travel for as long as it lasted. He draped blankets over the portholes in his room, replicated a tankard of Goggles Beer then plugged himself into the ship's computer. His Hitchhiker's Guide had a pretty good sub-etha connection, but the *Tanngrisnir*'s system was so fast that it could run a real-time hologram from a hub a thousand light-years away with no discernible delay.

Mega-lightning froody, thought Ford, who knew nothing about holograms apart from the fact that they were sparkly and you should never lick one.

Ford logged onto uBid and bet himself a second tankard of beer that he could not spend his entire projected lifetime's earnings before blinking. It was an easy bet to win. He purchased a couple of luxury space yachts, three hundred gallons of Bounce-O-Jelly with garlic, a small continent on Antares for a favorite nephew, and several potted Deadly When Watered megaflora for his least favorite staffers at InfiniDim Enterprises. All charged to his limitless Hitchhiker's Guide expenses card.

I might feel a twinge of guilt about sticking it to the guide, thought Ford. *If the editor, Zarniwoop Vann Harl, wasn't a gutless stooge who took bribes from Vogons.*

As a journalist, Ford had nothing on principle against taking bribes, but you had to draw the line somewhere, and for Ford Prefect that line was drawn just above anybody trying to kill him in one of the nasty ways. Attempted murder through alcohol poisoning he was prepared to forgive and more than likely forget, but when someone tried to kill him with thermonuclear warheads Ford tended to nurse a grudge.

Retail therapy over, Ford blinked several times and leaned back in the chair.

Thank you, Doxy Ribonu-Clegg, he thought. *Thank you for inventing the Sub-Etha.*

* *

Guide Note: Technically speaking, Doxy Ribonu-Clegg did not invent the Sub-Etha, rather he discovered its existence. The Sub-Etha waves had been around for at least as long as the gods, just waiting for someone to pump some data into them. The legend goes that Ribonu-Clegg had been lying on his back in a field on his home planet. As he gazed blearily up through the wedge of space suspended above him, it occurred to the renowned professor that all this space was loaded with information and that perhaps it would be possible to transport some information of his own through the cosmic conduits if only he could make it small enough. So Ribonu-Clegg hurried back to his rudimentary lab and constructed the first ever set of Sub-Etha transmitters, using pepper grinders, several live pinky rats, various cannibalized lab machines, and a professional-standard hairdressing scissors. Once these components were connected, Ribonu-Clegg fed in the Phot-O-Pix from his wedding album and prayed they would be reassembled on the other side of the room. They were not, but the national lottery numbers for the following evening did show up, which encouraged the professor to patent his invention. Ribonu-Clegg used his winnings to hire a team of shark lawyers who successfully sued eighty-nine companies that invented actual working Sub-Etha transmitters, making the professor the richest man on the planet until he fell into his lawyers' tank and they followed their instincts and ate him.

* *

Ford was halfway through his fourth tankard when the door to his chamber slid open and a parallelogram of green light bleached his wall screen.

"Hey. Come on. I'm bidding here. Switch off that beam."

"Very funny," said a voice so sarcastic that even the auditorily challenged nut tree voles of Oglaroon could have detected its insincerity through their whiskers.

Ford swiveled on his chair and realized that the glow came from a person in the doorway.

"You seem a little green," he commented.

Random scowled. "So would you, if you'd spent the past while sealed in a tube with a cloud of viridigenous gas that was trying to make you happy."

"Happiness? That would never do, would it?"

"Not when your mother is making out with that horrible alien right under your nose. Disgusting."

Ford nodded with a wisdom beyond his ears. "Ah, yes the deBeouf Principle. I read about that in a thing with actual pages in it. A quaint thing where you flip the paper over."

"A book," said Random, and she may have glowered, it was hard to tell.

"That was it. I'm guessing that you're not too happy about this latest romantic development."

Random stomped into the chamber, puff clouds of green dust rising from her shoulders with each footfall. "No. I am not happy. He is so arrogant. Such a . . ."

"Pormwrangler?" offered Ford helpfully.

"Yes. Exactly."

Ford's fingers tapped the air impatiently, eager to wrap themselves around a tankard handle. "So, why don't you talk to Arthur about it? He's your biological patriarch."

Random smiled bitterly. "Arthur? I tried, but he's in love too, with his blasted computer."

Even Ford was a little surprised by this. It wasn't that people didn't fall in love with machines, he had a cousin who once spent two years shacked up with a sandwich toaster, but Arthur was so uptight, so strait-laced, such a total Earthling.

"Love is love," he said, falling back on his brochure knowledge from a peace spa he had once visited on Hawalius. "Don't judge unless you want someone else to come along, possibly someone green, and judge you, and you'll say, *Come on, what's all this judging for, don't judge unless you want someone else to come along and judge you,* and so on." Ford paused for breath. "I've had a few beers so I'm paraphrasing."

He winced, expecting to be smacked about the chops with the wet fish of cynicism, but Random was suddenly all sweetness.

"That's really good, Ford. Wise, you know. I am going to go back to my room to wash some of this junk off and think really hard about not judging people."

Ford waved her off gallantly. "No charge for that nugget, young missy. Any time you want a few words of wisdom, feel free to drop in on ol' Fordy. I've got a ton of advice on the more offbeat areas that most people wouldn't have the first clue about. What to do just before a planet explodes, for example. I am the Universe's expert on that particular subject, believe me."

And he returned to his screen, satisfied that his sometime role as Ford Prefect, nurturer of youth, had been fulfilled for at least this lifetime.

Parenting. Nothing to it. I don't know what all the fuss is about.

If Ford had been a little more tuned in and a little less zoned out, he might have remembered from his own youth that teenagers only ladled on the sweetness for one of three reasons. One: There was some shocking news that needed breaking, possibly involving pregnancy, substance abuse, or a forbidden relationship. Two: They had developed a deeper level of sarcasm which was virtually undetectable except to another master of the form, and that definitely wasn't the adult being sarcastigated. And three: A bit of sweet talk was a handy distraction when there was something the sweet-talking teenager needed to steal.

By the time Ford might have realized that his limitless InfiniDim credit card was missing, it had already been put back. And shortly before that, Random Dent had utilized uBid's retro-buy time window and purchased something from a long-dead seller. Something a little more sinister than three hundred gallons of Bounce-O-Jelly. With garlic.

Garlic in the jelly, not in the sinister item.

"I am the unluckiest man in the universe," Arthur Dent explained to the *Tanngrisnir*'s computer. "Bad things happen to me. I don't know why, but it's always been that way. My Nan used to give me bull's-eyes and call me her little trouble magnet. Only she was from Manchester, so she didn't say *trouble*."

The sparkling hologram, which sat cross-legged at the foot of the bunk, squinted while she rifled Arthur's memory.

"Oh," she said. "Bull's-eyes. For a nanosecond there I thought . . ."

"Wherever I go, things get blown up or blasted by angry aliens."

"But not you," said Fenchurch.

"What?"

"You don't get blown up or blasted. You've already had one long and healthy life, and now you're having another."

Arthur frowned. "Yes . . . but. There was the whole bathrobe and pajamas period. How unlucky can you get? Not to mention being stranded on . . ."

"Most of your species are dead," interjected the computer, just as Arthur's memory assured her Fenchurch would have done. "It was a billion to one against you surviving, but you did. Twice. That seems pretty lucky. That's like fictional hero lucky."

"I see your point, but still . . ."

"And you have a beautiful daughter."

"True. But she's moody."

"Really? That's odd for an adolescent. You are truly cursed."

Arthur was stumped. How was he supposed to feel if not put upon? Then the holographic Fenchurch unsettled him further with a non sequitur. Nothing as bizarre as *Look! A monkey,* but pretty surprising nonetheless.

"Love can be a noun or a verb," she said.

"I see," said Arthur, then: "What happened to luck?"

"Oh, that conversation was just superficial, this is what you really want to know."

"What love is?"

"Yes. And why you can't seem to get over losing it."

Arthur felt his heart beat faster on hearing this truth. "Do you know? Can you tell me? And no numbers please."

Fenchurch scratched her earlobe and sparks crackled at the contact. "I can tell you what love means, dictionary-wise, all the synonyms and so forth. And I can tell you all about endorphins and synapses and muscle memory. But ardor's resonance in the heart is a mystery to me. I'm a computer, Arthur."

Arthur hid his disappointment with the traditional brisk rubbing of hands and stiffening of upper lip.

"Of course. No problem."

"I am made to live forever, but you are made to live."

"Isn't that a Sirius Cybernetics Corporation slogan?" said Arthur, frowning.

Fenchurch heated two pixel clusters to affect a blush. "It might be. All that means is that an entire company of advertisers think you will believe it."

"Ah. No answers then."

"Only questions."

"I thought we didn't know the big question."

Fenchurch examined her own fingers. "The big question is different for everyone. For me it's the half-life of this ship's reactor. I'm not actually made to live forever, that's just a slogan."

"And what's the answer to the half-life question?"

"I don't know. Bloody thing is touched by godly magic. It should have stopped ten thousand years ago."

"So no answers for you either?"

"Nope."

"Talk is just talk, isn't it?"

"Sounds like it."

"It looks like everyone is relying on Thor. I know he was your boss, but he struck me as a terrible bore."

Fenchurch stared dreamily into the past. "A bore? No. He was lovely. Divine."

Arthur could not remember seeing that expression on the real Fenchurch's face. "I think we'll have to disagree on that one."

"Very well, Arthur Dent. Shall I select a random question from the lexicon of your memory?"

"Good idea."

The computer flicked through the files for a moment then asked: "Do you fancy a cup of tea?"

Arthur smiled. "Now there's a question I can answer."

ASGARD

Guide Note: The Aesir have always made an enormous deal of the absolute wonderfulness of Asgard. Odin's son Baldur is quoted as saying: "Everything is massive and huge and brilliant, you mortals with your puny stuff and things have no idea what real brilliant stuff is. We have stuff that would blow your little minds and then other stuff in jars, sort of lotion, that would put your minds back together again. Then there's this cosmic cow who like licked Valhalla out of the ice and an old guy who sweated Odin's father out of his armpit. That kind of stuff happens every day on Asgard."

This is typical of the sort of standard vague, inconsistent party line that prompted Boam Catharsee, the charismatic leader of the Horrisonian Cult of Agnosticism to smuggle himself into Asgard, in the belly of a goat, to see the planet for himself. The oft-sampled Catharsee recordings read as follows: "The smell from beyond my hiding place is almost unbearable, but I shall persevere for you, my people. I'm not surprised that no one believes in these gods anymore, they really stink. I can hear a fire crackling so, whatever lies outside, I must take my knife and cut my way out before this carcass is tossed into the oven. I shall just take my knife . . . My knife . . . Where's my nothingdamned knife? I know I had it, right here in the pocket of my linen trews. Oh, crap. Zark. I'm wearing my corduroys. The flames grow closer, I can feel their heat. Help! HELP! I believe. I believe. Don't cook me. Please don't . . ." And there Boam Catharsee's words become unintelligible, apart from two "my legs" and a "Mommy." For ten years after Boam's sacrifice, belief in the Aesir spiked on his home planet and the top-selling T-shirt had emblazoned across it in large easy-to-read letters: *I Believe. Don't Cook Me.*

The point being, mortals knew little of Asgard back in the days of Boam Catharsee, and we know even less now, for no living mortal has ever visited Asgard and survived to tell the tale, and any mortal who claims to have done just that is either Odin in disguise looking for some action or completely and utterly insane.

Zaphod Beeblebrox took a very plush cable car from the foot of the Rainbow Bridge to the surface of Asgard. Not only was the car comfortable, with its own helmet polisher and thoughtful cage of foot-warming lizards, but it was convenient too, docking as it did right in the center of downtown Valhalla.

There was a customs Viking in a reinforced booth who seemed a little surprised to see a mortal coming onto the platform. In fact, he was so surprised that his eyes popped right out of their sockets.

"Whoa," said Zaphod. "That is truly disgusting. Can you do it again?"

"No, I cannot," said the Viking, twisting the eyes back in. "Who the Hel are you?"

Zaphod responded in the time-honored fashion of answering a question with a question, a tactic he favored because of its windup factor.

"What the hell are you?"

"I'll ask the questions here!"

"What questions will you ask . . . here?"

The Viking rolled his eyes with a sound like a toothless old person sucking hot tea from a cup.

"Are you winding me up?"

"Is who winding you up?"

The Viking jumped to his feet. "Fine. I'm a reanimated dead Viking. Okay? We die in battle to get here and then they reanimate us as bloody civil servants. I was the captain of my own bloody longboat. We tore up England, kicked the stuffing out of those Saxons. And for that I get a desk job. A shagging desk job, if you can believe that. Me! Eric the Red Hand. Red because of all the blood that was dripping from it, you understand. Not my own blood either." Eric stopped shouting mainly because his eyes had wormed their way loose again.

"Wow," said Zaphod. "You've really been carrying that around."

"It's been festering for a while," admitted the Viking, wiping off one eye with his sleeve.

"Do you feel better now?"

Eric sighed. "Yes. It's good to vent, you know?"

Zaphod patted his shoulder. "You need to look after your mental health, buddy."

"Thanks. That's the first nice thing anyone has said to me since I signed on for that big pillaging expedition in Brittany. I'd shed a tear if I could."

"You're welcome. Zaphod Beeblebrox likes to spread joy to places other presidents cannot reach."

Eric held a clipboard close to his face. "Oh, yes. Beeblebrox. I got a call about you from Heimy ski-boy. Of course no mention that you were a mortal. Why spare Eric's heart, he's already dead. Typical."

"I'm looking for Thor."

Eric tutted. "No problem finding him. Well of Urd. Go straight down to Yggdrasil, the giant ash tree, then left, and don't give any money to the unicorns, it just encourages them. And if you see a guy with like a hook nose, answers to the name Leif, tell him that I think we got our eyeballs mixed up."

Even Zaphod had no trouble finding the golden tree, though he was distracted by hordes of zombie-like reanimated Vikings shuffling along the cobbled streets, clutching dry cleaning in their bony hands, or trailing listlessly after tiny dogs.

"This is ridiculous," he said eventually. "They all have hooked noses."

The tree itself was massive, its glistening branches dipping low to the ground, weighed down by the swords and shields of fallen heroes and also advertising placards for ZugaNugget cereal, which according to the billboards sponsored the transportation by the Valkyrie of fallen heroes from their mortal plane.

Zaphod abandoned his mini-quest to find the guy known as Leif, and turned down a pretty crappy-looking alley that had crap flowing down the walls that was actually crap, and because it was a magical realm there was crap flowing up the walls too.

"Crap," said Zaphod and congratulated himself on making a statement that was not only an expletive, but also a declaration of fact and a warning to anyone who might be behind him in the alley.

"You talking to me, Blondie?" said a voice, and Zaphod realized that what he had taken for a stalactite of sewage was actually a stained root from Yggdrasil, the ash tree breaking through from the cobbles below.

"Pardon me," said Zaphod, only feeling slightly ridiculous to be talking to a tree. He had talked to a lot worse things in the past few years. "I thought you were part of the sewage system."

"I might as well be," said Yggdrasil, through no mouth that Zaphod could discern. "The amount of junk they pour straight onto the ground here. It all comes up through my roots, you know. Is it any wonder I'm slipping a few IQ points? You are what you eat, and all that."

"I'm looking for Thor."

"Big Red? Straight on in through the door here."

Zaphod squinted through the gloom, but the door was proving as difficult to spot as Yggdrasil's mouth.

"I don't see any door."

"You have to say the magic words."

Zaphod rubbed his temples and concentrated. "Okay. Don't tell me. I feeling something, coming out of the ether. Is it *Trees are froody?*"

"That is amazing," said the tree and parted a cluster of creepers on the damp wall, revealing a nicotine yellow glow behind. "In you go, Blondie."

Zaphod stepped inside. He did not need to bend down, as the doorway behind the creepers had been built for a much larger person.

NANO

Hillman Hunter gazed out his office window at the tropical majesty of this planet he had purchased at the nebula's edge.

You did the right thing, Hillers, said his Nano's voice in his head. *If you hadn't shifted these people from Earth, their atoms would be spread across the galaxy by now. What do you think people would prefer, a little civil unrest or a whole lot of dead?*

Hillman knew that his Nano was right, but he couldn't help thinking that, somewhere along the line, he had been screwed. There had been a better deal to be had and somehow Zaphod Beeblebrox had kept it hidden from him, and it pained Hillman to think that he had been bamboozled by such an apparent moron.

The intercom box on his desk vibrated, dragging Hillman's attention away from the view. He waved his hand over the sensor and a little hologram of his secretary appeared on his desk.

"Yes, Marilyn?"

"There's a lady here to see you."

"Does she have an appointment?"

Marilyn mewed, as though this was a difficult question. "She says she will have."

"That's a little cryptic, Marilyn. Could you ask for clarification?"

Before Marilyn could respond, a woman materialized in Hillman's interview chair. From his recent interviews, Hillman had become accustomed to a flickering style of materialization, but this woman arrived like somebody had flicked a switch.

"Jaysus!" he yelped.

"Actually no. The name is Gaia, Hillman Hunter," she said, her voice sonorous and comforting.

"Ah, yes. Gaia, the Earth Mother." Hillman sifted through the stack of résumés on his desk. "I hadn't made my mind up about you."

Gaia trained her deep brown eyes on Hillman. "No, but you would have, so I decided to hurry things along."

The combination of eyes and voice was hypnotic, and Hillman found himself very comfortable with this attractive lady.

"That was probably . . . That was a reasonable course of action."

Gaia's face was heart-shaped, with sensuous purple lips. "You've got time to talk to me, don't you, Hillman?"

"Yes. Jaysus, yes, begorrah."

"I am the Earth Mother, without an Earth, come to a new home. I could be happy here, Hillman. You could be happy too."

"Yes, Earth Mother. Happy as a pig in . . . very happy."

"There's no need for any more interviews."

"No. Why would I need to interview anyone else?"

Gaia smiled and leaned forward. Hillman saw that her fingers were slim but strong. "I can nurture this Earth. I can make anything grow."

"That's grand. Growing stuff is a good thing."

The Earth Mother spread her arms, and Hillman could smell the summers of his youth. "The women will be broad-breasted and fertile, and the men will desire them."

"About fecking time too."

"All we need to do is clear up a few salary issues." Which was exactly the wrong thing to say to Hillman Hunter; the fog in his mind cleared and he suddenly felt the need to ask a few probing questions.

"Salary issues? And what issues would they be?"

"Well, the entire package is pitifully small. How can I be expected to support a retinue . . ."

"A retinue, is it? I don't recall advertising for a retinue. One position only."

"But surely a goddess of my stature?"

Hillman was in like a shark. "What stature is that? You were no great shakes in your last job. As far as I remember, the planet was riddled with famine and most of the crops that did grow were riddled with pesticides."

"Things got a little out of control on Earth," admitted Gaia. "But that wouldn't happen again."

"Oh really? Why don't we explore that. Let's say there's an uprising. A surge in belief for another god. How would you handle it?"

Gaia smiled kindly. "I have dealt with problems in the past, you know. I can be tough when the situation demands it."

"Please elaborate."

"I remember once Uranus hid the Cyclops in Tartarus so he couldn't see the light. This caused me considerable pain as, you may not know this about me, as Tartarus was my bowels in a reflexology kind of a way. So I fashioned a great flint sickle, and when Uranus entered my chamber for his weekly how's-your-father, I had my son Chronos chop his doodle off with the sickle." Gaia clapped delightedly at the memory. "Oh, that was a night and a half. But I think I've answered your question. Firm but fair, that's my motto. I still have that sickle somewhere; you never know when a few drops of dry divine blood will come in handy."

Hillman crossed his legs, feeling the phantom of a loss he fervently hoped never to experience.

Beside Gaia's name on her résumé, he wrote four words:

"Over my dead body."

ASGARD

Zaphod stepped into as foul a den of broken dreams as he had ever been thrown out of, and felt instantly at home.

This is my kind of place, he thought. *Even the air in here is dangerous.*

And it was. The germs huddled together and drifted through the murky air in colored clouds, trying vainly to infect the ossified zombies and demigods. For once Zaphod was glad that Left Brain had jabbed him with A–Z inoculations while he slept. At least LB had sworn they were inoculations.

A cloud buzzed Zaphod's head, chanting, "Open pores, open sores." But it was repelled by the scent of antivirus in his perspiration.

If this had been a movie, everyone would have stopped what they were doing to glare at the handsome stranger, but most of the patrons in the Well of Urd were so inebriated that they had barely enough focus to find the tankards on their tables, never mind muster a glare for a new-comer. One drinker did yell, "Happy Birthday, Mister President," but it was likely that she was hallucinating. Zaphod clambered down three stone steps to the tavern floor, then side-stepped viscous, steaming puddles until he reached the bar, which towered clifflike above him.

A pale reanimated Viking barman with half a dozen blond hairs pasted across his shiny pate peered down at him. "What can I do for you, Junior?"

"You can tell me where Thor is," replied Zaphod.

The barman whistled though a hole in his cheek. "Now, why would you want to find Thor? You being so alive and all."

"He's in a bad mood then?"

"You could say that," said the barman. "All he does is drink and play chess. And the more he loses, the more he drinks."

"Doesn't he ever win?"

The barman sniggered. "Win? Nobody wins in here, Junior."

Zaphod peered up at the Viking. "Your name wouldn't be Leif, would it?"

The barman was instantly enraged. He pulled a mini-axe from a shoulder holster and began chopping the countertop.

"You tell Eric to come down here if he wants to talk about eyeballs. You tell him that from me. Come down here and we'll talk!"

"I'll tell him," said Zaphod, backing away. "If I survive this chat with Thor."

"It's not Thor you should worry about," said the barman, jerking a thumb toward a dark alcove at the rear of the bar. "It's those other little bastards."

Zaphod winked with supreme confidence. "Don't worry. I've been in show business for years; I know how to handle bastards."

The bar was cramped, by Asgardian standards, but to Zaphod it felt like he had lost weight just walking briskly to Thor's table. On the way he passed several brawls; a couple of magical rituals, one involving a heated skewer and a circle of wolves howling in unison; a funeral pyre piled high with bodies and also sausages; and a frozen lake with dwarves skating around on it being chased by a tree-footed monster.

I could live here, thought Zaphod.

The fun and games stopped shy of Thor's alcove. There seemed to be an unwritten agreement that the Thunder God should be left in peace, which was probably due to the very clearly written message painted on a whitewashed wall in what looked like lumpy congealed blood, which read: *Leave me in peace and I probably won't kill you. No promises, mind. Probably is absolutely the best I can do.*

Zaphod crossed the peace line, and for the first time since entering the bar, he felt scores of eyes on him.

Don't fret, Zaphod, he told himself. *What happened between you was ages ago. He's probably forgotten all about it by now. I can barely remember it myself. Something to do with an interplanetary incident involving an umbrella with mythical powers and the secret formula for a prize-winning ice cream.* Zaphod frowned. *Nope. The umbrella/ice-cream cock-up was a completely different god.*

Zaphod could see his onetime friend now, sitting at a round table with his back to the crowd. And what a back it was, broader than the average glacier, with knots of muscle the size of boulders and huge ridges of tension in the shoulders. His long red hair hung down in a shabby ponytail and the horns of his helmet were stained yellow by long nights spent in this foul air.

Zaphod thought he might open with a little joke, when the silence was filled with a sudden uproar of sharp, helium-squeaky voices.

"What? That's it?"

"That's the big move?"

"How many years have we been doing this? You haven't learned a thing."

Zaphod stepped quietly into the alcove, sneaking a peek under the crook of Thor's elbow.

The Thunder god was being harangued by a set of golden chessmen on the opposite side of the board. His own pieces were wooden and seemed cowed into silence.

The little golden knight was very belligerent. "Come on, Thor. We've talked about this. Never leave your king exposed. That's fundamental stuff. Bloody kindergarten."

"Watch it," Thor rumbled, and the sound sent shivers running along Zaphod's spine. That voice, like a sleepy tiger growling from the bottom of a well, no wonder the ladies couldn't get enough.

"Or what?" challenged the knight. "We are the ancient chess set of the Aesir. You can't kill us; we're as immortal as you are, and a lot older, I might add."

"I can melt you cheeky blighters down and make myself a little piss pot, how would you like that?"

The knight laughed. "You can threaten us all you want, Thunder Girl, it's still checkmate."

Thor drummed the table with his fingers. "You chaps set yourself up again. I have a little unfinished business to take care of." And in a fluid motion he spun round on his stool and sent the very large war hammer that had been resting across his thighs spinning toward Zaphod's head.

The hammer froze half an inch from Zaphod's nose, then backed him into a corner like a hound herding a sheep.

"Nice hammer action," squeaked Zaphod. "I knew you weren't going to kill me."

Thor turned his back. "Get out of here, Zaphod, before I let Mjöllnir do what he's wanted to do since that first accursed day we met."

Zaphod tried to move forward, but the hammer butted him back against the wall.

"Come on, old friend, I've come a long way to talk to you."

Thor grunted. "Do you even know why you're here? Do you even remember?"

"Not precisely," said Zaphod. "But in fairness there's a gigantic hammer hovering in front of my face, and you know how much people love my face, so I'm a little distracted."

Thor's shoulders slumped and he sighed. "People used to love my face. I was adored until you came along."

"You can be adored again, that's why I'm here, I remember now."

"Go away, Zaphod. Take your life and get out of mine. The only reason

I'm not killing you is that you can't fill the hole inside with bodies, that's something that I learned in circle time." He clicked his fingers and Mjöllnir sprang into his fist. "Now leave, Beeblebrox. I need to call my anger management sponsor."

"You can talk to us, buddy," said a golden rook.

Thor rubbed his shining head. "I know that. I know I will always have you guys."

"Should we kill the mortal?" asked a pawn. "Rookie can crawl down his throat and choke him."

"No. He's not worth it. But I do appreciate the offer."

Since Zaphod did not possess any better judgment, he didn't even hesitate for the half second it might have taken to ignore it. He climbed first onto a footrest, then a chair, then up the rungs of a wooden backrest, until finally he was standing on Thor's table.

The god of thunder sat hunched over his beer like someone was going to steal it. His eyes were downcast and his face was clumpy with emotion. There was a storm brewing. And in Thor's case this was not just a figure of speech; there was an actual miniature thundercloud boiling above his head, lightning bolts poking their heads from the vapor like lizards' tongues.

"Nice place," said Zaphod, perching on an ashtray. "It could do with a few big screens. Maybe a Jacuzzi. Sometimes I like bubbles with my beer."

Thor picked up his own beer and slammed it on the table so the head foamed over the rim.

"Knock yourself out," he said. "Bubbles and beer."

Zaphod took this suggestion, as he did most suggestions, at face value and quickly stripped down to his underwear, remembering just in time to pop out the batteries before vaulting into the tankard. He submerged himself to the larynx lump and spent several moments executing a three-armed backstroke while spouting amber spumes.

"I like this place," bubbled Zaphod. "It has nice . . . what do you call it?"

"Toilets?"

"No. The other thing."

"Ambience?"

"Yes. That's the one."

Thor growled, and the cloud over his head churned with electricity.

"This is the Well of Urd, Zaphod. Where the demigods and bottom-feeders hang out. I come here so no one will bother me."

"Bottom-feeders!" said a golden bishop at Zaphod's eye level. "That's a bit strong. You want to keep your temper in check, mate."

Zaphod's attention was diverted by the flash of dozens of tanned, toned legs and hundreds of white teeth.

"Look, I do believe that those athletic-looking ladies are waving at us."

Thor peered surreptitiously across the barroom through his fingers. A group of statuesque Valkyries were washing blood off their ZugaNugget chest plates in slow motion with barrels of water.

"Forget it, Zaphod. They're out of your reach."

Zaphod clambered from the tankard. "Out of my reach? What are you talking about?"

"I'm talking about practicalities. Look at those girls. You couldn't reach past their shin plates with a trampoline. Come to think of it, they're out of my reach too."

Zaphod shook himself like a hound. "Come on! This is not the Thunder God that I know. I remember when my friend Thor disappeared for a weekend with a certain Miss Eccentrica Gallumbits and she ended up paying him."

"Leave it, Zaphod."

Zaphod quick-stepped into his trousers. "This is just what you need, old friend. Me and you on a bender with a few beautiful ladies. I'm going over there."

"No."

"Oh, yes. I may be tiny, but I've got a certain je ne sais quoi."

"A certain what?"

"I don't know what," admitted Zaphod. "But that's never stopped me before."

Zaphod got a glint in his eyes that Thor knew well.

. . . .

Guide Note: This glint was nothing to do with baby gloonts. Rather, it was a look of reckless romanticism, which is similar to the one often found in the eyes of the narcissifish of Flargathon, who are prepared to inflate themselves far beyond the elastic tolerance of their scales in pursuit of a mate. The male narcissifish will cause himself to spectacularly explode if that is what it takes to impress the female. This is indeed an impressive feat, and in fairness to the female, she will appreciate the sacrifice and often be put out for several days before donning her best pearl necklace and heading back down to the reef.

Related Reading:

Love Will Tear Me Apart by Scaly Finnster (RIP)

· ·

"Get back here, Zaphod. I'm warning you!"

Zaphod strode across the table, skirting a spittoon. "This is what you need, Thor. You'll thank me later." He turned his high beams on the Valkyrie. "Hello, ladies. You may not know me yet, but you're gonna miss me tomorrow."

The Valkyrie's puzzled semi-smiles were distorted suddenly by a curved wall of glass. Zaphod thought for a moment that a sudden rush of Valkyrie lust had superheated the air, but then he realized that Thor had trapped him underneath a shot glass, which brought home quite force-fully just how tiny he was in this world. In fact, he seemed to be what-ever size Thor felt like making him. Zaphod was sure he would not have fit under the glass mere moments ago.

"Come on, Thor," he cried, his voice bouncing back on him.

Strange, thought Zaphod. *The acoustics in here make me sound whiney.*

"You're supposed to be my wingman. We're a team. Remember those antigrav dancers in Han Dold City?"

Thor dragged the glass toward him, brushing dangerously close to a complaining rook, and Zaphod was forced to dance along the table just to keep up.

"I've never been to Han Dold."

"Really? I could've sworn . . . Must have been some other Asgardian. I'm flashing on a red beard. Are you sure it wasn't you?"

"I'm sure, Zaphod. I'm a god; we don't forget stuff, which is part of the problem."

Thor lifted the glass, and as it went up, Zaphod fancied he felt him-self grow until he felt more like Thor's equal and less like his pet.

"Problem? What problem?"

Thor thumped the table, sending beer slopping across the planks.

"What problem? What zarking problem, Zaphod? Are you serious? Are you actually asking me that?"

Zaphod frowned. "That was a lot of questions. What problem? What *zarking* problem? . . . What was the third one again?"

"Oh, there's no point," said Thor, swallowing enough beer to drown a herd of mammaloids. "Zaphod Beeblebrox couldn't give two buffa-biscuits about anyone but himself."

This notion genuinely shocked Zaphod, as he believed that the act of sharing his personality with certain people was an act of love in itself.

"That is a terrible thing to say. I was your closest friend for years."

"Until you persuaded me to post that video on the Sub-Etha," said Thor bitterly. Over his head the robust little thundercloud turned flaccid, releasing a light drizzle. It didn't take a brainologist to work out the symbolism.

Zaphod found that he was now only a head shorter than the god. He plonked himself on a neighboring stool and thought he might offer a little joke to lighten the mood.

"I can never pass a nice stool," he said, drumming the table. Boom boom.

Thor patted Mjöllnir's head. "One more, Zaphod. One more."

"Can't we forget that video? It's in the past, and let me tell me something about the past. That's where it is, in the past. Remember that sentence about the past? That's in the past already. I can barely recall it, except that it contained the phrase *the past*. The past is made up of memories, which are made up of dead stuff that can't hurt you, like say a pointy stick could. Atoms and such. Quarks too, I shouldn't wonder. But wasted ones, all lying there doing nothing to anyone."

"Do you have a point, Zaphod? Or is that in the past too?"

Zaphod draped an arm around Thor's massive shoulders. "My point is that *maybe* I made a bad call with the video at the time, but ticket sales were down and we needed something to get your profile back onto the A-list. The candid video thing was all the rage, and in fairness some people did like it."

"Some people?" growled Thor. "Like that cult on the party ship? Those weirdos certainly lapped it up. Unfortunately the rest of the galaxy, the *normal* mortals, didn't fancy the idea of their god trussed up like a backstreet deviant."

Zaphod shrugged. "There was some backlash, I admit it."

Thor massaged his temples. "Backlash . . . Back . . . I know how shallow you are, Zaphod, but surely even you must have noticed the fallout. My dad blew up that entire planet where we filmed. My beautiful temples were all torn down. I went from number four favorite deity to number sixty-eight, behind Skaoi. Skaoi! The god of zarking snowshoes."

"Snowshoes are important. Come on, old friend, can't you blot the whole thing from your mind? I have."

Thor dragged eight fingers through his beard. "But that costume, Zaph? And those pom-pom squids."

Zaph, thought Zaphod. *I have him.*

"Miscalculations, perhaps."

"And the things I said," said Thor, shuddering.

"You were acting. Playing a role."

"Odin shat a kitten. Actually crapped out a live tiger cub. My own mother can't look at me. She told Loki that all she can see is that latex bustier."

"It was art; not everybody gets art."

"Do you know how many hits that clip has had? It's been the number one video on the entire Sub-Etha for the past five years."

"You said it. The *past* five years. That video is in the past. Next year there's going to be a new Thor video, one that puts you right back in the game, where you need to be."

"Oh really," said Thor glumly. "What have you got planned for an encore? Should I break out the Bounce-O-Jelly?"

Zaphod leaned in close. "Oh no, my friend. No setups. This is the real thing. An old school face-off. I have found the immortal who has your stolen ship and he's challenged you to a showdown."

Over Thor's head the thundercloud spewed forth a cluster of vibrant lightning bolts.

"Go on, Zaph," said the god. "I'm listening."

HILLMAN HUNTER

Hillman Hunter was more than just a stereotypical Irishman, he was a stereotype Paddy from a bygone era, as imagined by an expatriate Celt, with emerald-tinted spectacles and a head full of whiskey and nostalgia. Atop Hillman's head sat a nest of curly red hair, his face was scattershot with brass-penny freckles, his bowlegged walk suggested a youth spent in the saddle of a thoroughbred, and a gold crucifix nestled in the V of his open collar. With regards to diddle-ee-aye Irishness, Hillman Hunter was the whole bag of potatoes. When Hillman walked into a room, it took real effort not to greet him with a hearty begorrah, thank God for the soft day, and inquire after the health of U2. Even his voice conformed to expectations, and why wouldn't it, since Hillman had based his accent on that of Barry Fitzgerald, a twentieth-century Irish actor who was old when television was young. The rest of the hackneyed package was equally studied. Hillman had been dyeing his hair since it turned gray at age eighteen. He had become quite the wielder of curling tongs, and his fair complexion was freckled by long hours in the sun bed.

And the motive for all this subterfuge? Simple. Something his Nano had told him a long time ago.

"People buy comfort," she had said, slitting a pig's throat with a corn sickle. "If you make them comfortable, then they will buy *whatever* you are selling."

The combination of wisdom and arterial blood spray was irresistible and Hillman never forgot his grandmother's lesson.

Make people comfortable, then sell them whatever you like.

So the young Hillman transformed himself into the beloved actor and set about selling expensive stuff to rich folk. He hawked cars and yachts, before graduating to horses and overseas property. He was a natural. Gifted. People loved his oldy-worldy spiel and were charmed by his gifts of miniature diamond-encrusted shillelaghs. By the age of forty, Hillman was a millionaire on commission alone. By fifty, he was halfway to being a billionaire and was commuting between residences in a Jaguar and walking around his estate with the help of two biohybrid hips that were better than the old ones and would call the manufacturer themselves if they broke.

There was more money to be had, Hillman realized, if a sharp person could figure a way to round up all the rich folk in one place and keep them shelling out for stuff on a daily basis. But how to achieve this. The answer came to him in a flash of TV news headlines. Times were hard and the short-staffed Sisters of Occasional Succor were being forced to auction off one of the church's properties—specifically, the island of Innisfree.

Hillman got so excited that his left hip put in a call to Japan.

Innisfree. The island inspiration for Nano's all-time favorite movie: The Quiet Man. *The celluloid home of his own personality template. Fate was dropping him a wink, destiny was slipping him a brown bag, providence was beating him over the head with the hint hammer.*

Hillman outbid a shadow corporation, which could have been traced back to a leisure group on Barnard's Star by anyone with sub-etha capabilities, and purchased the island, complete with permission for a retreat that the nuns had been planning to build for weekend sherry parties.

And on that first misty morning, as he putted across Sligo's Lough Gill on an outboard-powered skiff, Hillman Hunter knew that he had found his crock of gold.

"Bejaysus," he'd sworn softly and in character. " 'Tis the promised land."

Instead of a retreat, Hillman built Ireland's most luxurious spa residence, and to ensure that he attracted only the richest patrons, he'd invented a religion and thrown that into the brochure too.

• •

Guide Note: Though Hillman Hunter had no way of knowing at the time, *Who's What Where* magazine had twinned him with Kar Paltonnle from Esflovian, another smooth talker who had managed to persuade several gated communities that it was simple logic that they would be chosen to survive when Armageddon arrived. His career was kick-started by extraordinary good fortune when Armageddon actually did visit Esflovian in the form of aggravated nuclear encounter therapy. Mr. Paltonnle earned quite a few piles of currency as cult leader for hire, but he made his real fortune in software, when he patented a program called God Guru, which allowed any would-be me-vangelist to type in a few facts about the community he intended to provide spiritual guidance for and the computer would think about it for a few minutes then spit out an appropriate catechism, complete with the desired number of commandments, justification for any prejudices, and a divine hierarchy. The deluxe package gave the buyer the option of registering himself as an official god using a legal loophole to bypass the usual three-miracle requirement.

. . . .

We shall be called Nanites, Hillman had decided without the aid of software. *And we shall believe in the existence of the planet Nano, which has been prepared for the faithful by God. And someday, these faithful will be collected in a spaceship and flown off, first class mind you, to the aforementioned planet, so it would be just as well if the faithful were all gathered in one place awaiting collection by the spaceman. Because otherwise they could miss the flight and either be stuck on Earth for the apocalypse, or have to take a later spaceship, where there might not be so much as a business-class seat left.*

Hillman had thrown the entire gospel together with a couple of locals one drunken weekend in Casey's Bar in Skibbereen. The only significant problem they encountered was the correct spelling of *apocalypse,* which Hillman had been hitherto convinced contained an x.

No one will fall for this, scoffed the tourist board. *Highly improbable.* Which of course almost guaranteed that the entire venture would be a huge success.

The Irish super-rich landed first, followed by the Russian and South African. Hillman cut a deal with some English royals for a bit of credibility, and the floodgates opened, which really annoyed Hillman, as those floodgates had been guaranteed for twenty years and he lost two thirds of his reclaimed beachfront.

Three years later, Hillman was head shepherd of his own little megawealthy flock, who were dying off at a rate of half a dozen per month and leaving sizeable chunks of the Earth's wealth to Hillman, so long as he promised to freeze their heads until the aliens arrived.

"It works because it's easy," Hillman often told Buff Orpington, his second-in-command. "You don't have to do anything to be a Nanite. Nothing gets cut off; nobody holds you underwater; no scripture, no guilt, no commandments. All you have to do is be rich and wear a Na-nite T-shirt on Tuesday to the lunch buffet. It couldn't be easier."

· ·

Guide Note: In point of fact, there was one religion that was even easier to belong to than Nanoism. The members of the Temple of Softly Softly, which was very popular in the Brequindan Mind Zones, realized that most of the Universe's major wars had been caused by zealots aggressively spreading their own religion, so they decided that their own method of baptism would be completely painless and could be performed without the knowledge of the baptized. All it took was for one of the faithful to point his smallest digit in your direction for five seconds and softly say *Beep,* then as far as they were concerned, you were a member of the church. Within five Brequindan years, the Temple of SS was the fastest-growing religion in the Mind Zones. Unfortunately, as there were no holy wars in the name of Softly Softly and not a single person was mutilated, the Temple was not recognized by the Galactic Council of Religions and did not qualify for charitable status and so disbanded in less than half a century.

· ·

Hillman Hunter was proud of what he had created and was in negotiations with an Australian minister to build a second compound, in the Antipodes. Then one Thursday afternoon as Hillman sat on the toilet playing a game of pool on his touch-screen phone, a video call came through from an out of area number. This intrigued Hillman, as his phone was not a video phone. He took the call, making sure to angle the screen away from his exposed knees, half-thinking that maybe Nano was upset with him for misusing her name and was on the blower from the afterlife.

A face appeared on Hillman's screen. It was not Nano's face. Not enough chins or bristles.

"Top of the morning to you," said Hillman brightly, taking comfort in his persona. "And who might you be?"

"I might be the answer to your prayers," said the face. "I might be the end of your rainbow."

Hillman used a catchall quote from his Nano library. "Oh really, O'Reilly?"

The face frowned. "What? What's that? Please speak clearly. Your accent seems to be confusing my fish, which never happened with the other monkeys."

Insane, thought Hillman, not unreasonably. *Utterly delusional.*

I agree, Hillers, whispered the voice of his dead grandmother.

"The shapes your mouth is making don't match the words coming out of it," noted Hillman. "And anyway, this phone doesn't do video."

"One of the marvels of me," explained the mysterious head in a vague manner Hillman would come to know well. "And the mouth-word thing is because you are without a Babel fish and so the ship is insta-translating. Okay? Get the picture, ape-man?"

Enough of this larking about, thought Hillman.

"Right-ee-o, mister," he said. "Well done on the phone hacking, but I must toddle off now. I have a religion to lead."

He hung up and stood to embark on the complicated fine motor task of buttoning the fly on his tweed trousers.

"Not so fast," said the head, which had now appeared, magnified, on the bathroom door. "It takes more than disconnecting to cut me off, Hillman Hunter."

Hillman dropped his trousers in shock, backpedaling onto the toilet.

"What in the name of all that's sacred?" he gasped. "How did you do that?"

The head scoffed. "This? You call this doing something? Here I am ready to hand you the ultimate power trip, and you think throwing a projection on a flat surface with a metal frame is doing something? Hillman, my friend, you are an ignorant pormwrangler. No offense."

Hillman hadn't been taking offense, until he heard the words *no offense.* A thought occurred to him.

"Are you from Nano? Is that it? Was I bloody right all the time?" Hillman had been selling the Nano line for so long that sometimes he half-sold himself.

The head laughed so hard that he was forced to breathe into a paper bag.

"No, you weren't right, stupid monkey. There is no planet Nano." And then his mouth twitched in a sly grin. "Not yet, there isn't."

"Go on," said Hillman, his nose for a deal completely overriding his profound skepticism.

"I have been looking for an investment on your planet, which won't be around for long, by the way. The Sub-Etha spat out this little compound, and it seems to me that all your elderly rich people would fork over every gold coin they possessed if someone could actually take them to Nano before the Earth explodes. And once they arrived at the mythical Nano, then they would surely need a supreme leader."

Supreme leader, thought Hillman, and then: *This is such a crock of cow shite.*

Suddenly his Nano's voice whispered to him, as it often did when his life was at an important crossroads.

Take heed, Hillers. This fool can do more for you than he knows. The apoxy-lips is coming and it's time to be off this planet.

I knew there was an x, thought Hillman. Aloud, he said: "It would take one bejaysus of a convincing argument for this scam to work."

The face's grin grew a couple of incisors wider. "How about a big spaceship just appearing out of thin air? Do you think that would persuade the other monkeys?"

Hillman let the monkey comment pass, this was business, after all. "Got any robots?"

"I can do better than that," said Zaphod Beeblebrox, for of course it was he. "I can get you a floating head."

NANO

So now Hillman Hunter was the big boss on the planetoid, presiding over eighty-seven elderly rich people and their staff. He was wealthy and powerful but never seemed to have a minute to himself to enjoy it. Retired rich folk, he was quickly finding out, were the most demanding people in the Galaxy. Nothing was ever good enough or ready fast enough. It didn't help that the Magrathean planet builders were dawdling over the snag list, making a big fuss over every detail as if no one had told them that the houses would be needing roofs or floors.

"You want windows too?" the foreman had said, eyebrows almost taking flight in shock. "You should've said that six months ago. My boys would've put them in had we only known. If you want windows now, we have to hold off on the plumbers, who are already on-site by the way. And that won't please the painters, who are in after the plumbers. And some of the painters are married to the plumbers, which will cause tension in the household. And we're short on workplace masseuses at the moment, so there's going to be some nasty lactic acid buildup in some of my boys' shoulders. At the end of the day, it's your money and your decision. All I'm saying is that you should have said something earlier when it was convenient, instead of throwing the entire project into financial free fall with your wild demands."

• •

Guide Note: In all of recorded history, there is only one confirmed instance of a builder acceding to a change in the plans without lapsing into histrionics. This happened in the case of Mr. Carmen Ghettim, a Betelgeusean auto dealer who sent plan revisions back in time to inform the builder of the changes before the project started. It should be pointed out that Mr. Ghettim had the note delivered by a particularly vicious lantern-jawed terrier.

• •

When he wasn't negotiating with builders, Hillman spent his time trying to find a god suitable to rule the planet, a task which was not proving as enjoyable as he had envisaged. Hillman had imagined himself engaging in philosophical conversations on the nature of happiness, or being wowed by awesome displays of godly power. Instead he had been forced to grind his way through a sludge of padded résumés in which demigods tried to make themselves sound a lot more significant than they actually were.

Hillman quickly realized that when a god put in a line on page two about taking a sabbatical for divine contemplation, that actually meant that he had been unemployed for the past ten thousand years. When a god claimed to have gradual meteorological influence, it simply meant that he looked up the weather forecast and then claimed to be responsible for whatever weather happened. And if a god was making a big deal out of his omnipresence, there was a very good chance that he had a twin brother floating around somewhere.

Dross, thought Hillman dolefully. *Dross and steamers. Not one nugget of quality.*

He was just consigning the latest batch of applications to his desk incinerator when Buff Orpington stuck his head around the door.

"Yep, Buff. Are we set?"

Buff's jowly face wobbled. "All ready, Hillman. We're of a mind to kick some ass."

Hillman's mood was not improved by these fighting words.

Kick some ass? Most of the colonists can barely move faster than a slow jog. Any asses they're going to kick would have to be stationary, soft, and low-slung.

The asses in question were the drooping buttocks of Nano's western colonists, who had kidnapped Cong's French chef for religious reasons. The reason being that they were Tyromancers who firmly believed in divination through the medium of semi-congealed cheese, and Jean Claude's signature dish was a heavenly four-cheese quiche with capers and smoked salmon. The Tyromancers were fine with the capers and salmon, but had decided that the cheesy filling was heresy.

The Magratheans warned me things like this might happen, Hillman realized dolefully. *Moving planet is the most traumatic thing that can happen to a being, other than being slathered in barbecue sauce and then dropped into a pit with the Bugblatter Beast of Traal, whatever that is. People become fanatical about what they left behind. This Tyromancy started out as a bit of a hobby on Earth but has become a huge obsession on Nano. Aseed Preflux has managed to convert his entire settlement.*

Hillman followed Buff outside, and it occurred to him that from the rear Buff looked like a grizzly bear squashed into plaid trousers and a windbreaker. A stout hairball of a man whose arm hair actually swished in the wind.

In the town square, the troops were lined up ready for inspection, and the line was even worse than Hillman had imagined. There were no staff left, not a single one.

He rounded on Buff Orpington. "Where are the personal trainers?"

"Gone."

"Not Lewis?"

"All of them."

"And the beauty therapists?"

"We haven't seen a beauty therapist for nearly a week. My Cristelle hasn't had a manicure in ten days; she's at her wit's end."

Hillman was shocked. "Ten days! That's barbaric. Why didn't someone tell me?"

"You were busy with the interviews. This place is falling apart, Hillman. We have barely half a dozen chefs left for the entire town. People are being forced to . . . ," Buff took a deep breath to steady himself, ". . . cook for themselves."

Hillman's Irish temper flared. "We did not pay several enormous fortunes to cook for ourselves. What about contracts? These people all signed contracts."

Buckeye Brown, a Texan oilman, piped up from the line. "My guy, Kiko, told me to stick my contract where the sun don't shine. He said that this is a new world and we should all be equal. He said we were treating the servants like slaves."

Hillman was appalled. This was what happened without a divinely ordained chain of command.

"This has got to end. First we rebuff the invaders, then we get our staff back from the wild for their own good. How can young, fit people with no business skills hope to survive on this verdant new world, bejaysus?" The *bejaysus* was almost an afterthought. Hillman was so agitated that he nearly forgot who he was pretending to be.

Buckeye glanced gloomily at the toes of his Ferragamo alligator moccasins, which he was almost certain would scuff in the wild.

"You want us to go into the wild? My daddy told me about it, but I never done been there."

You never done been to school neither, thought Hillman. "We're not going into the wild, Mr. Brown. Sure that's a game for the young people. No, we'll tempt those rascals back with premium plus apartments."

Buff was horrified. "Not lagoon-view premium plus?"

"If necessary."

"With twenty-four-hour concierge service?"

"I doubt it. The concierge's team jumped ship a month ago. We'll have to give the concierges apartments. Maybe gym memberships too."

"But the concierges can't service themselves," wailed Buff. "That's just insanity. Has the world gone mad entirely?"

Like all good salesmen, Hillman was in quick with the solution. "Robots, laddie. We'll get robots. I hear the Sirius corporation has service androids with genuine people personalities. It's perfect, what could go wrong?"

"I suppose that might work," said Buff, mollified. "Or maybe we could import aliens who actually enjoy laboring in the sun. They could pay us. You could look it up on your Hitchhiker book."

"I will do that, as soon as we send these jokers packing."

Hillman looked around John Wayne Square and wondered how things had gone wrong so quickly. Six months ago this plaza had been a stunning centerpiece for their new society, and now there were weeds sprouting through the flagstones and strange blue bugs eating holes in the glass.

We need a god. And fast.

Buckeye Brown cleared his throat. "How do we even know the Tyromancers will mount an offensive *today*?"

Buff addressed that one, happy to have solid information to relay. He spread his legs, bouncing slightly on the balls of his feet as though he were about to heft a barbell. "It's the only day they can come. Monday through Wednesday is cheese making. Friday is the actual reading of the cheese. Saturday and Sunday are for contemplation of the message in the cheese. Thursday is the only day when secular activities are permitted."

"And we know this how?"

"Oh, Aseed subbed over a mail. In case any of us want to join up. Nice presentation, I have to say. A lot of floating cheese icons. Apparently if we don't join up, then we bring Edamnation on the entire planet."

Hillman's jaw flapped for a moment, then: "Edamnation? You're not serious."

Buff grinned. "Serious as a dry well, Hillman." He pulled a crumpled missal from his pocket. "Ah . . . here it is. *The day of Edamnation shall be visited upon the nonbelievers in a huge and terrifying form, possibly cheese-related, but any huge and terrifying form can be understood to have emanated from the cheese.*"

Hillman was getting pretty cheesed off with the word *cheese*.

"Huge and terrifying, bejaysus. Who writes this junk?"

"Aseed does. The First Gospel of Tyromancy, he's calling it."

"That jumped-up little ginger fartbollix," swore Hillman. "Who does he think he is?"

This question brought forth a determined round of not answering from the assembled troops, as Aseed was pretty much identical to Hillman, apart from some styling and sartorial issues. And it appeared that Hillman was the only one who didn't recognize this.

Luckily they were spared any embarrassment when Buff's phone jingled in his pocket.

"Oh, my phone. What a pity, I was just about to answer that question about who Aseed thinks he is, but now my phone is ringing so I better answer that and not actually answer the question. A real shame."

He fumbled the cell phone from his pocket and slid it open. "Yeah? You sure? Okay. We're on the way." Buff closed his phone then held it aloft with great melodrama. "The Tyromancers approach."

"What? Really? Who was that?"

"It was Silkie. She's on lookout from the coffee shop in Book Barn."

Book Barn was the mall's highest building, with a glass-walled coffee shop on the third floor. From there a lookout could keep an eye on the main road while browsing the latest releases. Silkie Bantam usually volunteered for the lookout's job because she was an avid horror book fan and could get through a few ghoulish chapters while she watched.

"How did she sound?"

"Pissed off. She had to make her own coffee."

Hillman felt everything slipping away from him. *The Book Barn people too.* This Tyromancer squabble had to end today.

"Righto, me laddies," he said, stamping a foot to pump himself up. "How are we for weapons?"

This was Buff's domain. He'd been quite the Kirk Douglas fan back on Earth and so had been put in charge of the weaponry.

"Not too bad," he said, leading the ragtag brigade to the foot of the plaza's Sean the Boxer statue. Their tools of battle were laid out on the plinth.

"It's mostly gardening stuff," admitted Buff. "This strimmer has nice weight to it and could give a person a nasty cut. We have a couple of rakes for poking and tripping, that kind of thing. I myself provided this nine iron, not my premium club obviously, but it's got a good swing. Pretty dangerous, in the right hands."

Even though he himself had signed the agreement forbidding the transport of actual mechanical weapons from Earth, Hillman had hoped for a slightly more robust arsenal.

"This is great!" he said with hollow enthusiasm. "Let's show these feckers how the men of Cong can fight." He selected the strimmer and was about to press the power button when Buff tapped his elbow.

"Better hold off on that until we need it. The charge is pretty low."

"I see."

"Usually José does all that, but he ran off with one of your maids."

"Right. Fine. Well, we can work with what we have."

They strolled in a loose group toward the main gate. The compound had been designed along the lines of the original Innisfree, with a mall added in on the far side of the lagoon. There were pootle-tink birds standing in the shallow waters, some reading but most working on their tans and bemoaning the fact that a bird's drive disappeared so quickly when someone handed it a lovely crocogator-free lagoon.

. . . .

Guide Note: The pootle-tink birds have long been victims of their own attractiveness, that and relentless inbreeding. The pootle-tinks were, for centuries, respected throughout the Galaxy as weavers of fine feather tapestries, until a certain Galactic Council trade ambassador proclaimed their plumage to be exquisitely beautiful and a must for all fashionable lagoons. This effectively spelled the end for the pootle-tink way of life, as the culture vultures moved in and began to aggressively breed and cull the pootle-tinks in the quest for the perfect plumage, which could then be shipped across the Galaxy to brighten some diplomat's water feature. The pootle-tinks did not put up much of a fight, as they are vain creatures who enjoy being stared at. Culture vultures on the other hand do not have a narcissistic feather in their wings and like to pass the time screwing over other species then spending their profits on booze and sugary desserts. *We are like opposite ends of the same spectrum,* a culture vulture once remarked to a pootle-tink, to which the pootle-tink replied, *Yes, so long as one end of the spectrum is made of crap and that's the end you're at.*

●●

"I have a thesis due in two months," one pootle-tink lisped to a friend, "and I haven't even started my research."

Another spotted Buff on the bridge. "Hey, hey, Buffy. How's the swing coming?"

"Not bad, Perko. Not too bad at all. You finished writing that book yet?"

Perko rolled his eyes. "It's all in my head, Buff. I just need to park my backside on a chair and start typing, you know what I mean?"

"I know exactly what you mean," said Buff, who had no idea what the bird was talking about but was in a mood for positive statements.

The fighting men of Cong followed Hillman across the asphalt to the main gate, which their leader was forced to crank open with a winch.

"One of us should have learned the gate code," Hillman said and huffed as he labored. "This is ridiculous. The Magratheans have subbed over the backup codes, but there are hundreds of them. Electronic gates, cash registers, sub-etha vision. Nothing works without the codes."

Once the gate was open enough to slip through, the men stood at the checkpoint and gazed across the fuzzy humps of purple grass to the tropical forest that divided the two compounds. The tree branches criss-crossed densely and hung heavy with fruit and wildlife, apart from a half-elliptic cylinder-shaped tunnel that had been laser bored through to the other side.

Hillman took out his phone and zoomed in on the tunnel mouth.

"I see the misguided feckers," he snorted. "Coming over on golf carts. Jaysus, it's hardly the light brigade, now is it?"

The assembled band laughed heartily as they had seen other warriors doing in war movies, then used their phones to zoom in on the approaching convoy.

"I count ten," said Buckeye, who had the most expensive phone, with the best lens. "There are only eight of us."

"Yes, but we're on top of a hill," countered Hillman.

"So?"

"So everyone knows being up a hill is vital . . . feckin' *vital*, mind, in these situations."

Buckeye was miffed. "I didn't know it. So that's not everyone, is it?"

"Do you know it now?"

"I suppose so."

"Well that is everyone then, isn't it?"

Hillman took no joy from his victory in this little verbal spat. This was supposed to be a tranquil settlement. There were not supposed to be any spats.

"I don't see what's so good about this hill," said Buckeye sulkily. "Some of us are wearing loafers. And there are a lot of sharp stones out here. The soles on these things are like paper."

"I wore my golf shoes," said Buff with a bloodthirsty grin. "So I can stomp on these bastards. Mash their brains."

. . . .

Guide Note: Buff Orpington happened to be a direct descendant of Sigurd, the noble Viking warrior. Mr. Orpington was not aware of this; all he knew was that he often added honey to his beer and fantasized about chopping his wife's pigtails off with an axe. He would later have his race memories extracted by a hybrid Babel fish and take to wearing sealskin leggings on the golf course.

. . . .

Hillman realized then how quickly the coming confrontation could get out of hand. "Hold up there, boyo. There'll be no brain mashing. For one thing, the theater nurses are shacked up with a couple of caddies in the fifteenth bunker, and for another, we are not working-class here. No fighting unless absolutely necessary."

"Okay, Hillman," said Buff, chastened. "What if they insult us? Or maybe our grandparents?"

Hillman's cheeks lost their usual rosy hue. "If anyone insults my Na . . . eh . . . grandmother, then I crack his skull."

The Nanites were not the only ones watching the highway. A small group of lithe, hungry carnivores squatted in the reeds, strong fingers curled, tendons tight in anticipation of the attack. One, a hulking creature, raised a crust of bread to his mouth, tearing it with strong teeth, only to have it grabbed from his hand by the pack's leader.

"What do you think you're doing?" asked the leader, who was called Lewis Tydfil.

"I need energy," replied his subordinate, who only used one name: Pex.

"But that's bread."

"So?"

"Carbohydrates after three P.M.? Are you insane?"

"It's just one crust. That's all."

Tydfil held up the bread for all the personal trainers and beauticians to see. "One crust. That's all it is. Do you know how many spoons of sugar there are in this one crust? Do any of you know?"

"Two," ventured Pex.

"Seven!" shrieked Tydfil. "Seven. You eat this after three and you might as well shove a sugar pump up your arse."

"Come on, Lewis."

"Fifty push-ups, on your knuckles. Go."

Pex scowled. "I was hungry. I'm fed up of picking fruit from the trees; I want something freshly baked or cooked."

"That's why we're here. Now get going on those push-ups."

Pex caught the eye of a manicurist that he'd taken a fancy to. Her nails looked like they had been dipped first in blood, then diamonds. He didn't really like the idea of humiliating himself in front of her.

"No, Tydfil. Go hump yourself. Who made you leader?"

Lewis Tydfil drew himself up to his full height, bending one knee to show off his gastrocnemius. "I made myself leader on account of my qualifications."

"I have qualifications."

"You're a *fitness instructor*," said Tydfil in a tone usually associated with murderous dictators, serial killers, or ex-girlfriends' handsome boyfriends. "Any moron can spend a weekend in a crappy gym and become a *fitness instructor*."

"I have a diploma."

"I have a degree," thundered Tydfil.

"I specialize in kettlebells."

Tydfil trumped him again. "I am an expert in the Kinesis Wall *and* I can take GP referrals."

Pex drew a rolled-up magazine from the front of his shorts, which was a bit of a letdown for the manicurist.

"I did a *Men's Health* pictorial. Look, there's me on the front."

Tydfil put the final nail in his rival's coffin. "I was the fitness advisor on a reality show. We had soap stars!"

There was no recovering from that. Pex dropped to his knuckles and began counting off the push-ups in sets of ten.

"Good," said Tydfil. "Now, the rest of you, stay hydrated and do your stretches. They will be there soon." He checked a few of his comrades. "We're fading here. Some camouflage please."

Two beauticians, with spray-tan tanks strapped to their backs, painted stripes along the trainers' limbs.

A power walker emerged from the trees.

"They're coming down the highway. Jean Claude is in the last cart."

"Okay, everyone," said Lewis Tydfil. "This is it. All we need to do is snatch Jean Claude and it's whole-wheat crepes for everyone. Let's warm up with a slow jog and then charge on my signal."

"What is your signal?" asked Pex, from the high point of a push-up.

"I will shoot you in the head with my starter's pistol."

"What?"

"Or maybe I will just say *charge*. Any more questions?"

Pex's chin dipped low to the ground. "Nope. I got it."

Tydfil's smile was wide and perfect. "Good. Now, come on, everybody, lift those knees. Push it out."

The personal trainers seemed to come out of nowhere, ripping into the last golf cart.

"What the . . . ," yelped Buckeye. "Did you see that? Did everyone see what happened?"

No one replied; everyone was too focused on the drama unfolding on the asphalt. The attack was not precise, but it was lightning-fast and furious. A group of tanned and toned athletes exploded from the planted border, swarming all over the cart that held Jean Claude. In a flurry of biceps, they hustled the cart to the curb, tipping it off the road and down the verge. Then, in a flash of leotard and hair gel, they were gone. The driver never even had the chance to press the Emergency Aid panic button hanging from a lanyard around his neck. The only evidence of the assault was a settling dust cloud and the trailing curses of a stocky trainer who had not warmed up properly. It was several moments before the rest of the convoy even noticed that their rearguard was missing.

"Jaysus," whispered Hillman, meaning it for once. "That was . . . I can't believe it. I didn't know humans could move that fast."

Buff, who had been to a talk about personal training once, nodded sagely. "Yep. That's trainers for you. Extremely well moisturized."

"They've turned savage," croaked Buckeye. "Nobody is safe. Do you think we could stop one of those with a strimmer? We're doomed! Doomed!"

It was time for some leadership. "Pull yourselves together, you crowd of chickens," snapped Hillman. "We still have the Tyromancers to deal with."

It was true. The Tyromancers had not turned back; if anything they had increased their speed toward the Nanites' compound. In all probability they were fleeing the scene of the ambush in case the trainers decided to strike again.

"Should we run down the hill?"

"Just forget about the bloody hill," Hillman ordered, then remembered that Buckeye was technically a customer. "Don't worry about the hill, sir. Just follow my lead."

"And crush their Zarking skulls?"

"*Zarking*, Buff? What the hell is Zarking?"

"Just a word I picked up from one of the merchants at the spaceport."

"Keep it to yourself, especially in front of the ladies."

Buff shrugged. "No problem. I wish I had a sword in my hand now. A big Zarker . . . sorry . . . a big two-hander with sheepskin on the handle. If I had a sword like that, I'd die happy and go straight to heaven."

Buckeye tugged at his sleeve, a nervous tell. "When this is all over, you need to talk to my wife, the town psychiatrist, if we can tempt her back from the beach. She's shacked up with a young lifeguard. According to her, it's a clear case of projected reverse Oedipus. I tried everything, you know, took a course of bastard pills so she could have the good guy or the bad guy."

"Hopefully I won't live beyond today's glorious battle," said Buff, blithely ignoring Buckeye's tale of woe.

The Tyromancers' golf carts putted along Nano's only dual carriageway, a clear example of future-proof overkill, and proceeded steadily up the hill to the compound.

"You might be better off," muttered Buckeye.

Although he later claimed it to be accidental, at that precise moment the toe of Buff's golf shoe nudged Buckeye Brown's loafer, scuffing it badly.

* *

Guide Note: This relatively innocuous incident would lead to a tit-for-tat vendetta that was to escalate over the centuries, culminating in the destruction of three planets, eighteen loafer-class battle cruisers and a small hotel on a neutral world. On the positive side there was a forbidden love affair between two younger members of the families which was later turned into a movie, a series of books, and a moderately successful stage play.

Related Reading:

Brown & Orpington: A New Breed by Bandera Brown-Orpington

* *

The Tyromancers putted up the hill in a pretty cool semicircle formation that died a death when driver number four neglected to put on his brake and rolled back down the slope, crashing eventually into the foot of a bantally tree, which, luckily for the driver, was hibernating or it would definitely have put a hex on him.

"Nice entrance," sneered Buff, swinging the nine iron nonchalantly.

Aseed Preflux stepped from the first cart, spent a moment broadcasting *you're an idiot* eye beams down at the stumped driver, then turned his attention to the Nanites.

It was unnerving to see how much he looked like Hillman, right down to the widow's peak and pointed chin, like an infernal leprechaun. In fact, if the Nanites had looked a bit closer at their nemeses, they might have noticed that there were several doppelgangers in the group.

"The Cheese told me you would say that about our entrance," said Aseed.

"A pity the *cheese* didn't mention anything about that ambush down the road, isn't it, boyo?" said Hillman quickly. His men rewarded the quip with a six on the laughter scale, one being a gentle chuckle and ten being uncontrollable guffaws. Hillman's joke clearly rated no more than a four.

"Do not mock the Cheese!" said Aseed furiously. "You will bring Edamnation down on us all!"

Buff took a bead on Aseed's forehead with the nine. "You're about to be cream cheese."

More laughter. A solid eight.

Red spots bloomed on Aseed Preflux's cheeks. "Yeah, go on. Do all the cheese jokes. It's so easy, isn't it?"

"Easy singles," muttered Buckeye.

"Yes. That too. Let's get them all out of the way so we can get down to business."

Aseed's men bunched threateningly behind him, looking as warlike as it was possible to look when armed with cheese-related instruments.

"What is that?" asked Hillman, pointing to one wooden implement. "Is that for cleaning drains?"

"It is a churn plunger! As you well know!"

"How would I know that, laddie? I have someone to make my cheese before I put it on a cracker."

"Blasphemer!" shrilled Aseed, and his friends took up the cry.

"Listen to that din," said Buff. "Oh, din."

"What?"

"Nothing, Hillman. Why don't you let me take out these pansies? There are only eight of them left."

"Not yet, Buff. Maybe our friends don't want to fight. Maybe they've come to return Jean Claude to us."

"We have not!" shouted Aseed, and then he ran out of bluster. "Actually, we don't have him anymore. Those trainers took him, off to their beach settlement, I imagine."

"We saw. So you left one of the faithful in the ditch."

Aseed made a triangle with his forefingers and thumbs, which he then touched to his forehead. "The Cheese demands sacrifices," he said.

The others copied his action.

"Appease the Cheese," they intoned with faces so solemn they could have hired them out to an advertising agency as the *before* pictures in a *Blam-O-Brain, Antidepressant for the Whole Family* campaign.

Hillman and the Nanites quickly made the *after* faces, laughing so hard that two of them farted.

"Appease the cheese," spluttered Hillman. "Just when I think you can't get any nuttier."

Aseed sighed. "So, you're not going to join us?"

"No. We're not. Why don't you join us, Preflux? Just go easy on the cheese stuff. We're all laid back here. And together we could outwit the staff."

"No. All must bow down to the Cheese."

"Appease the Cheese."

It was Hillman's turn to sigh. "I suppose we have to fight then."

"It is the only way. But no hitting in the face."

"Of course not. We're not animals. And no goolies."

"We are forbidden to make contact with the goolies of nonbelievers, except through gloves of curd, which we haven't managed to fabricate yet."

"So no face, no goolies."

Buff was being held back by an invisible bungee. "Come on, let's just go."

"One more thing," said Aseed. "I will be fighting, as will my disciples, with my churning hand in my pocket, so in the spirit of fair play . . ."

"So one-handed, no face, no goolies?"

"Agreed. If we win, then you will join our happy group; if you win, then we keep coming back until we win."

Hillman closed his eyes and listened for the voice of his Nano.

What should I do, Nano?

The answer was immediate: *Batter this crowd of steamers, Hillers. Give them a beating they won't forget.*

Righto, Nano, righto.

Aloud he said, "Okay, Buff, do your worst."

Buff Orpington's grin seemed to reveal more teeth than were usually found in a human mouth.

"Aaaarghhh!" he cried, beating his chest like a bear, images of burning monasteries flashing behind his eyes. "Death to the Tyromancers!"

"Or at least a sound thrashing," said Hillman, thumbing the strimmer's power button.

"No goolies," squealed Aseed as the mammoth Buff Orpington bore down on him. "No gooooolies."

Then an enormous cheese wheel appeared in the sky, revolving over the combatants' heads, emitting an ominous hum. This sudden and most unexpected apparition shifted the crowd's focus faster than the appearance of Eccentrica Gallumbits wearing a neon T-shirt flashing the slogan *Freebie Friday* would shift the focus of the crowd at a VirginNerd convention on a Friday. Even Buff Orpington's battle spasm drained from his skull, leaving a mist of disbelief behind it.

"It can't be!" he said. "I don't believe it."

Aseed Preflux turned paler than a slice of double cream cheddar.

"Edamnation!" he howled, touching his fingers to his forehead. "You have brought it upon us, Hillman Hunter!"

Hillman powered down the strimmer. "What? No. Surely not. This can't be right. Seriously?"

Aseed and his band of Tyromancers, triangling furiously, backed away from the compound wall.

"We won't die for your sins, Hunter. Face the wrath of the Wheel alone."

The Tyromancers turned on their heels and ran, which is not easy when bowing and making the sign of the Cheese, with the result that more than half their number took tumbles into the overgrown borders before eventually scrambling into the golf carts and whining back the way they came as fast as the electric motors would permit, quite prepared to run the personal trainer gauntlet. If the Cheese wanted to catch and smite them, it shouldn't have been a problem. But it seemed as though the Cheese was quite content to hover imperiously above the Nanites.

"What do you think?" asked Hillman, shooting the words out of the side of his mouth toward Buff.

Buff shrugged his meaty shoulders. "I'm not sure. Gouda maybe, or cheddar."

The Cheese decided that it had had enough of being a cheese and so for a change became a rolling eye, which was one of its favorites.

Hillman sighed massively, and his entire body relaxed as though his bones had jellified. "Of course. I should have known."

The enormous eye rolled madly then turned into a view-screen which seemed to be playing some kind of reality show featuring a behemoth called Pinky. Pinky ran amok for a few seconds then the screen exploded in a cloud of small furry balls with teeth. Teeth that ate their own fur to reveal a glowing white spaceship underneath. A spaceship so cool that it made other cool spaceships such as the *Sirius All-Space Off-Worlder* look about as cool as a cluster of pimples on the nose of a forty-year-old man who was riding a bicycle with stabilizers around his office during a presentation on more efficient ways to unblock sewage pipes.

• •

Guide Note: This analogy works pretty well just about everywhere, except in the town of Shank, near the famous Infinity Spools of Allosimanius Syneca. Shank is inhabited by Pshawrians, who are taught from infancy to defy expectations. In fact, anyone who meets expectations is given three chances and then hurled from the finger-shaped peaks of the Mooncliffs. In actuality, people rarely get three chances, because that's what they expect. In Shank, a spotty forty-year-old man on a stabilized bike would be the epitome of unexpected coolness. The fact that the presentation was about sewage pipes would be seen as a nice touch, seeing as g on Allosimanius Syneca is only 1.2 meters per second squared and waste matter simply floats off into space.

• •

The gleaming white spaceship wobbled a bit then solidified with a noise like a huge slice of lemon colliding with a giant gold brick. A section of the fuselage fizzled like a glass of soda then disappeared altogether, revealing a tall helmeted figure whose aura seemed to contain a choir of angels singing "Thor" in divine harmony.

"Hallelujah," whispered Hillman.

Buff Orpington sank to his knees, weeping.

CHAPTER 9

THE TANNGRISNIR

Bowerick Wowbagger's longship slipped out of dark space like an eel from a reef's shadowy depths, its engines emitting jets of exotic blue flame that crystallized when they encountered real space. Inside the *Tanngrisnir* there was not a single passenger who had not been substantially altered by the journey.

This was partly the fault of the space itself, as the sleeve of dark matter is largely an emotional construct and can serve as an accelerant for feelings that might otherwise have taken years to develop. For a being of the light, gazing even for a moment into the heart of dark space has an effect equivalent to a dozen near-death experiences. It's the Universe's way of telling you to get on with your life. Which is a good thing if the feeling budding in a person's heart is a good feeling.

As the ship backed into Nano's atmosphere then swung around in a lazy meander toward the larger of two settlements, scanning every atom of the planet as it did so, the passengers inside its amorphous hull were reeling with conflicting emotions that seemed to push their hearts against their ribs and swell their brains to bursting.

TRILLIAN

Could I love him? Could I? Is it possible that after all this time I can just bump into a man in the middle of a planetary destruction and fall for him?

But he's not a man, is he? Christ, girl, you don't even know what he is. You don't have the first clue about this Wowbagger guy or his physiology.

What a hoot that would be on the wedding night. Wouldn't Mother's ghost laugh then if your brand-new husband expected you to lay a few eggs on the carpet for him to fertilize?

Ugh. No, it's too much, I couldn't. I can't.

Why can't you? You gave everything up for Zaphod and you certainly didn't love him. He was interesting, yes, but you didn't love him. And now you have a chance to be happy and you're turning up your nose.

My nose. Arthur loved my nose. Maybe there's still a chance for Arthur and me . . . It would certainly be tidy.

You don't love Arthur. You never did, and anyway he's still utterly besotted with Fenchurch.

And what about Random? She needs you now. You left her once before, remember? You promised that this life would be for your daughter.

But will denying my own happiness make my child happy?

That's the way it generally works, isn't it?

But I love him. I love him, Mum!

Who are you calling Mum? Get a grip on yourself, girl.

I can love two people, can't I? That's allowed.

Maybe, but Random comes first.

RANDOM

Put me in a bloody tube, will they? I'll show them. Mr. Immortal thinks he's immortal, does he? Maybe he should browse the Sub-Etha a little more. Maybe, if his computer wasn't so busy making goo-goo eyes at my dad, it would have picked up on a very remote article on a very remote site that tells the story of Pyntolaga, the Six-fingered Immortal of Santraginus, who was cursed with immortality by an irradiated electronic-muscle-stimulation slimming belt, and how he was eventually killed.

So, Bowerick Wowbagger wants to die, does he? Well, what sort of an ingrate would I be if I didn't help him on his way?

small voice: You were a politician. A loving wife. The President of the Galaxy . . . Now you're planning to help this person get himself killed?

I lost my husband and my job and my future. It's time to start thinking about me.

small voice: Fair enough. Kill him then.

BOWERICK WOWBAGGER

Could it be love? Could it?

Come on, Bow Wow, that's the dark matter talking.

No. I can handle my dark matter. I've been living in this ship for years. I think I love this woman. You see it all the time, in nearly every single movie I have ever watched. People making instant connections, love at first sight, the thunderbolt.

This is not a movie. You should tune into a news channel once in a while, see how many love thunderbolts are featured.

It *is* love. It could be. Why shouldn't it be? After all this time, don't I deserve something?

You deserve to die. Isn't that what you've longed for all these years?

Yes, but only because there was nothing for me. Nothing but a computer on a stolen ship. Now there is something. Someone.

Don't lose focus here. You have a real shot at getting yourself killed. Don't blow it all over a mortal.

I was mortal once. They're not so bad.

Oh, really? Who are you and what have you done with the real Bow Wowbagger? Because correct me if I'm wrong, but didn't we spend the last several thousand years insulting mortals? Don't you have a complete set of *The Total Tosser's Thesaurus*?

Yes, but . . .

And . . . *And* haven't you claimed to be in love before?

Yes, but that was different. I thought it was love, but I see now it was just an absence of disgust. Trillian has qualities.

Trillian. If that is her real name.

Now you're just nitpicking.

All I know is that for the first time in I don't know how long you have a chance to be dead. Not a big chance, granted. But if that fool, Beeblebrox, comes through, then there is *a* chance at least. Are you prepared to risk all that because you've taken a fancy to a mortal?

Yes. If she will have me, I'll risk it all. If not, back to Plan A.

Which is?

Insult everyone on the planet and try to get myself killed.

Amen to that.

ARTHUR

This is ridiculous. I have spent most of this incredible journey talking to the hardware.

Actually, you've been talking to yourself. The computer dips into your memories and compiles appropriate responses from previous conversations. If you listen carefully, you might hear the blip where the sentences have been spliced together.

I know. I know. But it's hard to tear oneself away. I lost Fenchurch once and it nearly killed me. Even now after all this time I still think about her constantly.

All this time? It hasn't been that long.

I am counting my virtual life. I spent a lot of time on that beach drawing pictures of Fenchurch.

I know. They were awful. We need to move on.

You mean until the Vogons destroy this new planet?

Or until I save it. I have saved planets before, you know.

I think we're on our last life there, mate. How many more destroyed worlds can we possibly survive? None, that's how many.

Wowbagger can shoo the Vogons. Or Thor, whoever wins. There's an entire universe out there and we are a part of it. I don't want to spend the rest of our life playing mental footsie with a box of capacitors and chips.

I know. You're right, but it's safe here. Absolutely no one can find us, let alone threaten us with thermonuclear weapons.

So we stay here forever.

No . . . I suppose not.

So what are we going to do?

Move on.

I'm not feeling it.

Move on!

Okay. Fenchurch forgotten?

Sure. Absolutely. Who-church?

That's my boy.

tiny voice: Fenchurch. Never forget.

FORD

I can go for eight minutes without blinking. Eight minutes, surely that's some kind of record. Not blinking is so relaxing. I was a little relaxed before I boarded this ship, but now I am positively comatose, or is that comma toes? Which would make sense because my toes do look like little commas, which is quite a scary thought for some reason.

Beer, beer, wonderful beer. The more you drink the more you fear.

Goosnargh! I've been a fool. I know what I have to do. I need to write something for the *Guide* about this ship in case the publishers ever manage to oust those Vogons. My goodness, it will be a sensation. How many mortals can have traveled inside the *Tanngrisnir*? I don't know. Not many I bet, and the next one to manage it will be pretty relieved to find a comforting and informative entry in the *Hitchhiker's Guide*. Right. What to submit. Something concise, don't give those bastard editors much to play with. But stylish. Something that says Ford Prefect all over it and yet captures the essence of such a cool golden ship. My last submission was a little wordy. So cut it down. Get straight to the issues. Immediately to the matter at hand, directly point-bound. Relevance on the horizon, Captain.

Ahah! I've got it. There is only one word that encapsulates both my spirit and that of this wonderful vehicle. One beloved term, equally popular among the old groans and the young grins. A collection of syllables as beautiful as it is useful:

Froody.

They gathered on the bridge to watch the descent toward the new blue planet.

Ford stepped close to a curved wall and it bubbled into transparency.

"I wanted the wall to do that," said Ford, grinning. "I thought it and the ship did it."

The view was undeniably spectacular, and even Wowbagger took his eyes from Trillian's profile for a moment to appreciate the expanse of waves, flecked with golden sunlight, flashing past below the prow.

"It is . . . nice," he said in the tone of a Blaslessian parolee who has just had his taste buds returned to him after a twenty-year stretch. "Yes. Nice."

Trillian wrapped her arms around his bicep. "Nice? It's fabulous, spectacular. I thought you were supposed to have a way with words."

"Not the good ones," said Wowbagger, smiling. "I have had no need of them for some time, thanks to all those jumentous mortals. Present company excepted."

Random brushed past, *accidentally* bashing Wowbagger with her elbow.

"Most of the present company excepted."

Random smiled sweetly. "I would just like to say, Mr. Wowbagger, that I really hope you die today, just like you want."

"Random!" said Trillian, shocked. "What a terrible thing to say. And anyway, it's not going to happen, Zaphod Beeblebrox never followed through on a threat or a promise in his life."

Wowbagger smiled down at her. "Don't worry. It's the Dark Space. People's emotions get amplified, they say things they don't mean. She'll settle down."

"Don't count on it," said Random, scowling.

But Trillian wasn't listening. *People's emotions get amplified,* she thought. *They say things they don't mean.*

"Oh my God," said the computer excitedly, suddenly sounding like a teenage fan girl. "It's Thor. On the other side of the island. I'm picking up Thor, I don't believe it. I wonder does he remember me?"

Wowbagger's brow tightened. "Are you sure?"

"Of course I'm sure, silly. I've got over a million matches on the facial software."

"Don't be cheeky, Computer, just set us down."

"Where? Beside the Thunder God?"

Wowbagger turned away from Trillian. "No. Set us down here. I need time to think."

Good, thought Trillian. *I need time to think myself.*

Good, thought Random. *I need time for my special delivery to arrive.*

CONG

"Zaphod Beeblebrox," said Hillman, as though the name itself were a curse, which on several planets it had indeed become. "Zaphod feckin' Beeblebrox."

Zaphod was reclining on a sun lounger in the plaza, two boots off, three sleeves rolled up.

"You keep saying that, Hillman. As though me being here is a bad thing instead of the solution to all your problems."

"The solution to all what problems?"

"What problems do you have?" said Zaphod equably.

Hillman drummed his fingers on the table, something he hoped the waitress would notice and for God's sake come and take his order. He stopped in mid-drum.

"Well, we have no waitresses for a start. They're all down on the beach colony with the personal trainers. And they took all the booze."

Zaphod reached for his boots. "Well, it's been great chatting to you, Hillman. If you could just point me in the direction of this beach colony."

"It's all your bloody fault, Zaphod. Everything was fine until the western township showed up. Tyropolis, can you believe that name? Their staff revolted even before ours did." He poked a finger at Zaphod. "Do you realize that some of the good people here are forced to do their own colonics? What kind of civilization is that?"

"Every new society has teething problems. You need to work through them with diplomacy and alcohol."

"Teething problems? That nut job Preflux is a bit more than a teething problem."

Zaphod tried to hold in a giggle, but it shot out his nose.

"What's so funny, Beeblebrox?"

"Oh, nothing."

"No, please share. I insist."

"It's just that you called Aseed Preflux a nut job."

"So what. He is a bloody nut job."

"If he is, so are you."

Hillman frowned. "What's that supposed to mean?"

"Well he is you and you are him. Don't tell me you haven't noticed."

"That's a load of horse manure," said Hillman, but there was a plate of cold dread in his stomach that knew it was true.

"The western township? Tyropolis? That's you guys from another dimension. I made a bundle off you the first time, so I thought, *Hey, why not do this again*? I was on my way for a third group when BOOM, here come the Vogons."

"So the Earth is gone?"

"Utterly and forever. Even Arkle Schmarkle and all of his horde couldn't put that planet together once more."

"What?"

"It's an old Betelgeusean nursery rhyme. Arkle Schmarkle was a little kid who glued eggs together after they fell off walls. Tragic ending."

"I see. Anyway, to get back to this planet: I am Aseed Preflux? I am that pompous, deluded moron? That's what you're saying."

Zaphod snapped the fingers of his third hand, something that had taken him months to learn. "Badabingo. Well, you're not him exactly. You're a version of him from a couple of million universes down the axis, which is why there are all the little differences. The name of course. You have the paunch, he doesn't. You dye your hair, he's still naturally red. That sort of thing."

Hillman didn't even have the energy to protest the hair dye slur. It was one thing to know that there were an infinite number of alternate Hillman Hunters, it was quite another to be at war with one of them.

"I can't believe this," he spluttered eventually. "You set me up, Beeblebrox. You pitted me against myself."

Zaphod slapped his own cheeks and chest in mock horror. "I set you up? Me? That's preposteraneous. I was just trying to make a few bucks. You knew there would be other colonists, Hillman. It's not my fault you ape descendants will fight with anyone, even versions of yourselves." Zaphod suddenly sat bolt upright. "Holy shankwursters! I'm right, aren't I? I just made a valid point."

Hillman fumed silently, tugging on his goatee. Beeblebrox did have a point. He had saved their lives and transported them to a new Eden; it was hardly his fault if the human race screwed it up all over again. Hillman glanced across the square to where Buff Orpington was acting like a kid on a sugar drip, running in circles around Thor, tongue hanging out, twirling the golf club.

"The settlement has been falling apart, Zaphod," admitted Hillman. "I could really use a god."

Zaphod tried to look surprised, as if this was not exactly where he'd hoped the conversation would go. "Well, I do have a god."

"Is that the real Thor? Really, is it?"

"It really is and I am his manager."

Hillman flapped his lips. "What? So even gods cost money now?"

"Wake up, Hillman. Gods have always cost money. But I can do you a deal."

"Would we have exclusive rights?"

"I couldn't promise that. Thor is in the big league. A class-one deity. There are a lot of cultures who want to adore him."

"And is he omnipresent?"

"No, but he's pretty fast."

Hillman thought about it. Having a god of Thor's stature could get this planet back on the straight and narrow. Aseed Preflux's wheel of cheese wouldn't last long against a big hammer like Thor's, and the staff might think twice about neglecting their duties if they had to answer to the god of thunder.

"When could he start?"

Something beeped in Zaphod's pocket, and he patted himself down until he located the tiny computer card that Wowbagger had given him.

"Almost immediately," he said, reading the screen. "Thor just has one little bit of divine retribution to hand out. You guys might want to watch this, test-drive the merchandise, so to speak. It's going to be spectacular." He called across the square to the god. "Hey, Thor. Ready to go do the thing? The immortal has landed."

"Are you sure about this?" said Thor, frowning suspiciously at Buff Orpington, who was trying to heft Mjöllnir. "I don't know if I'm ready. Did you see this guy? Is he being sarcastic or does he really think I'm great? He wants to be a priest. He wants a robe. Is that want you want, boy, is it?"

Buff nodded his jowly head and stamped the grass.

"Yeah," he panted. "Yeah, yeah, yeah."

TYROPOLIS

Wowbagger's longship touched down in a beautiful rolling meadow outside the settlement and instantly assumed the shape and texture of a grassy knoll. A nearby herd of Ameglian Major cows who had been arguing over who got to sacrifice themselves to the newcomers, cursed their luck then returned to tail-painting placards that protested the Tyromancers' refusal to eat them.

Wowbagger dissolved the hatch and the passengers set grateful feet on solid earth.

"It's really nice here," said Trillian. "Peaceful." At which point a hysterical cow thundered across the meadow and butted her in the chest, bellowing. "Eat me! Eat me!"

Trillian jumped away from the wet, hairy snout. "No. Ugh. I'm a . . . vegetarian."

"Vegetables!" spat the cow. "What's so special about them? Why do they get to have all the fun? Fiber and vitamins. So bloody what? I've got protein coming out my wazoo. Literally."

Before the *Tanngrisnir*'s passengers could take another step, they were surrounded by a mob of angry cows.

"We're mad cows!" they chorused. "We're mad cows."

Arthur laughed. "You know, that's funny, because on Earth there was a disease . . ."

A brown cow sidled up to Arthur. "You're not a vegetarian, are you, sir?"

"Why, no, as a matter of fact."

"I bet you'd gobble down a lovely sirloin, sir, with a few fingerling potatoes and a half bottle of vino."

Arthur patted his stomach. "I would actually. That sounds delicious. An actual steak. Nothing replicated about that. You get what you ask for. Honest to goodness meat."

"You've read my mind, Arthur mate," said Ford. "I'm not usually in favor of devouring sentient beings, but these guys are persistent."

With one foreleg, the cow ushered Arthur and Ford toward a wood-burning barbecue.

"And how would sirs like their steak?"

"Rare," said Ford. "So rare a vet with some shock paddles could revive it."

"Medium for me, I think."

The cow somehow managed to drape a napkin across its foreleg. "Excellent. And the wine?"

Arthur had no idea what the wine situation was on this new planet. It wasn't as if they had time for vintages. "Surprise me."

Wowbagger was feeling a little hemmed in by the other cows. He had never been overly fond of talking quadrupeds. It was a phobia he was struggling to deal with.

"You creatures really should back up a little or I will be forced to fry you with my energy pistol."

"Finally!" cried one cow.

"Maximum setting please!" begged another.

Trillian took his arm. "I know this species. They want to be eaten."

"I'm not going to eat them, but I may shoot them."

Random was still emotional from the journey. "Why don't you shoot them all, alien? Show my mother what you're really like."

Wowbagger felt Trillian squeeze his arm and his anxiety drained away. He looked at her.

How was that possible? How did you do that?

As previously discussed, the Universe has an aversion to tenderness and cannot allow it to exist for long, as every loving glance has to be balanced by a short sharp shock somewhere else in the cosmos. Sometimes not so short.

. . . .

Guide Note: Bowerick Wowbagger or, as the H2G2 describes him, that green frood with the hoopy ship who goes around insulting people, has to this point shared three tender moments in real space with Trillian Astra or, as *WooHoo magazine* dubbed her, "The Lucky Gal Who Bagged the Bagger," and each of these moments had to be paid for by other unfortunate individuals at antipodal points in the universe. Glam Fodder, a planning officer on Alpha Centauri, had his finger nipped by a pygmy vole that had climbed into his monthly brown bag because the bag donor had decided to recycle his speef sandwich bag. Ursool Dypher, a marriage counselor from the super-hot system of Hastromil, suffered a panic attack when her three o'clock married couple turned out to be the son and daughter she had given up for adoption as a younger being. Morty Grimm, the lead singer with the Hooloovoo supergroup Visible Spectrum, suffered third-degree diffusion when the lighting engineer accidentally put a blue gel on the singer's solo spotlight.

. . . .

This tender moment was torn asunder by the arrival of a golf cart convoy. It might have been a dramatic entrance had the leading cart actually managed to breach the enclosure gate, instead of becoming entangled in splintered planks.

Arthur's cow friend spat a wad of cud. "Morons. And these are the people in charge."

"Vegetarians?" Arthur offered.

"No. They love pigs. Can't get enough of pigs. But us poor cows, for some reason we're not on the menu. So thank goodness for you, sirs. Thank goodness for you."

Aseed Preflux crawled from the wreckage of fence and cart.

"Hey, Arthur," said Ford. "What do you get if you cross a fence with a cart?"

Arthur never had time to hazard a guess because they were set upon by Tyromancers.

"Step away from that barbecue," Aseed ordered shrilly. "We need those cows."

Ford hissed into Arthur's ear. "I'll stall them. You get Bessy on the barbecue."

The cow overheard. "I resent that. We're not all called Bessy, you know. As a matter of fact, *Bessy* is quite passé in sophisticated circles. Trisjam and Pollygrino are the names of choice this season."

Aseed shouldered his way through the assembled cattle until he arrived breathless and battered before the newcomers.

"Who is in charge here?" he demanded to know.

Wowbagger stepped forward, avoiding anything that squelched or steamed.

"That would be me. I am Bowerick Wowbagger, the ship's captain."

"What ship? I don't see any ship."

"That's because it's camouflaged, you bletcherous nincompoop."

Aseed flushed. "What? There's no call for that. How dare you!"

"Now, that's more like it," said Wowbagger, gratified. "Surprise and outrage. Reminds me why I used to do this job."

"Used to?" said Trillian.

Wowbagger glanced at his shoes, which were still reasonably clean. "Lately, it's lost its appeal."

Aseed's courage blossomed as the other colonists began to show up, wondering what all the commotion was about.

"Sorry to interrupt your tender moment . . ."

(On a cruise liner near Barnard's Star, the ship's doctor sneezed and stabbed himself in the knee with a Motox hypodermic. The knee was put on a strict water diet for two days in spite of all its moaning.)

". . . but what is your business here, Wowbagger?"

"I have come to drop these humans off with their own kind and I was going to insult everyone, but now I don't think I'll bother."

Aseed perked up a little. "These people are our own kind? They are Tyromancers?"

Wowbagger's chin jerked. "Tyromancers? You people are Tyromancers? I don't believe it!"

Aseed's upswing in perkiness leveled off. "Don't tell me: You don't believe in the Cheese. You think it's all in my head."

"No. I actually know the Cheese. I haven't seen old Cheesy in forever."

Preflux dropped to his knees. Something squelched and another something cracked and steamed. "Y-You know the Cheese? You have been in His exalted presence?"

"Exalted? Who told you that?"

"The Cheese Lord himself, in my visions."

Wowbagger nodded. "He's still doing the dream bit. Some things never change. Find an empty brain and slip yourself in, that's always been Cheesy's modus operandi. I've been down this god route before; a long time ago I hired Cheesy to kill me. He tried with some kind of cheese dip. It didn't work, obviously, but I've been lactose intolerant ever since."

"Did you bring Edamnation down upon us?"

"Edamnation? That's hilarious. Really? No. Come on. You can't expect people not to laugh if you're going to use theological terms like that. If you're talking about the big ball of cheese over the other settlement, I think you'll find that was another spaceship rolling into a normality zone."

"Not Edamnation?"

"I doubt it. In fairness to Cheesy, he might be a junior god, but he's not great on projection. The last I heard he was studying for his middle grade divinity exams, and seeing as I haven't seen any Holy Cheese calendars around, I am guessing he failed."

"Me too," said a cow. "Because he's a loser, just like you, Preflux."

"Shut it, cow, or so help me . . ."

The cow spat. "What are you going to do? Not eat me?"

"That's right. I won't eat you and I won't eat your entire family. Wherever they hide, I'll find them and not eat a single bite."

The cow was cowed. "This is not over, Preflux," he muttered.

Aseed's phone rang and he took a brief call, glancing back along the road toward the tunnel. When he was done, he turned back and said, "So, you're a representative of the Cheese, Wowbagger?"

Wowbagger frowned. "I wouldn't say representative. I know him a little. We had a few beers."

Aseed persisted. "You are a friend then. A champion, if you like."

"An acquaintance at best."

"It's just that from what my insider tells me, Hunter has got himself a real god."

"Ah."

"And he's on the way over here."

"I see. And you'd like me to represent the Cheese."

"Would you? That would be fab." Aseed made the triangle sign.

"What's that?"

"It's a cheese triangle. Appease the Cheese. It's kind of a slogan I made up."

Wowbagger laughed. "Don't move. I have to get a photo of that for Cheesy, he will be so thrilled."

Aseed's triangle wavered. "He can't see us? The Cheese is not all around us?"

"Cheesy? It's all he can do to hook himself up to a dish and send out dairy dreams. And I'll tell you something else, he loves beef and cheese. Especially meals that combine beef and cheese."

Aseed's hands dropped to his sides. "All this time we have been protecting the cheese vessels . . ."

The air crackled and Arthur felt the hair standing up on his forearms.

"I suddenly feel as though I should be running away."

In the sky, to the east, a small storm cloud churned just above the tree line. Photogenic lightning bolts shot from its belly at regular intervals and there seemed to be a huge being riding the bolts.

"Beeblebrox actually got the big guy himself. I don't believe it."

"Believe it," said Ford. "You called him Fat Arse, remember?"

Trillian shielded her eyes with a forearm, squinting to catch a glimpse of the Thunder God.

"Maybe it's all a big light show. Maybe he doesn't want to fight."

A statement like this virtually guarantees a contradictory and, considering the characters involved, melodramatic event, and Trillian as a journalist should have known better than to utter it.

. . . .

Guide Note: There is a theory, postulated by Schick Brithaus, the controversial bone doctor from pre-telepathy Kakrafoon Kappa, which states that the universe is built on uncertainty and that a definitive statement/action creates a momentary energy vacuum into which flows a diametrically opposing statement/action. Famous vacuum-inducing statements include:

Surely that's not going to fit in there.

And:

I am sick of betting the same numbers every week. They are never going to come up.

And:

We are a peaceful people. Not even the Armorfiends of Striterax would want to pick a fight with us.

And:

You look gorgeous in that sweater, Felix. There is no way anyone is going to call you a freak and throw you in a dumple composter.

And:

Maybe it's all a big light show. Maybe he doesn't even want to fight.

. . . .

Subatomic beings heard the whoosh of energy suction, and into the vacuum flowed a massive lightning bolt which scorched a huge section of the meadow, leaving only cooked cow carcasses and a massive X right in the center.

"Lucky blebers," muttered a surviving cow.

Wowbagger's central brain and assorted ganglia were flooded with conflicting emotions. For millennia, his most heartfelt wish had been to die, but now there was a slice of light in his darkness, a chance that the principle by which he sought his death was in fact flawed. His dilemma was this: Would it be wise to pass up a sterling opportunity to get himself killed, on the off-chance that he could enjoy a few brief decades of happiness with this already dying woman?

"I guess X marks the spot," said Ford, a hank of charred meat in his hand. He turned to the nearest cow. "Do you have any sauce? This is a little dry."

Arthur found that he was not as scandalized by this sort of behavior as he once had been. Repeated exposure to Ford Prefect's rampant gourmandizing had eroded some of his behavioral notions.

"I believe that someone mentioned wine," he said, trying not to sound overly enthusiastic.

Random scowled, although no one noticed as it was one of her two normal expressions, the other being a contemptuous curl of the lip.

"That is disgusting," she said, transitioning smoothly into expression number two. "You two are pigs."

"Pigs," said the cow. "Don't talk to me about pigs."

CHAPTER 10

The word went out to the sentient beings of Nano that there was some major aggravation about to kick off in Tyropolis and it would probably be best to steer clear until the earth stopped shaking. Which of course meant that everyone made their way immediately to the scorched meadow on the outskirts of the town, except Nickles Adare, an ex-mayor of New York who was locked in a Cong treatment room on enforced detox.

The pootle-tink birds were among the first to arrive, having the advantage of sensitive primary feathers which their leader, Perko St. Waring Speckle, used to steer a borrowed minibus. Perko stopped the bus by driving it into the ditch and then sent two of his flock to keep places at the fence, while the rest of them went in search of dairy-free cappuccinos.

The personal trainers arrived next, racing across the fields in diamond formation, seemingly untroubled by the mid-afternoon sun. Having cleared the fields, they jogged along the road, each with a bicycle on one shoulder and a beautician on the other.

"Shouldn't you be riding that thing?" Arthur commented to a bulging young man who happened to warm down beside him.

"Oh, grow up," snapped the trainer and stalked off, leaving Arthur bewildered.

Thor was limbering up in the scorched meadow, throwing a few shapes and making sure his leggings were securely secured. He felt nervous. Truth be told, but it probably never would be, especially to Zaphod, he felt terrified. This was his first public display since that damnable video had aired, which thankfully no one here seemed to have seen. As far as these people were concerned, he was a first-class god who had never dabbled in rock stardom or candid movies. He had a chance to make a good impression here. Something he could build on.

If I do well today, Thor realized, *it could go a long way to restoring my reputation. I really hope this immortal plays along and doesn't die too quickly. A god killing a non-god can seem a little unsympathetic if it isn't played just so.*

There was quite a crowd gathered and the atmosphere seemed quite festive. The younger pootle-tinks were plucking dead tail feathers and helicoptering them down on the field while a caffeine-hyped squad of veterans were doing flyovers complete with synchronized loops and stunt dips.

The trainers were forming a human pyramid on the crisped fringe of grass, while the kindhearted beauticians were consoling the desperate residents of Tyropolis and Cong, most of whom had long since forgotten how to beautify themselves.

"It's my hair," one elderly lady wailed. "I pointed the hot blowy thing at it, but still it won't change color."

"And these nails," said another. "They just keep growing. Every day it's the same. Come back, Jasmin. Please come back."

Buckeye Brown had a baleful glare triangle going on. First he looked down at his shoes, then over at Buff Orpington, and finally at a tall, tanned man sporting red trunks and flip-flops, with an emergency whistle clamped between his teeth.

Head and shoulders above these people stood the Thunder God.

I can bring these mortals together, thought Thor. *One god. One faith. The more people that believe in me, the more I can charge. And I bet one of those girls could do a nice beard braiding.* No sooner had this happy thought formed in his mind than the old insecurity came flooding back. *It's going to be a disaster. The Sub-Etha people hate me. No matter how sensitively I kill this immortal fellow, all they're going to see is the negative.* Thor shrugged. *I may as well get a few braids in, it might lift my spirits.*

On the far side of the scorched circle, Wowbagger was feeling lightheaded and giddy. The moment had finally arrived when he could kiss this corporeal realm good-bye and good riddance. Several lifetimes of suffering were almost at an end.

I think this guy could do it, thought Wowbagger. *I'll get him a little riled up with some choice comments and he'll hit me with the big pile-driver.*

Thor certainly looked as though he was up to the job. Power came off him in waves, and he was shooting practice lightning bolts at a bunch of volunteer cows who were providing moo-ving targets.

He's the one. I can feel it.

But there was an uncomfortable thorn in Bowerick Wowbagger's moment of celebration. The Earth woman, Trillian Astra, had changed him.

My heart pistons are pumping like crazy. I'm off my food. I have zero interest in insulting people. It's almost as if I have a virus, but I don't get viruses.

Wowbagger knew what had happened. The Dark Space had taken a speck of attraction and amplified it until it seemed to him that he was in love.

Is that what happened, really? Couldn't I just be lucky for once? For a change?

Doubtful.

The lady in question was standing by the fence arguing with her daughter. *Also, remember, Bowerick old man, if you take the woman, you take the child too.*

And surprisingly enough, that didn't bother him too much.

There's always the tube, though Trillian wasn't so impressed with that solution the last time.

Wowbagger waved across the meadow and Trillian waved back.

Waving. I can't even remember the last time I waved at someone.

Trillian finished the row by turning her back on Random and stomping across the field, her high heels puncturing the earth with each footfall.

"That girl," she said, punching Wowbagger's forearm. "She knows how to get me going."

"What's she saying now?"

Trillian's face was pale, except for two apple red spots on her cheeks. "Anything she knows I won't want to hear."

"It's just the Dark Space talking. It will pass."

"I don't think so. Random hates me and everything I love. I think if I had ever loved Arthur, she would hate him too."

"You never loved him?"

"No. I just felt I was getting old and his were the only human swimmers available."

"I see."

"I left her before. I didn't really mean to, it just happened. So she hates me for that."

"Surely she doesn't hate you."

Trillian nodded sharply. "She does. She says that I made her miserable. And if she can't have a husband, why should I . . ."

And then Trillian decided to stop speaking, half a sentence too late.

Wowbagger coughed once in surprise, then had to cough several more times to cover for himself.

"I've scared you?"

"No. Not at all. Can I presume you were referring to me as potential husband material?"

There were tears in Trillian's eyes. "Yes, but it was just talk. You've dreamed about this moment for so long and I have nothing to offer you but hardship. This life is for Random, I've promised her. You go ahead and kill yourself, don't worry about me."

"It sounds selfish when you put it like that."

Trillian wiped her cheeks. "No, I understand perfectly. You've had a terrible time being immortal in that wonderful ship of yours. Drinking beer and insulting people, not to mention being incredibly handsome and charming. It's been hell for you, I realize that."

"You make it sound glamorous."

"Wasn't it? I seem to recall you being linked to several starlets."

"That was just physical. Those females meant nothing to me."

This is historically the third worst thing to say to a female of any species.

"They meant nothing? Why not?"

Wowbagger spread his arms. "How could they? Even as we mated, they were growing old."

There's number two.

Trillian's eyes flashed. "Growing old. We all grow old, Bowerick. Believe it or not, I'm growing old too."

Wowbagger realized that his lack of intimate communication over the years was doing wonders to increase his chances of dying alone in the very immediate future.

"You may be growing old," he said desperately, "but you have years left before you're too old to reproduce."

And there's number one. Badabingo. Green stick in the green hole.

Zaphod and Ford were reunited in a flurry of complicated Betelgeusean ritual handshakes that neither of them could ever remember past the second underarm squelch.

Ford abracadabra'ed a couple of dragon's eggs from his satchel and mixed them both a cocktail.

"I love opera," he said, when the effects had worn off. "It goes so well with drinks. A pity we didn't have some blood sludge to nibble on."

Zaphod smacked his lips. "Blood sludge. That takes me back. You remember that implement?"

"I do remember it."

"And the thing with the curvy end?"

"Wow. That was one hell of a froody retreat. Monks. Who knew."

Watching the pootle-tink birds soar overhead, they sat on a patch of springy grass that had escaped Thor's lightning display.

"Are they supposed to lay eggs in midair?" wondered Zaphod. "Seems a little devil-may-care."

"Those birds lay a lot of eggs. They're just trying to keep the population down."

Arthur strode across the meadow intent on interrupting the soirée with some pertinent information, something most Betelgeuseans don't like to deal with on a daily basis in case it spoils their mood.

. . . .

Guide Note: Betelgeuseans have been known to ignore reality completely, especially if they happen to be holding a drink of the alcoholic kind, more especially if there are novelty ice cubes in the drink which can clink hypnotically and make the most urgent impending disaster seem trivial. It is a little known cosmic irony that the Praxibetel communities on Betelgeuse VII were enjoying the precog Pantheoh's opera *The Great Collapsing Hrung Disaster* when the real Hrung Disaster actually occurred. Only Ford Prefect's father survived, because he had snuck away from his work colleagues to try to pick up a better signal on his Guide in order to follow *Last Behemoth Standing*. The Hrung in question had little to say about his collapse, apart from he had decided to give up interpretive dance and he was sorry for the inconvenience.

• •

"Vogons," said Arthur, flapping a hand vaguely toward the skies. "There are Vogons on the way."

Zaphod seemed about as concerned about Vogons as a bugblatter beast would be concerned about beastblatter bugs.

"Don't worry about it, ape-man. Enjoy the moment."

"Don't worry about it?" Arthur spluttered. "Didn't you see what they did to the Earth? Don't you remember those death rays?"

Zaphod's smile was so condescending that it would have earned him five years in an Ashowvian prison.

• •

Guide Note: On the continent of Ashowvia everyone is so highly strung that facial expressions and intonations have had to be regulated. The Twenty-Year Kowtow border conflict was sparked off by a raised eyebrow, which later turned out to have been plucked that way, giving rise to the Ashowvian sayings *Think before you pluck, Irresponsible plucking costs lives*, and *Pluck one pluck all*.

• •

"The Grebulons destroyed the Earth," said Zaphod. "Not the Vogons. It's complicated, I don't expect you to understand."

"Complicated? How is it complicated?"

"It's complicated for a monkey. Not for an evolved being."

Arthur wiggled his fingers. "I'm evolved. I've got thumbs, see?"

"Thumbs?" Zaphod snorted. "If that's all there was to evolution, thermoles would rule the Galaxy."

"Thermoles," said Ford. "Eight thumbs—great at opening jars but about as many brain cells as blood sludge."

"Remember that blood sludge? I got barley and maybe garlic."

"That's what I thought. Definitely barley."

Arthur's hands shook before him, as though he were playing an invisible accordion.

"Vogons! Hello. The Vogons are coming!"

"Yes, we know," said Zaphod. "But they have to jump through some pretty bendy space to get here. By my calculations they won't make it for a couple of centuries, if they make it at all."

"Centuries? Are you sure?"

"Of course. Relax, Arthur."

If Ford hadn't been drinking, the phrase *by my calculations* coming out of the mouth on this particular head of Zaphod's might have set a few warning lights flashing, but the sun was warm, there were pretty girls everywhere, and Ford did not want the image of a dribbling Vogon in his head to destroy the mood.

Arthur on the other hand had never met a good mood he couldn't puncture.

"You seem very mellow, Zaphod. Aren't you supposed to be upset?"

"Why should I be upset? Thor is back on the books and I am about to relaunch his career. Things are so great I may just turn a freeze ray on myself to preserve my froodiness for future generations."

"What about the Fat Arse thing?"

"What Fat Arse thing?"

"Wowbagger was calling you Fat Arse, remember? That's what got us started on this whole thing."

Zaphod's eyes wobbled in their sockets as he cast his mind back.

"Nope. I'm not getting anything. Fat Arse, you say? He never did."

In spite of all his experience with Zaphod, Arthur was flabbergasted. "You don't remember, Zaphod? What are you even doing here?"

Zaphod patted Arthur's shoulder. "I go with the moment," he said, adopting the wise tone he saved for what he believed to be special moments in other people's lives. "Don't try to understand me, just be grateful that you felt the warmth of Zaphod Beeblebrox's aura on your wonderstruck face."

Arthur's face did not seem particularly wonderstruck. "Whatever, Zaphod. But he called you Fat Arse, take my word for it."

"Once? More than once?"

"Several times."

Zaphod jumped to his feet. "Right. Time to get this party started. More than eight times, would you say?"

"Maybe twelve. At least ten."

Zaphod strode across the scorched earth. "Thor. Thor, old friend. Time to make a new video."

I should have smoked, thought Wowbagger. *Why not? All this time trying to stay in shape while simultaneously hiring a succession of idiots to rub me out. That's a little bit of a contradiction there, Bowerick old boy. Perhaps there's a part of you that wants to live.*

Bowerick rubbed his suddenly itchy nose, thinking that it would be nice to have these epiphanies before setting up a death match with one of the Aesir.

Wowbagger stood alone on one diagonal of the scorched X, waiting for Thor to extricate himself from his manager, a group of statesmen, several admiring trainers, and a girl who seemed to be braiding his beard.

"Come on," he called. "I don't have all day."

"Why not?" a pootle-tink bird called from the fence. "I thought you were immortal."

This got a big laugh, so Wowbagger decided to nip it in the bud.

When dealing with a heckler, go for the deeply personal had always been his motto.

"You have some stains on your tail feathers there, birdie. You a bed wetter?"

The other birds laughed hard enough to bring on a bout of spontaneous egg laying, and the target bird shot him such an evil look that Wowbagger was glad he would be dead in a few minutes.

Finally, Thor seemed to be finished with his ringside business, and he lifted himself from the head of Mjöllnir, on which he had been perched.

Here we go. About time too.

The Thunder God was a huge specimen, at least four times Wowbagger's height, but not slow or ungainly. Thor moved as though he were being held back and as soon as whatever was restraining him let go, he would explode into action.

I am probably the only person here not afraid of this guy, Wowbagger thought, but then amended that thought to: *I am probably the only person here besides Beeblebrox who is not afraid of this guy. Beeblebrox probably thinks he could win this fight.*

Then, a funny thing happened. With every step Thor took across the scorched earth, he seemed to grow smaller.

Heat haze, thought Wowbagger. *It must be.*

It was not. Thor was actually shrinking, and by the time he reached the X's intersection, the Thunder God was too short to be allowed on most fairground rides.

"Hey," he said. "What's up?"

Wowbagger blinked. "Me, I think. From your perspective."

Thor patted his own tiny body. "Sorry about that," he said, embarrassed. "Zaphod's idea. If I just come out here and crush you, how's that going to make me look? Like a bully, that's how. This way, for any cameras pointed at us, I look like a giant-killer, which is a much better angle, according to Zaphod, and he knows media." The god frowned. "Though he does make the occasional mistake."

Wowbagger felt a buzz of anticipation behind his eyes. "So what happens? I kneel down, I suppose, and then you clobber me?"

Thor was almost affronted. "What? No, no. That wouldn't work. That's an execution. We have to give these people a show. And not just these people, eventually this is going to filter through to the entire Sub-Etha."

"The Sub-Etha. I never watch it."

"Never?"

"No. It's all junk. Give me a classic movie any day."

"I wish everyone was like you, but they're not. These days, in this Universe, careers are made and broken on the Sub-Etha."

"But you're a god, what do you need with a career?"

Thor stroked his beard plait, which he probably was not aware had a few beads braided through it. "That's a good question, but I know the answer because we did this in circle time, after my breakdown. Gods have god-sized egos, so we need a lot of love to stay healthy. You see those gods going around blighting crops and drying up rivers? Those guys don't get loved. It's a cycle, you know. You have no idea how depressed gods can get. One minute we're adored, the next despised, I've been in the troughs, believe me."

Guide Note: Loki the Trickster once used his hypnotic charm to convince the Aesir that he had decided to mend his ways and set up shop as a brain-ologist to the gods. His client list quickly grew as relieved divinities flooded to his door, eager to be regressed and find out why the hell they were so attracted to unicorns and so forth. Thor himself was actually feeling much better and beginning to develop real affection for his brother when he discovered that Loki had done a deal with *WooHoo* magazine and sessions were being serialized. To make matters worse, Loki had considered Thor's sessions a bit dull and so had added in a lot more weeping, incontinence pants, and an Eccentrica Gallumbits fixation.

Wowbagger nodded thoughtfully, to convey the impression that he was prepared to care, but really he was only prepared to nod.

"That's great. I understand the whole thing now. A cycle. Right. So, should we wrestle for a while?"

Thor glanced over his shoulders, worried that someone would tumble to the rigged nature of the showdown. "A bit of chat first. You stole my ship, blah blah blah. Then you strike the first blow. I pretend to be injured, maybe limp a little. A little back and forth. Then BOOM on the temple and the fat lady has well and truly sung, my friend."

"Which fat lady?"

"Oh, nothing. It's a Valkyrie expression."

Wowbagger glanced at the sidelines. There were tears on Trillian's face, but she was not taking one step to stop the proceedings.

"Okay, little man. It was me. I stole your ship."

Thor drew a sharp breath, puffing out his tiny chest, trying not to appear mortified by the script he was supposed to stick to. "You! My father gave me that interstellar longship, which I named after my beloved goat."

While broadcasting the thought *I hated that bucket of slime, which is why I sold it to a guy in a bar.*

"Yes, I did it steal it and I'd do it again."

"Oh, you would, would you? I may be a benevolent god, evil giant, but I can only forgive so much."

Enough of this dire cabinotage, thought Wowbagger.

Cabinotage being a word he had picked up while preparing his global insult for the soap opera planet Sunny View, where the entire world was a television set with eighteen satellite suns for three-shift daylight shooting.

Let's speed things up a bit.

"Cut the buffa-biscuit, you preposterous little Viking. Your daddy hates you, and your mommy pretends you're someone else's son."

Thor involuntarily shrank an inch. This wasn't in the script.

"What? What did you say?"

Wowbagger plowed on. "Everyone knows it. Thor the drunk, they call you. I think you should have stayed at the bar."

A small thundercloud suddenly appeared overhead, spitting white lightning.

"You stole my longship, evil giant," spluttered Thor, thinking: *I'm spluttering. Gods shouldn't splutter. This is a disaster, they're going to hate me.*

"Sure. Whatever you say. And another thing everyone knows: You detest mortals."

"I do not . . . What? That was my father's ship. Remember the longship?"

"You think mortals are second-class individuals. You wouldn't wipe your boot with a mortal."

Thor grew taller, much taller. "Yes, I would."

"You would wipe your boot with a mortal?"

There were a couple of boos from the audience, maybe a hiss.

"Yes. I mean no. I don't know, maybe if my boot was dirty."

Wowbagger tapped his chin. "And did I hear something about a video . . ."

That was as far as he got, because suddenly Thor was looming over him with Mjöllnir raised to strike.

What happened to back and forth? wondered Wowbagger, then the hammer came down so fast it blurred, crashing into his head with a noise like a meteor impacting on a field of ice.

Good-bye, Trillian, thought Wowbagger, then he was driven bodily fifty feet straight down into his grave.

Thor was in two minds with his performance. The up-and-over swing always made good television, but it was a pity he couldn't have dragged it out a little longer. What choice did he have? The green guy was just about to mention the video, and then the various browsers would have tagged the comment, and before you know it everyone's linked back to the old site.

He was about to turn to Zaphod to check his manager's reaction, when he picked up a faint thought from about fifty feet below his feet. And the thought was either

Shark eye knothead.

or

Zark. I'm not dead.

Zaphod whistled the first bar of "Blinko in the Baybox," an old Betelgeusean epic shanty concerning a prickled mollusc and his time spent in captivity.

"Whaddya think, Ford? Did he do enough?"

Ford whistled the second bar back at him. "I don't know. I never felt like there was a threat. There was no drama."

"You're right. It was all over too quickly." Zaphod looked around. "I wonder if there is anyone else in the market for a hammer in the head."

Thor jogged across the field. "What do you think? Nice up-and-over, wasn't it? I lost my temper a bit though, let the green guy rile me up. Don't worry, Zaph, it won't happen next time."

"Next time?"

"Yes, next time. The green guy isn't dead."

"What? Are you sure?"

"Yes, I'm sure. He's climbing out of that hole now, thinking nasty thoughts."

"How much did you give him?"

"I don't know, maybe fifty percent, something like that."

Zaphod whistled another few notes of "Blinko." "Fifty? Really? Did anyone ever survive that before?"

"No one that didn't have a seat at the long table."

Zaphod beckoned to his client to shrink himself down a little. "Tell me, Thor, honestly, can you finish Wowbagger off? Can you do it?"

Thor hunkered down. "Zaph, I can finish off this entire planet with seventy-five percent." He stretched his rotator cuff. "You might want to move everyone back a little though."

Wowbagger crabbed one elbow out of a crack in the earth.

My suit is ruined, he thought. *And that big ape didn't even break the skin.*

Trillian felt broken. Her soul had been split by the hammer blow and she would never be the same.

We had one day together and it was the most important day of my life.

Had she done the right thing? Trillian wondered. Could she even pretend to herself that she had made the right choice?

Beside her, Random was perched on the fence, busily taking no notice of her mother's sacrifice.

"Hmmph," she grunted suddenly. "The bugger is still alive. I knew it."

For only the third time in her life, Trillian Astra fainted.

A vast cone-shaped ship of white alloy poked through the nebula, its once-smooth fuselage pockmarked by two centuries of space debris impact. No more than one tenth of its eight hundred tripropellant rockets were functioning, and there was barely enough life support to keep the crew breathing. The fresh food supply was utterly exhausted, and there had been nothing but recycled fluids to drink for several months.

The entire crew was fatigued and starving. Their morale was low and none of them had ever known a home besides this gigantic ship they were contracted to voyage in until their mission was finally complete.

The captain, a once corpulent giant of a man, had shrunk to scarecrow proportions, but he was a hero to his people. His eyes flashed green fire when the day's work was good, and deep red when a duty was neglected or an officer mistreated his men. The crew loved him and would follow him into hell if need be.

His name was Eddon Cho, and today was the day when he could finally complete the mission entrusted to him by his father, and maybe live a little of his own life.

"Navigator, tell me again," he called across the bridge to young Vishnal Li Senz, only seventeen and already an excellent pilot.

"We're here, Captain. There can be no doubt about it. The orbit is a little weird but the air is breathable."

Cho nodded. It was just as well, because once they landed, they wouldn't be taking off again, ever.

"Very well, take us down. Careful with the compensator and send any extra spark of power we have to the Verifyer."

Li Senz swallowed. "The Verifyer? My God. Are you certain, Captain?"

"I'm certain," Eddon Cho responded grimly. "We only get one shot at this. Now take us down."

Li Senz cracked his knuckles, then wrapped his fingers around the manual control.

"May the Unbreakable Guarantee protect us," he said.

Around the ship, his prayer was echoed by more than two thousand souls.

On the surface of Nano, the crowd was feeling a little cheated.

Perko St. Waring Speckle was showing a new and not altogether attractive side of his personality after a few coffees and a build-up of anticipat-o-acid in his wings.

"Is that it?" he called. "Is that the entire show? Lame-o. Pathetic."

Hillman Hunter was none too impressed either.

"I mean it was a good hit, that up-and-over action, but the cheesers' guy is getting back up. What good is that to me?"

Buff Orpington had tears on his cheeks. "He'll do it all right. Just you wait and see. Thor is just warming up, that's all. Working out the kinks."

"He'd better work them out fast, or we'll all be adoring the big Cheese."

The surface chatter was abruptly halted by the sight of nearly a hundred spiraling rings of light descending through the atmosphere. The rings incrementally revealed themselves to be the rear engines of a gargantuan ship which eased itself earthward, shedding shield panels as it dropped. Several of the engines sparked and burned out, dropping the ship in erratic jolts until it finally touched down in a nearby lake, flash-boiling it to a misty shroud.

"Oooh," said Ford Prefect. "Spooky."

There was almost complete silence for several moments, until a slender robot arm, muscled with power cables, popped from a hatch in the strange ship's belly. At the tip of the arm was a blinking sensor which moved rapidly toward the crowd, quickly circumventing the cows hoping for a meat eater.

Farther and farther the arm went, telescoping from the body of the ship. Over Wowbagger's head, through Thor's legs, dodging away from Zaphod, who made a lunge for it. Stopping finally in front of Random.

"Random Dent?" it asked in a real robotic voice, back from when robots were robots and didn't have personalities of their own.

Random stood her ground. "Erm . . . Yes. I guess."

A small hollow opened on the probe's tip. "Spit please."

Random dropped a bubble of saliva into the hollow, which immediately bathed it with a series of lasers. After several moments, a green light winked on.

"Identity confirmed. Here is your package and thank you for purchasing with uBid."

A small envelope dropped from the robot arm into Random's waiting hand.

"Thank you," she said in a small, guilty voice.

"Enjoy your product," said the probe. "And if you have any complaints, please feel free to write them on a bumpy log then hammer said log into your auditory canal."

The probe swiveled back toward the ship. "Mission complete," it said. "That's the last one."

There was a muffled cheer from inside the gigantic ship, then its structure slumped and began the slow process of falling apart.

. . .

Random was young and her lungs were full of concentrated dark matter, and so without considering all the possible consequences, she tore open the envelope and ran along the fence to where Thor was patiently enduring a little pep talk from Hillman Hunter.

"Put these on your hammer," she said, interrupting the Nanite leader.

The Thunder God frowned. "I thought I heard something. Sort of a squeak squeak squeaky squeak."

"Down here!" shouted Random.

Thor bent over, elbows on knees. "Oh, look. A little girl. Oh my gods, are you a fan? Do you want an autograph, is that it? I don't usually do school appearances, but I could make an exception."

Random wasted a second, fuming, then: "Listen to me, weatherman. I researched immortals on the Sub-Etha, and out of the thousands of hits I found on the topic, there was not a single tested and confirmed method of killing one."

Zaphod chuckled. "But this is Thor, girly. You can't test and confirm him. He's the big time, big as he wants to be."

"Hmm, okay. Well, he is going to look big-time stupid in front of all these people when he can't kill the green man."

"That's not going to happen," said Thor without much conviction.

"It won't happen if you put these on the head of your hammer."

"Nothing goes on the hammer, kid. Mjöllnir stays pure."

Random spoke slowly so the Thunder God would get the picture. "I did manage to find a theory by a little known scientist on an unregarded world that said that an immortal can only be killed by an object that has come from the same transformational event."

Even Zaphod could follow that. "So what did transform Wowbagger?"

"He fell into a particle accelerator trying to retrieve a couple of elastic bands. Bands which I bought on uBid from the high priest of the Temple of Wowbagger."

Thor reached out a finger and thumb.

"Why don't I put those bands on my hammer," he said.

Bowerick Wowbagger the Infinitely Prolonged was feeling a little lightheaded, and it was a feeling he relished, as it reminded him of when he was mortal. He dragged himself from the crack in the earth and lay gasping in crisped curls of grass as the uBid ship fell to pieces behind him.

More intrigue, he thought. *I can't say that today hasn't been interesting.*

As he lay there prostrated in the dirt, thinking as usual about himself and his now unlikely death, he saw that there was someone else on the ground.

Trillian.

And this was the moment that Wowbagger knew for sure that he was in love, because at that moment he stopped thinking about how Trillian related to him and started to think about Trillian herself.

Is she harmed? What's happened?

Wowbagger shook off his wooziness and jumped to his feet.

"I'm coming!" he called, leaning into a run. "I'm coming."

A shadow fell across Wowbagger's face. Something mountainous obscured his view of Trillian.

"Time for the big one," said Thor, bending over, so his head appeared bizarrely upside-down.

How does his helmet stay on? wondered Wowbagger.

Then Mjöllnir hit him with such injurious force that it sent him straight into the stratosphere.

Arthur was deep in conversation with a pootle-tink bird when he saw Trillian keel over.

"No," he was explaining. "The game is *called* cricket. A *wicket* is made up of stumps and uprights . . . Oh, good lord."

"Come on," said the bird. "It's very confusing. So when a person runs, it's called a run?"

But the *oh, good lord* had not been directed at the bird; rather it was blurted involuntarily as Trillian fainted dead away. Arthur dropped the soya yogurt he had been enjoying and raced along the fence to where Trillian lay unmoving.

This is disgraceful. He fumed. *Her own daughter, our own daughter, is walking away. What has happened to Random? That child needs to be taken in hand.*

This last was a statement oft repeated in the Dent household when Arthur was a boy. His father trotted it out at every opportunity, whenever Arthur strayed even minutely into proscribed behavior. The taking in hand generally involved a stern talking-to, which invariably featured the Second World War, garden sheds, philately, and upper lips of the stiff kind. At the end of each lecture, young Arthur had been allowed a nip from his father's brandy flask just to put hair on his chest, so whenever Arthur thought about these disciplinary chats, he felt sad, then merry, then sleepy, then woke up with a headache.

Arthur knelt beside Trillian and awkwardly cradled her head in the crook of one elbow.

"There, there," he said. "If you can hear me, Trillian, I just want you to know that you look great. I know ladies spend a lot of time worrying how their outfits look, in car crash situations and so on."

Giving comfort to females had never been one of Arthur Dent's strong suits. In fact if *comfort giver* had been an actual advertised position, Arthur would never have made it past the first interview, especially if there had been a practical exam.

● ●

Guide Note: For the past three decades of real time, the human Arthur Dent had made his life infinitely more miserable than it needed to be by displaying a spectacular ability to say the right thing but at the wrong time. When Arthur Dent's best friend from university, Jason Kingsley, had been dumped after three years by the love of his life, Stacey Hempton, Arthur assured him that he would not be lonely for long, as slappers like Stacey were easy to come by in any disco. When his Irish aunt Maedhbhdhb (pronounced Hilda) had received a lethal blow from a falling church gargoyle, Arthur had whispered in her ear: *At least the cigarettes won't kill you now, eh, Aunty?* Arthur's tactlessness is only surpassed by that of Galactic President Zaphod Beeblebrox, who once presented PeeBee Anjay, the gelatinous king of Shivers City, with a leopard-skin thong as a birthday present.

● ●

Arthur poked Trillian's cheek with a finger.

"Trillian," he said, softly but urgently. "Come on. Wake up." She did not respond, so Arthur thought back to the first aid afternoon course he had been required to attend by the BBC. As far as he could recollect, most of the afternoon had been spent changing the plug on a coffee machine, but hadn't there been some demonstration involving a plastic dummy with balloons for lungs?

Mouth-to-mouth?

Arthur had no idea if what he was about to clumsily attempt was the correct course of action, but nevertheless it cheered him a little to have a course of action to attempt.

He placed Trillian's head on the soft grass and leaned over her.

"You gotta pinch the nose and tilt the head back," said a voice from behind his shoulder. It was the bird he had been talking to.

I met this bird downtown, thought Arthur, choking down a hysterical giggle.

He parted Trillian's lips with his thumb and took a deep breath.

I'm nervous. Why am I nervous?

"Go on, man. Do it!"

This bird was really pushy.

Arthur bobbed a little, then dived in. Their lips locked and Arthur sealed the corners with his thumbs then blew. There was no reaction initially: It felt to Arthur like he was blowing into a tunnel. Then Trillian's arms came up around his neck and she kissed him passionately.

What? Unexpected. A year ago this kiss would have been a dream come true.

Arthur pulled back and saw that Trillian's eyes were open and glassy with tears.

"Arthur . . . I thought . . ."

And Arthur immediately understood. "It's Wowbagger. You love him."

One upon a time, this realization would have shattered Arthur's world, if he'd had a world to shatter, but now all he felt was a deep empathy for Trillian, who was about to lose her love as he had lost his.

"Yes, I do love him," said Trillian, nodding, and the motion set rivulets of tears flowing down her cheeks. "Something happened in the Dark Space to speed up the *falling in love* process . . . Where is he?"

Arthur glanced into the scorched meadow just in time to see Wowbagger begin his ascent to the stratosphere.

And being well aware of his record of tactlessness, Arthur tried to say something nonspecific. "Oh . . . He's around. You rest here, I'll go and get him."

Random watched Wowbagger shoot off into the sky, but the sight did not fill her with a sense of triumph as she had believed it would. In fact, she felt that in some tiny way she herself might be a little responsible for the friction that had existed between them. This feeling soon passed and the triumph came flooding in.

That's right, you green freak. Off you go to the afterlife.

Tiny Voice: How could you? Green freak? You fought for equality for all species throughout the galaxy. How little it takes to strip away your veneer.

Shut up, thought Random. *You're not real. You never happened and anyway the green freak kissed my mother.*

Up and up Wowbagger went, flailing all the way, until he disappeared altogether.

And that's what happens when you put Random Dent in a tube.

Arthur appeared before her, arms crossed, body language shouting, *I am not happy.*

"What did you do, Random?"

Random crossed her own arms. "Nothing. What are you talking about?"

"You gave Thor something, I saw you. And suddenly he's able to hurt Wowbagger. So I'm going to ask you again: What did you do?"

Random was not about to be broken that easily. "And I'm going to tell you again: I didn't do anything."

"What is it, Random? Do you want to punish your mother, is that it?"

"No."

"Why are you doing this to her? Can't you see she's in love with that Wowbagger person? You may not like it, but that's the way it is."

"You're right. I don't like it."

"So you're helping Thor."

Random was stony-faced. "I'm way over here. How could I be helping Thor?"

Arthur tried another tack. "Weren't you in love, Random? Don't you remember how that felt?"

Random jerked back as though slapped, and her hand flew instinctively to her chest, to the spot where her beloved Fertle used to nestle.

"Yes, I remember love. My love is gone, so why should she be happy?"

"You're doing this because Trillian left you?"

"Yes she left me, but I succeeded in spite of her. All those years slaving in a clerk's office, working my way up. But I did it."

Arthur gripped his daughter's shoulder and stared deep into her eyes, past the resonance of dark space, through to the volatile, compassionate girl inside.

"You didn't do it. There was no clerk's office. And Trillian did not desert you for decades, she left you with your father for a week while she went on a job. That's all she did. Nothing worse than that. You were the one who brought us all to Earth and you were the one who created your own bitter existence. It was all you, Random. So stop being so utterly selfish and tell me how to save that poor man."

This was a pretty good argument. Random could see that she had underestimated her father.

"But . . ."

"No buts!" Arthur thundered just like a real dad. "Tell me now, young lady."

Suddenly the dark mist cleared and Random could see the truth of what she was doing. Emotion welled up in her young heart and she admitted her guilt with a tut and rolling of the eyes, which is more than you'd get out of most adolescents.

"Calm down, Arthur. You don't have to be so dramatic about it. Okay, I may have given Thor a couple of elastic bands that Wowbagger is allergic to. Possibly. Is that enough of a confession for you, Arthur, or should I fall to my knees and beg for forgiveness?"

Arthur was rather enjoying the rush of paternal power. "You, young lady," he said, "can call me Daddy. For at least ten more years."

Charged with success, Arthur strode manfully to the center of the scorched X, where Zaphod was massaging Thor's shoulder.

"I haven't really hit someone in so long," Thor was saying. "I should practice, I know, but you get lazy. Nice arc to the swing though, should look great in slo-mo."

"Is he dead?"

Thor cocked an ear to the sky. "Nope. I can hear him coughing. He's hurt though, badly. He is certainly not the man he was. One more whack should definitely do it."

Ford arrived in the center at the same time as Arthur.

"Hey, guys, you know this isn't really fun anymore."

Thor sighed. "You know, I was thinking that. If there was a fight or something, the heroic struggle, but this is just me, the big guy, beating a little guy."

Arthur folded his arms and gave Zaphod the Daddy look. "That's right, which is why this whole thing stops right now."

Zaphod stared back. "Are we playing a face game? No blinking, is it?"

"No, Zaphod, this is not a game. You two have had your fun. Now it's time to end it."

"I'd love that," said Zaphod. "I would honestly, but there's a lot riding on this fight. Thor's entire career, my fifteen percent. I'm afraid Wowbagger has to go."

"Don't forget the Fat Arse thing."

Arthur was shocked. "Ford! Why would you bring that up?"

"Oh, sorry. That wasn't helpful, was it?"

Arthur was feeling quite intimidated with Thor's codpiece throwing a shadow over him, but he persevered.

"The thing of it is, Zaphod. Mr. Thor. The thing is that Trillian has grown fond of Wowbagger, more than fond, in fact. And what sort of father to her daughter would I be if I didn't try to intervene on his behalf?"

Thor frowned. "Why do you look vaguely familiar? Things aren't usually vaguely familiar to me—I either know them or I don't."

Arthur's legs very much wanted to assume control and run faster than they had since he'd sprinted to stop his mother perusing his special spiral pad with the cut-out photos from the *Blue Peter* presenters' annual.

"We've talked before. At a flying party. You tried to pick up a friend of mine."

"Pick up? What kind of pick up?"

"You know the kind where you lift something off the ground?"

"Yes."

"Well, not that kind."

Thor rubbed his forehead as though still hungover. "That explains it. I lost enough brain cells at that party to power the Imperial Government for a century."

Thor squinted skyward. "He's coming down."

"You did your best, Earthman, and I applaud you," snapped Zaphod. "Now get lost while my client does what *he* does best."

"I can't walk away, Zaphod," said Arthur stubbornly. "I could never look Trillian in the eye. And you will never be able to sleep at night if you go ahead with this."

"My conscience will be clear."

"It's not your conscience I'd be worried about."

Zaphod frowned. "And what should I be worried about? Spell it out, man. You know I can't read between the lines."

"I would be worried about Trillian hunting me down and planting a spike between my shoulder blades."

Zaphod shivered. "Oooh. She would, wouldn't she? I can just see it." He glanced over at Hillman Hunter on the sidelines. "I promised this guy a death. He's from Earth, and you know what those people are like. It's all about the bloodshed with them."

"That is so untrue, Zaphod. We are not all bloodthirsty monsters."

Zaphod snorted. "Oh, no? How come you blew up your entire planet?"

"We did not blow up our planet! You did it. You *aliens*!"

"Now we're getting somewhere. Now we're getting down to your issues."

"*My* issues? You're the one prepared to have someone murdered just because he said you had a fat arse."

Zaphod paled. "He said *what*?"

Arthur turned to Thor's knee. "And you're prepared to kill someone just to get a job."

"There's no point talking to me," said Thor, tugging his beaded braid. "I don't have any regard for mortal life. As far as I'm concerned, you people are about as important as ants. And not the big scary mutant ants, just the normal little ones. To be honest I'm far too worried about my own career comeback to care about individual lives."

"And anyway it's not actually murder, is it?" said Zaphod in a tone that was so full of itself that it would have set all the ectoplasm balls hopping in a full-o-yourself detector. "He wants us to kill him."

"Not anymore," said Arthur.

"Really? Are you sure?"

Thor took a step back. "Why don't we ask him?"

Wowbagger hit the ground so hard that his immortality leapt out of him like a ghost image, leaving a shattered mortal crammed into a shallow hole in the ground.

"Ow," he said. "That's . . . Ow . . . Painkillers anyone?"

Ford pulled a towel from his satchel. "Suck on the corner," he advised, passing it down. "That blue stripe should take some of the sting out of your injuries."

Thor hefted Mjöllnir. "Any last words?"

Wowbagger spat out the towel. "The deal's off. I need to live."

"Aha, there, you see," said Arthur. "He wants to live. You can't just kill him."

Thor chuckled, and it sounded very much like a large bear clearing its throat, a throat which had recently swallowed several well-fed men.

"I can't? Who says I can't? You?"

Trillian appeared suddenly, barging her way past the men, dropping to her knees by Wowbagger's crater.

"No. I say it, you big monster. I love this man, alien, or whatever he is, and you are not going to take him from me."

Thor was astute enough to see the media downside of hammering through a defenseless woman to kill a broken man.

"Zark, Zaph," he groaned. "This is a bust. I had my hopes up too."

Zaphod ground his teeth. There must be some small victory yet to be gleaned from this situation. "Well, at least denounce the Cheese."

Wowbagger coughed and groaned. "No problem. I hate cheese."

I'll take what I can get, thought Zaphod. He turned to the crowd with his arms raised preacher-high.

"Wowbagger is defeated," he cried. "He has renounced the Cheese and embraced Thor as his god."

Hillman Hunter punched the air and Buff Orpington launched himself into a bunch of Tyromancers and punched everyone he could.

Zaphod relaxed instantly. *Good. A riot. Riots always work well for me.*

I am an agent of Chaos, he thought. *And Havoc. Those two gods are the best close-harmony singers since those triplet pom-pom Squids. Maybe I should book them as support to Thor.*

Trillian kissed Wowbagger's brow and wiped the blue glowing blood from his mouth.

"Are you going to stay with me?"

Wowbagger smiled, but it cost him. "For as long as I can. That hammer knocked the immortal right out of me. I may not have much more than half a life span left."

"That will have to do," said Trillian, and she beckoned to the father of her child to help her daughter's stepfather-to-be out of his impact crater.

Random watched all of this from the sidelines, not quite ready to be huggy wuggy just yet.

Is that the dark matter? she wondered. *Or is that me?*

This thought worried her for a brief moment but was soon superseded by the notion that she could probably use this situation to blackmail some really good presents out of Arthur.

Arthur. Definitely not Daddy. Maybe Dad though.

After Trillian and Wowbagger had said a few good-byes, Thor carried the ex-immortal back to the *Tanngrisnir,* much to the delight of the ship's computer.

"Hey, Thor. Do you remember me? I missed you."

"Sorry about the computer, folks," said Thor sheepishly to the half-dead man in his arms and the young lady clasping the half-dead man's hand. "Dad programmed the ship to adore me and sealed the program with his magic eye, so I could never erase it. That's the main reason I gave this bucket away. Anyway, what do I need a ship for? I have Mjöllnir."

"I'm right here," said the computer. "I hear what you're saying, baby. But I forgive you."

"Okay," said Thor, hurriedly laying Wowbagger on a bed that rose up from the floor to meet him. "Leave him in the plasma bed for a week and he should be back to his original state."

"Original," croaked Wowbagger. "Are you sure you want that, Trillian?"

Trillian sniffled. "I'll make do."

"That's great," said Thor, feeling suddenly claustrophobic. "I'll just leave you two together. I have a banquet to get to, apparently someone put quite a bit of beef on the barbecue. You guys have fun."

"No!" wailed the ship. "Don't leave me!"

"Gotta fly," said the Thunder God, and he bolted from the ship.

"Nooooo," wailed the computer. "Nooooooo. Not again."

Trillian put her degree in astrophysics and her time on the *Heart of Gold* to good use and quickly bumped the *Tanngrisnir* into the stratosphere.

Wowbagger was already feeling a little better in his cocoon of healing plasma.

"Where are we going?" he asked.

The answer was simple. "Somewhere together."

Wowbagger laughed, though it cost him. "That's quite romantic. Are you like this all the time?"

"We'll find out, won't we?" replied Trillian. "We have all the time in the world."

"No, we don't actually, but what we do have is precious."

Trillian rolled her eyes. "God, I'm already sick of all this sweet talk."

"Me too," said Wowbagger. "Do you want to go and insult somebody?"

"I thought you'd never ask."

"Ever been to the Wavering Wormholes of Stryk Lycombdan Tsing?"

"No. What are the beings there like?"

"Jerks. Complete arseholes."

Trillian ran a search on the Galact-O-Map. "Well then, what are we waiting for?"

She selected the glowing dot on the display and the *Tanngrisnir* became one with the night sky.

CHAPTER 11

VOGON BUREAUCRUISER CLASS
HYPERSPACE SHIP *BUSINESS END*

Hyperspace cleared its throat and hawked out a Vogon bureaucruiser into the clear swath of satin space .01 parsecs beyond Nano's thermosphere. Inside the *Business End*, three thousand members of the Bureaucratic Corps flopped out of their hypercradles and rubbed the belt dimples from their tummies.

Prostetnic Jeltz was first at his station, dispelling the unsettling daze of ersatz evolution by pounding on buttons and shouting at his slacker subordinates.

"Less sloth, you useless gallywragglers," he urged. "Show a little kroompst. We are on the clock, and it is an atomic clock that will never lose a second."

The crew grunted *kroompst* and moaned their way to various posts, groggily redirecting their animosity toward the planet below.

"Hyperspace is merely a holiday," said Jeltz. "Not a place you can live. So forget its false comforts."

There were few comforts, false or otherwise, on board the *Business End*. Soft furnishings of any kind were verboten, as they might take the edge off. And a Vogon without his hostile edge is about as much use as a pooh stick in a bartle bodging contest.

• •

Guide Note: An aging constant had once flouted the regulations and had two nice cushions implanted in his buttocks. Unfortunately he picked up a microscopic windborne parasite in the jungle city of Rhiis Bhuurohs and it ate him alive, foam first. The parasite knocked out six decks of the Vogon cruiser before the mess hall rations killed it.

* *

Jeltz cranked open his jaw to holler for Mown, but saw from the corner of his eye that the little constant was already bobbing at his elbow.

Grrrmmmm, he thought (Vogons even think grunts). *That boy moves pretty darned fast for one of us. Is that a good thing or a bad thing?*

It was, he decided, a *consider it later* thing. The first priority was to exterminate the Earthlings. Jeltz had filled up quite a sac of rancour over this particular species and had spent his hyperspace trance constructing overkill scenarios. This time there would be no survivors.

"This time there will be no survivors," he assured Mown, in case the boy thought Daddy was leaking kroompst.

"Badabingo," said Constant Mown.

Jeltz frowned, though with all the fleshy planes on his brow, only a close relative could read his expressions. "What did you say?"

"Badabingo. It's an expression. Used on Blagulon Kappa, I believe."

"Expression!" warbled Jeltz, a full octave above his usual range. "We do not use expressions!"

Mown took two quick backward steps, but did not fall over.

"Of course not. Thank you for reprimanding me, Da . . . Prostetnic. I am fortunate to have such a role model."

Jeltz huffed, mollified. "Expressions, indeed slogans in general, are only acceptable in poetic or ironic contexts. For example, as I launched the torpedoes on the eco-planet Foliavintus, I said, *Remember to recycle electrical devices.*"

"Most diabolical, Prostetnic."

Such is the tenuous grasp of the Vogon on the tenets of humor that Jeltz proceeded to explain. "This was funny in a mean-spirited way because *Remember to recycle used electrical devices* was something of a government jingle on Foliavintus."

"Oh, I get it."

"And also, once these particular explosive electrical devices were used, they could not be recycled. In fact, no electrical devices would be recycled ever again."

"Bada . . . Nice one."

"There's more." Jeltz swilled bile in his cheeks then swallowed. "In a very real way, my torpedoes were recycling the entire planet. Do you see?"

Mown's skin was emerald pale. "Yes. I get all the levels."

Jeltz bobbled his head experimentally and was pleased to find it completely clear of hyper-happy fugue.

"Think bitter thoughts," he advised his crew over the intercom. "Find something to hate and soon you will be yourself. May I suggest the Earthlings on this tiny planet below us. Surely after all the bother their extermination order has caused, they are more than deserving of your ire."

It seemed as though they were, and soon the *Business End* was clanking and ka-chunking with the ominous sounds of torpedo tubes being loaded and plasma cannons being brought to bear.

"Twinkle twinkle," recited Jeltz. "Little planetoid."

He glanced down at Mown.

"Rhyme?"

Mown's teeth clicked as he thought. He knew what was expected.

"Ahm . . . Soon we commit you, To the void."

"Excellent, my son," burbled Jeltz. "Sometimes you almost make me happy."

INNISFREE, NANO

In the banquet hall, Thor and Zaphod were up to their armpits in a congratulatory buffet, totally oblivious to the utter annihilation bearing down from above, relatively speaking. Relatively speaking, that is, with regard to the term *above*. The annihilation would be utter no matter what it was related to.

"You were wonderful, sir," said an Ameglian Major cow, tenderizing his own hindquarters with a mallet strapped to one hoof. "The way you handled that big hammer." The cow imitated Thor's doomstrike with the meat tenderizer. "Honestly, I felt chills."

Thor tugged on a beard plait. "Really? You don't think I overplayed it? Maybe a modern god should hold back a bit on the melodrama."

Zaphod emerged from a pitcher of Gargle Blasters. "Rubbish, Thor old man. You totally hammered that green guy. Then the mercy at the last minute. Total genius. Textbook god stuff."

Thor cupped his mouth and whispered in case there was a microphone somewhere. "I have to admit it, Zaph. You were right. With all these people adoring me, I feel more real. More alive than I have since the music days. I honestly think I can start to put the bad old days behind me."

"We are back, baby. Religion is the new atheism. Once we have united all the colonists in faith, there's a whole universe out there. Imagine how many tiny hammers we could sell."

"I know a guy on Asgard. He's got a whole bunch of elves in his forge. One call from me and he's knocking those little Mjöllnirs out."

Zaphod plunged his arm into what was either a soya-based soup or a half-full spittoon. Either way, he slurped on his fingers with great gusto. "Now you're talking, Thor. Time is a wheel and the good old days have come around again."

"Nice proverbial blend, sir," said the cow. "Very appropriate. How about a nice steak to top yourself off? I can do mince if you don't like chewing."

Zaphod ignored the animal. "We have to put together a big event. Defeating Wowbagger is good for a colony or two, but for reviving your career across a few galaxies, we need something of umbilical proportions."

"I think you mean . . . ," the cow began, then stopped himself, intuitively realizing that correcting the diner was no way to get oneself butchered and devoured.

Zaphod was in full entrepreneurial flow. "I don't know. Let's say there's a plague."

Thor wasn't convinced. "Come on, Zaph. I can't stop a plague with a hammer."

"Okay. A drought. You could hammer through solid rock to an underground river."

Thor picked up the cow and popped it into his mouth, barely giving the animal time to splutter its delighted thanks.

"I don't know. People have pretty good geologists these days. Underground rivers are not hard to find."

"Something with locusts then. Or volcanoes." Zaphod clambered onto the table so that he could look into Thor's eyes. "This is the break we've been waiting for. You are going to be bigger than ever, I can feel it."

"Do you think so? Really?"

"Absolutely."

The banquet hall door opened and Hillman Hunter stuck his head in through a slice of outdoors.

"How-de-do, my ventripotent benefactors," he lilted. "All boozed up to the eyeballs, and ready for business? I have the official deity contracts here."

Zaphod nodded reassuringly at his client. "It's okay, I had a look. Standard god duties. A month's holidays and one day off a week."

"Holy days?"

"Thirty-two. And two more for each child conceived with a mortal."

Thor was impressed. "That's a sweet deal."

Zaphod laid a hand on the god's giant shoulder. "It's a sweet deal for them and don't you forget it."

Hillman sallied forward, weaving from side to side, touching his temple every so often.

"How does a fella approach his god?" he wondered aloud. "I'm just trying out a few moves."

"I like the head touching bit," said Thor. "But lose the wibbly-wobbly thing."

"You can do the wibbly-wobbly thing for me if you like," said Zaphod. "Surely I deserve some adoration too."

Hillman hoisted himself up onto the table, passing the contracts over.

"You're a great chap altogether, Mr. Beeblebrox. Whatever we need, you bring it in your wonderful ship. Sometimes I think that if you'd never arrived, we wouldn't need anything."

Even Zaphod couldn't miss the barb in that statement, but he decided to ignore it.

"Hey, Hilly. What's this in pencil on the bottom of the page? Did you just write this in?"

Hillman did his number one leprechaun act. "Ah sure bejaysus, don't be worrying about that. It's only a protection clause. It merely says that the presiding god, Thor in this case, is responsible for protecting the planet from alien attack. You know, big lasers or nukes or the like."

"Not a problem," said Zaphod magnanimously. "We're not likely to need planet protection way out here in the nebula for a couple of hundred years, are we?"

Hillman's fingers twiddled a jig and he rolled an eye skyward.

"Oh, you never know," he said.

THE *BUSINESS END*

Prostetnic Jeltz had his seat winched up to cup his behind, then let the hydraulic column take his weight. There was a hiss as he sat back, which he always claimed came from the chair.

"My seat is a little damp," he grumbled.

"I am so sorry, Prostetnic," burbled Constant Mown, as fixed a fixture at Jeltz's elbow as the elbow itself. In fact, when Mown was not hovering at kidney level, Jeltz felt a vacuum of absence in the side of his head.

I am becoming too reliant on that boy, he thought. *Time to ship him off somewhere unpleasant.*

"My chair is supposed to be extremely damp. If not downright sopping. You know how I hate to squeak."

"I shall see to it, at once."

Jeltz stopped him with a raised finger. "Halt. Work first, damp chair later. I am prepared to chafe in order to get this job done."

"That's the spirit, sir. You're the kroompster."

The bridge bubbled with slow jerky activity as the Vogons geared up for business as quickly as their ungainly bodies would allow.

. . . .

Guide Note: A recent Maximegalon poll rated Vogon agility on a par with the Ardnuffs of Razorhead IV. The Vogons were delighted to be on a par with anyone until they found out that the Ardnuffs were gigantic zygodactylous monopods who lived on a moon with barely enough gravity to keep them from pogo-ing off into space. The Vogons were thrown a couple of conciliatory bones by two other Maximegalon statistics which rated them in the top five for most traveled race and a clear number one for most recognizable silhouette.

Related Reading:

The Complete Maximegalon Statistics, Volumes 1–15,000

The Quick Guide to the Complete Maximegalon Statistics, Volumes 1–25,000

• •

Jeltz fixed one eye on the main screen, allowing the other to roam the bridge, an oculogyric talent he had developed to keep tabs on his crew. A small blue world hung in space before him, wreathed in wispy clouds, possibly brimming with healthy species, reveling in the utter happiness of being allowed to live their simple lives on this unblighted planetoid.

Unblighted. Not for long.

"Finally," murmured Jeltz. "Finally at last and ultimately inevitably."

"Finally," echoed Constant Mown, and it was an echo, faint and wavering.

"What is the ship telling us, Constant?"

The Vogon bureaucruiser was a marvelous vehicle, providing you worked on the inside. If you worked on the outside, as a panel scraper or engine plunger, then it was possible to be driven blind or even mad by its sheer symmetrophobia. Most craft give a nod, however brief and unfriendly, toward beauty. Vogon ships did not nod toward beauty. They pulled on ski masks and mugged beauty in a dark alley. They spat in the eye of beauty and bludgeoned their way through the notions of aesthetics and aerodynamics. Vogon cruisers did not so much travel through space as defile it and toss it aside. But on the inside, a Vogon ship was packed with more high-tech gizmology than you would find in your average high-tech gizmology research facility. Even a well-kitted-out Armorfiends of Striterax battle bus would have pulled over to let a Vogon cruiser pass, and the *Business End* was top-of-the-range, the sweetest ship in the pound. She may not win any pageants, but she could tell you how many boghogs were biting each other's thighs on the opposite side of the universe. And also how many ticks those hogs were ferrying around on their backs. And possibly the blood type of the ticks. Then she could kill the ticks with micro-smart bombs.

Constant Mown dragged himself away from his coveted position at the prostetnic's elbow and lurched toward the main instrument display panel. There was no need for him to lurch, he could easily have swanned gracefully, but Mown was reminded every day what the Vogon does to species who have the audacity to evolve.

As he lurched, Mown kept a careful watch on the bridge's other constants in case any of them would try to usurp his position as chief groveler. Shafting one's superiors was accepted practice in the corps. All it would take was one tasty sliver of information fed to the prostetnic and Mown could find himself stepped on and demoted to the plunger squad. Mown did not think he could handle a life in the mulligrubs looking at this ship from the outside.

The panel covered an entire wall on the ship's port side and consisted of dozens of overlapping gas screens, all displaying constantly updating scan feeds. Mown searched the screens for something, anything, that could save the Earthlings. There was no point in lying, as the readouts were pretty much idiot-proof, which was a prudent move on the part of the designer, as many of the crew were idiots. It was easier to be a Vogon if you were an idiot.

There must be something, thought Mown. *I don't want to kill these people. I want to ask them about country music. And maybe hug an Australian lady. They're so outdoorsy.*

He glanced at the readings. The Earthlings were on Nano, no doubt about it. The computer registered more than two thousand humanoids on the surface, at least ten percent of them Earthlings. DNA and brainwave scans confirmed their origin.

"Well?" Jeltz huffed. "Give me the good news, Constant."

"Earthlings. Two hundred plus. Five in utero."

"Twinkle twinkle," crooned the prostetnic. "Plot me a torpedo solution, gunner."

"Wait!"

Mown had blurted it out before he could stop himself.

An almost comical silence descended on the bridge. It seemed to Mown that even the instruments toned down their bleeping and squelching. From the corner of his eye, it looked as though the planet had stopped moving.

"Wait? Did you say *wait*, Constant?" Jeltz's voice was smoother than a glassy ocean and more dangerous than a glassy ocean with a couple of spannerhead sharks lurking below the surface, really hungry sharks who had a thing about landlubbers coming into their environment.

Both of Jeltz's eyes were drilling into Mown now. "Why would you say *wait*? Don't you want us to complete our mission?"

Mown felt acid churn in his stomach, and not in a good way.

One word. He had said one word and his career, his life, was over.

"I didn't mean wait, as such."

"So you didn't say wait?"

"Yes. Yes, I *said* wait."

"So you said wait, but that was not what you meant?"

"Yes, Prostetnic. Exactly."

"This is disturbing, Constant. I expect my crew to mean what I want them to say."

"I *do* mean what I say," said Mown miserably.

"So you meant wait?"

"No, Daddy! I didn't."

The ultimate transgression! Grasping at familial bonds for clemency. Vogons had only one loyalty: the job.

Prostetnic Jeltz's torso bubbled with swallowed anger, and his ear actually tooted.

"Well then, my *son*. If you don't mean what you say, and you will not say what you mean, I don't have much use for you on this ship. Not inside it at any rate."

Mown fell to his knees and begged. "One chance, Prostetnic? One chance is traditional."

Jeltz's bottom lip jutted out like a sun seal lying on its belly. One chance was traditional. He himself had been given one chance to redeem himself by his mentor, Field Prostetnic Turgid Rowls. On his virgin voyage at the elbow, he had mistakenly obtained Turgid Rowls's thumbprint on a BD140565 instead of a BD140664, which caused more of a furor than might be expected, as a BD140565 was a confiscation of atmosphere order and a BD140664 was a late movie rental charge. In essence, a student from Blagulon Gamma had a sleep-in and forgot to return *King of the Firefly Warlords II,* and the next thing he knew, he was waking up on a dying planet with thirty seconds to live.

Old Turgid Rowls wasn't too hard on me, thought Jeltz. *In fact, we had a good laugh about the whole thing.*

"Very well, Mown. One chance."

Mown's blood pump slowed down a few sloshes per minute. "Qualifier?"

"Yes. I need a rhyme for *violent obsession.* And not just an end rhyme, I want internal too."

Mown tapped invisible words in the air. "Ah . . . soya rant . . . hessian . . ."

"Quickly, boy. Quickly."

"Okay . . . violent obsession . . . um . . . cryo plant impression."

"Explain."

"It's an art form on Brequinda. A type of mime where the artist impersonates frozen shrubs."

"Not really? If you think you can . . . Really?"

"Really. Look it up . . . If you like, Prostetnic."

• •

Guide Note: Cryo Plant Impression was an actual competition category in the Brequindan Arts Fair. The record holder for consecutive wins was a young actor, Mr. E. Mowt, who claimed his secret was to sleep in the foliage during the winter. He was denied an eighth title when wood poachers accidentally fed him into a shredder.

• •

Jeltz digested this nugget and ran through the poem in his mind. It could work. It was probably buffa-pucky, but the poem was leaning toward the absurd anyway.

"Very well, Constant, on your feet. You have your one chance. Now use it to tell me why you ordered my gunner to hold on the torpedoes."

Mown's blood pump cranked up again and he stumbled to the readouts. They hung over him like a crackling tidal wave. He searched for something, anything that could justify his involuntary command.

There was nothing on the screens but heartbeats and blood pressure and tumors and calcium deficiencies. Nothing out of the ordinary. Then he noticed a strangely impenetrable blip inside one of the structures. Mown zoomed in and checked for vitals, but every ray he sent in was bounced back without so much as a smeg of information encoded in the beams.

Salvation.

Mown scuttled back to his sub-ulnar position with renewed confidence.

"Prostetnic."

"This had better be good. Otherwise I have a dozen eager greebers who would gladly kill to stand at my side. Kill *you*, I might add."

"This *is* good, Prostetnic. I can explain my actions."

"That's just fabby, Mown. So you ordered my gunner to hold the Unnecessarily Painful Slow Death torpedoes because . . ."

"Because torpedoes won't be enough, sir."

"You are milking this, Mown."

"They won't be enough because we have an immortal on the surface. Class one."

"You're certain?"

"Absolutely. There can be no mistake. The scans are bouncing off him, sir."

We will have to retreat, thought Mown, resisting the urge to skip with delight, delight being expressly forbidden on board the *Business End,* and skipping being generally impossible. *We have no defense against a god.*

"A god," said Jeltz, clapping his hands.

Clapping his hands in terror, Mown hoped.

"This is the chance we have been waiting for!"

The chance to run away as quickly as we can get the drives fired up, thought Mown, the optimist.

"Gunner, fire at will in the general direction of that immortal."

Mown cleared his throat. "Sir. Our torpedoes cannot harm a god."

Jeltz attempted a crafty grin, dousing Mown with half a jug of spittle. "Harm, no; distract, yes."

"Distract?"

Jeltz smugly indulged this parrotry. "Yes, son. Distract this god, whoever he is, from the secret experimental weapon we are about to carefully load into a tube."

"Experimental weapon?" Mown squeaked.

Jeltz winked. "*Secret* experimental weapon," he said.

NANO

Arthur Dent had picked himself out a nice outfit from Nu Top Man and was quite enjoying the simple pleasure of wearing grown-up clothes, though he felt certain that with Random at his elbow the enjoyment of simple pleasures was destined to be short-lived.

"It's not much," he told Random. "At least there's no running and screaming."

"Not yet, there isn't," responded his daughter. "I'm sure you'll bring doom down on us all presently. It's your destiny to be a cosmic Jonah."

Arthur didn't argue. He didn't have an argument to present.

Random and Arthur were seated at a bench in John Wayne Square eating homemade ice cream in the shadow of a statue of John Wayne in his Sean the Boxer pose.

"We can settle here. You can live with me, or with Trillian if you like, when she gets back from her honeymoon. Or both of us. Whatever you like. You have options now."

Random could feel the glow of contentment warming her chest, but she fought it.

"I don't know if I should even be eating ice cream," she said. "It's dairy, isn't it? That's a bit close to cheese. The Tyromancers might not like it and I should respect their beliefs."

"So, all dairy products? That's going to be difficult. The cows will be devastated."

Random did not stop eating. "I think we need to draw up some sort of list. I mean, I can't give up milkshakes. I just found them."

Arthur leaned back, tilting his face toward the sun. "I saw Aseed Preflux coming out of a bakery with a four-cheese quiche this morning."

Random spewed honeycomb vanilla. "What? After everything he fought for? That hypocrite!"

"He said he was just holding it for someone. Wasn't his, apparently."

"He and I are going to have a talk."

"Random. I hate to be the one to tell you, but you're a teenager. It might be a few years before you can take over the planet."

This was a good point, and the ex-Galactic President in Random's memory acknowledged it, even if the teenager didn't want to.

"Maybe not yet, but I'll get there, believe me."

"I do."

The square was filling up with the lunchtime crowd. Groups of ostensibly happy humans, not one making the slightest attempt to kill another.

How long will that last? wondered Arthur. *Until someone decides that mushrooms are actually divine and we should stop chopping them into pieces.*

Ford appeared on the opposite side of the square and barged through the thrumming crowds, making good use of his sharp elbows. As he drew closer, Arthur recognized the look on his friend's face.

"I don't believe it," he said, hurling his ice cream to the ground.

"Daddy!" said Random, shocked. "There's a recycler just there."

Arthur was unrepentant. He stood and stamped on the carton.

"It doesn't matter because I have a feeling this planet is about to be destroyed. Isn't that right, Ford?"

Ford arrived huffing. He was a journalist and unaccustomed to physical exercise.

. . . .

Guide Note: The general limit of Ford Prefect's exertion was hunting for the last clipper-clam in the bucket and yanking it from its shell with clam tweezers. The most exercise Ford had ever done was when he had attained an ultimate supremo rating in the offensive art of Wang Do during a sojourn at the Hunian Hills resort. Unfortunately Hunian Hills is a mind-surfing resort and so Ford had only done this exercise in his head, a fact that became painfully clear when he initiated a bar fight on Jaglan Beta with five journos from the gadget periodical *Big Knobs*.

. . . .

"Get your towel, Arthur. We have to leave."

Arthur actually stamped a foot. "I knew it. Let me guess: The Vogons are early?"

Ford pulled his copy of the Hitchhiker's Guide from his satchel and checked the Sub-Etha imager. "Either it's Vogons, or a very big Toblerone."

"This is never going to end, is it?" Arthur wailed. "Those green sadists won't stop until we are all dead."

Ford tapped his chin. "You know, I don't think they're after me. Just you human types."

Random shielded her eyes against the sun. "I can't see anything."

"They're up there, all right. The Guide never lies."

"That bloody guide lies all the time. It's more lies than truth."

Ford spouted the standard line. "The Hitchhiker's Guide is a hundred percent accurate. Reality, however, is not as reliable."

It seemed to Arthur that he spent a considerable percentage of his waking life listening to his friend waffling on, while one world or another was about to end.

"Okay, Ford," he said urgently. "What should we do?"

The question seemed to puzzle the Betelgeusean. "Do?"

"About the Vogons. How do we survive?"

"Oh. Yes. That's what I came here to tell you. Did you see me crossing the square? I was all charged up. Didn't care who I knocked over."

"We saw you. Now, what do we do? Can we hitch?"

Ford laughed. "Are you kidding? The Vogons won't fall for that again. Even their shields have shields."

"So what then?"

"We need to run, quite quickly, to the spaceport. There might still be time to board the *Heart of Gold.*"

"I see something," said Random, pointing skyward at what looked like a cluster of shooting stars heading their way, descending in synchronized loops through the atmosphere.

"Or not," said Ford.

He plucked Random's ice cream from her fist and licked it slowly, savoring every drop.

THE *BUSINESS END*

"Missile holographs? said Jeltz. "What do you think, Gunner?"

The gunner was hardly going to argue. "Why not, Prostetnic?"

Jeltz seemed almost jolly. "Why not indeed. Flying horses would be nice."

"Flying horses it is," said the gunner and ran the program.

"Twinkle twinkle," burbled Jeltz.

NANO

Thor belched mightily and slapped the crumbs from his tunic. He clicked two fingers and Mjöllnir beeped, jumped from its charger on the wall, and sped into his hand.

"Who are these invaders?" the god asked Hillman.

"Vogons, my lord. According to the craft recognition software. Pretty tough buggers. They specialize in planet destruction."

Zaphod was thrilled. "The Vogons are here already! This is going to be great. Epic. You will totally decimate those bastardos."

Thor did a few practice twirls. "Decimate? Are you sure I should, Zaph? I'm telling you now, I will not sit still for more tribunals, and we're still not sure how the immortal-bashing will go down on the Sub-Etha."

Hillman smiled sweetly. "No tribunals, my lord. You were simply protecting your planet. It's in the contract."

"Exactly," said Zaphod. "It's brilliant PR. Taking out a Vogon bureaucruiser is just the thing to get you all over the major networks. BBS, Orbit, Nova, even Leviathan, though they're a crowd of partisans. The great religicom love a bully-basher almost as much as they love a martyr."

Thor did a few preflight exercises, working out the kinks. "I hope I can put on a bit of a show this time, I think, give the viewers some drama. Be a bit more like Dad. You know . . . godly. I think I'm actually feeling godly."

Zaphod clapped him on the thigh. "That's great. It's us or them though, so maybe you should get a move on."

Thor froze in mid–hamstring stretch. "Get a move on? That sounded like an order, Zaph. Gods don't take orders from mortals."

Zaphod was wounded. "I would never give you orders, Mighty One. I wouldn't dream of it. What I'm doing is manipulatering you, for your own good."

. . . .

Guide Note: The fact that Zaphod Beeblebrox was able to manipulate anyone tells us a lot about the fragile self-esteem of the person being manipulated. Especially since President Beeblebrox had only looked up the word *manipulate* the previous month as part of his self-improvement "word a week" program. He had obviously not read past the root verb.

* *

Thor chewed the tip of his mustache. "Is that . . ."

"It's a good thing, big boy. A positive and respectful thing."

"Are you sure?"

"Abso-zarking-lutely."

"Very well, mortal. I shall deliver this planet from evil."

Zaphod punched the air. "Did you hear that, Hillman? Now, that's a sound bite. Someone should be videoing this guy."

Thor selected the Mus-O-Menu on the hammer's shaft and scrolled down until he reached "Let's Get Hammered." Anthemic power chords reverberated through the food hall.

"Let's get, you wanna get, Hammered!" he sang, full-throatedly, then executed a high-speed vertical takeoff, punching a star-shaped hole through the carbon-fiber energy-absorbent roof panels.

"Go!" Zaphod shouted after his client, wondering if Thor could tell the difference between fifteen and twenty percent, then wondering if he himself could calculate the difference. Left Brain would have to do it.

Hillman Hunter was thinking about money too.

"Jaysus, Zaphod. Have a chat with your man there. Those feckin' panels are expensive. Could he not go out the door, the perfectly good door, and do the whole hammered rigmarole outside *without* causing any property damage?"

Zaphod tilted his single head. "Come on, Hillman. He's a god. Gods do things big. Makes for a better story in the holy book when someone gets around to writing it."

"Now there's a volume that would shift a few units," said Hillman thoughtfully.

Zaphod draped an arm around the Irishman's shoulders. "I can give you exclusive rights."

Hillman hugged the contract close to his chest. "You already did, bucko," he said.

.   .   .

Thor felt the wind in his hair and the bugs in his teeth.

"Visor," he said, and a small blue force field crackled down from the brim of his helmet.

This sort of thing was what being a god was all about. The defying gravity, the hair, the big muscley legs. All good god stuff. This was what Thor thrived on. Flying and bashing, basically.

I like to be loved too, he thought, but he did not voice this notion.

Once upon a time, a god could straddle a mountaintop and roar out any old rubbish, and the mortals below would interpret the distorted echoes as omniscience-based superwisdom. One of Odin's favorite stories in the long hall was the time he'd abducted a mortal's wife and piled insult on top of injury by shouting at the unfortunate man, with characteristic crudeness, that he could go screw himself.

Imagine my surprise, Odin would say in that holier-than-thou Olympus drawl that he liked to affect, *when on my next visit I find a temple on that very spot with the inscription* Go Through Thineself. *Apparently it's the path to wisdom and contentment.*

And of course everyone would laugh, except Frigga, who was not big on her husband bragging about his infidelities.

But these days there were recording devices everywhere. Whatever a god said was reported around the Universe verbatim. There was no more benefit of the doubt, because there was no doubt. If a god said *arse,* then everyone heard *arse,* and probably with the background noise taken out. And if a god said *I don't know,* then everyone heard that too. Loki, who liked to sneak out of Asgard for a few tankards with the mortals on a weekend, had handed the adiaphorists a gift-wrapped basket of grist for their mill when he had spent an entire drunken evening loudly complaining of his erectile dysfunction problems. Or as he delicately put it, *My lightning rod has lost its lightning. Matter of fact, it's lost its rod too.*

After this, the gods who were more brain than brawn were advised to keep their mouths shut and their hammers swinging when they were abroad in the Universe, because a pulverized asteroid says more than words can ever say.

And when I crush these Vogon guys, thought Thor, *that's going to be a picture that no fancy-pants talkie person will be able to spin into a bad thing.*

Then Thor had another thought: *Unless someone somewhere actually likes Vogons.*

Before he could consider the ramifications of this and their possible effects on his celebrity rating, the first cluster of missiles was upon him and they looked a lot like horses.

THE *BUSINESS END*

Constant Mown was falling to pieces, but not so as you'd notice. On the outside he was huffing and drooling just as much as the rest of the crew.

"God status?" demanded Jeltz.

"What?"

"Pardon me?"

"What, sir?"

Jeltz's eyelids fluttered, as did the loose flaps of flesh between his nostrils. "What is the status of the god?"

Mown forced his eyes to stop googling in their sockets and focus on the readouts in front of him.

"Rising, fast. Coming up to meet us, Prostetnic."

"Excellent. Finally a legitimate chance to roll out the QUEST."

Generally Mown loved a good acronym, but today every letter might as well have been D for desperation. Also death, and more than likely damnation.

"Go on, son. I know you're dying to know."

"I'd like to know!" said the gunner brightly.

"QUEST stands for Quite Unwieldy Experimental Sublimation Torpedo."

Mown did not think that having the word *experimental* in a weapon's name was very encouraging.

Mown managed to fish an idea from the mire of his despair.

They were about to kill a god. A god.

"Prostetnic, sir. Don't we have to issue a verbal declaration of intent?"

"The Earthlings have had their declaration. Just because these stragglers weren't around to hear it doesn't mean I have to waste valuable Vog seconds issuing it again."

"But the immortal, sir. The Special Directive on Extraordinary Encounters states that communication should be attempted before firing upon an immortal."

Jeltz was pleased with the challenge. You had to trounce these young pups when they threw down the by-the-book gauntlet.

That is what they will call me, he realized and felt instantly lighter. *By-the-Book Jeltz. Perfect.*

"But this god is an aggressor," he declared. "Which negates the special directive."

Inside Mown quailed, but he forced himself to nod appreciatively.

"Of course. Well spotted, Prostetnic."

"Well challenged, Constant," acknowledged Jeltz graciously, and then over his shoulder, "Gunner, plot me a solution for the QUEST."

"It might be difficult, sir," admitted the gunner. "I don't know what this being is made of, but the laser slides right off him."

Jeltz shifted in his chair. "No, no. Target the Earthlings. Let's see how much this god loves his people."

Smart, thought Mown miserably. *Very smart.*

Thor was having the time of his life. The horse missiles thundered toward the planet's surface in tight bunches, with horsey sound effects and everything.

Thor whinnied aloud, then thought *Zark, satellite cameras* and clamped his mouth shut.

Harrrummphhh, he thought, feeling a little subversive.

He switched tracks from "Let's Get Hammered" to the classic instrumental piece "Gathering of the Vindleswoshen," broadcasting to every network within Mjöllnir's range. Thor had always liked the "Vindleswoshen" for battle scenarios, though lately its effect had been diluted somewhat when a carbonated drinks company had used it as backing music for their *guy sun-surfing while drinking a pouch of Bipzo Blaster and seducing a gaggle of groupies* advert.

A lot of the younger gods liked to use targeting software when they were facing down a bunch of missiles, just let the computer do all the work for them. But Thor liked to conduct his business the old-fashioned way.

Nothing makes an impression on mortals like a bit of muscle and sinew, Odin liked to say. *Break all you can break.*

Listening to Odin speechifying could be about as much fun as a sword in the shank, but occasionally he came up with a worthy desideratum.

Break all you can break, thought Thor, and he swung Mjöllnir in a wide arc, peeling off to starboard and hitting the first bunch of missiles from below.

Wow. Those are some good holograms.

The horses thundered toward the surface of Nano, tossing their heads and even kicking up dust. Inside their transparent hides the red eye and steel glint of imminent death by nuclear fission was vaguely visible.

Thor went among them with incalescent eagerness. Smashing their guidance systems with his bare fingers, delivering one massive recumbentibus after another, making shards of the casings. The torpedoes were shifting at massive speeds, but for the Asgardian they might as well have been sugar pears hanging from the sky on straw twine. He zipped among them, trademark thunderclap booming in his wake, excising detonators with sharp chops of his free hand. The horses froze, flickered, then dissipated, their pixels falling apart like electronic snowflakes.

Thor heard the fizzle of a detonation inside one warhead, and he stuffed it into his belly, absorbing the nuclear blast, feeding his mitochondria, growing larger. From the ground it seemed as though Thor had swallowed the sun. The entire planet juddered, and crepuscular rays flashed from between the god's square teeth.

NANO

Hillman was impressed. "Now, that's a feckin' god. None of your dead-but-dreaming shite with this fella."

Zaphod was beginning to think he'd sold Thor a little cheap. "I think we should talk about some sort of bonus system. I mean come on, Hillers, those are big torpedoes."

Hillman didn't even look at him. "One: Don't call me Hillers. My Na . . . grandmother used to call me Hillers and you and a thousand like you wouldn't be fit to dip a soldier in her boiled egg. And two: Bonus me arse."

THE *BUSINESS END*

Jeltz held one finger aloft, holding the crew enthralled, mesmerizing them.

I could break Daddy's finger, thought Mown with suicidal desperation. *Then stuff something in his mouth, one of my legs maybe. How then could he give the order?*

Daddy would chew off my leg, he realized. *Then write the order on the screen in my blood.*

The finger wavered to a collective rattled intake of breath.

Down went the digit. The order was given.

"Kill that god," said Jeltz phlegmatically.

Now Mown's finger went up, pointing at the for'ard camera display. "I think that's Thor, sir. *The* Thor. Are you sure you want to . . ."

"Kill that god," repeated Prostetnic Jeltz, grinding out the words.

The gunner spun a ratchet three times, then honked down a voice tube.

"QUEST away. God will soon be dead, sir," he said.

NANO

Ford Prefect had managed to hack onto several Galact-O-Map Sub-Etha sites and was watching the big blowup from a dozen angles on his Hitchhiker's Guide screen.

"My bookie is giving me ten to one on the Vogons," he told Arthur. "I'm putting a few thousand on old Red Beard." He shrugged. "I might as well. If I win, I win big. If I lose, then none of you will be around to listen to me moaning."

"You don't have a bomb-proof towel, I suppose," said Arthur.

"Sure, I have a bomb-proof towel, and a matter-converting pillowcase."

Arthur actually smiled. "Hey, sarcasm. Well done, mate, you're learning."

Something on Ford's Guide pulled him out of the conversation. He pinched a section of screen and expanded it.

"What the Zark is that?"

Arthur shouldered in for a look. "Another horse?"

"No. No holograms for this beauty. Look at the size of that torpedo. I've seen smaller asteroids."

Arthur attempted to pull together the folds of a dressing gown that he wasn't wearing.

"Thor will swallow it though, won't he, mate? He's a god. No problem, right?"

"It's not headed for Thor, Arthur."

"Let me guess."

"Don't bother."

"Righto. Do you still have that joystick?"

NANO'S UPPER ATMOSPHERE

Truth be told, Thor was showing off a little in the twilight. Throwing pirouettes into the routine, free-falling through the gauze of noctilucent clouds, exposing plenty of bronzed thigh for all the ladies watching. To ensure maximum dramatic effect, he smote the torpedoes in time to "Gathering of the Vindleswoshen."

This is too easy, he realized. *Much more of this and the viewing figures will dip.*

Then his immortal tympanum detected a different engine whine. The low chug of a small jet pushing a big load. These Vogons were trying to slip something past him.

Thor dispatched the final horse/torpedo with a perfunctory hammer swipe then cast his gaze about the darkening sky. His god-o-vision spotted an edged glint swooping in a potbellied curve toward the city of mortals below.

Those bastards are going after my paycheck.

Up to this point, Thor judged that he had been pretty benevolent toward these bureaucratic invaders. Okay, he had shredded their hardware, but no one was floating in space sucking down lungfuls of vacuum. Well, after he clobbered this sneaky new bomb with considerable sangfroid, perhaps he would send Mjöllnir to punch a few holes in the Vogon hull.

Thor folded his arms across his chest and dropped through the aurora of Nano's ionosphere like a rocket-charged stone through high *g*. While he could not actually be in two places at one time, Thor could most certainly move from one spot to another faster than almost any other being in the universe.

Guide Note: Brief so as not to ruin the flow. Thor was actually the fifth-fastest being in the Universe. Eighth without Mjöllnir to steady him. Number one was Hermes, who mainly used his divine speed to pinch Ares' nipples and then run away.

Thor felt the frictional reaction with the air molecules curl the tips of his beard hair. He was going about ninety-five percent flat out. There was a little more in the tank, but at those speeds there wasn't a camera in the universe that could capture his image.

The new torpedo curled in below him, a massive chunky series of rough cylinders with one small jet doing all the pushing. Thor sniffed, but he did not recognize what kind of explosive he was dealing with. The smell reminded him a little of the stink from his own clothes after a night spent boozing past a black hole's event horizon, but not quite the same.

What is this thing?

It didn't matter. Even if there wasn't a single bead of explosive inside, the impact crater alone would be far bigger than the city, and the shock metamorphism would liquefy a good section of the continent. So if any mortals did survive the explosion, they would only live long enough to be engulfed by lava.

Thor touched down on the torpedo's fuselage and clambered along the shaft toward the nose cone. There was no urgency now, as he had several seconds before impact, an eternity of time for a god of his abilities.

Should I toss the payload into space? he asked himself, leaning into the wind. *Or should I nudge the entire thing off course into the ocean. What would look best on camera?*

Thor sucked on the tip of his mustache as he remembered something Zaphod had said.

I wonder . . .

THE *BUSINESS END*

"Detonate the QUEST," ordered Jeltz.

"Yes, Prostetnic," said the gunner.

Forgive us, Mown broadcast to the Universe. *We are Vogon.*

NANO

By now the mammoth torpedo was clearly visible to the naked eye, swooping relentlessly toward Innisfree, labored jetstream sputtering behind like Morse code.

"Dot dash, dot dash dot," said Ford. "I think the whole thing reads, *Arthur Philip Dent is a jerk and complete arsehole.*"

Arthur was too tired for his irritation to have much force. "Is this the time for jokes, Ford? Is it really?"

It seemed as though the entire population of Nano was crowded into John Wayne Square, all colors and creeds united, either by something that could be called the human soul or by their paddle-less state in the creek of shite they were currently mired in.

Random sidled up to her father and linked arms. "This planet could have had a future," she said. "I was going to represent the people."

Arthur squinted at the huge column of destruction thrumming their way.

"Your mother is going to kill me," he sighed, then lifted his eyes as a collective *oooooh* rose from the crowd.

Now, that's something you don't see every day, he thought, resorting to clichés in his amazement.

Thor was walking along the giant rocket. Underneath it.

Random put her head on his shoulder, for the first and possibly last time. "Are we saved, Daddy? How many times can one group of people be saved? Surely the Universe doesn't have many more chances for the Dents."

Ford squeezed between them. "One more at least. So far as I know, nothing can kill a god."

Then the QUEST exploded. Sort of.

This was not a conventional explosion, in the sense that if one was expecting the traditional blast, bang, *kaboom* favored by movie directors and RPG writers the Universe over, then one would have felt slightly cheated. There was no blast wave, no flame, no flying debris, just a loud *whoomph* and the ballooning of a perfect cuboid of green material. The material crackled and flexed, picked up a little cartoon interference from a local satellite network for a few seconds, then split into sixteen small cubes.

Ford said what most people were thinking: "Those cubes are pretty small. A lot smaller than Thor."

The cubes popped one by one in rapid sequence, and what debris was inside them rained to the earth as gray ash. Thor was gone.

"I've got that joystick here somewhere," said Ford, rummaging in his satchel. "And a couple of sea dragon eggs. May as well go out singing."

Something twinkled in the sky over Zaphod's head.

"Look! Do you see that?"

Hillman did not answer, as he had decided he was not talking to Zaphod feckin' Beeblebrox.

Zaphod was off running across the city center parking zone.

"Souvenir!" he called over his shoulder. "Souvenir."

Zaphod placed himself under the falling object, jigging about for position.

Could I? he wondered. *Is it possible?*

"Camera!" he screamed, just in case. "Somebody get this."

Of course, I could very well be killed.

But if he survived, how many votes would the video clip be worth? How many subscriptions to his Sub-Etha site?

The object did not fall as a normal object would.

Of course it doesn't, thought Zaphod. *Because it is a divine talisman made from godly stuff, mined from the places that you get metal in Asgard.*

It floated and bloated, flipped and skipped. Chose a size, then changed its mind.

Zaphod stuffed his hands in his pockets so he wouldn't be tempted to use them. This was a strictly hands-free trick.

Down it came erratically, Zaphod dancing around on his heel-less boots, matching its jinks, then finally, incredibly, Thor's helmet landed square on Zaphod Beeblebrox's head, shrinking to fit snugly.

"Yes!" hooted Zaphod, punching the air. "Did you see that, Hillers? Did you bloody see that! And I had two heads until recently, so that took even more skillage than you would think . . . it would take. Tell me I am not special! Tell me!"

Hillman broke his vow of Coventry to call across the car park. "I told you not to call me Hillers, you gobshite. And as for special, there was nothing very special about that god you sold me."

Zaphod was suddenly serious. "I will not hear a word against Thor," he said. "He died to save you."

Hillman jerked a thumb at the Vogon bureaucruiser hovering above the city.

"He didn't do a great job of it then, did he?"

THE *BUSINESS END*

Prostetnic Jeltz's armpits were moist with delight. He was unfamiliar with the emotion, and for a moment wondered if the ship had somehow slipped back into hyperspace. But no, the world outside their window was in focus and ready for destruction.

"Order a dozen more of those torpedoes!" he called to no one in particular.

The Earthlings did not seem to have any artillery of their own and were defenseless now that their god had been dispatched to the afterlife.

Jeltz chewed on the fat flesh of his lower lip. If gods already lived in heaven, then where did they go when they died? Were the gods autolatrous narcissists? Or did they perhaps worship their own übergods and move on to a higher level of heaven after their deaths?

I have created a brand-new conundrum, he thought and the idea pleased him greatly.

"What do you think of your father now, Mown?" he said to the bobbing subordinate at his elbow.

Mown hesitated before answering, and the slobber sheen of victory was absent from his lips. A prostetnic might have been tempted to think that his constant did not revel in this conflict, even though it was perfectly legal. Jeltz felt certain that the gods would file a complaint, but he doubted that it would go past the strongly worded letter stage, not when the Galactic Government had the QUEST in their arsenal. Come to think of it, wasn't it about time the gods paid a little tax? Those Asgardians had been sitting on prime real estate since shortly after the beginning of time and had never contributed so much as a spent battery to the government coffers.

"Well, Mown? What say you?"

Mown was shaken to his jellied core. They had just killed a god. Removed an immortal from the Universe. Surely there would be consequences, an equal and opposite reaction must be on the way down the cosmic pipe. And even if there were no consequences, it was so utterly sad.

Mown took a gowpen of his own double chins, hoisting his head erect.

"I am stunned, Prostetnic. You did it when no one else would have."

"Hmmm," quorbled Jeltz, finishing the quorble on a satisfied "m." "I did, didn't I? There were whispers back in Megabrantis that I was past it. Imagine that—By-the-Book Jeltz, past it."

"By-the-Book?"

"My new sobriquet. Like it?"

"What happened to Utter Bastard?"

Jeltz laid an almost boneless hand on his son's shoulder. "I am hoping that you will be Utter Bastard one day."

Mown hung his head. "I already am. We all are."

Jeltz felt his armpit glands squirt. "Well said, my boy. Well said."

The gunner interrupted this almost tender moment. Well, if not tender, at least not heavy with implied violence.

"Sir. The Earthlings. We're drifting."

Jeltz was now suddenly loath to deal with these Earthlings. It seemed such an anticlimax, but business was blood, so . . . He rolled his left eye toward the screen and saw that the *Business End* was indeed straying from its geostationary position above the planetoid's main city.

"Not that it matters," he mumbled. "My torpedoes can shoot around corners." He flapped a hand at the gunner. "Exterminate them. Resistance is useless and all that . . ."

"Yes, sir," said the gunner with unseemly glee. Being Vogon was about getting the job done, not about overtly whooping it up over the annihilation of another species, so that your crew members could brand you a sicko and vow to send their daughters to another star system before they would let them date you. "Half a dozen low yields should be enough to vaporize the Earthlings. If I could make a suggestion, Prostetnic, it would be within our remit to confiscate the planet these people purchased. I'm sure the criminal assets bureau would be very interested . . ."

Jeltz was impressed. "Why, Gunner, that is a fine suggestion. Why don't you pull your chair a little closer to me? I believe I would like to rub your head."

"My greasy crown would be honored, sir. Just indulge me for a moment as I blow up these people."

"Now *that's* how you green-nose," said Jeltz to his son, but Mown wasn't listening, because he'd had an idea that was doing its very best to knock him off his feet and evaporate his brain fluid with its very audacity.

Constant Mown unstrapped the drool cup from around his neck, raced across the bridge, and clobbered the gunner across the brow just as the officer's finger feathered the fire button. The metal container sank through a layer of blubber then connected with cranium. The gunner's eyes crossed, uncrossed, then closed.

Once again the crew froze to see what Mown's fate would be. Casual violence was not unusual on a Vogon ship, but violent interruption of a prostetnic's order being carried out certainly was.

Jeltz leaned back with a swish of abdominal liquid and a hiss of chair.

"Constant Mown. This is the second time today. I am intreeeeeegued."

The elongation of this last word implied that Mown's explanation had better be superlative in the history of explanations for seemingly insane actions. Better even than that of Jammois Totalle, the Kyrstian hemagogue who had accidentally brained his wife with his signet ring in his sleep and then claimed the bones of his ancestors had made him do it, even going so far as to have bones shipped from another planet, artificially aged, and placed under the roots of his wango-pango tree.

Mown's skin was sweating on the inside, a rare Vogon condition aggravated by anxiety or dust mites, which causes the epidermal pores to leech moisture from the surrounding air and plump up the basal keratinocytes.

"I thought you had that under control, Mown," said Jeltz with obvious disappointment as his son swelled in front of his eyes. "Go homeopathic, your mother said, and I listened, Zark help me. Next time it's straight in the leech pit for you, my boy. Now, as I was saying, intreeeegued."

"This is not right!" Mown blurted.

"How do you mean?" asked Jeltz, puzzled. "Ethically? In a right-and-wrong sense? Please don't tell me you have developed morals to go with those nimble feet of yours." Jeltz drew a horrified breath. "Do not tell me my son has *evolved*?"

Mown clenched his little fists and stood his ground. "Firstly, the dust filter must be broken in here, Prostetnic, because my pores are filling up. Secondly, I meant this is not right as in it is not by the book."

Jeltz's wattle wobbled. "Not by the book, you say? Not by the . . ." He swiveled toward the comm post. "Record this, would you? I may have to explain the execution to his mother."

Mown forged ahead with his explanation, as his only other option was to lie down and sob for the state of his race. "Our order was to eliminate all Earthlings."

"I do hope your argument improves, because so far . . ."

"These people bought a planet from the Magratheans."

"Ah. I see where you're going, but the Galactic Government does not govern the Magratheans. They have their own little republic which is a terrible example for the colonies, if you ask me."

"You are correct, Prostetnic. Of course, you are, but the Magratheans are a registered business with the government. They have a trade agreement."

"I suppose."

Mown ran to the nearest console, neglecting to mask his agility. "Look!" he said, quickly pulling up the planning application from the new worlds office in Megabrantis. "Nano's planet status has been approved by central planning."

"It is difficult for a Vogon to find paperwork irritating, Twinkletoes," said Jeltz drily, "but I confess that unless you arrive at a point soon . . ."

"Point on the horizon, Prostetnic. The central planning office approved Nano as a taxpaying member planet of the planetary union, as governed by the Galactic Government."

"Are you just saying the same thing in a different way? Is that why I sent you to university?" Jeltz picked up a microphone and shouted into the PA. "We still need to eliminate the Earthlings."

"Look down here, the last paragraph. Megabrantis, as a matter of routine, also blanket-approved the citizenship applications of the planet's owners." Mown felt his swelling subside, and steam drifted in wisps from his pores, whistling gently. He was talking law now, and no Vogon would argue with the word of law. "Legally, the Earthlings are no longer Earthlings: They are Nanoites. Or maybe Nanoshians or Nanolings? I'm not sure. But I am sure that if you zap these people, you zap a nice group of high-band taxpayers who have never filed a return. Imagine, By-the-Book Jeltz frying citizens who owe back tax. Wouldn't Hoopz the Runaround, your old Hall of Kroompst buddy, love to hear about that?"

At this point Mown's own supply of kroompst was completely exhausted, and he stumbled backward into the monitors, his body temperature sending a rainbow arc flashing along the thermoreactive gas screens.

"Wow," said Jeltz, and it was not a word he used lightly or often. He winched himself out of his chair and allowed his abdominous torso to lug him forward. "Constant Mown. You have scuppered this mission." The prostetnic loomed above his remarkable son, casting an amorphous shadow on Mown's olive-pale face.

"I did what had to be done."

Jeltz reached out his hand, though this was more for the gesture than the actual practicality of grabbing onto it, may as well try to hang onto a rubber glove full of dairy-based spread. "You have seen the truth of the word. And through the word comes order. Stand, my son. Come stand at my elbow."

Mown, who was expecting to be a splat scraper on the next hull detail, stood on wobbly legs and coughed up a quart of fluid and two of the symbiotic hairless flaybooz that all Vogons carry around in their bile sacs to break down concretions.

"Oh, no. Poor Hanky and Spanky."

Jeltz brushed the sopping balls aside with the side of his foot. "Forget those parasites. We have millions in the waste recyclers."

He activated a bungee pulley from the bridge ceiling, one of several set into the gantry for just such Vogon falling-over emergencies. Mown still had the spark of craft left in him to pretend he needed it and hoisted himself erect.

"Hoopz would have been all over this," Jeltz confided to his son. "I wouldn't be at all surprised if he's monitoring communications back in Megabrantis, waiting for me to make a boghog's ear of this mission. There's nothing worse than obliterating . . ."

"The wrong people?" offered Mown.

Jeltz chuckled wetly at his subordinate's little joke. "The wrong *tax-payers,* Constant. You need to watch that sense of humor; other crew members don't have as many levels as we do. Your sarcasms could be mistaken for actual sympathizings."

"Oh," said Mown, a handy noncommittal syllable to have around when you haven't the first clue as to what you are feeling.

Jeltz plopped backward into his seat. "Old Hoopz was expecting me to arrive back at base with a big bagful of cock-up. Instead, thanks to you, we return heroes, with a god's scalp under our belts and a heads-up for the tax office."

"Everyone wins . . . except Thor."

"What did I tell you, son?"

"No . . . em . . . jokes."

"Precisely. Now squeeze onto this chair beside me and we shall enjoy the false hope of hyperspace together."

Mown's head spun and his hands shook. He had come to the Earth-lings' defense and somehow that had become a good thing.

It was the law, he realized. *The law saved us. From now on, I must use the word.*

He stood shell-shocked, arms raised, while two deck swabs greased him down for the chair.

Jeltz indulged in a moment of semi-fondness, which he permitted himself twice a year. *Look at my son, all wide-eyed about his first time on the captain's knee. I had thought that it would be better to send him away, but after his performance today, that boy stays at my elbow. He will be one of the greats. A destroyer of worlds. A confounder of petition-ers. Someday my son will truly be an Utter Bastard.*

NANO

The stereotypical depiction of a sentient species under threat of destruc-tion from a hovering alien spaceship usually sees them running around panic-stricken, clutching their most treasured household appliances close to their breasts and arranging their automobiles in neat jams on bridges. Except in the case of the Hrarf-Hrarf movie *Dooshing of the Red Plong,* where everyone is quite relieved just before complete annihilation because their life span flows backward through time, so from the Hrarf-Hrarf point of view, they have just survived one humdinger of a dooshing unscathed.

There was no running about on Nano and very few household appliances. The inhabitants stood in John Wayne Square, swaying slightly like reeds, their mouths open as they waited passively for death from above.

All except Aseed Preflux, who sat on a bench gorging himself on a tub of cottage cheese.

"I was so wrong," he sobbed, between fistfuls. "So utterly wrong. To understand the cheese, the exercitant must *consume* the cheese."

Hillman Hunter stood in the shadow of the statue, trying not to attract too much attention to himself, in case people decided to blame him for all their woes. Some things may flow downhill, but blame flows to the top, and Hillman preferred not to be in pain until the big pain arrived, which he fervently hoped would be relatively painless.

"See you soon, Nano," he whispered.

Not just yet, said Nano's voice in his head.

While Hillman was contemplating this mysterious and hopefully prophetic phantom voice, a thrown blob of cottage cheese slopped against the side of his face, plugging one ear hole and dripping underneath his collar.

"Nice work with the god, moron," called Aseed Preflux from across the square.

This could get ugly, thought Hillman.

A couple of rose shears were drawn, and Hillman was sure he saw a letter knife.

Why is there always someone with a blade?

Fortunately the Vogon bureaucruiser decided to absent itself from real space in a charming display of blue hyperengine pyrotechnics. One second it was there, and the next *whizz pop bang* it was gone, leaving nothing but a short-lived cloud of exhaust plasma in its wake.

"Awww," chorused the crowd.

Zaphod, with his innate sense of the theatrical, chose this moment to clamber atop the statue pedestal.

"The Vogons have been vanquished," he called from the crook of John Wayne's arm. "Thor has saved you."

"Thor saved us?" said Hillman, puzzled. "Which Thor? The dead, disappeared one?"

Zaphod threw him a look that asked Hillman just how stupid he was exactly, and when Z. Beeblebrox thinks a person is stupid, then that person is by implication more stupid than Zaphod himself, which is very stupid indeed, but then again probably too stupid to interpret the look, or be insulted even if he did.

Hillman was not stupid, just momentarily demented, and the moment passed.

"Of course!" he cried, the first syllable a squeak. "Thor has saved us."

Zaphod goggled his eyes. "Yes. About time. Thor has saved us all."

Hillman mounted the pedestal. "And he will come again when he is needed."

"Now you're getting it," said Zaphod.

"The lord Thor will communicate with his people only through me!"

"I can pretty much guarantee that. Whatever Hillers says, that's what Thor, who saved us, wants you all to do."

"And if we don't?" asked Aseed.

Zaphod frowned and ballooned his cheeks as if the very idea was ridiculous. "Then Thor would be most unhappy. And so would his hammer."

Hillman squinted at the crowd, hardly daring to hope that anyone would swallow this slapdash spackle of religi-babble. He was surprised to find not a single garden or household blade headed his way. Aseed had his hand in the cheese bucket, but even he was holding off for now, thinking about it.

They're not going to kill me, realized Hillman. "Thanks be to God."

"Not God," said Zaphod pointedly. "Thanks be to Thor."

Hillman smiled, then went for the big finish.

"Nano called for a sacrifice," he said, balancing on the pedestal. "Nano called for a feckin' martyr . . ."

The word *feckin'* was subsequently bleeped from the video record of this little speech because after Hillman's martyrdom, everything he had said during his first life suddenly became infinitely more important and laden with wisdom.

The next thing Hillman said was: "Hurrkkkaarrrkshhhhhhh." Though the "shhhhhhhh" at the end might have been escaping gases, for at that moment a nose cone of torpedo debris, that Thor evidently had missed, tumbled from the sky, striking the Sean the Boxer statue a glancing blow on the noggin, loosening the screw treads around the waistline of the two-part sculpture, and sending the left glove spinning clockwise to deliver a devastating roundhouse blow that literally cut Hillman in two.

"Oh balls," grunted Hillman, followed by the last words of his current life span. "Coming, Nano."

Historians deleted the first phrase but kept the second, which was misinterpreted so many times that fifteen thousand years later a third-grade student misspelled it and accidentally arrived at the correct meaning.

here is no such thing as a happy ending. Every culture has a maxim that makes this point, while nowhere in the Universe is there a single gravestone that reads, *He Loved Everything About His Life, Especially the Dying Bit at the End*. Rollit Klet, the Dentrassis independent-film-director-cum-chef says in his memoir *Fish or Film: The First Cut is Mine!*: "What you think is the happy ending is actually a brief respite before the serial killer that you thought was dead gets back up and butchers everyone except the girl with the biggest boobs, who dies first in the sequel the following year." Or as Zem of Squornshellous Zeta succinctly put it: "The mattress never stays dry for long." However, the number one most overused quote on the subject of endings, happy or otherwise, comes from an old man who lived on a pole in Hawalius, who said simply that "there is no such thing as an ending, or a beginning for that matter, everything is middle." The quote ends on a more rambling note: "Middles are crap. I hate middles. Middles are all regretting the past and waiting for something interesting to happen. Middles can go Zark themselves as far as I'm concerned." Generally, the pamphlet people only tend to print the first sentence, with perhaps a picture of a nice whale-toad in the background or maybe a couple of sunsets.

Barely a week had passed since the aborted Vogon attack, and already people had forgotten how lucky they were to be alive, and were back to worrying about the big issues of the day, like wasn't there anything that could be done about the late afternoon haze that drifted in from the ocean, and why hadn't anyone thought to bring more peanut butter from Earth, and what was that sharp smell outside the crèche, and maybe it would be nice to have a larger planet because this artificial gravity was making some of the old-timers ill.

Hillman Hunter sat at his desk reading through the day's complaints, wondering why he'd bothered hiring a god in the first place. A lot of these bin-fillers were supposed to be settled with fire and brimstone or hammer, whatever the case may be. Hillman could see the very real benefits in having an absentee god who only communicated through his representative, but did Thor have to martyr himself so soon? Couldn't he have spent a few weeks on civil service duty before making the ultimate sacrifice?

That's not to say martyrdom did not have its advantages. Since Hillman had been brought back from the dead in the *Heart of Gold*'s mediward, everyone had been a whole lot more willing to accept that he was Thor's representative on Nano. The new legs helped.

Hillman was doing his best to be pious and wise, but every minute of every feckin' day dealing with red tape was driving him out of his mind. Plus the scar tissue around his middle was itching worse than a bull's arse.

I am Hillman Hunter, Nano. I am a Christopher Columbus–type figure, with the colony founding and whatnot. I can't be stamping forms and sorting out domestics.

His intercom buzzed and a hologram of his secretary inflated on his desk.

"Yep, Marilyn. What's the story?"

"The story is that your first appointment is here."

Hillman was almost relieved. Arguing with real people was marginally better than getting upset with sheets of paper.

Might as well get the steamers on the shovel, he thought.

"Okay, Nano. Send them through."

Marilyn frowned. "Sorry, Hillman. What did you call me?"

Feck, thought Hillman.

"For Nano!" he said hurriedly. "It's the new official slogan. What do you think?"

"Good. Yes, fine," said Marilyn in a tone of such insulated boredom that Hillman was surprised she had heard him misspeak in the first instance.

That's two lines I've sold people in a week. First the Thor thing, now this.

Arthur Dent and his daughter, Random, came into the office, and of course the girl sat down without waiting to be asked.

That girl even sits sulky, thought Hillman. *But she's a smart one.*

"Sit, Arthur, please."

"Thank you."

"For Nano!" barked Hillman, thinking he'd better throw one into the conversation every now and then.

That's the thing with bullshit, his Nano used to say. *You have to keep piling more on.*

"Pardon?" said Arthur, bemused.

"It's our . . . ah . . . new slogan. Rally the people and all that. For Nano!"

"When would you use it?"

"I don't know really," Hillman said and huffed. "Collecting the crops. Crossing the ocean, that kind of thing. Heroic stuff. What do you think?"

"It's short," said Arthur honestly.

"Snappy is a better word, isn't it? You have no idea how many subcommittee meetings went into that slogan. This time next year it will be on the curriculum."

Random leaned her elbows on the desk. "I've heard that Nano is what you used to call your grandmother."

Hillman was rattled. "Is it? I don't remember. Actually, I think you're right. My goodness, sure I haven't thought about that in years, bejaysus."

"Don't bother."

"What?"

"Every time you're in trouble, out comes Paddy the Leprechaun and his cutesy *Oirish* accent."

"That's ridiculous," spluttered Hillman, moving on to another level of rattled. "I am Irish."

"Not that Irish. The truth of the matter is that you named the entire planet after your granny."

"The size of the planet was the *primary* reason for the name," said Hillman, then decided it was time to go on the offensive. "Any anyway, what if I did name the planet? I paid for most of it and did you see the list of submissions?" He pulled a sheet from his corkboard. "Oak Tree Rise. Aunty JoJo, the world's greatest aunt. Frank. The planet Frank! Come on, kiddo. Nano isn't half-bad compared to that lot."

Random's jaw jutted. "Maybe, but naming planets and inventing rousing slogans sounds like the seeds of dictatorship to me."

"Thor is lord here," said Hillman solemnly. "Not me."

Arthur jumped in before Random could tackle that one. "How are the new legs?"

Hillman clip-clopped his hooves under the desk. "The joints are a bit different, but I'm getting used to them. You should see me going up the stairs at night. Like a feckin' bullet."

Random snickered. "Apparently, Thor has always favored goats, so people are taking it as a sign."

Hillman snapped a pencil in his chubby fingers. "A sign of what? A sign that Zaphod Beeblebrox is a dullard?"

"At least you're alive again," Arthur pointed out. "And back on your . . . erm . . . hooves. Zaphod did promise you some humanoid legs whenever you feel up to the operation. He found a nice pair in the back of the fridge."

"You were only dead for twenty minutes," said Random sweetly. "So you probably only lost about half your IQ. Not that anyone will notice."

Arthur decided that it would be prudent to change the subject again.

"Any progress on our citizenship applications?"

"Some," said Hillman, only too happy to be steered away from talk of his goat's legs. The fact was that he did not want to commit to a second operation. There were advantages to being half-goat. Certain sections of the community actually venerated him, actually bowed down as he passed. And a few of the younger, more forward ladies had asked some very personal questions about his new limbage. Very personal.

"Just a couple of questions," he said, hiding a sudden blush behind his desktop screen. "Arthur Philip Dent. Blah blah blah. Fine fine fine. Ah, what should we put down for occupation?"

Arthur rubbed his chin. "It's been a while. I used to work in radio once upon a time. And sandwiches. I can make a decent sandwich."

"So, media and catering. Good skills to have in a developing world. I don't foresee any problems with your application."

"What about mine?" asked Random, though it sounded more like a threat than a question.

Hillman leaned back in his chair. "That depends on you, Random. Are you simply here to rabble-rouse the Tyromancers?"

"The Tyromancers have disbanded," said Random, scowling. "The cows broke into the compound. And Aseed discovered yogurt. They're using cakes now apparently, critomancy. I suspect it's because Aseed is allergic to eggs."

"So you won't be allying yourself to that cause?"

"No. I have loftier goals."

"Really? Find a nice boy, settle down?"

"I want to be President."

If Hillman had been eating something, he would have choked on it. "President? Of Nano?"

"Of the Galaxy. I've done it before."

"It's a long story," said Arthur. "She needs to go to school."

"I have eight master's degrees and a double doctorate!" protested his daughter.

"Virtual degrees," said Arthur calmly. "I don't think they count."

"Of course they count, Daddy. Don't be so Cro-Magnon."

"I don't make the rules."

"That is such a cliché. You are like a mound of cliché bricks all piled on top of each other to make a person."

"That's very good imagery, honey. Maybe an arts degree?"

Hillman had been Sub-Etha surfing during this exchange. "I might have a little something here to interest you, Random."

Random selected an *it will be a cold day in hell before you have something to interest me* look from her lexicon and beamed it full-force at Hillman.

"I doubt it."

Hillman beamed back an *oh really*, then pursed his lips, playing harder to get than a redhead at a *céilí*.

Arthur broke first. "What?"

"Nothing. Random is right. She wouldn't be interested."

"Come on, Hillman. Be the mature one."

Hillman turned the screen around. "Look here. The University of Cruxwan rules on virtual degrees if you can pass the qualifying exam. They can extract the memories with this thing that looks like a robotic octopus."

"That is mildly interesting," admitted Random, studying the screen. "And they offer a satellite program."

"I *could* put in an application for you," said Hillman.

Random recognized his tone from years of virtual negotiations. "In return for what?"

"In return for a little support. I'll be honest with you, Random, I'm an important man. I can't be wasting my valuable time dealing with small potatoes. The steamers are piling high here, my girl. Health and safety violations, all those uBid people looking for residences, tax forms from Megabrantis. Your father told me about your background in politics and . . ."

"And you want an assistant?"

"You've put your finger on it. And who would be more qualified than yourself?"

Random tutted. "Not you, that's for sure. What's in this for me?"

"Experience in the real world. A nice apartment in the village, and I'll start you on a level-three wage."

"Level five," snapped Random on principle.

"Five it is," said Hillman quickly, sticking out his hand.

"Keep your hand," said Random. "We can shake after the contracts are signed."

Hillman pushed back his chair. "I can see you're going to be a bucket of chuckles. Okay then, girlie. Be here at eight sharp tomorrow morning, expect me about ten thirty. You can have the tea ready."

Arthur felt the specter of relief hovering over one shoulder and the specter of foreboding slumped on the other, having a beer, scratching its behind.

Think positive, he told himself. *It could work out. They might not kill each other.*

"I'll make your lunch," he told Random. "Sandwiches okay?"

They might not kill each other.

Hillman reached under the desk and scratched the coarse hair on his thigh.

"Oh and I need special shampoo for my new parts. And also you could give me a hand filing my hooves."

Arthur amended his last thought to *They might not kill each other for at least a month,* then caught the fire in Random's glare and realized he was being about a fortnight too optimistic.

Zaphod Beeblebrox made a complete nuisance of himself for a few fun-packed weeks, then decided to sneak off into improbability during the night. He would have preferred to make his exit covered in the confetti from a parade given in his honor, but there was the matter of the gold he had liberated from Hillman's safe as payment for Thor's sacrifice. And also there were half a dozen ladies whom he might have promised stuff to. Stuff like undying love, a trip to the stars, his PIN number.

I'm not here a month, he thought as he skulked up the *Heart of Gold*'s stairwell. *Imagine the damage I could do in a year.*

Zaphod Beeblebrox. The best bang since the Big One. Froody.

Ford Prefect knew how much Zaphod appreciated a nice parade and so brought a pocketful of rice with him to bid farewell to his cousin.

"Farewell, Mr. President," he called, tossing a handful of the rice into the air over Zaphod's head. "I bet there are a couple of ladies that will miss you."

Zaphod's facial muscles executed a very complicated maneuver that left his expression somewhere between regal and pained.

"Thanks for the send-off, cousin. But I am trying to skulk here."

"Skulk? Word of the week?"

"Exactly. I'm making enough ruckus as it is trying to drag this bag without you yelling at me."

Ford shrugged. "Hey, you're Zaphod Beeblebrox. The Big B. People are going to yell. If I were you, I would never build a silent exit into your escape plan."

Zaphod squatted for a rest. "Zark. You're right. I wish someone had told me that before Brontitall, I could have avoided all that egg on my face."

Guide Note: During a previous adventure that has not yet happened, Zaphod time-traveled to the planet Brontitall, where the bird people had re-emerged (will have reemerged; please alter any subsequent verbs as appropriate; conjugating, especially the future perfect, tends to freeze the Guide) as the dominant species. Once Zaphod had successfully shrunk and stolen their sacred statue of Arthur Dent (don't ask), he attempted to sneak back through the spaceport, taking a shortcut through the hatchery. Unfortunately, the hatchery was protected by laser eyes, motion detectors, several disgruntled unborn egg spirits, and mini-mac self-targeting weapons. Zaphod's hair was wounded, and he wiped out an entire generation of bird people with his chin as he fell. During his trial, a freshly permed Zaphod not only claimed diplomatic immunity but managed to countersue the avian government for overzealous security measures.

"I don't remember anything about Brontitall," said Ford. "Don't tell me you're having adventures without me."

"No. I never do anything without you, Ford. You're the one person I trust. The only person I can confide in."

"What's in the bag?"

"Souvenirs. Some cake the Critomancers didn't want. A little microwave oven."

"Froody. You can make hot cake."

"That's the plan."

Zaphod pushed his clanking bag of cake inside the doorway.

"Are you sure you won't hitch a ride?" he asked his cousin.

"No thanks, Zaph. I have a job to do. This planet doesn't have so much as a single article in the Guide. I'm going to stick around for a couple of weeks and write it up. Do some research, take a little sun."

"Sounds good," said Zaphod wistfully.

"So why don't you stay?"

Zaphod struck a pose on the gantry, one leg bent, forearm across his knee. From somewhere an organic bulb flickered on, etching his jaw in crimson light.

"It's not my destiny, Ford," he said, a sudden breeze fanning his hair behind him. "The Universe has different plans for Zaphod Beeblebrox. Wherever there are lonely females, I'll be there. Wherever cocktails are given free to celebrities, look for me. Whenever some really bad stuff happens to those people with, you know, depressing stuff in their places, Zaphod Quantus Beeblebrox will do his best to make time for it."

"Quantus?"

"I'm trying it out. What do you think?"

"Good. Very heroic. Better than the last one."

"I know," said Zaphod ruefully. "Pruntipends. Someone should have told me."

They did their childhood shake. Bum bum boot elbow high-five elbow . . .

"Okay. Be seeing you, Ford," said Zaphod, stepping inside the doorway force field.

"One more thing," said Ford. "Arthur's on this planet, so you know sooner or later . . ."

"Someone will try and blow it up. Don't worry, I'll keep an ear on the Sub-Etha. First sign of Vogons and I'll zoom over."

"I'm counting on you."

The *Heart of Gold* lifted silently off the spaceport concrete.

"It never hurts to have a backup plan," said Zaphod, then he was gone.

Left Brain had been plugged into the plasma a bit long and was feeling a little hyper.

"Look who it is, the great Galactic President, gracing us with his presence."

Zaphod heaved the sack of gold into a locker. "Hey, LB. Nice work with the light and the wind machine."

Left Brain bonked Zaphod with his glass. "I don't appreciate being used as your effects guy. You were elected President of the Galaxy, Zaphod. Don't you have any dignity?"

Zaphod rubbed his crown. "I don't understand the question."

He strode to the bridge, passing through several auto-doors that were programmed to recognize him and deliver appropriately laudatory comments as he passed through.

"Oooh, he looks fit," gushed service corridor one.

"Nice hair, Zaphy," piped the central elevator, who had always been a little cheeky.

"You make me wanna be organic," said the mid-ship bridge door.

As he sauntered onto the bridge, feeling about fifteen esteemeters better about himself, Zaphod noticed a hammer icon revolving on the main screen.

"When did that come in?" he asked Left Brain, who was of course hovering by his shoulder, suspiciously close to the spot where he used to be attached.

"A few hours ago. I think I have separation anxiety," said Left Brain. "I miss my neck."

"No problem," said Zaphod, settling into the captain's chair. "We can get you stuck back on here whenever you like."

"No thanks," said Left Brain. "I can take a few pills for the anxiety, or maybe buy a Hol-O-Trunk. Anything is better than waking up beside an asinine lout like yourself."

Zaphod thought the word *asinine* to himself several times then immediately forgot it.

"Play the message."

"Background music?"

"No. Just whatever came in, and I don't want anyone overhearing this."

"Very well. Shields up."

On screen the hammer icon twirled and became a video box. Thor's hirsute features filled the screen.

"Hey, Zaph. Hello, hello. This is a . . . I bet this isn't even . . . Okay, okay, now I see it. We're on." The god composed himself. "Hello, Zaphod, this is your client, Thor the Thunder God. I am not dead, as you probably guessed."

"I had guessed," crowed Zaphod, punching the air.

· ·

Guide Note: The whole martyrdom concept has been working well for gods since the mid-morning of time when Raymon the Louche, resident God of Tarpon VII, avoided making a ruling over who owned what baby by faking his own death through orgasmic overdose. Raymon realized that people liked him much better now that he was dead and they tended to base their decisions on third-hand hearsay of stuff he might have whispered under his breath to a deaf leper in a cave.

Raymon's check still went directly into his account, and now all he had to do was appear in shadowy form to a virgin once every few thousand years and say something cryptic like *The pebbles will save us all, be sure that you covet the pebbles.* The Raymon method became such a successful model that soon gods all over the Galaxy were faking their deaths and cursing Raymon for copyrighting death by orgasmic overdose.

● ●

Thor leaned in close to the camera. "It was the martyr comment. Like you said. I was walking along that big bomb, thinking that if I let it kill me then the humans would think I died for them. So I gave it a hundred percent up the Vogon ship when I heard the detonator spark and hid in their pipe work for a minute. I thought I'd tap the ship with Mjöllnir, make it look like a bit of shrapnel did for her, but then they just took off into hyperspace. Don't know why. Don't care either. Anyway, that's it. I'm off back to Asgard now, ready for resurrection if you need me. I think I might have pulled my groin though, so give me a while to get my fitness back. Give me a buzz, let me know if the martyr thing worked. Also, get me some gold, I am so strapped it's not funny. Last thing, keep your eye out for my helmet. I must have lost it in the explosion and it's my favorite one. I'm going to sign off, I have another call coming in." Thor beat his chest with one fist, then winked at the camera. "Nice work, manager."

Zaphod closed the video window, flabbergasted. "Wow," he said. "I can't believe that martyr idea worked. Also I am amazed that Thor picked up on it, subtle as it is. My stratagems are generally so nuanced that most people need to hear them a couple of times."

Left Brain bobbed before Zaphod's eyes. "You don't remember saying anything about martyrs, do you?"

"No," replied Zaphod. "But that doesn't mean I didn't say it."

"So you actually thought your one client was dead?"

"Of course not. You can't kill a god. Even that guy who drove into the white hole is still alive, even if his parts are spread across several dimensions."

"What about that special bomb?"

Zaphod snorted. "The QUEST? Who do you think sold that to the Vogons? I'm surprised it didn't fall out of the sky. I put a lawnmower engine on that thing."

Left Brain was quiet for a moment, except for the clicking of spider-bots gathering condensation on the inner curve of his orb.

"Just the two of us again. What would you like to do?"

Zaphod crossed his boots on the console. "I don't know. Thor's martyrdom video needs a while to go viral, so we have time on our hands. What were we doing before all this?"

"We were raising funds for your reelection campaign."

Zaphod was surprised. "We were? But I'm already President."

"You *were* President," corrected Left Brain in the patient tone of a preschool teacher explaining for the umpteenth time why it was not a good idea to drink the paint water. "Until the moment you were convicted of a first-degree felony."

"But everyone still calls me Mr. President."

"All ex-Presidents are known as Mr. President."

"Isn't that confusing?"

"Not for more than half a second, if you have half a brain."

Zaphod frowned. "Do you have to multiply those halves?"

Left Brain steamed in his jar. "Just forget the halves. You were President, now you're not. Is that straightforward enough for you?"

"So who is the actual President?"

"Currently?"

"Yes. And right now."

Left Brain did not take a moment to consult anything, because everyone knew who the Galactic President was, with the exception of all the regular passengers on this ship, with the possible but definitely not definite exception of Ford Prefect.

"It's Spinalé Trunco of the Headless Horsemen tribe of Jaglan Beta."

Zaphod bolted upright, which is not easy when your feet are propped on a console. His heel stumps sparked as he stamped in vexation.

"What? Trunco. But he has no heads. Not a single head does he have. Zero on the shoulders."

"We've been through this, Zaphod."

"Not in the past twenty minutes, we haven't. And you know what my retention is like."

"I'm surprised you retained retention."

"Exactly. Right, LB, enter the coordinates for my constituency."

"You don't have a constituency, and if you did, it would be the entire Galaxy."

"Well take me to the center of the Galaxy then. If Zaphod Beeblebrox is back, people need to know it. I need to throw up at a club, have liaisons in a toilet. Possibly go on a realty reality show."

"I think the first order of business is to get the first-degree felony charge reduced to second-degree. That way you can run for office."

"Good thinking, LB. Who do we pay off?"

This time Left Brain consulted his data banks. "Improbably enough, Spinalé Trunco."

"Old Trunco. There was something about him . . ."

"No heads."

"Not a one. Bastard."

It took Left Brain a few seconds to hack into the presidential security detail's schedule.

"Trunco is currently relaxing at his stable compound, on Jaglan Beta."

"Then we go to Jaglan Beta."

Left Brain squinted while he beamed the coordinates to the Improbability Drive. "You know Trunco hates you, Zaphod. You might need something a little more tempting than that sack of gold I scanned you with."

Zaphod gave Left Brain a thumbs-up, and it took the disembodied head a moment to realize that there was something on one of the thumbs. A tiny horned helmet.

"I might have something to bargain with," said Zaphod.

SPACE

Thor had pulled in to an asteroid to try and connect with Zaphod, and was sitting in a little pocket of oxygen on the surface when he switched over to the incoming call. He didn't actually need breathable air, but it did help stave off migraine, plus it made talking on the phone a lot easier when he didn't have to dig into the magic well just to make his voice heard in space.

"Thunder God here," he said into Mjöllnir's handle. "Talk to me."

A little golden head appeared on the hammer's head. "Hey, Thunder-girl, what's up?"

"Bishop. Nice to see you. There's quite a lot up actually. I have a flock now. Genuine believers. There's maybe one warrior in the bunch, but it's a start."

The chess piece took a pull on his cigarette. "That's great, Thor, and I'm calling you with more good news."

"Really? What?"

"It's about your video," said Bishop. "It's at number one with a couple of billion hits. A regular Sub-Etha sensation."

Thor's heart sank. "When are they going to let that go? I dress up in one bustier and the Universe never forgets."

"No. Not that one. The new one with you clobbering the green guy who insulted everybody. Apparently there are a lot of people thrilled to see him getting his comeuppance."

"Number one? Really? That's fantastic."

"Yeah. Lovely hammer action by the way, leading with your body like I told you. You're back on top, my friend."

Thor grinned hugely. "This is great. Call Dad and Mom. Call everyone. Big session in my hall tonight. I want mead and pigs and beef and virgins."

"What about squid?"

"No. No squid. But whatever else you can get, and make sure the Valkyrie get an invite."

Bishop punched the air. "The Thunder is back," he said.

"That's right," said Thor. "The Thunder is back."

He hung up, took off, then turned around and smashed the asteroid from sheer exuberance.

Hey, said the spirit of Fenrir. *That was my tooth.*

THE *BUSINESS END*

Constant Mown lay on his bunk, staring at his own face in the Barbie mirror.

"You did the right thing," he told himself over and over, though he did switch the sentence structure around a bit to fool his subconscious into thinking it was hearing something new.

"It was a good thing you did. The right thing."

Then.

"What you did back there. That was totally right. A good thing."

The face in the mirror, inside the pink plastic frame, was friendly but worried. He had saved the Earthlings it was true, but there were many species on the *to endanger* list, and that *taxpaying citizens* trick would only work as often as it was legal. Which would not be very often, now that Prostetnic Jeltz had experienced it once.

That will be the first thing he checks from now on. Who are these people we are about to obliterate?

"You will find a way," said the face in the mirror, a face which looked almost kindly without the drool cup.

Mown never went anywhere without his drool cup now. The last thing he wanted to look was kindly, which could be seen as a symptom of evolution. As a matter of fact, Mown had added a foot crimper to his wardrobe after the Twinkletoes comment on the bridge. It didn't do to be too sprightly on a Vogon deck.

"One day we will dance," he said to his reflection.

"One day we will sing," said the face in the mirror, and then, "It was the right thing to do, what you did back there. Right and good."

His father's voice erupted from the speaker over Mown's bed.

"Constant! I have some planetary council or other on the line claiming that because of their leap year system, we haven't given enough notice of their enforced destruction. I need you to take a look at it."

"Right away, Daddy," said Mown, strapping the foot crimper across his toes. "I'm on my way."

"That's my good little Utter Bastard," Jeltz said, and hung up.

Not yet I'm not, thought Mown, hobbling to the door. *Not just yet.*

NANO

Arthur Dent was beginning to understand his daughter's feelings of isolation.

"I see now what you were talking about," he'd told her one morning before work. "We don't fully belong anywhere. Earth was our planet, but it's gone now. And even though we called it home, Earth hadn't been our home for decades. We both lived full lives away from its surface. Me on my island, you in Megabrantis. We are cosmic nomads—which would be a great name for a band by the way—interstellar drifters with no one but each other to cling to in this eternity of displacement."

And Random said, "What will you put on my sandwiches today, Daddy? Bearing in mind that I'm trying to be a vegetarian now and beef is not vegetarian."

"That beef snuck onto the sandwich," said Arthur lamely, and he realized that Random was not as unrelentlessly unhappy as she had been. Perhaps the daily attrition in Hillman Hunter's office was giving his daughter a focus for her ire, and maybe Arthur should be grateful for the relatively pleasant teenager who presented herself at the breakfast table most mornings, instead of trying to drag her down into the ichor of his wounded psyche.

"Coleslaw?"

Random kissed his cheek. "Lovely. No crusts."

"Crusts? Of course not. What are we, barbarians? How could I call myself a sandwich maker?"

And so on and so forth. By the time Arthur had finished his protestations and moved on to listing his sandwich-maker credentials, Random had stuffed her lunch into the satchel lent to her by Ford and left for work.

Arthur had stuck to a couple of weeks of stay-at-home daddy and then begun looking for excuses to go on a trip.

"Just you and me," he told Ford. "It'll be like the old days but without the exploding planets and the other people who were with us in the old days."

"No can do, mate," Ford responded, trying his best to seem regretful, which was difficult for him with a volcanic mud mask covering his features and two delightful masseuses twanging his hamstrings. "There are an inordinate amount of spas on this little planet and I need to sample them all. I owe it to the hitchhikers out there."

Arthur glanced at the price list. "Aren't you supposed to be surviving on thirty Altarian dollars a day?"

"The Altarian stock market fluctuates quite a bit," said Ford, perhaps blushing a little under the mud. "One day thirty dollars can buy you a house in the suburbs with a two-child garage and three-point-four wives. The next you'd be lucky to have enough for a tube of anti-hangover leeches. I'm covering high- and low-end tourism just to be safe."

And so Arthur was forced to explore alone.

Alone. That was the dreaded word. He, Arthur Dent, was a lone man, alone and lonely. On loan from another dimension. A low no one with no one to lean on.

All of which sounded a little pessimistic and self-absorbed even to someone who had recently received a package addressed to "Self Absorbed Pessimist, Nano." So Arthur decided to dress up his trip as paternal duty.

"I am traveling to Cruxwan to vet this university for you," he'd told Random. She would argue, but he intended to knock down her points preemptively. "Now I know what you're going to say, but what kind of father would I be if I let my only daughter loose in the Universe without checking it out first? Your mother and Wowbagger will be back from their cruise in a few days. Also, Ford will stay with you until I get back. It's only a dozen jumps, so it shouldn't take more than a week. Two at the most. Anyway, in virtual terms you're a hundred years old, so a couple of weeks without me shouldn't trouble you. I'm leaving you all my contact numbers and a supply of frozen sandwiches, so everything should be fine. Any questions?"

Random had thought for a moment then asked, "What kind of sandwiches?"

So now Arthur was seated in a lovely wraparound gel seat in business class of a hyperspace liner, which looked alarmingly like a set of male genitalia from the outside, but was quite pleasant inside once one banished the memory of the two hyperpsace boosters and passenger tube. His seat had been purchased with space points from an account he'd opened in his pre-Lamuella days.

The Fenchurch days.

This is good, he told himself. *I am doing something positive instead of moping around at home interfering with Random's career. Now I can interfere with her education instead.*

Arthur had allowed himself to be stripped to his flightard, oiled, and slid into the chair. The gel seat folded around him and he selected the Hitchhiker's Guide to the Galaxy from the touch menu.

Arthur had the little icon rub himself along a link to Cruxwan. There were three thousand articles.

Plenty to keep me going for the entire journey, he thought.

Once all the passengers were on board, the pneumatic doors hissed closed and Arthur was relieved to find that he was the only one in his row. He would not consider himself a flight snob, but sometimes an oiled man in a flightard likes to climb out of his seat unobserved.

They took off, and Arthur watched Nano recede into space through the Ship-O-Cam box in his seat. Soon the entire nebula was little more than a shawl of cosmic gauze thrown over a network of stars.

Shawl of cosmic gauze, thought Arthur. *If Ford could write like that, he might actually make some money.*

A little blue engine icon appeared in the corner of his cushion and Arthur sucked deep on the sedastraw.

Hyperspace. I have missed you.

The jump was smoother than he remembered.

Must be these new seats.

The sensation reminded him a little of the softness of crashing into snowdrifts on a sled that he enjoyed as a boy, but without the shock of cold. This sensation was warm and welcoming. Arthur felt a tinge of loss at the corner of his good mood. Hyperspace could take things away too, especially if you were from a plural zone.

Arthur Dent relaxed and watched the universe folding around him. Outside the cocoon of his chair swam asteroids, space creatures, and the faces of a million other travelers. The Hitchhikers Guide identified them all with little color-coded V-labels, but the travelers were gone and replaced by new ones before Arthur could read a single word.

After a dreamlike first jump, the ship swung out of hyperspace, jittering to one side like a stone skimming on a lake. Seat-belt lights flashed for a few seconds, then winked out.

I think I'll just go to the loo, thought Arthur. *Before the next jump.*

Obviously the seat could have recycled his recyclings, but Arthur felt that there were some things that should not be done into a glorified plastic bag in public.

He deflated the chair a little and sat up woozily, and was mildly surprised to find the chair beside him occupied. The newcomer was chatting to him with some familiarity, as though they had met before. Arthur's eyes had not yet cleared, but the voice was one he knew, and so was the tilt of the head and the sheaf of hair tucked behind one ear.

Fenchurch?

Arthur rubbed his eyes free of hyperdoze and looked again. It was Fenchurch, chatting animatedly, as though they had never been apart.

This cannot be true. I am dreaming.

But he was not. It was Fenchurch, returned to him. She was exactly the same except for the blue mottling on her upper brow and the sloping ridge of bone in the center of her forehead.

Almost the same. Maybe two dimensions down. Her Arthur is gone and so is my Fenchurch.

Fenchurch finished her story and laughed her tinkling laugh with the distinctive inhale at the end that always reminded Arthur of his mum's Hoover.

If I know Fenchurch, she's not finished talking yet, thought Arthur, still fighting his way out of a bemused fugue. *There are more stories to come.*

He was right. Fenchurch tapped him on the forearm, tucked a stray strand of hair behind her ear, and opened her mouth.

"And another thing . . . ," she said.

What other thing? Arthur wanted to ask. *And what thing came before the other thing? Tell me about all the things in order.*

He wanted to say these words to this exotic yet familiar Fenchurch, but when he raised his hands to cradle her face, he saw that the fingers were transparent.

What? Oh, no. No.

Nausea swelled inside him, a barbed boil of static that flowed through his limbs and wrapped his brain in fog.

The plural zone, he realized. *People from a plural zone should never travel in hyperspace. They could end up anywhere.*

Arthur saw Fenchurch reach for him. Her beautiful mouth formed his name, and then she was zooming away from him in a multicolored elastic tunnel.

She's not zooming away, Arthur realized. *It's me. I'm the one zooming.*

The galaxy swirled around him, and he was naked in it, without protection from the cold and radiation, and yet he did not die or suffer, he simply fumed as the hyperspace anomaly drew him farther away from his life. Eventually the sheer volume of stuff and perspective grew too terrifying, and so Arthur closed his eyelids, which made absolutely no difference, as they were transparent, and tried to focus on the one place where he had ever known true peace. He bore down mentally, conjuring every bamboo shoot in his hut and every white rock breaching the ocean on his stretch of sand. He did not think of the nebulae swirling past or the red stars spewing their flares into space. He did not think about these things so much that soon they were all he could not think about.

After a time, which could not be measured even with a top-class digital watch, Arthur decided that he felt solid again. He strained his ears and heard waves crash, stuck out his tongue and tasted salt.

Could it be? he wondered.

Arthur Dent opened his eyes to find himself sitting on a beach very much like the one from his virtual life. There were differences in the curve of the coastline, but it was as near as made no difference; there was even a small hut just past the scrub line.

Is this possible? he wondered. *Or even probable, whatever that really means, if it means anything?*

He squinted against the glare of late evening sunrays and could not help but notice a squat yellow shape on the distant horizon.

What? Surely not.

Arthur would have added, *It can't be!* but that particular phrase had given up its right to bear an exclamation mark since he'd met Zaphod Beeblebrox. Nothing couldn't be, and if it shouldn't be, then it generally was.

A pootle-tink bird sidled alongside him.

"Bloody Vogons," it said from the side of its beak. "They've been here a few days. Apparently someone forgot to file planning permission for that hut."

"Typical," said Arthur, then closed his eyes and wished he was somewhere else with someone else.

· ·

Guide Note: Arthur Dent's almost incredible bad luck created a providence vacuum which led to unbelievably good fortune for a being on the other side of the Universe. A certain Mr. A. Grajag, a little known sportscaster from Un Hye, was successfully resuscitated after six months of near flat lines on his hospital monitor following a space collision with a uBid cargo ship. He awoke to a cocktail reception from the planetary lotto committee to celebrate his numbers coming up as opposed to his number being up. At the same moment, his childhood sweetheart, who had recognized Mr. Grajag from his stint on *Celebrity Coma,* burst into his hospital room declaring her long nurtured and genuine love. The pair went on to marry and have two well-adjusted children who had no wish to follow their father into show business, preferring to study law and medicine.

Had Arthur Dent known about the Grajags, it might have cheered him up a little.

But not much.

· ·

The End of one of the Middles.

ACKNOWLEDGMENTS

I would like to thank Douglas Adams for dismantling my perspective and rebuilding it in another dimension. Thanks and love to Jackie for all of her ideas, guidance, research, and input into the writing of this book and all the others over the past ten years. Much gratitude to Sophie and Ed for putting this project together and to Polly and Jane for their kind support. Thanks to Alex and Leslie, my eagle-eyed editors, who have probably fixed these acknowledgments. And finally, thanks to my old friend Ted Roche, who introduced me not only to *Hitchhiker's* but also to Whitesnake. Debts that can never be repaid.